D0296783

IN THE KINGDOM
ØF MEN

IN THE KINGDOM OF MEN

Kim Barnes

First published 2012
by Hutchinson
This Large Print edition published 2012
by AudioGO Ltd
by arrangement with
The Random House Group Ltd

Hardcover   ISBN: 978 1 4713 1073 7
Softcover   ISBN: 978 1 4713 1075 1

British Library Cataloguing in Publication Data available

1 7 3 9 4 9 8 21

Printed and bound in Great Britain by
MPG Books Group Limited

For my brave and beautiful mother,
Claudette Barnes,

and with special thanks to
Coleen and Wayne Cook—
because of you, this adventure

We travel, some of us forever, to seek other states, other lives, other souls.

—ANAÏS NIN

Let me have all things, let me have nothing.
—WESLEY COVENANT PRAYER

This is one way to make a new world.
—WALLACE STEGNER

Rome, Italy

Here is the first thing you need to know about me: I'm a barefoot girl from red-dirt Oklahoma, and all the marble floors in the world will never change that.

Here is the second thing: that young woman they pulled from the Arabian shore, her hair tangled with mangrove—my husband didn't kill her, not the way they say he did.

There is so much, now, that you will want to know, that you believe I will be able to tell you. If not, why even begin?

Because I can't stop thinking of her, not yet eighteen, perfectly, immutably silent, just as they wanted her to be. It is the dream of her face shining up from the sea like a watery moon that still haunts me. Not even her mother will speak her name.

Because, among these Roman people whose language flows like a river over rocks, my own name drops heavy as a stone, no husband, no father, no family or tribe to tether me.

Because I don't know who I am anymore and have forgotten who it was I meant to be.

Let me tell it from the beginning, then, remember the truths of my own story so that I might better bear witness to hers, trace the threads to that place where our lives intertwined—one of us birthed to iron-steeped clay, the other to fallow sand, each of us brought to this place by men born of oil.

CHAPTER ONE

In the beginning—these three words my daily
bread, recited at the kitchen table in our shack in
Shawnee, the Bible open in front of me. Before
then, just as the Korean War was beginning, I
remember my mother humming honky-tonk as she
fried spuds for our dinner, two-stepping to the table
in an imaginary waltz. She was the daughter of a
Methodist circuit preacher who extolled separation
from the world, and his wife, who bowed her head
in submission and held her tongue even as she
secreted away the money she made selling eggs, a
penny at a time added to the sock hidden beneath
the nest of her beloved Rhode Island Red, a hen so
fierce and prone to peck that my grandfather gave
it wide berth.

My mother loved to tell the story: how my
grandmother scraped and saved until she had
enough for a train ticket back to her family in
Pawhuska, then rose one morning, fixed her
husband a big pot of pork hocks and brown beans—
enough to last him a week—made bacon and
extra biscuits so he wouldn't have to go without
breakfast, ironed his handkerchiefs and starched
his shirts, then told him that one of the ladies of
the church was having female troubles and needed
her care. My grandmother walked out the door
with a bundle of biscuits under one arm, her infant
daughter in the other, went straight to the train
station, didn't even leave a note. My grandfather
refused to divorce her, would never forgive the
way she had deceived him, but maybe he should

1

have known—the way that women have always lied, risking their souls to save their sorry lives.

It was eighteen years later when my father, two weeks hitchhiking Route 66 and still no job, came looking for work at the Osage County Fair and first laid eyes on my mother—a rodeo princess pitching cow chips for charity. He must have fallen in love with her right then—the way she could clean up pretty as a new nickel or muck down on her knees in manure, that sunshine smile never breaking. She brought him home to meet her mother, and I like to imagine that moment: the three of them at the table, the late light warm through the window, and all of them laughing at their good fortune—to have found one another, to share the sweet fruit of that pie.

My parents were married that winter, and the next winter, I was born. When my father was drafted, my mother and I moved in with my grandmother to wait out the war. Two years later, the official from the State Department arrived, telling how my father had died in the Home-by-Christmas Offensive, that the president was sorry, as was the nation. My only memories of him reside in the stories my mother told.

And then, that summer I turned seven, the cancer came up through my mother's bones like it had been biding its time, took what smile was left, took her teeth and blanched her skin to parchment. I would lie in our bed and cradle my dolly in a tea towel while my mother wept and prayed that God would take her and my grandmother offered another spoonful of laudanum. When, finally, God answered my mother's prayers, and then, only a few months later, my grandmother was felled by a blood clot that the doctor said had bubbled up from her broken heart, I was ordered into my grandfather's custody.

He came to the city orphanage in his old Ford pickup, and I watched from the doorway as he approached, a lean man, sinewy and straight, with a strong way of moving forward, like he was forcing his way through water. Pinched felt hat, starched white shirt, black tie and trousers—only the seams of his brogans, caked with mud, gave him away for the scabland farmer he was when not in the pulpit.

My nurse had dressed me in a modest blouse and jumper, but I refused the hard shoes she offered and wore instead my mother's old riding boots, an extra sock stuffed in each toe. The first thing my grandfather did was have me open my suitcase. My doll, my mother's rhinestone tiara, her wedding ring—all worldly, my grandfather said, the devil's tricks and trinkets, and he left them with the orphanage to pawn.

I wailed all the way to Shawnee, but my grandfather didn't speak a word. By the time we took the road south that led to the flat edge of town—that marginal land where the poorest whites and poorer blacks scraped out a living—I had cried myself into a snubbing stupor. He held my door, waited patiently as I climbed down and stood facing the narrow two-room shack with its broken foundation and sagging roof, the outhouse in back a haphazard construction of split pine. I trailed him through the kitchen, its walls papered with newsprint, pasted with flour and water, stained dark with soot, and into the bedroom, where he placed my suitcase on the horsehair mattress. He peered down at me, laid his hand on top of my head. 'God

3

will keep us,' he said, pulled the door shut, and left me alone.

From the room's single window, I saw that he had changed into his patched work clothes, and I watched as he hitched the jenny mule, threw the reins over his shoulders, and returned to the plot he'd been plowing. What I found in that house was little: tenpenny nails in the wall, hung with my grandfather's good hat and suit; a two-door cupboard that held Karo, flour, sugar, a salted ham hock; an oilcloth-covered table and two weak chairs; a short-wicked kerosene lantern; a potbellied stove streaked with creosote; the cot that my grandfather had set in the kitchen and covered with an old wool blanket so that I might have the bed. I moved to the porch, found the washbasin, the straight razor, the leather strop, and a cropped piece of flannel that he used for a towel. I sat on the single-plank step and watched him chuck the mule up one row and down another until he put the plow away, came and stood in front of me, wiping the sweat from his brow.

'Where's my dinner, sister?' he asked gently. I hadn't thought to feed him, didn't know how. He led me back to the cupboard, showed me the cast-iron skillet, the knife, how to make red-eye gravy with the ham drippings, flour, and salt. Over the next week, we would eat that ham right down to the bone, boil it for soup on Saturday, crack it for marrow. I learned what it meant to be hungry, learned that Sundays meant more food and a healthy helping of God's word.

Because he now had a child to care for, my grandfather left the circuit, and he counted it as God's goodwill that a small congregation east of the city was in need of a pastor. The parishioners, some white, most black, folded us in, and though I had no siblings, they called me Sister Gin. I wasn't yet old enough to understand what the townspeople might think—*that poor little white girl*—and spent the Sabbath wedged in a hard oak pew between skin that ran from pale pink to sallow, dusky to dark. My grandfather's dictates were absolute, but in his eyes, all of God's children, *red and yellow, black and white,* were bound by the same mortal sin, given the same chance at redemption. I sat in fascinated horror, the sanctified moaning around me, as I listened to my grandfather's hellfire sermons that foretold the woe of every unsaved soul. Blood to the horse's bridle, flames licking the flesh—the punishment that would come my way if I didn't repent, but no matter how hard I considered my deeds, I didn't yet know what sins to confess.

After the hymns had been sung—*happy are the faithful dead!*—the churchwomen prepared a fellowship meal at one shack or another. Your color didn't matter when it came to who was served and where, but whether you were male or female did. The men were fed where they sat, their wives fixing their plates before their own, wise to their husbands' predilections: Brother Fink ate only the chicken's legs, thighs, and the tail he called the pope's nose; Brother Jackson required that his food be layered—a mound of potatoes topped with meat and smothered with a generosity of gravy. The boys not old enough to be in the men's circle and the girls too young for kitchen help were called in next, made to scrub their faces, and put to the table. Only after the men and the children were served did the women eat: bread heels, chicken backs,

5

the wateriest remains of corn pudding. They ate with babies nursing at their breasts and whispered their hushed stories of hard births and tumorous wombs, jumping up when called to bring another biscuit or glass of sweet tea to the men, whose talk was of dropping wheat prices, Nazi spies, and the local criminal element that ran bootleg out of the bottoms and carried razor-sharp knives. I sat quiet in whatever corner I could find, acting like I wasn't listening, but what I heard told me all that I needed to know: that the world was fallen, that my only hope lay in the grace and glory of God, that Satan was waiting for me to falter at every turn, that he might appear to me as the Angel of Light, deceive me with his wicked tongue, and lead me to hell as his bride.

How many times did I rouse from some nightmare, call out for my mother to save me? I might have left the trappings of my old life behind, but my grief had packed up and moved right along with me, shaped and weighted as though it had a life of its own. I woke one night so sure that the devil had found me that I ran to the cot in the kitchen, told my grandfather that I could feel that grief lying right there beside me like a panting black dog. He lit a candle, took a vial of oil from the corner of the cupboard, made the sign of the cross on my forehead, and pressed his palms to my ears. 'Demon, by the authority given to me by the Lord Jesus Christ, I command that you leave this child!' He gripped my head tighter, shook it like a gourd. 'In the name of the Father, the Son, and the Holy Ghost, come out of her, I command you!' He drew his hands away so quickly that the suction nearly deafened me. When I opened my eyes, I

6

saw the tears pooling in the dark shallows of his face, his mouth arched as though that demon had leaped right out of me and into him. I went back to my bed, now cold, and wished I had never left it, had kept my hurt to myself. Silence was a lesson I learned well—how to mute my body, my voice, my heart.

That fall, my first day of school, my grandfather rode me to town on the mule because the pickup had broken down and no amount of prayer would fix it. As we approached the playground, I saw all the white children pointing and laughing until the pretty young teacher came out to scold them. If I hadn't understood it before, I knew it then: we were different, *I* was different, not only a member of the Holy Roller church but an orphan from the south edge of town who lived where most whites wouldn't. I slid from the mule's broad back, kept my head down, and followed the teacher into the room, where she showed me my desk and placed a picture book in my hands. 'You can read for a while,' she said kindly, and left me to lose myself in the pages even as the other students filed in and began reciting their numbers. From that point on, books became my solace, my escape. I brought them home from the library, hid them from the eyes of my grandfather, who believed that only the word of God had a place in his house, that stories outside of the scripture might lead me astray.

I completed elementary, kept growing, went with the junior high nurse to buy what my grandfather called my unmentionables—soft-cupped brassieres, panties, sanitary belts and napkins—then stood in my bedroom, confounded by the hooks and straps, ashamed that my grandfather would no longer meet my eyes when I came in from the outhouse. From him, I learned that I was the daughter of Eve, a danger to myself, a temptation to those around me. Couldn't wear pants, only skirts that covered my knees. Couldn't wear makeup or jewelry to draw the attention of men. Couldn't cut my hair, which was my veil of modesty. Couldn't preach because Paul said so. Suffer not a woman. When revival came and the Spirit descended, the sisters who were slain fell flat on their backs, arms raised to heaven, ecstatic in their possession, and I was the one whose charge it was to hasten forward and cover their legs with the lap cloths that they themselves had sewn so that their modesty might be maintained. What would it feel like, I wondered, to give myself over so completely, to fall under such a spell? But not even the fear that I would spend my eternal life in hell brought the call that would lead me to kneel at the altar, lay myself at the feet of the Lord, and the church people noticed. I learned to pretend the conviction I did not feel, to pray with my mouth open, my eyes closed, my hands raised to heaven. I was saved—couldn't they see? Born again. It was a lie I didn't realize I was living, a way to survive the surly dictates of that thing called faith.

Who knows what gives rise to our sensibilities? Maybe it was some seed of resistance sown in me by my grandmother that allowed me to keep my soul to myself. Maybe it was just the way I was—*turned funny*, I heard them say. They didn't even bother to hide their mouths. No matter the color of my skin, I was the kind of girl they watched from the corners of their eyes, the kind of girl that brought them to predictions—headed to ruin if I didn't get my head straight, my heart right with God. I wasn't like them, wasn't like anybody I knew.

It was the characters in books who spoke to me, reflected some secret part of myself. When the librarian handed me *To Kill a Mockingbird,* I read it straight through, then hid it beneath my bed. 'I lost it,' I told the librarian. 'I'll work check-in and checkout during recess to pay.' She was satisfied, and so was I. It was a sin that I was jealous of and wanted to keep—the worst sin of all.

Walking home from school one afternoon, the September air thick with gray aphids, *Anne of Green Gables* open in my hands, I found a girl asleep on her sack, cotton tufting her hair. Fall harvest meant more hours in the field for the black children of South Town, the season's sun beating down, the long, long sack trailing behind like an earthbound anchor. Maybe that was when I began to understand that, no matter how different I was, my life would never be as hard as hers. I sat at the edge of the patch and watched her for a long time, then tore away one page of the book and then another, planting them in the soil beneath her bare feet as though they might sprout like Jack's magic beanstalk and carry her aloft, as though I were feeding the girl her dreams.

When the librarian discovered the ruined book, she said that two was too many and sent me home with a bill. That was the first time I lied outright to my grandfather. Ignoring any lessons I might have learned about false accusation, I described in detail how Tug Larson, the schoolyard bully, had knocked the novel from my hands. 'He grabbed me,' I said, 'and pushed me down.' I cried and showed my grandfather the bruises I had pinched on my arms to convince him how wounded I was.

He grew solemn, said he would talk with the boy, but I insisted it would only make things worse, that he was already being given detention, and shouldn't I forgive? My grandfather was placated, and I felt a surge of relief and tingling possibility. I had transgressed, might confess and be forgiven, but I had discovered something that intrigued me even more: I could lie and not be struck dead in my shoes.

I remembered my grandmother's ways, used the last of our flour and lard to bake half a batch of sugar cookies, told my grandfather I was taking them to Sister Woody, an elderly parishioner who lived down the road, and he nodded his approval at my charity. I felt like skipping as I made my way out the door. I had no destination, only a desire to be free. I walked an easy two miles, ate half the cookies, fed the rest to the crows, turned around, and came home happy with the news that Sister Woody's health was improving.

I became braver, told bigger lies, and walked the farmland for hours or hid with my book in the neighbor's barn. In gym class, I let my body have its joy, leaping and sprinting ahead of my classmates. When my teacher suggested I try out for girls' basketball, I forged a careful note home that said I was helping clean the blackboards after school. I made the team and for the first time felt part of something, like I might be someone's friend, running up and down the half-court and hollering back and forth like it was a normal thing for a girl to do. I skipped the communal showers, unable to imagine letting myself be seen naked, left my knee-length trunks and sleeveless top in my locker, and ran as fast as I could, hoping to beat my grandfather home. He would sit down to the dinner I made him and never say a word about my wild hair, my ruddy skin, and I believed I had fooled him until the evening he rode into town on the mule and appeared at practice still in his farm clothes, pulled out the worn Bible, and filled the gymnasium with his voice. '"The woman shall not wear that which pertaineth unto a man, neither shall a man put on a woman's garment: for all that do so are an abomination unto the *Lord* thy God!"' He clapped the good book closed, pointed me to the door, and I slunk out, shamed not by my sin but by the looks of pity on the faces of my teammates. Once home, he sent me to my room and sat at the foot of my bed, studying me with intense sadness, as though he might see the workings of my deceitful soul. 'I can't let you burn in hell,' he said, and raised the leather strop. The fierceness of his whipping came up through my bones, rattled like dry seeds in my ears. After, he held me and cried. Maybe that's why I can forgive him. He only meant to save me.

Why couldn't I just obey? Drinking, smoking, dancing, bowling, playing cards, going to movies, wading with the Butler boys down at the creek—all sins. To question my grandfather's rules and the law of his God was mutiny, any plans to rebel an act of treason. Yet even with the punishment I knew was coming, I'd slide open the sash I'd waxed with paraffin, drop to the ground, and walk to Chester's Drug, where I would sit at the end of the counter and watch the boys peacock, the girls preen while the jukebox played Elvis, Roy Orbison, the Miracles.

The only one who paid me any mind those times was Juney Clooney, a white girl too pretty for her

11

own good, the church ladies said, but I envied her grace, the way she tipped back her soda, ponytail hanging down like a plumb bob. She would pour me a glass of her Nehi, something in her smile almost sad. Maybe I was the only one who wasn't surprised when her place at the counter came up empty, one of the few who knew the truth of what had happened between her and Baby Buckle.

Buckle was a childlike man, rolled flesh at his neck, rounded shoulders and soft hips, waist cinched by a wide leather belt and a brass buckle the size of a saucer. He worked right there at Chester's Drug as a delivery boy. Chester and his wife always said that Buckle showed up one Christmas Eve, abandoned as a baby on their doorstep, cold as slab marble, but rumor held he was Chester's son by Hazel Twig, a young mixed-race woman from our side of town who cleaned the store once a week until she up and disappeared. Because that is what happened when girls got themselves in trouble. They were sent to the home for unwed mothers or simply sent away, anything to erase the family's shame, absolve the father's guilt.

It was Juney's twin brother, Jules, who came stumbling into the store one day, his shotgun loaded, hollering that he'd gone home for lunch and found Juney crying. She told him that Buckle had come to make a delivery, caught her alone frying gizzards, and dragged her into the pantry. I sat stone still as the other boys piled into their pickups. They found him beneath that big walnut tree at Bowman's Corner, asleep with his pants at his ankles. They didn't stop to ask, just noosed him up with his own belt, buckle splitting his mouth like

12

a bit. It wasn't but a few days later that I came in on Juney's mother, confessing to my grandfather that it wasn't Buckle who had raped her daughter but Juney's own daddy, who told her to blame Buckle or he'd kill her and her mother too. All that Buckle did was pick the wrong tree to do his business behind. But what good would it have done for me to tell, and who would believe me? I had read the stories of courage and conviction, but sometimes the truth seemed worse than the lie. I sat quiet at the counter, kept my secrets to myself.

What I remember of high school: not the football games and dances I wasn't allowed to attend, not overnights with the girlfriends I didn't have, but the romances and mysteries that kept me company. My grandfather demanded from me humility, modesty, and temperance, but when I read *Little Women, Gone with the Wind, Murder on the Orient Express,* I entered into the realm of everything knowable, anything possible, if only I were smart enough, pretty enough, and brave.

In my imagination, I had traveled to that place of dark-haired princes and veiled sultanas, knew the thousand and one tales that kept Scheherazade alive, dreamed that I might do the same, weave a web of stories so enthralling that the man I loved would be spared the agony of having to kill me, but if someone had told me that I would soon be living in Arabia, I would have laughed. And no matter the number of romances I read, I never dreamed that someone like Mason McPhee would kiss me— my long skirt, those awful shoes, straw from the henhouse tasseling my socks. But Mason. Highest-scoring point guard, on full-ride scholarship to Oklahoma State, once and former prom king, the

13

pride of Shawnee! Homecoming, the first parade of my life, Mason an honored guest riding high in a convertible Chevrolet, everyone calling his name. Only our hometown astronaut, Gordo Cooper, had a bigger crowd, and he'd orbited the Earth in a spaceship.

I wore my best wool skirt, rolled it up just a little. If my grandfather had seen me that way, he'd have whipped me into next Sunday. I thought I might look like Rita Hayworth, auburn hair to my waist, loose and undone, and maybe I did. Maybe that's what Mason saw. 'Virginia!' He cupped his hands like a megaphone. 'Ginny Mae Mitchell!' I was struck dumb, as though he were the first ever to call my name.

Here's the truth of it: watching him smile and wave from that car, I made the decision right then. When he asked me out for a Coke, I thought, This is it, my one chance with a man like Mason McPhee. I waited until my grandfather was asleep and slid open my window, not a creak or scratch to betray me.

That Coke was the sweetest thing. I couldn't believe I was there at the soda fountain with Mason, the other boys slapping his shoulder. The girls looked at me like they'd never seen me before. Maybe because I didn't know what to say, Mason talked and talked. About basketball, all the hours he had practiced in back of his house, a bicycle rim bolted to a pine. How his sharecropper father would come in off the tractor, challenge him to a game of Horse, and they would play past dark, nine games, ten, until Mason's mother called that she was feeding their dinner to the hogs. Mason always knew he would go to college and was studying

14

prelaw, meant to be the finest public defender to come out of Pottawatomie County, maybe even a judge. He was sure that he could make a difference. He railed against the war in Vietnam and segregation, told me about the marches and protests he attended. 'This world right here isn't real,' he said, and tapped the café table. 'You,' he said, resting his hand over mine, 'you can never be what you ought to be until I am what I ought to be. We've got to think bigger, do bigger things, like the Reverend King says.'

I didn't know the words of famous men, only the verses of the Bible I had been raised on, but I believed everything that Mason told me, as though they were truths I had felt but never knew how to say. All I could do was nod, take in the shock of light hair fallen across his forehead, those blue, blue eyes, his only flaw a small scar at the right corner of his mouth that folded in like a dimple. He hadn't seen it coming, pitched by the boy picking rocks, the two of them sweating for ten cents an hour, clearing the Cooks' field free of stones. Even that wound seemed worthy, a testament to work and withstanding.

'I should get you on home,' he said. He held my eyes for a moment, and when I didn't look away, he brought my palm to his lips. And then it was easy enough to slide into his old sprung sedan, ride that road out of town, find that little stand of post oak. He ran his hand beneath my hair. 'You smell just like ripe wheat,' he said, 'just like honey from the hive.'

I should say I tried to stop him, but what reason would I have now to lie? Another few days and he would be gone back to the city, another world, but after we finished, he held me close like he feared I might slip away. When he lit a cigarette, I lifted my face.

'Can I have one?' It was the first thing I had asked of him, as though opening my body had loosened my tongue.

'I bet you don't even know how,' he said.

I moved my hand to his, eased the cigarette from his fingers, and he crooked a smile. 'You're damned determined, aren't you?'

Maybe just damned, I thought, but not a single cell of my body believed it was true.

After I told him to, he dropped me at Bowman's Corner, and I walked the flat mile back home. I wanted to keep the night inside me a little while longer. All those stars. That piece of moon. 'You only think you know what you want,' my grandfather once said to me, but this time, I was sure.

By Christmas, I couldn't lie anymore—my grandfather had been watching my rags. He wasn't crying when he whipped me but making sounds like he was dying. I couldn't help but curl up, even though some part of me wanted to give him my belly, let him beat the baby right out of me. Maybe he was more afraid than I was, and the truth is, I wasn't afraid at all. I believed that I was done being afraid.

That night, I waited until he fell asleep in his cot, the strop still coiling his fist like a copperhead, before pulling on my mother's old riding boots, soft and slick in the soles, and sliding out of my window. When my feet hit the ground, I was running, cutting straight across those open fields, leaping the ditches, falling over stones. By the time I reached

Chester's Drug, my knees were bleeding, my palms burning raw. I called from the pay phone at the corner, nickels dropping down, heard Christmas carols, men's laughter in the background. When I told Mason, he didn't even hesitate, just said he would do right by me. It was an honorable thing. I knew it then and I know it now. A right and honorable thing.

He drove in from Stillwater, picked me up at the corner, and took me to Oklahoma City, where we lied about my age to the justice of the peace. A thin band from the pawnshop, a little bit of gold, and I was Mrs. Mason McPhee. There was nothing my grandfather could do but what he did—he shunned me, wouldn't even speak my name.

Mason's parents offered that I could live with them while he went back to college, but he said he wanted to do this on his own, it was his responsibility, and I knew he meant me. He told his coach he'd lay out for a while, get a job and save up, return in the fall, but when a slicker came up from Texas, recruiting for Zapata Off-Shore, fanning money and mouthing promises of plenty, Mason didn't hesitate, signed on as a roughneck, and said we were headed to Houston. I wish now I had talked whatever sense I had left, insisted that he go back to school, but I believed that, as a wife, I had only two choices: follow his lead, or leave.

We packed up everything we owned, made the trip in a day, and found a little rental behind Basta's Funeral Parlor, peach-colored stucco with a redbud out front. I kept the back curtains closed against the hearse pulling away, the parade of cars with their lights on. But the parking lot had a basketball hoop, the mortician watered the lawn green, and

17

the tulip trees lining the lane filled the evening air with their sweet perfume. Sometimes I wish we had stayed right there, making our way dollar by dollar, but Mason never let the grass grow under his feet. The only way he knew how to move was up.

Those first weeks, he'd come home from the oil rig black as a coal miner, all the shininess of his life gone. We lived on stew meat, sacks of beans, thought an onion was a special thing. I'd get up each morning, pull on his old jeans and long-tailed shirt, sweep the floor, sew a little, then fry spuds for dinner just like my mother did, the baby in me heavy and kicking, already wanting out. Mason, he'd eat the food right down to the plate, tell me how good it was, then go to bed, asleep before his head hit the pillow. I'd start scrubbing his clothes because they were the only ones he had, hang them by the stove to dry, iron them in the morning. Only when I tucked into our single bed, borax still burning my knuckles, did he wake, just long enough to kiss my neck, make love in that tired, sweet way, and then we would sleep.

Mason believed in giving his all no matter what, never complained, just did his job better than the next guy, kept the muscle moving the metal that pumped the oil that kept the profit and every man's paycheck coming in. Some of the drillers were Okies like us, others Creoles trucked in off the bayous, Czechs just off the boat—to Mason, all the same. I'd never known a white man to step aside for a black, but that's what Mason did. Like me, he sometimes forgot to even think of color, and I loved him more for it, but I knew what some of the other men were thinking as they watched him, gauging his sympathies, their mouths twisting with

18

the names they called him behind his back. If I had first been drawn to the vision of him sitting high in that convertible Chevrolet, what I came to cherish was his fairness, his compassion and belief that he could change things, make the world a better place, so different from what I had been taught: that man had fallen so far, there was no way to pick him up again.

When a Chickasaw running a cable got sliced clean through and his pregnant widow lay in the dirt at the base of the rig for two days until her family came to carry her away, I wrote her a letter, and Mason sealed in what money we'd saved. 'She's lucky they found him at all. Sometimes there isn't much left,' he said, and I remembered a woman in Shawnee whose husband had disappeared in the oil patch, vanished without a trace, she told my grandfather, like he'd been caught up in the Rapture. She'd come to our shack for assurance that she hadn't been left behind, and I watched the two of them kneel in the kitchen, my grandfather's hands on her shoulders, her lips quivering in prayer. The next day they found her husband, who had fallen through the floor of the platform and been impaled on a rod, thigh to throat. 'Just like a scarecrow,' the crew boss said. 'Even his hat was still on.' I learned early that people can disappear just like that—the wink of an eye and they're gone.

Houston seemed like the center of the world back then, people coming in from all over, derrickhands, engineers, toolpushers, and boiler-men—Mason's friends, every one. Weekends meant cocktail parties, pinochle parties, jamborees at the Bill Mraz Dance Hall, where Mason taught me to polka, my maternity smock billowing as we

19

twirled. I watched the other women smoke their cigarettes, drink whiskey sours, cross their legs, nylons swishing. They belonged to that world that my grandfather had feared would find me. I didn't know how to talk to them, what to say, but Mason, he fit right in. That smile, quick and easy. Sometimes, when he grew quiet, refilled his whiskey again, I feared he was thinking about the way things might have been if he hadn't married me but Sally Richardson, his prom queen, blond hair, narrow waist, a daddy who owned the Buick dealership. No man wanted a ruined woman—wasn't that what I'd been told? Yet there I was, dancing the night away with Mason McPhee, having the time of my life.

We bought a white bassinet, a pale yellow blanket with satin trim, set up the extra bedroom as a nursery, and I spent my days washing walls, sewing curtains, until all I had to do was sit and wait, even as the near-spring air perked the robins into frenzies and the redbuds swelled fat. When I told Mason I wanted to learn how to drive, have some way to get out when he was gone, he veed his forehead. 'Streets are too busy around here,' he said. 'I'll take you to the country one of these days, let you bust around where nothing can get in your way.' I bided my time, beat him out of bed one Saturday before dawn, climbed behind the wheel of his old sedan, and eased it around the block. I thought I could steal those minutes, the sky just beginning to pink, teach myself all that I needed to know, but when Mason stepped out later that morning to find the car bumped up onto the curb, he lit a cigarette, looked at me with one eye squinted shut, but didn't say a word. He got in, drove away, and I thought he was angry,

20

but he returned an hour later from the used-car lot in a pretty little two-tone Fairlane. 'Best to go along with whatever you set your mind to,' he said, grinning as he moved to the passenger seat. 'Telling you no is like pouring gas on a fire.'

I slid behind the wheel, drove twice around the block, and felt right at home, as though I were meant to hit the road a little faster. Mason pointed to the highway, and we headed south, Dean Martin on the radio, past the new domed stadium, so big I couldn't take it in, and on to where pumpjacks levered the horizon, the ranchland split open and paved into cul-de-sacs, fresh-built houses strung out like charms on a bracelet, NASA families in every one. I checked the rearview, saw the new high-rises, steel beams piercing the haze, and thought of our dead president's call to put a man on the moon. Even then, some part of me understood we wanted to own it all, up, down, earth to sky.

When Mason pointed to the Mobil, I slowed and turned in, afraid I'd dent the fender if I pulled too close, but the attendant motioned me forward. While Mason got out and helped clean the windshield, I focused on the flying red horse. Pegasus, I remembered. I had wanted to go to college and become an English teacher, but even if I hadn't gotten in trouble, my grandfather wouldn't have let me. Worldly education hardened your heart against God, he said, and filled your head with ideas.

I watched Mason walk back to the Fairlane, tipping a bottle of Dr Pepper still dripping ice, the heat shirring the air between us. His hair grown a little too long, a pack of cigarettes rolled in the sleeve of his white T-shirt, his jeans riding low on

21

his hips—I felt a lick of lust mixed with guilt, that baby right there inside me.

'Hey, doll.' He slipped in, handed me the soda, and I drank in deep swallows. I toed the accelerator, directing the car away from the attendant, who stood in his billed cap like a soldier at attention.

My stomach pressed against the rub of the steering wheel brought me back to the road. I had been thinking about names and considered the constellations I'd memorized, library book and flashlight held beneath the covers so that my grandfather wouldn't know that I was studying the stars like a necromancer.

'What about Cassie for a girl?' I asked. 'Cassiopeia.'

Mason sucked his teeth. 'Boy?'

'Percy? Perseus McPhee.' I signaled left, then changed my mind, kept going.

'Where are you coming up with these names, anyway?' Mason began drumming the car top, singing along with the radio, his voice an easy blend in the low keys as I guided us through the evening streets, taking the long way, air through the windows heavy with the smoke of backyard barbecues.

That night, I woke to the sheets slick and cooling beneath me, the pain gripping my back, the ache in my thighs. At the hospital, while the doctor scraped and pulled then called for his ether, the nun held my shoulders. It was just as well, she said— something had been wrong for the baby to die like that, as though I should feel lucky. 'Do you want him baptized?' she asked, but I turned my head away. I didn't have the words for what I was feeling,

22

raw and empty, nothing that I could name. When the doctor told me I could no longer bear children, I thought, This is the punishment my grandfather promised me. This is what I deserve.

When, a few days later, Mason drove me home from the hospital, he circled around, kept the tulip trees between us and the funeral home. He went in ahead, pulled shut the door to the nursery. I'd never see that room again. He set the blue ceramic baby bootie that the nun had given us on the kitchen sill, a small tangle of variegated ivy sprouting from its center.

I quit the cocktail parties, spent my days with the doors and windows closed. When the *Chronicle* landed on our porch with its stories of race riots, women burning their bras, men burning their draft cards, the flag, burning, I let it lay. When the evening news gave a tally of the weekly body count in Vietnam, I turned it off because I didn't want to know. I focused on my chores, what I was made for. By the time Mason came home from work, I had the bed tucked tight, the floors scrubbed, the laundry on the line, a brambleberry pie bubbling in the oven. I'd once filled my diary with stories of romance, imagined I might someday be a writer, but what right did I have to dream? Only at night, Mason shooting baskets for hours, the sound of the ball hitting asphalt, bouncing, hitting again, did I allow myself to sit on the couch and read. The Texas sky clouding over, a storm moving in— those seemed the stillest of times, as though I were suspended, hovering outside my own life.

I looked up one evening to see Mason standing there and felt the old fear, my grandfather snatching the book from my hands. But Mason,

23

he sat down beside me, touched my forehead as though I were a child sick with fever, pushed the hair from my face. He smelled like the fields after spring burn. Out the window, I saw the sun not yet set, the days grown longer without me.

'You need more than this,' he said, and pulled me to him. 'We got to get you better.'

The next morning, he told me to get dressed, that we were going to town. It seemed like the hardest thing I had ever done. Gordo Cooper had set the record, eight days in orbit, long enough to fly a man to the moon, yet I couldn't even step out my door. I stood in my slip for a good half hour, staring at the closet, nothing to wear but the schoolgirl's wool skirt I'd brought with me from Shawnee and a few maternity dresses—the trappings of someone else's life. I picked out the smock I'd worn to the polka, belted it with a sash, found my one pair of flats and realized I'd been barefoot for weeks. I tied my hair, traced my eyebrows with the burned head of a match, added a little rouge—enough sin, my grandfather would say, to bring on more. He didn't know his great-grandson was dead. Maybe he never would.

The first thing Mason did was to drive me to the Sonic for lunch. He held my hand while the carhop skated out and took our order.

'You look real nice, Gin,' Mason said.

I straightened my sash, kept my eyes down. 'It's not much,' I said.

'It doesn't take much. You're always beautiful.' He pulled me to his shoulder, let his burger get cold while I cried, then drove me to Foley's, sat and watched while I tried on dresses, blouses, a new kind of stretch pants, the saleswomen clucking. By

24

the time we got home, I had a wardrobe, a word I'd never spoken before. I used every hanger we owned. We made love standing up in the kitchen, me in my shiny patent leathers. Shameless, I thought, but who was there to see? Any remnant of belief I might have had in an all-knowing God was gone.

Mason had me sit down while he scrambled some eggs. I watched as he cut my toast into triangles, thought how he wasn't like any man I'd ever known, then raised my eyes to the ivy that had grown and tacked itself to the wall above the sink. I'd started to pull it free once, but I couldn't bear the noise of it ripping, the rusty imprint of its rooting like dabs of dried blood. Every time I started to feel happy, the world came back to knock me down like happiness was something I had to pay for.

'I don't want to be here anymore,' I said. I didn't know if I meant in that house or in Houston. Maybe I meant my own life. 'I wish we could leave this all behind.'

Mason didn't say a word. He didn't have to. My dead mother's voice was already in my head: *Be careful what you wish for.*

The next day, Mason came home lit up like a firecracker. His supervisor had recommended him to an Aramco recruiter. 'Drilling foreman,' he said. 'Double my salary, maybe more, tax-free. All we have to do is move to Arabia.'

I couldn't hear what he was telling me, so he said it again. 'Saudi Arabia, a place called Abqaiq, all fenced and guarded. Everything we want, just like living in a country club.' He sat me down, had me imagine: our own home, private swimming pool, golf course, movie theater, the best doctors money could buy—and all of it paid for by the Arabian American Oil Company. 'When we get back, we'll have enough money to buy you all the new clothes you want.' He held my shoulders, bent a little to look into my eyes. 'Nice house, big diamond ring, that's what you want, isn't it, Gin?' I tried to remember if I had ever wanted such things. He gave me a squeeze, a little shake as though he needed to get something out of me. 'I don't want to be just scraping by for the rest of my life,' he said. 'I was on my way somewhere. I need to feel that again.'

I rested my ear against his chest, felt his heart pounding fast, already racing ahead.

Over the next few weeks, what we couldn't sell, we gave away. When Mason carried the bassinet out the door, free to a derrickman whose wife was expecting their third, I watched through the kitchen window, gave the ivy a little more water. Maybe the next wife would find it there, let it grow. Maybe she'd think it too much trouble and tear it free, planning wallpaper, a double coat of eggshell enamel.

I packed all the clothes I owned, my new pair of shoes, my mother's old boots. 'Best to leave the books at home,' Mason said, but I folded *Gone with the Wind* into my sweater anyway. Valentine's Day, 1967, the redbuds near bursting, I boarded the first plane of my life, smart in my new Jantzen suit. Other passengers arranged their blankets and pillows, settling in for the flight to New York. Behind us, several rows of women chatted and laughed.

Mason motioned to the back. 'Aramco wives being shipped over. You could be with them instead of me.'

I stole a glance to where they giggled like schoolgirls, then turned and rested my head on Mason's shoulder. I'd never been comfortable in the company of women, unsure of what they expected of me. With men, at least, I knew.

Mason pulled my knuckles to his lips, kissed them twice. 'For luck,' he said. I clutched his hand a little tighter, smelled the aftershave he'd slapped on the back of his neck where the barber had clipped him too close. 'I look like a farm boy,' he had said, fingering the line where his tan met the pale stripe of skin. 'That's because you are,' I answered, and he had grown quiet, as though that were a part of himself he wanted to forget.

I peered out the small window of the plane, saw the gray Gulf of Mexico falling away. Our layover in New York I remember only as a dim hotel room filled with the noise of the bar below, Aramco and Bechtel men laying in a last good drunk before hitting the dry desert. A short stop in Montreal, where we took on more passengers, and then the ocean crossing.

It was like a dream, flying through that night. I remember Mason held in a white pool of light, studying his book of Arabic phrases, and then people leaving their seats, gathering in the aisles to smoke and drink until the plane took on the feel of a flying lounge, Johnny Rivers piping through the speakers. I thought I wouldn't be able to sleep, but I did. When Mason lifted the shade, we were landing in Amsterdam, the sun spreading across the horizon like paint spilled from a can. A stop in Athens to refuel, and then on to Beirut, where we left the jet and boarded a four-engine prop scoured shiny by sand.

'From here, it's the milk run to Dhahran,' Mason said. 'Six countries in three days—not bad for a couple of Okies from Shawnee.' He still looked crisp in his new Arrow shirt, but I felt woozy, my cheeks flushed.

We crossed into Arabia and followed the Trans-Arabian Pipeline, leapfrogging along, scattering herds of camels from the water wells Aramco had drilled, landing on oiled strips to unload geologists, small engines, and crates of eggs that were replaced by bundles of letters, trunks, and packages, grinning American golfers carrying their clubs, a single Arab in gold rings and flowing robes. When the plane abruptly banked, sending everything that wasn't strapped or bolted to the lee of the fuselage, I screamed and grabbed for Mason's arm. The Arab man smiled. 'It is only the wind,' he said simply, as though it were the answer to any number of things, and I felt myself blush. I wanted to tell him what I knew of wind— the tornadoes tipping from the yellowing sky, hot gales that sapped the sweet from the corn. How my grandfather would strip an ear, scrape a few kernels with his teeth. 'Could be worse,' he'd say. He remembered the powder-dry soil, the roof-high drifts, his own family's house buried in the till of once-fertile fields. I looked out the window, saw the dunes undulating for miles. Like the sand, that dust was everywhere, sifted into the cavities and creases of everything living and dead, and I understood how it was that the Okies and Texans might find the desert familiar, the suffocating heat a manageable thing.

The Tapline ran before us like an ink-dark tattoo, broken only by mounds of sand bridging the

28

routes of nomadic migration. In the distance, a vast pool of light, the sun, and the sea that melded with the sky to a single canvas. And then I saw the flares. Mason had told me that even the astronauts could see them from space, giant flames burning off gas at the wellheads. The Dhahran Airport appeared like a white cathedral: pillars, arches like wings, control tower shaped like a minaret. All that light flowing in. We stepped off the plane, and it was like opening an oven. A furnace blast. A heat you had to lean into or be knocked down.

I stood stunned by the hours we'd lost in flight until Mason took my arm and steered me across the tarmac. Inside, I watched the Arab official search through my clothes while a clutch of women cloaked in black silently waited to board. The Saudi man who accompanied them, dressed in a fine-cut suit and white head scarf, sat placidly, intent upon the activity my luggage elicited. The customs official took one look at the cover of my book— Scarlett and Rhett in an ardent embrace—handed it to an attendant, and clapped the suitcase closed before flourishing a stick of chalk between us and marking my bags with bold checks. When I started to protest, Mason tapped my elbow, shook his head.

The company driver who waited for us outside of customs stood with his hands folded, calm as a monk, as though the weight of his garments didn't bother him a bit. Red-and-white-checked head scarf secured with a black leather cord, a creamy ankle-length nightshirt that buttoned from neck to hem—he must be suffocating, I thought, and remembered how my mother had wrapped me in sheets to break fever.

'Peace be upon you.' His took off his dark

29

glasses, and his eyes wrinkled at the corners as he shook our hands. 'I am Abdullah al-Jahni. Welcome among friends.'

'And upon you peace.' Mason motioned me forward. 'This is my wife, Mrs. Virginia McPhee.'

Abdullah reached out, gave my hand a warm, single shake. I had imagined Arab men as either rough and brutish or courtly and cosseted, draped in the robes of a prince, but Abdullah was neither. He seemed a few years older than Mason, his face not as handsome but somehow more interesting, as though I might study it for a long time and discover something new each second. I took in his angular profile and steeply sloped nose, his thin mustache and carefully groomed beard that followed the line of his jaw, his wide mouth full of impossibly white teeth, but it was his eyes, half-lidded and deeply set, that intrigued me. His gaze moved from me to Mason to the baggage handlers and beyond in fluid and precise observation, as though he were committing each detail to memory or guarding himself against surprise. He led us to a dun-colored Land Cruiser that might once have been green, where he instructed the airport workers on the loading of our luggage. When he stepped off the curb, he gathered his skirts like a woman, and I realized that I was staring. He opened the door so that I could climb into the backseat, Mason in front. I lifted my nose to the cracked window as we passed a series of raw buildings and rough settlements before heading southwest, deeper into the desert. What I smelled was almost nothing. I opened my mouth to taste it, and a memory came to me. Fourth of July, a church potluck and fireworks over the creek, and it was my job to sit on the ice-cream maker as my grandfather cranked, my patience helped along by the chipped knobs of salted ice that I sucked and savored like candy.

The land humped and flattened, broken by bunches of yellowing grass plowed through with sand. The dry streambeds bristled with spring flowers, their oranges and purples and reds like the burst of fireworks. Even now, I don't know how to describe the sudden emptiness that crowded in once we left the airport. No trees, no mountains, just the horizon ribboned with clouds that seemed to smoke right off the desert floor and into the sapphire sky. The minimal traffic—a black Jeep, a large white donkey laden with palm fronds, a few people on foot—seemed oblivious to the rules of the road: no sidewalks, no lanes, no limits. I braced myself against the seat as Abdullah veered to miss a rattletrap pickup, men packing the bed, balanced on the bumpers, clinging to any handhold. He never slowed, just kept a steady speed to pull us out of the sand and back onto the road.

'I thought Texas drivers were bad,' Mason said.

'Better than an American driving a camel.' Abdullah grinned. 'Truly, that is sad.'

I noted the way the men sat the humped animals, some with one leg crooked like they were riding sidesaddle, others kneeling astride or straddling with their ankles crossed at the camel's neck. They urged their mounts faster by lifting their arms, shaking the reins until the animals broke into a jarring canter, and I wondered how they kept their seats. Other camels roamed free like cattle on open range, their colors the colors of the desert: bone, buff, and straw. Flies rose thick off a road-killed carcass—a young camel left to rot, Abdullah

31

told us, because it hadn't been slaughtered in accordance with Islamic law and was therefore *haram*—forbidden—and could not be eaten.

Mason and Abdullah began an easy conversation about the hierarchies of the Saudi royalty, future drilling sites, and new machinery, and I relaxed back, happy to be left to my study until I saw a wavering dark line in the distance that seemed to loom large, then small, like a film out of focus. I squinted but couldn't tell how far away we were—a half mile? Five? It was as though the desert existed in two dimensions and nothing in my vision was true. I sat forward and pointed.

'What is that?' I asked Abdullah.

'Bedu,' Abdullah answered. 'People of the tent. With the new opportunities, there are fewer of us who remain in the desert.'

As we drew closer, I peered at the caravan, the men in their robes and white scarves, daggers belted at their waists, the women in long colorful skirts, their hair, faces, and shoulders draped in black, balancing baskets and buckets on top of their heads. Young girls herded the long-eared goats, laughing and calling freely. I could see how thin they were, the children's bones showing through, the adults short and wiry, yet compared to the somber group in the airport, they seemed jaunty as a band of Gypsies.

'Where are they going?' I asked Abdullah.

His chuckle, low and easy, made me feel happy. 'Farther,' he said.

A few miles more and a maze of geometric houses broke the soft sand swells—Dammam, Abdullah told us, new homes for Saudi workers, part of the Aramco housing program that allowed purchase through loans and payroll deduction.

'A company town,' Mason observed.

'Some might say that the entire country is a company town,' Abdullah said.

I scooted forward, took in the warm smell of his woody cologne. 'Where do you live?' I asked.

'In the black tent,' Abdullah said.

Mason considered. 'But you've been with the company for a while?'

'First as an errand boy in Dhahran,' Abdullah said, 'where I was allowed into school.' He offered a modest smile. 'I was selected to attend university in Texas.'

Mason squinted against the smoke of his cigarette. 'You have a degree?'

'Petroleum engineering,' Abdullah said.

Mason studied him for a moment before going back to his cigarette, and I knew that he was thinking about that life he had left behind, who he might have been if not for me.

More miles, more sand, and we all grew quiet, as though the heat that screwed down and the expanding emptiness were nothing worth noting. I had seen stretches of barren plain in Oklahoma and Texas but never the kind of infinite sweep that lay before me, the sand that moved like an animal rippling its hide, sloughing its skin, shifting, lying down, rising again. We were thirty minutes southwest of the airport when I saw a settlement erupting from the flatness.

'Abqaiq,' Abdullah said, and steered us toward the compound, backlit by the steady blow of flames from the nearby plant that filled the air with the stench of sulfur.

'Will it always smell like that?' I asked.

33

'It is the smell of money,' Abdullah said. 'Abqaiq is where the crude oil from the southern fields is piped to be stabilized before being pumped on to the port at Ras Tanura.'

Mason eyed the intricate network of valves, drums, spheres, and columns. 'That's one big operation,' he said.

'The largest in the world,' Abdullah said.

Mason nodded. 'Like everything else in this place.'

Sand gave way to portable trailers and a series of small apartments. As we neared the main gate, I saw the bunkerlike *suqs* that functioned as a private marketplace, enclosed and attached to the main compound, Abdullah said, so that the company wives could shop without leaving camp. We approached the tall *gareed* fence made of chain-link woven with palm fronds, where Abdullah nodded to the pleasantly rotund Arab manning the guard station. He was no taller than I was, his mustache like twin exclamation points punctuating his mouth. He smiled broadly and waved us through.

'His name is Habib walud Tariq walud Khalid Al-Jahni,' Abdullah said, 'but with Americans, he goes by Habib. He is my cousin. We Bedu are like the sand, you see. We are everywhere, part of everything, beginning to end.'

Abqaiq opened itself like an onion, at its center an oasis of green. Sand drifted against the buildings' foundations, powdered the driveways, sidewalks, and lawns that were broken by hedges of jasmine, clutches of periwinkle, hibiscus, and oleander. The road, lined with acacia and date palms, smoothed into an avenue wide enough to land an airplane in case of emergency. In the distance, we could see the golf course, barren as a moonscape, its greens nothing more than oiled sand.

Abdullah gave us a motor tour past the post office, commissary, medical clinic, fire station, taxi stand, and bus stop. He pointed to a flat-roofed complex. 'Your recreation center and pool,' he said, then circled around to a large ranch-style that sat a little more separate from the others: white stucco, flowering vines creeping up its sheltering veranda, a row of young roses just beginning to bud. Mason pointed across the street to where a basketball hoop stood anchored in asphalt and gave me a thumbs-up.

'Your new home,' Abdullah said. 'With your permission, the houseboy and gardener who attended the previous residents have asked if you will consider keeping them on.'

Mason looked at me, shrugged. 'Guess they know the place.'

Abdullah removed his dark glasses. 'Please,' he said, and led us from the car to where two men appeared on the front lawn. He gestured respectfully to the elder. 'This is Faris bin Ahmad, who will tend your flowers.'

The old Arab, grizzled beard resting on his chest, mumbled a few words before dipping away and disappearing around the back of the house. I looked to Abdullah, who nodded, his manner more stiff. 'And this is Yash Sharma,' he said, 'the houseboy.'

I expected to see just that—a boy—but Yash was older than Mason by a decade, his dark hair fixed with pomade. He gave a slight bow while balancing a rusty bicycle against his hip. 'I have left a light meal for you and will arrive in the morning

35

to prepare your breakfast,' he said. He straddled his bike and rode for the gate, wheels squeaking, the creases of his white shirt and khaki pants still crisp despite the sweltering humidity. I looked to Abdullah, who tightened his smile. 'The departure of their previous employer was unexpected,' he said. 'The furniture, too, has been left behind. You may decide whether or not to keep it.'

He waited as we stepped to the porch. When I turned to invite him in, Mason caught my arm. 'We don't know the rules,' he whispered. It seemed rude to leave Abdullah in the heat, but I followed Mason inside. On our left, a gilded mirror hung above a burled console table, across from a deep coat closet, empty except for a large umbrella whose use I could not imagine. Straight ahead was the big kitchen with its four-burner range, frost-free Frigidaire, breakfast bar, and walk-in pantry stocked with flour, sugar, spices, and canned goods. On our left, the living room with its TV, console hi-fi, red ginger-jar lamp, matching easy chairs, and sofa positioned atop a Persian rug, and then the dining room with its swinging doors back to the kitchen. Down the hallway hung with an elaborately embroidered tapestry of a white unicorn in a pen, past the linen closet that held plush towels and percale sheets, was the guest bathroom and bedroom, a furnished study, and then the master bedroom with its double closet and our very own tub and shower. Mason rested his hands on my shoulders.

'Think it will do?' he asked.

'I've never been inside a place this nice,' I said, as though he might not know.

'Well, it's ours now.' Mason smiled so big that

36

the scar at his mouth disappeared. 'I'll tell Abdullah we'll take it,' he said.

The meal that Yash had left in the refrigerator was neatly arranged on a platter that I pulled out and placed on the counter. When Mason returned, he lifted a sandwich wedge, sniffed, took a bite, and shrugged. I savored the meat mixed with tart pickles and spices. We ate standing, cleaning the plate of everything, including every slice of whatever it was that wasn't apple or orange or even pear but something like a peach that wasn't a peach. I washed the dishes before following Mason to the shower, confused by the twin toilets, or the toilet that wasn't a toilet but a porcelain bowl that seemed something I might wash my feet in, then crawled between the sheets that were somehow crisp and soft at the same time. We kissed and rolled to our backs, still holding to each other's hand as though we were tethered and might float apart if we dared to let go. I thought I was tired, but I lay awake for a long time, listening to the sounds outside our window, rustles and reeps and mewls. Lizards, Mason said when I asked, or maybe a desert fox.

Instead of feeling frightened by the foreignness of it, I felt a kind of anticipation I hadn't known since stealing away to his car, the world larger than it was before. Already, our last night in Houston seemed years ago, and I remember how Mason had taken me to see *The Sound of Music,* how I had been mesmerized by the dream unfolding before me. When I look back and think of us in that dark theater, I feel the air beginning to shift. Mason was still the man I thought I knew. And who was I? A girl I no longer recognize, her blank face flickering

37

in the light of the movie screen.

If I could stop this story right here, would I? 'The education of Mrs. Gin,' Yash once answered when I asked him what it all would come to. It would be the last time I saw Yash, but I didn't understand that then. All I knew was that he could sometimes tell me what I wanted to know, and sometimes what I needed to know, and, in the end, nothing that would save me from myself.

CHAPTER TWO

I don't remember falling asleep that first night in the desert, only Mason up and showered, prodding me awake. I heard an echoing chant, resonant as the distant chorus of a choir, and rose up on my elbows to listen. White walls, white ceiling, the room as big as the shack in Shawnee and filling with muted light—it took me a moment to recall where I was, to believe what I remembered. 'Arabia,' I whispered, as though saying the word would make it true.

I stumbled into the bathroom and washed my face, thinking how wondrous it was to have the toilet and sink *right there,* not even a hallway to wander down, so unlike the bellyaching cold of early morning visits to the outhouse, the candle set to burn in a cutout Folgers can doing little to break the chill. Sometimes I stole wads of paper from the girls' restroom at school, hid them in my coat, welcome relief from the rough cobs and ripped catalogs that my grandfather hoarded and stored in a wooden crate.

What to wear? I dug through my disheveled

suitcase for a modest skirt and blouse, did my best to snap out the wrinkles, thinking about all the ironing I had to do, then joined Mason in the dining room, where I found the table set with eggs sprinkled with bits of chive, strange little biscuits and jam, Yash pouring our coffee. His Mother Hubbard apron embarrassed me for reasons I couldn't quite explain except that I had never seen a man wear one before. When I shyly asked for cream, he returned with a little pitcher of it, so thick that I dipped it out with a miniature spoon. All of the silverware shiny as new, the china we ate on slip-thin, goblets of water reflecting the light—everything I touched rang like a bell.

Mason rested back in his chair, didn't seem to mind a bit that someone was cooking his meal, refilling his coffee, and why would he? Even though his own household had been only a scratch and a peck less poor than mine, he had been waited on all of his life, first by his mother and then by his sisters and then by me. He lifted his cup.

'Guess we got lucky,' he said. 'Abdullah told me that this place just came open, so they moved us to the head of the line.'

'It's not real,' I said.

'It's real, all right.' He wrinkled his eyes. 'They'll work me hard enough to earn it, but that's what I'm here for.'

Behind him, the sun slanted beneath the heavy drapes. When I finished my breakfast, I rose to draw them back, see what the day was made of, but Yash was quick at my side.

'Oh, not good,' he said, and lowered the blinds. 'AC is much better.' And that was when I realized that every window was sealed and slatted, battened

39

tight against the sun and sand. It made me feel like I was suffocating. When I followed Yash into the kitchen, he looked at me from the corners of his eyes.

'Why two separate taps?' I asked, working the faucets.

'One is sweet water,' he instructed, 'for drinking and cooking. The other is unfiltered for laundry and dishes.' He watched me as I perused the cabinets, as though he suspected I was up to no good.

'Do you need help with anything?' I offered.

'No, *memsahib,* thank you.' He waited stiffly until I took my leave and went into the living room, where I stood for a long moment, disoriented, not sure which way to turn. Even with the heat, I was glad when Abdullah came to the door to fetch us for orientation, glad to step out of the close house and into the Land Cruiser. I sat in back—the place I would always be when outside the compounds unless my husband was driving—studying Abdullah's draped head, Mason's shoulders and neck, the sunburned tips of his ears.

Again, the open desert, the sand-dusted road. We were alone, whipping up a rooster tail of dust behind us, until we drew closer to Dhahran, and the traffic increased. A commotion broke out in front of us as a brilliant white Mercedes, windshields tinted, bullied its way toward us, taking its half of the road right down the middle, my grandfather would say. Abdullah slowed to the side.

'One of our many princes,' he said.

Mason craned to see. 'How many princes are there?'

Abdullah rested his wrist on the wheel. 'I fear

40

we have lost count,' he said. 'Nonetheless, the wealth that is divided among them seems never to diminish.'

Mason shifted in his seat, lit a cigarette, and looked at Abdullah. 'Have you ever been to one of these orientation meetings?'

'This is senior staff only. It is like your country,' he said, and made descending hash marks with his hand, 'upper class, middle class, lower class. American senior staff are at the top. Intermediate staff are internationals such as Yash who live outside the compounds. And then there is general staff, which is made up of Arab laborers and service workers. You, of course, are senior staff.'

'And you?' Mason asked.

Abdullah hiked his chin. 'I am Bedu,' he said, and then more seriously, 'They say we must work our way up, and so we shall.' He pulled around a fenderless pickup, a full-grown camel crouched in its bed. 'At first, it was very difficult. The company needed information to pay us, but we didn't understand the reason for their questions. They wanted the names and ages of our mothers and our wives, our girl children.' He blinked as though he still could hardly believe it. 'They didn't understand that to talk of our women in front of an unrelated male is *haram*.' He glanced at Mason. 'Of course, all progress is precarious.'

Mason's face lit up with recognition. 'Martin Luther King,' he said, and Abdullah nodded.

I scooted forward. 'So I can't ask you about your wife while Mason is here?' I asked.

Mason scowled at me, but I held my place.

'I don't yet have a wife,' Abdullah answered evenly. 'I am my mother's only son, and my father

41

is dead.' The muscle of his jaw flexed, and I saw his eyes move to the side mirror as though there were something more that he wasn't willing to say. I tried to imagine him among the Bedouins we had seen the day before, living out in the open desert, and my head flooded with questions—How did he get water? What did he eat? How did he keep his clothes so clean?—but I feared another warning look from Mason. Instead, I peered out the window and listened to them talk, taking in the long road ahead, thinking that the drive from one compound to the other was more like a journey from outpost to outpost. If the sand had been snow, we might be in Antarctica. I was relieved when the desert gave way to a crush of tight, flat-roofed buildings outside of what looked like a small city that was enclosed by a high fence, gridded as a military base. The tidy homes gleamed in the sun.

'Dhahran,' Abdullah said, 'and the Prosperity Well, where Aramco first struck oil. Like a prize she-camel, it still produces. Here, executives and engineers live. It is the capital of Aramco operations.' He held up his fingers. 'Three camps: Dhahran, the stabilization plant at Abqaiq, and the port at Ras Tanura.'

Mason turned in his seat. 'What do you think, doll?'

I wanted to say not what I thought but what I felt, that our car was a boat, the desert an ocean, Dhahran a small island, sand lipping its shores, but I lifted my shoulders and smiled, saw Abdullah's eyes flick up in the rearview then back to the road. I wondered what he thought of me—that I was pretty or plain, too forward, too shy? Always as a girl I was warned to be seen and not heard, that even to be seen was too much. I had learned to fold my hands in my lap, cross my legs at the ankles, suppress whatever glee possessed me because a woman who laughed with her mouth open was inviting the demons in.

Abdullah stopped for a moment to chat with the uniformed Bedouin who stepped from the guardhouse before driving through the fenced main gate with its overhead arch that read in both English and Arabic: take safety home. We passed an area of industrial buildings and went into the main compound, where the sidewalks were swept clean, the hedges trimmed into uniform neatness. The few American men I saw braving the heat were dressed in crisp shirts and smart pants, the women in stylish culottes and bright floral dresses. The palm trees lining the avenues, the green lawns and modern houses—it struck me as a movie set, as though I had stepped into a postcard of Hollywood.

Abdullah dropped us at the Oil Exhibit building, where we were handed our copy of *Aramco and Its World* and joined other new employees and their wives, along with a welcoming committee of Aramcons who had lived in Arabia for years. I held close to Mason as we settled into a row of folding chairs. A large American man, flushed in his Western-cut suit and red-and-white-checked head scarf, took the microphone.

'I'm Ross Fullerton,' he said, 'district manager of Abqaiq. Welcome to the Aramco family!' His Sunday-go-to-meeting cowboy boots clapped across the stage as he pumped his fist in the air like he was preaching a revival. 'We are your home away from home, and you will never find a better one!'

He called several men to the front of the room

43

and introduced them like an auctioneer lining up his stock. I focused on Burt Cane, a silver-haired man with the posture of a colonel who managed personnel and stood in stark contrast to Swede Olson, Mason's drilling superintendent, an aging giant with a brawler's face whose fists hung like hams at his sides, and his assistant, Tiny Doty, who stood a foot shorter and had the grin of a naughty schoolboy.

The lights dimmed for a film, *What Aramco Is All About*. The booming voice of the narrator related the story of discovery, how in the beginning, there was nothing but the sand and the promise of oil beneath it, the Bedu who journeyed for centuries through the steep *jabals* and over the carbonate Dammam Dome. And then, in the 1930s, the American engineers and geologists, the tinkerers and gadgeteers filtering in a few at a time, their women following like the pioneer wives they were. We saw old photos of King Ibn Saud, already blind with trachoma, signing the concession, footage of the Standard Oil rigs drilling down through layers of grainstone, mudstone, limestone. What they found was *exceptional porosity*, the narrator said, *exceptional.* Texas Oil joined in, and the Arabian American Oil Company was born, not a corporation, the voice reminded us, but a special friendship. The Aramco family went to work with a single-minded objective: two million barrels of oil a day.

But first, the roads, platforms, derricks, refineries, eight hundred miles of pipeline—all had to be built atop the dunes, the evaporated lakebeds and dry wadis. We watched grainy footage of the Aramco Mobile Drilling Platform No. 1

44

being tugged ten thousand miles from Vicksburg, Mississippi, at a steady three and a half knots to the Persian Gulf, the largest offshore oil field in the world—Safinaya, where Mason would work. Impossible tasks, the labors of Hercules, but we had won the war, the narrator reminded us, would someday land a man on the moon. What challenges could the desert present that we could not meet? The call went out for operators to man the machinery, men to oversee the men. Roughnecks from Halliburton, Standard, and Shell. Farmers from the Philippines, Danish journeymen, an entire village of Italians from Eritrea. Laborers to build the camps and compounds where the laborers and supervisors would live. Gardeners and houseboys, drivers and cooks—a cadre of servants and servers. Aramco enticed the Bedouins from their caravans with the promise of pay and all the water their camels could drink, imported Palestinians, Syrians, Jordanians. Who could resist the promise of such prosperity? Workers from every continent and of every faith flowed in as readily as the oil flowed out. The American dream became the dream of the world.

'There were some naysayers,' Ross said as the lights were raised, 'but never tell an American there's something he can't do.' He pulled down maps from their rollers: the region, the area, the three districts. A discussion of the dollar versus the riyal, the market in al-Khobar, the food in the commissary, health clinic hours, Dhahran's state-of-the-art hospital. A phone directory of services and emergency numbers. How to get mail, the weekly *Sun and Flare* tabloid newsletter, and *Aramco World,* the slick bimonthly magazine—all read and

45

censored by the Saudis. He popped open a large black briefcase, passed around various forms, told us that the company would hold our passports and where we should go for our photo IDs. A quick slide show of customs and traditions. The woman's *abaya*, the head covering and face veil called *hijab*, the man's *thobe*, and the scarf called a *ghutra*. Ross unwrapped his own to demonstrate its construction, revealing a thin skullcap that masked his balding pate. He flapped the scarf into an open square, folded it into a triangle, spread it evenly atop his head, and secured it with a black leather *agal*. He told us about the Five Pillars of Islam, including the *hajj* to Mecca and the five daily calls to prayer. Muslim bus drivers, drillers, soldiers, sheikhs, even the king—all were obligated to stop whatever they were doing and kneel facing Mecca. We would get used to the singsong calls of the muezzin broadcast from the mosques' minarets, Ross said, if we would just think of it as radio.

'It's a heck of a good life, but never forget that we're guests in this country. They overlook a lot when it comes to us gringos, but you got to be respectful.' Ross had worked himself into a rolling sweat and mopped at his brow with the hem of his scarf. 'The Arabs are known for their hospitality, but they are particular about their watering holes. Out in the desert, the wells are hard to spot, just old mounds of camel dung, but they belong to specific tribes. Stealing a Bedouin's water is like stealing a man's horse. He'll shoot you for it.' He picked up his glass and took a long swallow, sopped his mouth. 'Now, as you all know, there are some things that are okay *inside* the compound but verboten *outside*. The Arabs call these things

46

haram—forbidden by the laws of *shariah.*'

I listened to the familiar list of sins: dancing, gambling, drinking. Ross loudly whispered into the microphone that a bootleg instruction booklet, *The Blue Flame,* was available on how to build your own kitchen still. He winked. 'Or you might just ask your neighbor if he's finished with his cooker.'

'Never!' a big man shouted, and everyone laughed.

Pork was illegal, its handling and consumption *haram,* but sometimes rations could be found in the commissary's pork room. 'Chops, roasts, bacon. What's Easter without a ham?' Ross paced the platform, became more solemn. 'Men, as you know, the local women don't show themselves. If you happen to see one, don't talk, don't touch. Don't even look at them. We've got the best lawyers money can buy, but this isn't the U. S. of A. The Saudis are serious about this stuff, and you'd better be too. We're talking jail time, deportation, and that's if you're lucky.' He looked around the room to make sure he'd made his point, snapped his briefcase closed, pushed it aside, and settled one ample hip on the table. 'Now,' he said, 'let's go over the rules for the gals.'

It is forbidden for any woman to drive outside the compounds. No women allowed on the crew launches. No women allowed on the rigs. No women in the men's section of cafés and coffeehouses. No women in the men's suqs. *No women outside the gates alone.*

'But'—Ross lifted his finger—'the Ladies' Limo runs from Abqaiq to Dhahran and right into al-Khobar. You want to shop, get the girlfriends and hop on. Just don't go wandering off or we might never find you.'

Women who leave the compounds should dress in modest attire.

'Leave the golf skirts at home, girls. These Arab boys aren't used to seeing bare skin, and they might not be able to control themselves. They'd like you to wear the *abaya,* but we negotiated special dispensation. Best to look like you're going to church. Back inside the compound, you can put on those swimsuits, dive into that pool!'

The big man gave a loud wolf whistle, eliciting a chorus of snickers.

'It's the job of the *mutaween,'* Ross went on, 'the Committee for the Propagation of Virtue and the Prevention of Vice, to enforce the laws of *shariah.* You won't often see them, but they do carry canes. They leave us Aramcons alone, but no need to spur them.' Ross straightened and hoisted his trousers, which had worked their way below his belly. 'Questions?'

Mason looked at me, but I was remembering my grandfather, how he'd switched me for cutting the sleeves from my dress. August in Oklahoma, and I thought I'd die of the heat. No neighbors for miles, and still my bare shoulders were an insult to the Lord.

When Ross directed us to the refreshment table, Mason was stopped by Burt Cane, and I saw them fall into easy conversation. I moved into line, but before I could get my coffee, a woman minced up to me, her feet swollen in the clench of high heels. A fall of blond hair framed her heart-shaped face. I'd thought she might be my age until I saw the heavy makeup caking the corners of her mouth.

'Hi,' she said in a chirpy Texas drawl. 'I'm Candy

48

Fullerton, Ross's wife. Welcome to the Aramco family!' She held out her hand, sharp as a hatchet.

'Gin McPhee,' I said, and shook the fingertips she offered.

'Are you all liking your new house?' Her eyes canvassed the room behind me.

'It's wonderful,' I said.

'Give it a year, and you won't be so easy to please.' She looked at me from the corners of her eyes. 'Buck and Betsy Bodeen lived there until three days ago, you know. He was the head of Materials Supply. I'm sure you'll want to redecorate. Those marble floors are so gauche.' I stole a glance to locate Mason, saw that Burt Cane had his full attention, but Candy ignored my distraction. 'As soon as Ross gets promoted to general manager, we're moving to Dhahran,' she said. 'Abqaiq is in the middle of nowhere.' She pursed her lips. 'Watch out for the houseboys. They always try to take advantage of newcomers.'

'Yash seems fine,' I said.

'He's uppity.' The corners of her mouth winced, then lifted as her eyes took on new focus. 'Carlo is here,' she said.

I followed her gaze to where a compact man with a camera crouched on his heels. Green silk scarf tied across his high forehead, dark beard sharpening his chin, gold hoop earrings, bloused white shirt undone and exposing a thatched chest, buccaneer's boots to his knees—how I could have missed him, I wasn't sure.

'He's Italian,' Candy said. 'Isn't he cute?' She toggled her fingers his way, but when he didn't seem to notice, she turned back to me. 'Listen,' she said, 'how about a round of golf tomorrow?'

49

'I don't—'

'You can learn.' She glanced behind me and touched my wrist. 'I'll send you a personal invitation to the club.'

I watched her hone in on Mason, her voice rising as she extended her hand and smiled brightly, edging in until her breasts brushed his arm. I was glad when he looked up, saw me watching, and shifted away. I turned to the coffee and was adding powdered creamer when I felt someone touch my back.

'Hi,' the woman said. 'I'm Ruthie Doucet.' She spread her arms wide. 'Welcome to the Aramco family!' She rolled her dark eyes to where Candy Fullerton was laughing openmouthed at something Mason had said. 'Did she ask you to join the Ladies' Golf Club?'

'Yes, but—'

'Don't,' Ruthie said. 'There's better company to keep.' She hooked my arm. 'Come on. I'm dying for a cigarette.'

We sat at a table decorated with little flags stabbed into half-moons of Styrofoam: the Stars and Stripes, the green Arabic script and sword, Aramco's rust-colored circled double A, bold as a cattle brand. Ruthie crossed her legs as she scouted the crowd. Brunette bouffant, blue eye shadow, pearly lipstick, a tartan skirt and cap-sleeved pullover—she was nearing forty, I guessed, but had the electric air of a teenager.

'How long?' she asked.

'We flew in yesterday.'

She offered me a cigarette. I hadn't smoked since that first seductive puff in Mason's car, but I figured I could fake it. She loosened one high heel

50

and rubbed the arch of her foot. 'From?'

'Houston. Oklahoma before that.' I held the smoke in my cheeks, let it out in a puff.

'I met Lucky in Beirut,' she said, 'We moved here from the States after he got out of the air force, fifteen years now. Any kids?' When I hesitated, she dipped her hand as though in understanding and went on. 'We've got one son, Joey. He's in boarding school at Hargrave.' She pointed her cigarette to where a man nearly twice her size was filling his mouth with cookies, and I recognized him as the one who had shouted his answers at Ross. 'Lucky!' she called. 'Lucky Doucet! Come and meet Gin.'

Sandy hair clipped into a crew cut, brown eyes, a chip-toothed smile that made him look younger than he was, Lucky, tanned brown as a beechnut, rolled toward us, a slight limp in his stride. He shook my hand gently, as though he were afraid he might hurt me.

'My husband . . .' I said, and cast about for Mason.

'. . . is already taking his job too serious.' He chuckled the kind of laugh that could turn into a full-bellied guffaw without notice, his words fast and thick, their staccato rhythm both strange and familiar. He motioned to where Mason was deep in conversation with Burt Cane. 'I can see we're going to have to loosen that guy up.'

Mason worked his way to our table, shaking hands as he came. When he saw me with the cigarette in my hand and hiked an eyebrow, I smiled and took another drag. Ruthie introduced him to Lucky, and the two men began discussing their jobs as drilling foremen, Lucky over a crew of Arabs in the desert, Mason a new recruit on

51

the sea—and then moved easily into banter about the recent formation of the New Orleans Saints. I leaned in closer to Ruthie, nodded to where the man with the camera stood near the door as though trying to steal away.

'He looks like a pirate,' I said.

Ruthie followed my eyes. 'Carlo Leoni? He's Aramco's official photographer,' she said, then in a low whisper, 'and gigolo.'

'Here?' I asked, my mouth gone slack.

'Where better?' Ruthie gave a knowing smile. 'Boredom is the desire for desires, you know.' When Mason turned our way, she drew back. 'Let's have lunch on Monday,' she said. 'I'm dying to see what you've done with the place.'

I hesitated, wondering whether I had done anything at all with the place and what I would fix for our meal. I'd never learned to make the little sandwiches Houston wives favored, cucumbers sliced paper-thin, cold soup alongside. Each luncheon, each tea, I'd find myself reaching for the salt, spooning more sugar, just to taste something. I'd go home, put on a big pot of brown beans, boil up a ham bone, cut in a slab of bacon, bake cornbread in a cast-iron skillet, sheen it with lard. If it was cucumber I wanted, then chunks of it with rings of sweet onion, floated in vinegar and oil, doused with salt.

'I'll bring dessert,' Ruthie said, and was off to chat with a group of wives. I missed her immediately.

Abdullah waited for us after the meeting, leaning against the Land Cruiser, talking with a few other Arab men, who lowered their gazes and moved away as we approached. I stopped until Mason

52

touched my arm.

'What's the matter?' he asked.

'They make me feel so strange,' I whispered, 'like I'm poison or something.'

He lifted his shoulders. 'I think they do it out of respect.'

I forced a smile for Abdullah as I ducked into the back of the Land Cruiser. I looked around at the other women coming from the building, most dressed in light summer clothing that showed their arms and legs, and wondered whether the Arab men who worked inside the compound believed themselves in heaven or in hell. I flapped my program against the heat, imagining that Abdullah had been talking about me. Mason sat quiet, lost in thought, but Abdullah motioned to the horizon as though he could see something brewing in the clear blue sky.

'Tonight, there will be one last rain,' he said.

'In the desert?' I asked. 'How do you know?'

'Because I am Bedu,' he said, and looked at me in the rearview. 'You will learn.' I recognized a hint of teasing and grinned back until Mason began quizzing him on the correct pronunciation and meaning of Arabic phrases—the early salutation *morning of light,* the night's greeting *evening of goodness.* I listened without hearing, Abdullah's promise still ringing in my ears.

Back home, the rooms were redolent of . . . what? Something I had never smelled before. Yash greeted us at the door. 'Dinner at six, *memsahib.*'

I followed him into the kitchen. 'Ruthie Doucet is coming for lunch on Monday,' I said.

'Perhaps I will make a cold carrot soup,' he said.

'You will?'

He lifted his eyes at my surprise. 'I am your houseboy and your cook,' he said. 'I prepare your meals, clean your rooms, do your laundry, and run your errands.' He saw the look on my face and allowed a thin smile. 'You will get used to it, believe me.'

'Ruthie says she will bring dessert,' I offered.

Yash waved the thought away. 'Her houseboy is from Pakistan. What does he know of sweet?' He turned to the sink. 'Besides, he is leaving the country, as she will discover soon enough.'

I stood for a moment, watching him rinse the vegetables, before moving to our bedroom, where the blankets were smoothed, the pillows tucked. Yash had unpacked the rest of our luggage, ironed and hung Mason's shirts, slacks, and my dresses, and folded away our underwear. I stood staring into the drawer, imagining Yash's handling of what my grandfather had called my unmentionables. When Mason came in, I showed him the clothes neatly stowed.

'Even my panties and garter belts,' I whispered.

He gave a one-sided smile. 'Not bad work if you can get it.'

That evening, I found the table set with small bowls of sliced bananas, dates, and nuts, a tureen of chicken stew that smelled of bay leaves, garlic, cinnamon. I sat across from Mason, folded my hands, and felt something like a prayer coming on. And maybe a prayer is what I should have offered right then, some gratitude for the grace of that moment. Instead, I dipped my finger into the stew and sucked like I had been starving all my life. I looked up to see Mason watching me.

'You just go ahead, Ginny Mae. You go right

54

ahead and enjoy.' He spooned the rice and curry. 'The pool looks nice. You can get your tan.'

'I don't own a swimsuit,' I said. He knew I never had.

'I bet Ruthie's got one you can borrow.' He tapped a few more raisins into his stew. 'I've been craving a cobbler. Make me a pie, why don't you?'

'I'm thinking I'll plant a garden,' I said. 'The backyard is nothing but sand. Maybe I can bring in some manure.'

Mason focused on his coffee, stirred in a spoonful of sugar. 'You heard what Ross was saying today. Maybe it's best if you stay in the compound while I'm gone.' When he saw the look on my face, he raised his hand. 'Just this first time,' he said. 'Two weeks isn't so long.'

I lowered my fork, tried to keep my voice steady. 'Two weeks?'

'That's my shift,' he said, 'my tour. Two weeks on the rig, but then a whole week back here in camp with you.'

Two weeks, I thought. I had never been separated from Mason for more than the few nights I had spent in the hospital. When Yash stepped in with more coffee, his mouth arched in dismay, I forced a smile.

'Is it not good?' he asked, and hovered over the tureen, sniffing.

'Very good,' I said, 'thank you.' But all I could think about were those hours without Mason.

When Yash disappeared back into the kitchen, Mason reached out and placed his hand over mine.

'Listen,' he said. 'There's plenty to do right here in Abqaiq. Get to know some of the other wives, play some cards, find your way around.' He ducked his head to catch my eyes. 'Okay?'

I lifted my shoulders.

'Good girl.' He gave my fingers a final squeeze. 'I'm going to check out that study,' he said. 'Makes me feel more important than I am.'

I moved into the living room and turned on the television. Channel 3 was showing the *Alfred Hitchcock Hour,* but the sound was distorted, as though a storm were blowing through the studio. When Yash came to tell me he was leaving for the night, I rose from the couch, not sure what was appropriate to say.

'I will return in the morning. Sleep well,' he offered, and quietly pulled the door closed behind him.

I joined Mason in the study, where he was surveying the large framed map of the Middle East hanging on the wall, one corner pulled away as though someone had tried to peek underneath. 'See where it broke the landmass,' Mason said, and traced the country's boundaries, the shorelines on either side like the pieces of a puzzle, perfectly fitted, the peninsula straining at its borders as though it might let go its tenuous connections, set itself adrift. He thumb-shined the already gleaming heads of the brass horses that held up a matching set of red leather books, each scripted in gold Arabic.

'You're wondering the same thing I am,' I said, 'about the Bodeens.'

Mason nodded. 'Maybe they just needed a change of scenery,' he said.

'It's strange, isn't it?' I said. 'Having servants?'

'Yeah,' he said. 'It's strange.'

'I hate that you'll be so far away.'

56

'Not so far.' He pulled me into his lap, and I rested my head on his shoulder, felt him lapsing into thought. 'Burt Cane says he's going to be retiring soon. Hate to see him go. I can tell he's one of the good ones, open to new ideas.' He stroked my arm. 'When I get back, let's take a little trip. Abdullah says the desert is full of ruins. Maybe we can dig up some old pots or something.'

'Ruthie's coming for lunch on Monday,' I said.

'See?' he said. 'You're already finding stuff to do.' He rocked forward, hefted me into his arms. 'Time for our Arabian honeymoon,' he said, and carried me to the bed.

He made love to me, then, in that slow way he had of letting me know he was sure, our rhythms familiar, not so different from that first night in the back of his sedan when we fit together, he had said, like tongue and groove. He tucked me up against him, the heat between us cooling in the refrigerated air. I clung to him for a long time, as though I felt he might be torn away. I didn't want him to leave me behind, not the next day, not ever.

'You are my anchor,' I whispered to him.

'You float my boat,' he said, and kissed me so deeply I fell out of myself and forgot I had meant to hold on.

I listened to his breathing even and slow, and then I heard it—the rain hitting the roof. I slipped from bed and walked down the hallway, stepped out the back door of the kitchen. At first, it was like standing downwind of a sprinkler, a mist of warm water, and then it came hard enough to hurt.

I tucked back under the eave, closed my eyes, breathed in the smell of what had been nothing but now was peat and dung, new grass, the smell of my

57

grandfather's rifle shot for rabbit, the blood of the rabbit itself. When I opened my eyes, the flare in the distance burned a hole in the night. My gown hung cold and wet at my shoulders, slicked to my legs, but I didn't want to go in.

I need to remember this, I thought. By morning, every drop would be gone.

CHAPTER THREE

Early that Sunday, the first day of the Muslim workweek, I helped Mason pack his duffel and saw him to the door. I waved to Abdullah, who waited to drive him sixty miles north to the port at Ras Tanura, where he would catch the launch that would ferry him more than one hundred miles to the drilling platform. I had no sense at all of what it might be like to work, eat, and sleep on a mechanical island in the middle of the sea. None of it seemed real as I watched the Land Cruiser disappear down the street, fighting the flutter of panic in my chest. I was too shy to consider calling some of the other wives, joining them for card games that I didn't know how to play. Yash seemed busy in the kitchen, raising his head only once to smile at me pleasantly, and I turned back to the empty house.

I rearranged the living room furniture, moved it back again, then spent twenty minutes at the linen closet, refolding the bath towels the way my mother and grandmother had taught me—three times down, three across—and then the sheets, each corner pocketed, creased tight. I moved to the study and surveyed the operating manuals and old atlases that lined the shelves, but not a single novel.

In the corner sat a small chair and worktable, a large lighted magnifying glass clamped to its edge, and a shallow drawer full of long-handled tweezers, picks, and scalpels as fine as the tools of a dentist. An empty whiskey bottle, mounted on its side, contained the half-finished body of a ship, its masts still tucked, strings leading into the bottle's mouth as though, at the very moment the sails were to be sprung, the maker had been called away, dropped his instruments, and left the schooner in limbo. Next to the small jars of paint and miniature brushes lay a pipe still redolent of sweet tobacco. I set the stem between my lips, and the bite brought water to my mouth. I picked up the framed photo that anchored the table's corner: an older couple, lifting glasses of champagne in front of a pretty red speedboat that looked like it was about to be launched, painted along its bow, *Arabesque.* His hair a wispy ring of silvery gray, hers a short mass of ash blond curls cut tight to her head, both of them smiling—the Bodeens seemed happy enough, leaning into each other. I studied the photo, looking for clues. Maybe one had taken ill, I thought, or maybe there had been a death in the family, or maybe they had simply had enough of the desert. I laid the picture in the drawer with the bits of sailcloth and compact spools of thread, slid it out of sight.

I sat in Mason's chair and opened the first of the red leather books, ran my finger along the gold script like I was reading Braille. I wondered what the intricate pattern of dots and swooping dashes had meant to the Bodeens, or maybe the set was nothing more than decor. The lush illustrations indicated an epic tale or maybe ancient history. I put the volume back, then pulled out another, let it fall open. I rubbed the paper between my fingers—like the diaphanous pages of a Bible—then flipped through the illustrations until I came to the end, where I found several pieces of ledger paper glued over the last pages, just like my grandmother had pasted the cutout recipes from ladies' magazines to the pages of *Amy Vanderbilt's Complete Book of Etiquette.* I read down the columns of penciled numbers, but the equations were as indecipherable to me as the Arabic script, and I placed the book back with its mates.

I walked a circuit through the bedrooms, then back down the hallway to the living room, where I frumped down on the couch and read through a dated stack of *Aramco World* magazines, the pages filled with colorful photographs of Arabs and Americans, building, paving, extracting, standing back to admire the progress they had made. Arabs raising radio antennae, Arabs driving drilling rigs, Arabs in the classroom and the laboratory—the harmony and utility perfectly captured, the desert no more impossible than any frontier had ever been, the ingenious Americans and their Saudi allies headed for sure victory over whatever lay between them and the massive fields of oil. 'If it's there, we'll find it,' one explorationist proclaimed, and who wouldn't believe him? Spread across the centerfold, a sleek supertanker rested at anchor near Sidon, its streamlined efficiency set against the clear beauty of the sea. A portrait of its smartly uniformed captain, pipe in hand, handsome as a movie star, filled the next page. 'A big man,' the caption read, 'with broad shoulders, hair the color of brass, a lopsided grin, a lively wit, a taste for strong tobacco and Dutch gin, and a gift for running a taut ship with a minimum of effort.' I was halfway in love with him myself and maybe even more so with the journalist who had dared to embed such titillating details and somehow sneak them by the censors. I read cover to cover, hard and too fast, soaking up every word, forgetting to save some for later. When I looked at the clock, I saw that it wasn't even noon.

'Don't be a slugabed,' I told myself. 'Get up and do something.' I pushed from the couch, tied my hair in a ponytail, and went to survey the sparse backyard, wondering what vegetables might root in sand. Okra would love the humidity, potatoes and yams the porous soil. When I saw Faris watching me from the corner of the house, I lifted my hand, but he ducked away.

As I paced off the plot, I kept my eyes open for anything that might strike, remembering how, in Shawnee, I once had stepped off the porch without looking. The scorpion had hit my bare heel sharp and quick, not much more than a bee sting at first, but by midnight, I was burning with fever, my leg swollen to the knee. My grandfather began to pray and didn't stop, right there beside me for two days and two nights, until the tremors lessened and I fell into sleep. When I woke, he stood from his hard chair, rested his hand against my cheek, and looked at me with his watery eyes. 'What doesn't kill you makes you strong,' he said, then turned for the door and the chores he had left undone.

When I went inside and announced to Yash that I would walk to the commissary, he protested that shopping had always been a part of his job.

'But I want to plant a garden,' I said, 'and I need seeds.'

'You'll not find garden supplies at the grocery store,' he said.

'Not okra?'

'What is okra?'

I described the small fibrous pods.

'Ah,' he said, *'bhindi!'* His smile dropped to a frown. 'You will not find that either.'

When I insisted, he handed me a basket and the umbrella, its shade little help against the heat that rose from the blacktop, gumming the soles of my shoes. I stopped to peer out over the compound, its low-roofed houses, the young trees piecing the sidewalk into lacy shade, the homely fence, the stacks lifting their incendiary flares against the blazing sun. I checked out the recreation center with its swimming pool, the bowling alley where Bedouin boys set the pins, and the movie theater with its schedule of censored Hollywood films, traveling operas, symphonies, plays, and meetings held each Friday, one for Protestants, another for Catholics, although, in deference to the laws of the land, the word *church* was never mentioned. The small auditorium seemed the heart of the compound, everything illegal all in one place.

There was a small library inside the center, but I knew about small libraries—I could exhaust the stacks in no time if I weren't careful to ration. When I walked into the single room with its few shelves of books, I saw that it wasn't small but tiny, its volumes dog-eared and stained with coffee. I opened an issue of *Good Housekeeping* to find the pages limp and scissored, whether by the censors or wives hunting recipes, I wasn't sure. I sighed and turned to see a young teenage girl watching me, her nose brindled with freckles, hair the color of flax.

'Hi,' she said, her voice so high she sounded as though she had inhaled helium. 'Is the new *Seventeen* in?'

I smiled and shrugged. She plopped down cross-legged and groaned at the dated covers. When she turned back to me, I peered at the magazine in my hands.

'Are you new?' she asked.

'I've only been here a few days,' I said.

She eyed me wisely. 'You must be out of school.'

'I just moved here with my husband,' I said.

She wrinkled her nose. 'I'm never getting married,' she said. 'I'm going to be a stewardess for Pan Am.' She dusted off the seat of her pedal pushers, as though she'd been sitting in dirt, and left me in the library alone.

I moved outside and walked to the playground, where I watched the younger children tussle. I wondered how my life might be different here if I had a son or a daughter to join the romp and holler of the group, some experience to share with the other young women. I felt in-between, somehow, out of rhythm with the world, and tried to remember whether I had ever known another childless woman, but only the biblical stories of Sarah and Rachel and Rebekah came to me— women who prayed and obeyed and believed until they were old and still their wombs opened and their sons were conceived. Sometimes I wondered why I had opened my own womb so soon, what had possessed me to give myself away. I remembered Mason, all that talk, all that sweetness, and couldn't help but smile. Even knowing what it had cost me, it was a mistake I might be willing to make again.

I twirled the umbrella like a parasol and strolled to the compound's entrance, where I stood at the fence, peering into the distance while Habib peered back. As far as I could see, there was nothing but the golf course, where a Bedouin caddy, *thobe* fluttering, waited patiently while an American dressed in bermudas teed off. A turnstile at the fence led me to the narrow lane of *suqs*, the smell a mix of sour lanolin and cinnamon. Spun fleece, daggers, silver bracelets, camel bags, honey, bolts of bright cloth—each small store had its specialty. I chose a handful of thimble-size strawberries, which the Arab clerk weighed on a balance scale and poured into a twisted paper funnel. I ate them as I walked to the commissary, which was little more than a line shack built of cement blocks. Cases of soft drinks stacked one wall. Shelves along the center held canned goods and cleaning supplies. I inspected the long open freezer as the two Arabs manning the checkout watched. One cleared his throat.

'Australian beef,' he said, his words heavily accented. 'It is very good.'

I nodded and moved to the produce, where I found several bunches of wilted green onions that might yet revive if planted, softening potatoes and yams sprouting eyes that I could quarter and bury, and a miraculous handful of okra pods. A deep freeze held frozen vegetables and fruit, including a battered bag of sliced peaches, good enough for a cobbler. In the back of the building, I saw a doorway leading to a smaller room, where an enormous Nubian man, his head wrapped in a

64

turban, cut pork into chops. He smiled down at me when I requested a pound of bacon and wrapped it carefully in butcher paper as though diapering an infant. On the way back to the checkout, I stopped at the small rack of used books and magazines and picked up a worn copy of *The Count of Monte Cristo,* censored but unabridged—a week of reading if I took it slow.

The Arab clerk who tallied and bagged my few groceries fingered the book's pages, brought it to his face, and sniffed. The novel felt like contraband, enough to convict me, but the man seemed patient, even kind. He bound the book in brown paper, tied it with twine, then pointed me down the street to a small bakery, its interior roaring with the heat of a wood-fired oven, where the baker, gesturing to caution me that it was hot, pulled out a puffed loaf of bread that quickly flattened. It was then that I realized what had struck me as odd: only men worked the shops, sold the groceries, fired the ovens. I stepped back out, the sun like a heat lamp, and retraced my steps home, my stride falling in time to the muezzin's second call to prayer. The entire outing had taken less than an hour. Already, the day seemed like it had stretched on forever.

Yash greeted me at the door, fretful as a brood hen. He approved of the bread and bacon, expressed surprise over the okra, and cut his eyes at the heavy paper package that I secreted to my room. I hid the book beneath the head of the bed, snugged against the wall—a childhood habit still familiar—before going back to the kitchen, where I found Yash considering the bag of thawing peaches.

'I'm going to make a cobbler,' I said. I opened

the drawer that held tea towels and found six of them, each embroidered with a day of the week and a little Indian child, buckskin dress or leggings and breechcloth, engaged in the day's corresponding chore—Monday, Wash Day, Tuesday, Ironing . . . only Sunday was missing, but since Saturday was Baking Day, I pulled it out, touched the precise, even stitches—the work of a superior seamstress—then raised the towel to my face, breathed in the smell of clean cotton, and tucked it at my waist.

Yash pursed his lips. 'I will make you the perfect crust.'

We considered each other a moment before he reached for the lard and I made a move for the sugar. We worked tentatively at first, careful not to brush a shoulder, an arm. I mixed the peaches with sugar and a little flour before spreading the fruit in the baking dish, dotting it with butter, lemon juice, and a dash of cinnamon. Yash unrolled the dough from his rolling pin as easily as laying a baby's blanket. We began at opposite corners, finger-thumb fluting the edges, his calm intent something I felt with the appreciation of a child, hot afternoons, my mother making pies as I napped, my bed an old quilt spread in the coolest corner of the kitchen.

'Tell me about your family,' I said.

Yash took a paring knife and slit pretty petals in the crust, added a border of tendrils and vines. 'My family is Punjabi with a tradition of military service.' One eyebrow arched up. 'We are, after all, a martial race, according to our lords and commanders.'

'What about a wife?' I asked.

He didn't answer but gave a slight nod, then

66

pinched a piece of dough. When he held it out to me, I drew back.

'That will give me worms,' I said.

'What?' Yash looked shocked.

'That's what my grandmother always told me.'

He popped the bit into his mouth, looked at me slyly. 'There are no worms in my dough,' he said, 'but perhaps the same cannot be said of your peaches.' I caught the hint of a smile.

Yash was lowering the dish into the oven when the knock came so hard that I jumped, but he seemed hardly to notice. 'One moment,' he called, but I beat him to the door and looked down to see a legless Bedouin garbed in pinned-up trousers and a faded tunic, riding atop a little wooden platform with wheels, balancing an enormous basket on his head.

'Is-salaam 'alaykum!' he cried.

Yash appeared behind me, wiping his hands. 'No,' he said, and turned to me. 'I apologize, *memsahib*. I have no idea how the beggar found his way past the gate.'

I gave him a sharp look before addressing the peddler. 'And upon you peace,' I said to the man, who smiled broadly, two black teeth stubbing his gums. He presented the basket, fanning the flies, and I saw that it was full of glistening pink shrimp. I knelt and ran my fingers through the briny casings, cupped two hands full, then watched as the man spread a newspaper and cleaned the shrimp on the spot before handing me the tidy package, smiling his painful smile. He looked parched to me, his mouth puckered and dusty.

'Would you like a drink?' I asked. 'Water?'

Yash left and returned with a few riyals and a

67

glass, which I handed to the peddler. He drank in one long swallow before thanking me repeatedly and rolling his way down the street.

'The Muslim won't eat them himself, but he's happy to sell them to us infidels.' Yash dumped the shrimp into a colander.

'That water was warm,' I said. I was remembering the two taps in the kitchen—remembering, too, the separate drinking fountains in Shawnee, one for blacks, one for whites.

'You do not give a Bedouin sweet water to drink. It is a taste he is not used to.' Yash stirred the shrimp with his fingers. 'It is the way of every American home.'

'Not this one,' I said.

He looked at me quickly, then away. 'Of course, *memsahib.*'

I scrunched my shoulders. 'Could you just call me Gin?'

He considered for a moment. 'Perhaps Mrs. Gin,' he said, and I smiled.

'We can make shrimp cocktail,' I said, but Yash pulled back as though I had uttered a shocking profanity.

'If you will allow me,' he said delicately, and I hesitated before abandoning my station and wandering through the house as though there were something I had lost.

When Yash finally called me to the table, my mouth was watering, my hunger whetted by the delicious smells wafting from the kitchen. He served me the shrimp sautéed in butter, spiced with ginger and garlic, and I ate them every one. The air conditioner kicked on, and I shivered in the cooler air. While Yash was making tea, I pulled back the

68

curtain, louvered the blind's slats. I could feel his immediate dismay as he positioned my saucer.

'It is not simply the heat,' he said. 'If a Muslim sees what is forbidden, we will be the ones who are punished.'

'But we're not doing anything,' I said.

'It takes very little,' he said. 'I've known houseboys who were thrashed and deported for being observed playing a simple game of cards. The Americans believe that the fence is to protect them from the Arabs, but, truly, it is to protect the Arabs from the Americans and their myriad temptations.' He began clearing the table.

'Let me help,' I said, and stood to gather my plate.

'Mrs. Gin,' he said, stopping me in my tracks. 'Without a job, I will be the one deported.' I let him take the dishes from my hands, then trailed him into the kitchen.

'What about the Bodeens?' I asked. 'What were they like?'

He scraped our plates, ran hot water. 'They were Americans,' he said, 'like you.'

'Why did they leave the way they did?'

Yash lifted his shoulders but didn't answer.

'All right then,' I said, too stubborn to stop. 'How did you meet your wife?'

He lifted his chin but not his eyes. 'We met at university. I spied her across the courtyard and was immediately smitten, but she was beautiful and a very serious student. I mistakenly believed that my soldier's uniform might spark her interest, but she took no notice of me.'

'So what did you do?'

'What young men have always done in the face

69

of love. I made a fool of myself.' He smiled, and I smiled with him. 'I had been to the library, and my arms were full of Plato and Curie, Rumi, of course, and even Lord Byron. I fancied myself not only an officer, philosopher, and physicist but a poet as well. She was with her girlfriends at the fountain, and I thought to drop my books in front of her so she could see the brilliance of my study.'

I waited, imagining Yash, a mop of dark hair, dressed in a crisp white shirt, little different than he looked now, only younger.

'I tripped in realistic fashion,' he continued, 'and succeeded in scattering my books at her feet. Misfortune that the trajectory of my fall propelled the weightiest of the tomes into the waters of the fountain.'

'Oh, no,' I said. 'The books were ruined.'

'Only the rarest of them, the ones I would spend the next year paying for.' He paused for a moment, fixed his eyes on the dishwater. 'To see her take off her shoes, hike up her skirts, and wade into the fountain—this was worth all the world's wisdom that day.'

'It worked,' I said. 'You won her heart.'

He brought his eyes to mine for a quick moment, then dropped them back to his hands. 'Yes, I won her heart.'

I waited, but whatever story he had in him was done. 'I guess I'll plant the garden,' I said, 'if Faris will let me.'

In the plot of yard, I shoveled and rooted, lined out rows, dug my fingers deep into what was little more than sand, the sweat that dripped from my nose evaporating the second it hit the ground. I seeded the okra and cut the potatoes and yams into

70

eyed sections. When I heard someone behind me, I thought it was Faris, but I turned to see Yash, carrying a perfectly arranged tray of hot tea and the bread he called chapati.

'Can you pour that tea over ice,' I asked, 'and throw in some sugar? It's baking out here.'

He looked down at the tray then back at me, sighed, and turned for the kitchen.

'Bring yourself some too,' I called, but the door had already clapped shut.

By the time Monday rolled around, I was so eager for Ruthie's arrival that I could hardly sit still for breakfast. On my way to the shower, I stopped at the linen closet for a fresh towel and found all my work undone, each item carefully refolded to its original configuration. Yash stepped into the hallway as though he knew what I was thinking.

'Dinner this evening is masala lamb, my mother's specialty. It is the first time I have chosen to make it,' he said, and smiled his way back into the kitchen.

I stood for a moment with my hand on the knob before quietly closing the door. The house was clean, dinner planned—even the folding of the laundry was now out of my hands. A lady of leisure, I thought to myself. I couldn't imagine what my grandfather would say.

A little after noon, the doorbell chimed, and Yash hurried to the entry as though he feared I might get there first. Ruthie breezed in and handed him a bottle of pineapple wine. 'Dessert,' she said. 'Better stick it in the freezer.' She turned to me. 'My houseboy has gone off to find a wife, and until he gets back, my place is off-limits. I haven't cleaned a toilet for fifteen years, and I'm not going

71

to start now.' She dabbed her upper lip free of sweat. 'Give me a tour, will you? I've never been past the living room.'

Yash carried the bottle into the kitchen while I showed Ruthie the house, still surprised by the number of closets, the paintings on the walls, Mason's study with its mahogany desk.

In the bathroom, Ruthie exclaimed, 'Oh, you lucky duck! I've always wanted a bidet.' I stared at the porcelain fixture next to the toilet, and Ruthie laughed. 'For rinsing your bottom.' When she straddled the bowl like she was sitting a horse, I couldn't help but cover my mouth. 'After sex,' Ruthie said matter-of-factly, 'to cleanse.' It made my skin prickle to think of it: a woman opening herself so shamelessly, with such practicality.

'It's a beautiful home,' Ruthie said as we moved down the hallway.

'I'm sure yours is just as nice,' I said.

'You're kidding, right?' When she saw my blank look, she gave a short laugh. 'You've got one of the best.'

'I guess we got lucky,' I said, but she shook her head.

'Nothing around here happens by luck unless it's bad.' She stopped at the tapestry, ran her fingers over its thread. 'You'll earn more money here than you'll know what to do with. Some people save, and some people spend. Buck and Betsy were spenders. They poured everything into this place, then left it all behind. Betsy and I weren't the closest of friends, but I thought she would at least take the time to say good-bye.' She waved her hand between us. 'It won't do any good to ask why because no one will tell you a damn thing. Usually, it's best not to know. Around here, rumor is king and as close as you'll ever get to the truth. Best to take what you inherit and shut up about it.' She settled in at the dining table, searching for an ashtray, which Yash brought as though summoned by a bell. When she handed me a cigarette, I didn't hesitate, seduced by the pearly lighter she pulled from her case, the leaning into the flame, the first inhalation and blood rush.

'Next door,' Ruthie said, and pointed north, 'you've got Chuck and Starla Cunningham. He's ramrodding a job in Venezuela and won't be back until after Christmas. On this side, Don Perry and his wife, Inga. He dug her up in Denmark. She is always in bed with a headache.' She moved her cigarette in a circle. 'The Perrys keep to themselves, but most of us use any excuse we can to get together—birthday parties, baby showers, full moon, you name it. That's why they call Abqaiq the Friendly City. If the Welcoming Committee comes by, act like you're not home or they'll tote in their casseroles and swill all your booze. If you don't want company, don't answer your door.'

Yash returned with fragrant dishes of beef *biryani* flavored with whole spices, a curry made with potatoes, eggplant, and green beans, tomato chutney, and homemade yogurt with a dash of sugar. For dessert, he presented rose-flavored dumplings in cardamom-scented syrup along with a glass of the pineapple wine that was cold but smelled like sulfur. He watched carefully as we tasted the dumplings until Ruthie pointed to her cup. 'Tea?'

'Of course, *memsahib*.' Yash went to heat water, carrying with him an air of mild disappointment.

73

She peeked back to make sure he was gone. 'Always remember,' she whispered, 'the houseboys hear everything.'

'He's really smart,' I said.

'They are *all* smart,' Ruthie answered, 'or at least they think they are. Yash was with the Bodeens for years, so I'm sure he has learned a trick or two.'

'He went to college,' I said. 'That's where he met his wife.'

'He's a Brahmin?' Ruthie narrowed her eyes. 'Who did he murder to end up here?'

I lifted my shoulders. 'Maybe he just likes being a houseboy.'

'Now, that's a joke,' she said, then motioned to the kitchen. 'Let's go see what's left of the still. You know that Buck had the best.'

Yash stepped aside as we surveyed the large pantry and discovered the various pots, tubes, and condensers. Tucked beneath a crocheted tea cozy, I found a stained copy of *The Blue Flame,* detailing with scientific exactitude the fermentation and distillation of spirits.

'Throw in potatoes, fruit, whatever you've got, but all you really need is yeast and sugar,' Ruthie said. 'It's like running a pressure cooker full of gasoline, so let Yash do it.'

'*Sadiqi,*' Yash said pleasantly.

'*Sadiqi* means "my friend,"' Ruthie said. 'It's code for booze. The truth is that if you don't have a still, you've got nothing.' She dropped her cigarettes into her purse, pulled out a bright yellow scarf, tied it beneath her chin. 'Listen,' she said, 'you'll want to see more than these walls every day. Most wives are Casual Employees, typing, transcribing, that kind of thing. I go into Dhahran every now and then and

74

help with vaccination records.'

'I read,' I said.

She smiled indulgently and patted my arm. 'I'll call you in the morning,' she said. 'We've got to do something about that hair. It makes you look like you're ten.' She stepped out to where her once-blue Volkswagen, sun-bleached to milky gray, hunkered on its oversize tires, more dune buggy than car. 'See you later, alligator,' she called.

It took me a moment to remember what I had heard the other teenagers say in Shawnee, to raise my hand and respond, 'After 'while, crocodile.' Such a simple thing, but it filled me with more happiness than I had felt for a long time.

CHAPTER FOUR

The next day found me sitting in the eye-watering haze of perm solution and cigarette smoke of the Abqaiq Beauty Salon, still savoring the memory of the dinner Yash had made me: tender masala lamb that had filled my mouth with the sweetness of tomatoes and the tart surprise of lemon, nothing like the tallowy mutton I'd been forced to eat as a girl. When I told Yash that I wished I could cook like he did, he had lifted his nose in mock arrogance. 'You must first be Punjabi,' he said, genuinely pleased as he carried my empty plate to the kitchen.

I looked around the shop to where Candy Fullerton and Burt Cane's wife, Maddy, waited their turn, purling their needles through baby booties, part of their charity work for native

75

children. Soft blue sweaters, pale pink caps, green-and-yellow afghans—the Christian Women's Fellowship Group sent out donations each week, but Ruthie said she had yet to see a Bedouin child dressed in knitted pastel. Except for Ruthie, I felt shy around the women. Many, like Candy, carried the airs of Southern debutantes, while others seemed more like aging matrons, including Maddy, whose hair had been teased and sprayed into a helmet meant to defy the stiffest of desert winds.

Rafiq, the lean Lebanese beautician, worked at the rats in Ruthie's bouffant, combing his way up from ends to scalp, and I was next. I needed a new style, Ruthie had insisted, for my interview with *Sun and Flare* in Dhahran. 'I know the editor, Nestor Reedy,' she had said when I opened my mouth in surprise, 'and you need a hobby so you don't go bonkers.' I wondered whether she somehow sensed in me that desire I had felt as a girl to be the maker of my own stories. All those diary pages, all that dreaming . . . 'Your head is in the clouds,' my grandfather said to me, 'and that's not the same as heaven.'

The dryer's heat made the beauty shop hotter than the air outside. 'The bathroom faucet broke,' Maddy was complaining, 'but do you think Burt could fix it? No, sir. He can drill a well a mile deep but can't plumb a faucet. I had to call in the coolies.' I focused on the familiar pages of *Aramco World*, then used it as a fan. I had garbed myself in slacks and a seersucker blouse, but Ruthie sat cool in her sleeveless white shell, black capris, and pearly red flats.

'Did you hear about Katie Johnson?' Candy leaned in, her voice breathy and sharp. 'They flew her out last night. Nervous breakdown.'

Maddy started to respond, then cut her eyes my way, needles clicking. I pretended to be absorbed in the magazine, imagining the articles I might write if I could report what I heard at the beauty shop.

'Gin is going to be reporting for *Sun and Flare,*' Ruthie announced as though reading my mind.

'I've always wanted to be a writer,' Candy said, her voice tipped with jealousy, 'but Ross won't let me work.'

'Ross is crazy,' Ruthie said, and nodded to me. 'Your turn.' She slid from the chair before Rafiq could release the foot pump. He dusted the seat, snapped a fresh cape, and motioned for me to sit. He palmed the ends of my hair, cocked his head in the mirror. Ruthie lit a cigarette, circled around, then said a few words that I didn't understand. Rafiq nodded his agreement before leading me to the sink, where he lowered my head gently, testing the spray against his wrist. I relaxed as he worked the lather with the tips of his fingers. When he caught a snarl, he went at it with the precision of a lace maker, teasing the strands free. I kept my eyes closed as he rinsed, moisturized, then gathered my hair in a towel and squeezed. When I looked up, I saw him gazing down at me with the beneficence of a monk. I returned to the chair, and he combed my hair into sections, made a cut in the back. When he lifted the thick hank, I caught my breath.

'Oh,' I protested, 'not that much,' but he just shrugged. I closed my eyes and didn't open them again until he had my hair in large rollers and was leading me to the dryer, where I sat with the hot wind blowing across my ears and watched the mouths of the other women. When Rafiq combed

77

me out, my hair fell into a flip at my shoulders. He stood back, presenting me to Ruthie for inspection.

'Just gorgeous.' She turned to Candy and Maddy, who had been stealing glances all along. 'You've got to have high cheekbones to pull off this cut. Just look at yourself, Gin. So sophisticated.'

I stared in the mirror, my eyes different somehow, not mine at all. Rafiq caught my gaze in the reflection, smiled, then busied himself with his broom.

Outside, the sun hit my head like an anvil. I walked stiff-necked to Ruthie's VW, fearing the wind that would twist my hair into knots.

'Don't be a goose,' she said, wrapping her own new style with a scarf. 'It's the kind of cut that falls right into place.' She checked her lipstick in the rearview, handed the tube to me. 'Candy is jealous of you already.'

'Why would she be jealous of me?' I touched the lipstick to my mouth, tasted its bitter perfume.

'Because you're young and beautiful, and she's mutton dressed as lamb,' Ruthie said. 'She married late and has never gotten over it. When Ross Junior was born, you would have thought we had a new prince.' She waved to a passing car. 'Candy will do anything to make sure that Ross gets promoted to general manager. I just try to stay out of her way.'

'What about Maddy?' I asked. 'She seems kind of sour.'

'She's more than sour. She's a mean old bitch.' I startled at Ruthie's words. I had never heard a woman cuss before. 'Maddy never wanted to be in Arabia in the first place and has hated every minute of it.' She waved her hand as though clearing away a bad smell. 'All I know is that I've got good friends here. She's not one of them. Listen,' she said, checking her purse for cigarettes. 'After we get done with your interview, let's take the bus to al-Khobar and do some shopping.'

I raised my face in surprise. 'But I didn't ask Mason,' I said.

'Do you have to ask him about everything?' Ruthie rolled her eyes. 'I hate planning out every hour. Better to be spontaneous. Besides, what else are you going to do? Go home and read?' She snapped her gum. 'Mason won't even know.'

I considered her arms. 'What about the Virtue Police?'

'Al-Khobar is an oil town,' she said. 'They won't bother us there.'

When I hesitated, she winged her eyebrows, said, 'Now what?' and I lifted my shoulders. 'I don't have any money,' I said.

'You don't need money. If you see something you want, they send your husband the bill. I don't even carry a wallet. Come on,' she said. 'We'll have fun.'

We parked at the bus stop, and Ruthie nodded to where a tall Arab man, ten-gallon hat settled onto his jug-handle ears, leaned against a two-tone Chevrolet. Instead of a *thobe* and *ghutra,* he wore a Western snap-button shirt and blousy cotton trousers tucked into a pair of boots whose gaucho heels added two inches to his height.

'That's Yousef,' she said. 'Some of us girls pitched in and bought him that outfit. I insisted on the Stetson. He doesn't speak English, but he knows how to get you where you're going.' As we walked by, Yousef tipped his hat and smiled a big cowboy smile. 'Give him a smoke, and sometimes you ride free,' Ruthie murmured. 'Nobody loves tobacco more than a Bedouin.'

We waited for the bus with Cindy Moe and Ronda Taylor, two of the other wives who looked to be in their thirties, all of us wilting in the heat. I listened to them and Ruthie catching up on news of children, plans for a company trip to Ceylon, the preparations already beginning for the annual Christmas pageant. Christian holidays were officially outlawed, they told me, but even the Arabs looked forward to watching the annual pageant enacted on the Dhahran baseball diamond: the American wise men dressed in robes and *ghutras*, arriving at the stable on camels to pay homage to the blond Virgin Mary, the pale baby Jesus wailing in his manger.

The old Mercedes bus bucked to a halt in front of us, and we climbed aboard, then followed the wide asphalt street onto the sand-humped road. I couldn't imagine how the Empty Quarter could be any emptier than this desert expanse and remembered Candy's words—*the middle of nowhere.* Miles and miles of nothing but sun and sand as far as I could see. As we neared Dhahran, traffic picked up, and the ride became less sedate as we dodged donkey carts and swerved around the hulk of a car abandoned along the roadside. The other drivers tailgated before ripping past, blaring their horns all the while.

'The Ladies' Limo,' Ruthie said, and sighed. 'Sometimes I just want to get in the Volkswagen and gun it right through the gate.'

'What if you did?' I asked.

'If Aramco got to me first, a good scolding, I'd guess.' She peered at the back of the driver's head.

'If the Saudis discovered I'm an Israeli Jew, they would ship me out for sure.'

I looked at her quickly, then away. The only Jews I knew were in the Bible, and I wasn't sure what I had expected one to look like—just not like Ruthie. I glanced up at the bus driver, who was smiling at us in his mirror.

'Don't worry,' Ruthie said. 'He's Somali. You can tell by the scars on his face. They mutilate themselves.'

I sat quietly until we reached Dhahran, where the bus dropped us near a blocky concrete building holding a proliferation of Cairo grass at bay. The coolness of the interior hit as hard as the heat. I followed Ruthie down the hallway to an office where a man in black trousers and white shirt sat amid stacks of newsprint and photos, file cabinets left open, a wastebasket overflowing with crumpled papers. He jumped to his feet when we entered.

'Nessie!' Ruthie wrapped his long frame in a tight hug. 'Nestor Reedy, this is the friend I told you about, Gin McPhee.'

He thumbed his black-framed glasses back up his nose before turning to me. 'You're the writer,' he said.

I looked at Ruthie, who widened her eyes and gave a tight nod.

'I've written some stories,' I said, remembering my diary, my wishful attempts.

'If that's enough for Ruthie, that's enough for me.' He puffed his chest and tucked his shirt, which seemed too short for his torso. 'Please, ladies. Sit.'

'I need to use the little girls' room,' Ruthie said. 'You two go ahead and take care of business.' She stepped out, and I saw how Nestor watched her and knew he felt as I did: a little bereft.

He righted himself, turned to his desk. 'So, you see what we're up to. Production news, food drives, sports, that kind of thing. We like a few cartoons and jokes sprinkled around. Everyone can use a good laugh.' He mustered a smile that dropped quickly. 'The Saudis read and censor everything. Just because we do it doesn't mean we can write about it. Parties are illegal in Arabia, so don't use that word. We call dances shindigs or steppers or do-si-dos, and never mention drinking or gambling. Problem is, that's all we do around here.' He ran the eraser of his pencil down a coffee-stained desk calendar before standing and escorting me to the door. 'First assignment, Beachcomber's Ball,' he said.

The latch clicked shut behind me just as I saw Ruthie laughing with a tall woman about her age, dressed in a nurse's uniform—platinum hair pinned into a beehive beneath her pointed cap, a way of switching her hips that made her sturdy white shoes bap like a rumba. Ruthie kissed the woman's cheeks and walked toward me.

'Who was that?' I asked.

'Linda Dalton.' She stripped a stick of gum, offered me half. 'I like Linda. She can talk about something other than casseroles. She followed her fiancé here. He missed Kentucky. She didn't. She works at the Dhahran hospital and lives in Singles.'

'She lives in Arabia by herself?' I asked.

'Why not?' Ruthie asked, snapping her gum. 'If Lucky ever left me, I'd kill him first, then find a good job. A girl has got to have something to fall back on. What's your first assignment?'

'The Beachcomber's Ball.'

82

'It's a ball, all right. The Yachting Association puts it on.' She applied fresh powder to her nose. 'Let's see what's new at Fawzi Jishi's.'

We climbed back on the bus and sweated in the torrid heat through the long minutes it took the driver to finish his prayers. When we finally began moving, I held my face to the open window, welcoming the hot breeze. As we passed the police station, Ruthie tapped the window and pointed to where a tall T-post was strung with what looked like blackened leaves.

'There,' she said. 'Do know what that is?'

I shook my head.

'Saudi justice,' she said. 'If someone gets caught stealing, they cut off his hand.'

I peered at the pole as we passed. 'Are you sure?' I asked.

She wrinkled her eyes. 'What do you think, I'm lying?'

I settled back against the seat, pressed my palms into my lap. 'That's awful,' I said.

'If you're looking to feel sorry for someone,' Ruthie said, 'you've come to the right place. Sometimes it's like a stalag around here.'

I sat quiet, trying to absorb all that Ruthie was telling me, even as I charted the empty miles of sand that separated the compounds. To see al-Khobar on the horizon felt like a discovery, a new planet in the vast solar system of the desert. The bus dropped us near a small courtyard, and a whipping breeze gusted up around us, clearing the littered street. If I'd believed that the desert smelled like nothing, the market smelled like everything: coffee, incense, roasted meat, cardamom. Adobe-like buildings of mud and mortar, some centuries old and faded to the color of sand, others newly constructed and limed a brilliant white, one-story, two-story, three, many with suspended covered walkways along the front, Arab men peering down from the open windows— al-Khobar reminded me of an Old West town, a mix of what once was and what was about to be. Cars rattled past the long-eared goats that bleated and scattered, Arab children close behind. The date palms and jasmine that had been planted along the thoroughfare had somehow taken hold, their roots sinking deep beneath the sand that had been scraped and bladed smooth. Ruthie gestured to where a group of women, some blond and blistered with sun, others tanned the color of sandalwood, laughed over a monkey that dashed to the end of its leash and pinched almonds from their fingers.

'Those are single girls, hired into the secretarial pool,' Ruthie said. 'German, Dutch, one way or the other, they have their pick of men. Aramco started shipping them in when the Indian clerks wanted more money. Women will always work for less, especially if they can get a husband in the bargain.'

I listened to the languages that mixed and swirled with the dust, the sounds and smells like the chaos of a carnival. As we moved away from the group, Ruthie touched my elbow. 'Watch for the *mutaween*. You'll know if they're coming because everyone will start acting nervous.'

'I thought you said they would leave us alone.'

'Don't worry. They're just a bunch of bullies,' she said, 'prowling around, trying to take everyone by surprise. Even the natives hate them.'

But I did worry as I followed Ruthie through the nut store, the egg store, the carpet store, the toy

84

store, the stationery store—the hair at the back of my neck electric with foreboding. At the material store, Ruthie did her best to distract me by pointing out the canvas and lace, Dynel, and imitation fur. And then the refrigerators, transistor radios, fingernail polish, electric shavers, shelves of Danish meats, brown-and-serve rolls, powder bleach, and Spangles chewing gum that held their place alongside tooled leather sandals, antique urns, tapestries, and melons. At the As-Sharq Record Store, Ruthie squealed like a teenager over the Beatles' album *Revolver*.

'I didn't think this would *ever* get here,' she said, hugging it to her chest, and I remembered my grandfather in Shawnee, calling for the destruction of all the Beatles' records. 'We're more popular than Jesus,' John Lennon had said—blasphemy enough for good Christian people to call for his death. The bonfire we built in the little gravel lot lit up the sky, fueled by blackjack and scrap and the lone LP found in our congregation, pried from the fingers of twelve-year-old Maggie Dahl, who cried as her record burned.

At Fawzi Jishi's, I told Ruthie that I needed a new swimsuit. Amid knit jackets from Italy, Lusso chiffon blouses, and Jacques Fath ball gowns, Ruthie found an emerald green bikini, a tie at the back of the neck and at each hip. She held it against me. 'Adorable,' she said. 'It will match your eyes.'

'I don't know if I can wear that,' I said. 'Don't they have any one-pieces?'

She blinked. 'Are you even twenty?'

I clamped my mouth shut.

'Then quit acting like an old lady.'

The bearded Saudi clerk, dapper in a Western

suit coat buttoned over his white *thobe,* smiled broadly as he wrapped the package and wrote up the charge. Outside, the sky above us pilled with clouds, just enough to parse the sun's bite. Ruthie pointed me to a little sidewalk café with a private room where women could sit closed off from the men. She sank into her chair, took off her shoes, dug her thumbs into the arch of one foot, and groaned. The old Arab man who brought our coffee took his time, arranging the sugar and spoons, mesmerized by Ruthie's bare legs. It might have made me anxious if not for her nonchalance, as though we were not in the middle of Arabia but shopping the mild avenues of Oklahoma City, flirting with shop boys. I kept my knees tucked beneath the small table, took a sip of the thick black brew spiked with cardamom—a taste like nutmeg or mace. When two black-cloaked women came in, moving around us like our own animate shadows, only their kohl-lined eyes visible, I lowered my gaze, made shy by their modesty and sharp glances.

'Have you ever met one?' I whispered to Ruthie.

She flicked her lighter. 'Once. The Fullertons invited some sheikh to dinner, and he brought his first wife along. She just sat there in her *abaya* and didn't say a word. We couldn't drink while they were there, so the whole evening was a bust.' She brushed the flies from the sugar. 'Some Arab women spend their entire lives in one house, never leave, not even for groceries. It's a mark of status because it means all of their needs have been met. Can you imagine?'

Just thinking about it made my throat tighten, my chest constrict. 'They must be so lonely.'

'I'm not sure a woman is ever alone,' Ruthie

86

said. 'If a Muslim has enough money, he can take four wives and all the concubines he can feed. Women always have to be in the care of a man, so men marry widows just to take care of them, and they all have their kids and relatives, so it's a mob, a big family, but the men and women are always segregated. The only real time a wife spends with her husband is when it's her turn in his bed.' She shrugged. 'Guess that in some ways they're not much different from us.'

'Except for the more-than-one-wife part,' I said, 'and the concubines.'

Ruthie blew out a smoky breath. 'You take a bunch of healthy men and women, fence them up in the middle of the desert, throw in some *sadiqi* juice, and see what happens. It's like Peyton Place around here.' She sat back, crossed one arm at her waist. 'The difference is what happens if you get caught. If a Saudi woman is even seen with a man she's not related to, she can lose her virtue, and if she loses her virtue, she may as well be dead. You know, honor killings.' I nodded as though I did know. Ruthie lowered her eyes, thought for a moment. 'Then again,' she said, 'there's Charlene Whitaker.'

I ran through my mental list of names and faces. 'Charlene? I don't think I've met her.'

'That's because her husband strangled her to death, then buried her body in the desert. He was always sure she was having an affair whenever he was on the platform, but she never dared even look at another man.' Ruthie ran one finger along the edge of the ashtray. 'She always blamed her bruises on bumping into things, tripping, but we all knew. They locked him up in the Dhahran hospital until they could ship him back to the States.' She lifted her face. 'But it doesn't do any good to think about things like that. What's done is done.' She looked around, waved her cigarette like a censer. 'When we first came to Arabia,' she said, 'this was nothing but sand and a few mud houses. Next thing you know, they'll be putting in a Bloomingdale's.' She brought her gaze back to mine. 'But you're not like the other girls. Shopping isn't really what you want to do, is it?'

I dropped my eyes. 'I'm just turned funny,' I said, and Ruthie laughed.

'I think you've got more adventurous things in mind,' she said. 'The trick is learning how to spend your time so that it doesn't spend you.' She stubbed her cigarette, checked her watch. 'We had better get going,' she said, 'before the shops close down for prayer.'

We sauntered back, stopping along the way at a *suq* strung with Mexican peso pins and baby bangles, where a veiled woman, hands crippled with age, stood with her basket of fruit. When I reached to examine the bananas and dates, she touched her fingers to my face.

'*Latifa,*' she said. I looked at Ruthie.

'She thinks you're pretty,' Ruthie said. 'She'll want to give you something now.'

As if on cue, the woman lifted a persimmon from her basket. 'She's offering you a gift,' Ruthie said. 'You have to take it.'

The persimmon nested in my hand, soft as an Easter chick. 'Thank you,' I said. The old woman's eyes wrinkled with pleasure, but then I saw them widen. She pulled up the hem of her scarf and hobbled away. I turned to see two Arab men approaching, their long beards untrimmed, their *thobes* cut short at the knees.

'What in the hell are they doing here?' Ruthie hooked her arm through mine. 'Don't look. Just start walking.'

I matched my quick steps to hers, and we headed back to where the bus would pick us up, weaving past crates, kicking up the sand that had drifted in and around the buildings. Maybe it was Ruthie's bare shoulders that caught their attention, or maybe it was the way we brushed against the Arab men in our path, but when one of the *mutaween* let out a shout, I knew we were in trouble.

Ruthie pulled me into a jog, and then we were running, our bags belling our elbows, the quickening slap of the men's sandals against the ancient stone street echoing behind us. We dodged between a donkey cart and an oncoming Mercedes, the young prince laying on the horn as he passed. Shopkeepers appeared at their doors and windows, calling loudly, but I couldn't understand what they were saying. I felt the strength in my legs come back to me, all those sprints across the open fields, running to beat my grandfather home, but Ruthie was lagging. I looked back and saw the two men barreling down upon us, skirts flapping, people and chickens and goats scattering from their path.

'I can't,' Ruthie gasped. 'I'm out of breath.'

I dragged her a little bit farther, wishing I could pick her up and carry her like a sack of potatoes, but when she staggered to a stop, I held on to her, turned, and stood as tall as I could.

A crowd of shopkeepers was joined by the curious men who had left their coffee and bargains on the tables and begun to gather as the *mutaween* slowed and approached, their canes held out like they were goading hogs. I could see now that one of our pursuers was a bit younger than the other, his voice shrill and excited. The elder, his face pitted with smallpox scars, stepped toward us, angrily gesturing to the group of men for support. I looked around, hoping for help, but the few women in their *abayas* had disappeared. I considered our bags and purses, some token we might offer—a Beatles LP, an emerald bikini—and then I remembered the persimmon.

I moved carefully, showing that I meant no harm, and extended my hand, the fruit balanced in my palm. 'Peace be upon you,' I said, and offered a modest smile.

The elder looked at me with such disdain that I thought he might spit. Before I could move, he raised his staff and struck the fruit from my fingers. I pressed my throbbing hand to my chest and heard a murmur go up from the ring of men who surrounded us. Ruthie pinched my elbow.

'Don't do it,' she whispered, but it was too late. The pain sparked a flash of anger that flared in me so fast, I didn't even stop to think. I reached down, snatched up the persimmon, and threw it as hard as I could.

Mason had always said that I had a good arm for a girl, and maybe he was right because the persimmon smacked the *mutawa* right in the forehead. I pulled back, hardly believing what I had done, although if I had had a bag of persimmons, I would have pitched them every one.

The *mutawa* stumbled back. When he lifted his hand as though he might find blood and found instead a spatter of sweet fruit, the surprised look on his face turned murderous. He raised his cane to

90

strike again, but I ducked away and pulled Ruthie behind me. I heard shouts and jeers, felt the crowd of men pressing in.

'Oh, shit,' Ruthie said. She huddled against me, and I draped my arms around her and tucked my shoulders, expecting a shower of stones. It took me a moment to realize that it wasn't me and Ruthie who were being taunted but the robed police. The shopkeepers and other men crowded in, separating us from the *mutaween,* urging us away.

'Hurry,' Ruthie said, 'the bus.' She took my hand, and we ran together, gasping our way past the fountain, banging up the bus's stairs, startling the driver. We ignored the curious looks from the few other women and collapsed into seats near the front. I peered out my window and saw the angry eyes of the elder *mutawa* glaring back as he watched us pull onto the main road.

Ruthie let out a cackle of relief, reached into her purse, and tapped out two cigarettes, her hands trembling.

'See?' she said. 'I told you we'd have fun.'

I dropped my head back, blew a stream of smoke. 'Not the kind of fun I want to have every day,' I said, even though it wasn't true.

She bumped against my shoulder. 'Thanks,' she said. 'You're the best.' When I ducked my head, pleased and a little embarrassed, she laughed. 'Listen, meet me and Linda at the pool tomorrow morning. We'll work on our tans.'

By the time we arrived back in Abqaiq, the adrenaline had drained away, leaving me with a pounding headache. Yash eyed me coolly when I dropped my bags to the floor, splayed on the couch, and kicked off my shoes.

91

'We went to al-Khobar,' I said, grinning. 'The Virtue Police tried to catch us, but we got away.'

He lifted his chin, whether in disbelief or disapproval, I couldn't tell. 'You are welcome to freshen up a bit before dinner,' he said.

I watched him back into the kitchen, then gathered my shoes and bags and half swaggered to the bedroom. I laid out the swimsuit and spent an hour in the tub, shaving my legs, smoothing my heels. In the bottom vanity drawer, I had discovered an abandoned stash of Betsy's makeup, and I lined my mouth with Strawberry Meringue, then opened a bottle of polish and painted my toenails Jungle Red. I couldn't quit looking at them, pleased by the bright flash of color. I pulled on the bikini and appraised myself in the mirror, turning to see my naked shoulders, the bare expanse of each leg. 'You've got gams like a filly,' Mason often cooed to me. 'Want to take me for a ride?' I tucked my arms against my sides, hoping for more cleavage, stood on my tiptoes, sauntered back and forth, tipped my chin like Marilyn Monroe. I pulled up my hair, let it fall back around my face. 'You're such a tease,' I said aloud, and pretended a flirty laugh, leaned in until my breath fogged the mirror, and pressed my lips to the glass. The perfect bow, the ghosting condensation—I decided to leave it, just to see what Yash would do. Some part of me liked the idea of his finding it there as he cleaned, hesitating just a moment, maybe two, before wiping it away.

CHAPTER FIVE

Abqaiq buzzed with electric heat as I walked to the pool the next morning, the coolest hours already boiled dry. Mynah birds panted in the deep forks of trees, whistling their distress, sometimes mimicking the beep of a car horn. The Bedouin boy at the snack bar nodded as I passed, shyly offering his greeting, his eyes never lifting from that place where my sundress dipped toward cleavage. I wondered at the stories he must tell his friends—whether he spoke of the Aramco wives with admiration or contempt—and thought of Abdullah. How did he move between one world and the other, compound to tent to compound? Did he tell his mother of all that he witnessed or keep it from her like a teenage boy who took his visions to bed?

'Gin, over here!' I saw Ruthie, laid out on her chaise longue, sleek as a seal, Linda Dalton beside her, all legs and décolletage, a cigarette in one hand, a Pepsi in the other, her beehive perfectly coiffed. They waved me past a passel of children gathered in the shallow end, splashing and screeching their delight. A few of the young mothers raised their faces to see who I was, then dropped back to their magazines. I smiled down as I walked by, the knot in my stomach bunching. I counted the months, as I had done so many times before. Come June, my son would have been born.

Ruthie introduced me to Linda, who pointed at a bottle of coconut oil. 'Help yourself,' she said.

'Thanks.' I sat on the longue and kicked loose my sandals, working up the courage to strip my dress. I looked at Ruthie and smiled when she handed me a soda.

'Just take it off,' she said.

I stood and turned in a half circle, trying to find the position that would afford me the greatest privacy before letting the dress fall. I folded it quickly and reclined on the longue, my arms crossed, the sexy confidence I had felt the night before gone.

Ruthie rubbed a bit more oil onto her already glistening thighs. 'Linda was just telling me about this engineer from Morocco,' she said. 'Sounds cute.'

'He's rich,' Linda said. 'Too bad he's not white.'

'He's whiter than some you've dated.' Ruthie pulled back her neck strap to check her tan line.

'Not close enough to take home to Daddy.'

'You don't have to marry him, you know,' Ruthie said. 'Why buy the pig when you can get the sausage for free?'

'Easy for you to say.' Linda rolled to her stomach and undid her top, let the straps fall to each side. 'You don't eat pork.'

'That puts me with the majority here,' Ruthie said. 'You're just a common infidel.'

'There's nothing common about me, Miss Ruthie.'

I took a sip of Pepsi and listened to their banter, fascinated by the easy give and take I had never heard between women. I remembered Carlo Leoni and looked around the pool, wondering how many of the women he had bedded.

'Don't forget to turn over, Gin,' Ruthie cautioned. 'You'll broil instead of bake.'

The thought of rolling to my stomach, exposing

94

my backside, filled me with misery, but I did it anyway, hooking my fingers in the elastic legs of my bottoms to gain an inch more coverage.

Ruthie snorted. 'You're funny.'

'Leave her alone.' Linda, her cheek against the chaise, sounded drowsy. 'She's shy.'

'Look at her,' Ruthie said. 'How could you ever be ashamed of that body? I'd be showing it off every chance I got.'

'She's not you,' Linda said.

'She's repressed,' Ruthie said, 'just like you.'

Linda raised her head. 'You think I'm repressed?'

'Well, maybe not you.' Ruthie pulled a Thermos from her beach bag, glanced around to make sure no one was watching, and filled her pop bottle. 'Ginny Mae?'

I hesitated before handing her my soda. 'Just a little, please.'

'That's what we all say. Drink what you want, and I'll finish the rest.' She tipped the Thermos, then tucked it back in her bag. 'If no one sees it, it doesn't exist, just like everything else in this place.'

'What's the word on Katie Johnson?' Linda asked.

'Candy says nervous breakdown.' Ruthie sucked on her cigarette. 'I say home abortion.'

'True?' Linda asked, although she didn't seem surprised.

'What do you think?' Ruthie blew a stream of smoke from the side of her mouth. 'She's fifty if she's a day, with six kids already. I'd just kill myself and get it over with.'

Linda clucked her tongue. 'You have to admit that Clyde's still got it.'

95

'Clyde needs to keep it in his pants.' Ruthie looked at me. 'Linda decided it wasn't worth having a husband just to have children. It's very enlightened of her.'

'Shut up, Ruthie,' Linda said.

'That's what you told me.'

Linda flipped to her back, her top falling away to reveal a full breast and pink nipple. I looked down until she got herself fastened. 'What are you and Lucky up to these days, anyway?' she asked.

Ruthie lifted her sunglasses. 'Short leave in Bahrain, then Christmas break in Ceylon. Joey is going to meet us for Hanukkah.' She gestured to me with her lighter. 'You and Mason need to start thinking about where you want to go. The company will fly you anywhere. Every two years, you get a full month's home leave.' She smirked at Linda. 'That's when we're supposed to reconnect with the mother country.'

'Right,' Linda said. 'Why would you go back to the States when you can go to Morocco?' She rested her arm across her eyes. 'How about your husband, Gin? He's offshore, right?'

'Ten more days,' I said. The liquor made me feel light-headed, a little giddy. 'Seems like forever.'

Linda peeked one eye my way. 'You'll get used to it. There's more than enough to do around here. The problem is what not to do.'

'Boy, that's the truth,' Ruthie said. 'The wives who spend their hours making spaetzle are nuts. Lucky knows better than to expect me to meet him at the door, all cooey.' She snapped her eyes like a doll. '"Here's your martini, dear, and your slippers, and dinner is on the table." Blah. He's lucky if he can find me at all.'

'He just follows the trail of booze bottles,' Linda said.

'Funny.' Ruthie waved her magazine. 'All I know is that when he gets home, he wants food, sex, and sleep, not necessarily in that order, and if I don't give it to him, someone else will.' She cocked her head my way. 'You'll want to keep your eye on Mason, especially around Candy.'

I felt my scalp tighten. 'Mason would never . . .'

Ruthie sucked in her cheeks. 'There are some things no man can resist.'

'Like what?' I asked.

She crooked a grin Linda's way. 'More wine, more time, we'll talk.' She pushed on her sunglasses, brought up her magazine, and I was left to the lull of the sun, the pleasant hum in my ears. I closed my eyes, drifted in and out with the rise and fall of the children's laughter until Ruthie swung her feet to the ground. 'You're getting pink, Gin. You'll have good color for the ball.'

Linda sat up. 'Who's going?'

'We are,' Ruthie said. 'Come with us.'

'Maybe.' Linda swallowed the last of her Pepsi.

'I like your earrings,' I said. I'd been admiring the little coins that dangled at her jaw.

'Want to try them?' Linda pulled one loose, held it out. I clipped it on, wishing I had a mirror.

Ruthie looked at Linda. 'I thought your ears were pierced.'

'I've never gotten around to it.'

'You?' When Ruthie squinted at my lobes, I shook my head. She pondered for a moment, then pulled on her dress and slipped into her sandals. 'Let's do it.'

'What?' I asked.

'Pierce your ears.'

I looked at Linda, who looked at me and grinned. 'Why not?' she said.

How could I answer? Because my grandfather said that only ruined women pierced their ears? Because I had to ask Mason first?

'Why not?' I echoed, and shook out my sundress, let it slide over my shoulders, felt the tacky catch of tanning oil, the prickle of sunburn. 'Where?'

'Your house,' Ruthie said. 'Yash can feed us one of his fabulous lunches.' She directed her voice at Linda. 'Gin's got a dream of a houseboy. Waits on her hand and foot.'

'My houseboy can't cook worth beans,' Linda said. 'All he wants to do is sit on the porch and smoke his stinky brown cigarettes. Maybe I need a new one.'

Ruthie motioned for us to follow her. 'Come on,' she said. 'We're going to make this fun.'

I climbed in back, and we drove to the little *suq,* where we found a pack of darning needles. The Arab clerks watched us openly as we tittered over our purchases, but I didn't care, buoyed by the liquor and sun. A quick stop at Ruthie's house, where Linda and I waited in the car while she ran in and returned with an armload of formal gowns and a jewelry case that she piled on top of me. When we pushed into the foyer of my house, hot and smelling like fruit salad, Yash stopped his meal preparations long enough to look from Ruthie to Linda and then to me. I attempted an encouraging smile that slipped sideways as I followed Ruthie and Linda into the bedroom. Ruthie stripped naked before I could step out of my sundress, and I kept my eyes averted as she considered the gowns.

98

'The midnight blue,' Ruthie said, pointing Linda to a floor-length dress with a plunging neckline and ruched waist. 'I'm taking the red empire.'

I chose the emerald ball gown made of taffeta with a sweetheart neckline and three-quarter sleeves. Ruthie helped with my makeup while Linda pinned my hair. When I looked into the mirror, I hardly recognized the woman there: hair swept into a chignon, face full of color. Like the prom queen I'd never been.

Yash, wary as a cat, stiffened when we came back into the kitchen.

'We need *sadiqi* and clothespins and a potato cut in half,' Ruthie ordered. She struck a match and ran the flame over a large darning needle. 'Who's first?'

'I want to get it over with.' Linda scooted onto the high stool, the blue iridescence of her dress shimmering, and downed several swallows. I tipped my own glass, my throat burning. Ruthie clamped Linda's earlobes with the clothespins Yash had mustered.

'We'll leave these there for a minute,' she said, 'and then you'll be numb.'

'May I ask,' Yash queried, 'what is happening?'

'I'm piercing their ears,' Ruthie said.

He moved closer as Ruthie removed one of the clothespins. 'There will be infection,' he said.

'That's what this is for.' She poured a saucer full of moonshine and dropped in two sets of studs from the jewelry box. 'Are you ready?'

Linda took a long drag off her cigarette. 'Ready as I'll ever be.'

Ruthie pressed the potato half against the back of Linda's left earlobe and positioned the needle.

99

Yash's eyes had widened, whether with horror or fascination, I couldn't tell.

'Here it goes,' Ruthie said, and punched the needle through.

'Ouch,' Linda said.

'Almost done with this one.' She withdrew the needle, wiped the blood, and pressed a gold stud into the tiny hole.

'Ouch again.' Linda said. 'Now it's throbbing.'

'Keep drinking,' Ruthie said, and repeated the procedure on the other side. When she was done, Linda's earlobes were red and beginning to swell. She slid from the stool, hiked her dress, said, 'Your turn,' and wobbled toward the bathroom, taking her glass with her.

'One more drink,' I said, and took as much into my mouth as I could swallow.

'You do not have to do this,' Yash said.

I nodded as Ruthie applied the clothespins, felt them pinch and swing heavy at my jaw. 'It's fun,' I said.

He scowled. 'This does not look like fun.'

'Hush,' Ruthie said. 'She's fine.'

He drew back, picked up his knife, and began slicing a cucumber. 'It is not easy to prepare a meal in the face of such bloodletting.'

When Ruthie pulled the clothespin from my left ear, I closed my eyes, felt the raw coolness of the potato and then the hot sting of the needle. The throb was immediate, as though the lobe were pulsing, inflating with fire. When the post of the earring popped through the tough tissue, my stomach rolled.

'Are you okay?' Ruthie asked.

I opened my eyes, swallowed the water pooling

beneath my tongue. 'I think so.'

'Take another drink. You're almost done.'

It was all I could do to keep my seat as she pulled loose the second clothespin and positioned the potato. I looked at Yash, who shook his head and turned away.

'Here it goes,' Ruthie said. I winced, felt a cool sweat break out across my chest. By the time it was over, I was shaking. Ruthie lit a cigarette and placed it between my lips. 'Good girl. Let's go sit in the living room until lunch is ready.'

Linda was on the couch, the color back in her face. Ruthie dropped the Beatles album she had brought along onto the hi-fi, then plopped down between us, pulling at the waist of her dress as George Harrison sang about the taxman.

'Just keep swabbing your earlobes with alcohol,' Ruthie said. 'In a few days, you'll be all healed.'

Yash came in with what remained of the pineapple wine and a tray of chapati, dal, and fresh vegetables.

'No, thanks,' Linda said. 'I need to get home and take some aspirin.' She waited until Yash had left the room, then lowered her voice. 'He's not like any houseboy I've ever seen.'

'Told you,' Ruthie said.

I smiled as though I had won some kind of prize. 'He's more like a friend,' I said.

Linda glanced at Ruthie, then back at me. 'I wouldn't let it get around,' she said, then gathered her purse. 'I'll see you two kids at the ball.'

'With the Moroccan?' Ruthie asked.

'You know they wouldn't let him in,' she said, 'any more than they'd let Yash walk through the door.' She pulled out her sunglasses, touched my shoulder. 'We're like blood sisters,' she said. 'Take care of yourself, sweetheart.'

When latch clicked shut, I reached for the bottle, feeling like I had survived some kind of ritual. 'Linda's nice,' I said.

'She's not "nice."' Ruthie snapped a carrot between her teeth. 'She's smart and she's beautiful. But I'll tell you this'—she pointed the severed carrot—'if she ever lays a hand on my Lucky, I'll snatch her bald.'

I tried to imagine Linda Dalton, smooth and polished as a racehorse, taking a shine to Lucky Doucet. I looked down at my bare feet, thought I saw drops of blood before remembering I'd painted my toenails red. I tried to focus, closed my eyes, opened them again.

Yash came in to tighten the blinds and stack a few more records on the hi-fi, Pat Boone crooning his love as Ruthie poured another glass of wine. She leaned back, lolling her head to the music. 'So I'm a college student in Beirut, dating this putz named Reuben. Reuben the Rat, that's what my girlfriends called him, because he had this sharp little face.' She crinkled her nose, bucked her teeth, then laughed and clapped as though to dispel his memory. 'Anyway, we're at this dance club, and in walks Lucky Doucet in his dress blues, out on leave. Bigger than anyone else in the room.' She reached for a piece of bread, dipped it in dal, kept talking. 'He came right at me like no one else was around. Didn't say a word to Reuben, just took my hand and led me to the dance floor. We didn't stop until the club shut down.' She rocked forward, lowered her voice. 'Then he took me to his hotel, pattering to me in that sexy Cajun French the whole time.

102

We started the minute the door closed, right there on the floor. Made love in every corner of that room before the night was over. I never heard from Reuben again.' Her fingers traced the single strand of pearls at her neck, and she smiled, looked at me sideways. 'Your turn. Tell me about Mason.'

I hesitated. I didn't know how to tell my own story, how to make sense of any of it. I felt like if I started pulling the thread, it would all unravel into a pile of nothing. Ruthie touched my knee.

'We've got time,' she said. 'Start at the beginning.'

So I did. I told her about my mother's illness and death, about my grandfather's whippings. I told her about Mason and the only baby I would ever have. Ruthie dabbed at my mascara with her napkin.

'You're in a good place to start over, Gin. We all are.' She held her cigarette to my lips, and I inhaled, felt the bite of tobacco. 'Believe me, it could always be worse. The girls around here could be stoned for doing some of the stuff we did.' She lowered her gaze, ran one thumb around the rim of her glass. 'My parents and brothers all died in the death camps. Everyone except me.' When I started to react, she shook her head. 'Old news,' she said. 'Maybe that's why I like it here. Most of us have some grief we're leaving behind.' She clinked her glass against mine. 'Cheers,' she said, and tipped it back. 'Now, let's talk about something fun. Tell me a joke.'

I sat for a moment. 'I don't think I know any jokes,' I said.

'Then here's one,' Ruthie said. 'So Issy and Sadie were not having a good sex life. "How come you never tell me when you have an orgasm?" asks Issy.

103

Sadie looks at him and says, "Because you're never home!"'

I cracked up, maybe a little too loudly because Ruthie straightened and peered at me, sly-eyed. 'Don't tell me,' she said, 'don't tell me you've never had one.'

'I have them all the time,' I said, then clapped my hand over my mouth, and we both fell back laughing. I jerked upright when I heard Yash step into the room.

'What do you have when a Pakistani is buried to his neck in sand?' he asked.

We shook our heads.

'Not enough sand.' He chuckled, then composed himself. 'I'm going to market,' he said. 'Is there anything that you need?'

'Oh, please.' Ruthie hiccuped. 'Don't get us started.'

He tucked his lips, but the smile broke before he could turn. Ruthie and I lay against each other, catching our breath, listening to his footsteps fade away.

'He's a nice guy, Yash is.' Ruthie pushed herself back against the couch, rubbing her ribs. 'He'd make someone a good wife.'

'He's a better wife than I am,' I said. 'I don't do anything around here.'

'It's what you do in bed that counts,' Ruthie said. She dragged her purse up off the floor, pulled out her compact. I took her wrist, peered into the little mirror.

'I look awful,' I said, and dabbed my mouth with her lipstick.

Ruthie looked at her reflection and sighed. 'Next to you, I look like a dried-up old prune.'

'That's not true,' I said, and focused on her eyes. 'You're beautiful.'

Ruthie cupped her breasts, let them drop. 'Everything is heading south.'

'If I stick out my tongue,' I said, 'I look like a zipper.'

'You're like the French,' she said. 'More than a champagne coupe is a waste.'

I fell back against the couch, plucked at the bodice of my gown. 'Now what are we going to do?'

'I've seen all the movies,' she said. 'Lucky promised he'll take me to *Under the Yum Yum Tree* when it gets here. I just love Jack Lemmon.' She tilted against me. 'We could go to the bowling alley and seduce the pin boys.'

I rolled my head to meet her eyes. 'You could tell me what no man can resist,' I said.

She drew back and considered me for a moment. 'What's the nastiest thing you've ever done with a man?'

I tried to focus, felt my vision waver. 'Mason is the only man I've ever been with.'

'I should have known,' Ruthie said. 'Okay, then, what's the nastiest thing you've ever done with Mason?'

I tipped forward a little, held my glass close. 'We made love once standing up in the kitchen,' I said.

'That's not nasty.' She chuffed. 'That's wholesome.' She tilted her head. 'You really are that innocent, aren't you?'

I gave a slow blink. 'Weren't you a virgin when you met Lucky?'

Ruthie's face went blank for a moment before breaking into a smirk. 'Oh, kid,' she said, 'you're a case.' She sucked in an ice cube, let it drop back

105

into the glass. 'You've got to keep them guessing or they get smug and then they're boring.' She took a drag off her cigarette, cast her eyes to the ceiling, let the smoke out in a smooth stream. 'What about fellatio?'

I scrunched my shoulders. I had never heard the word before, thought it might be somebody's name, a character in a book I hadn't yet read.

'You know, blow job?' Ruthie said. 'Your mouth on his thingy? Lucky loves it. All men do.'

I sat silent for a moment, trying to imagine. 'You just put your mouth on it?'

Ruthie picked up the empty booze bottle. 'Watch.' She closed her eyes and let the glass slide in, then bobbed her head up and down, and I saw the pink of her tongue flick along the underside, circle the neck. When she licked her lips and winked at me, I barked out a laugh.

'See? That's all you have to do,' Ruthie said. 'Get your mouth on a man, and he's yours for life.' She wiped the lipstick from the bottle and passed it to me. 'Just imagine you're sucking on a Popsicle,' she said. 'You're hot, and it's melting.'

I swallowed the last of my drink, held my cigarette away from my face. The bottle clinked against my teeth.

'Fold your lips over,' Ruthie said, 'like you don't have a tooth in your head.'

I was making another attempt when the door swung open in a hot whirl of air. Ruthie and I let out yelps of surprise when Lucky swaggered in.

'What the hell?' he said. 'You girls expecting company?' Mason stood beside him, looking at me like I had grown horns.

'Why are you home?' I asked, and touched my

106

lips, swollen and raw, felt my earlobes burning. 'What's wrong?'

'They hauled us in for a meeting with the emir,' Lucky said. 'You know the Saudis. Everything's got to be on their time.' He gave Ruthie a squeeze. 'Grab your wraps, ladies. The head honcho wants to meet the wives. We've got a *real* party to go to.' He swiped Ruthie's flask, emptied it in one swallow.

Mason took in the table, the overflowing ashtrays, the empty bottle with its smear of red lipstick, then looked back at me. His eyes settled on my newly styled hair. 'Guess we're ready,' he said.

'But our clothes,' I said.

'You're fine,' Ruthie said. 'It's a party, after all.' She threw me a scarf, and I attempted to tuck myself into some semblance of decency as we hiked our gowns and stumbled out to the Land Cruiser, where Abdullah waited, dressed in a fine *thobe* and crisp white *ghutra*. He looked at me quickly, then away as I climbed into the back between Mason and Ruthie, and I flushed with embarrassment, as though he knew everything I had been doing.

'Here,' Ruthie said, and held out a stick of gum. 'Just don't breathe on anybody.'

'Now, you girls remember.' Lucky threw the words back over his shoulder. 'If the emir takes a shine, we got to give you to him. Ain't that right, Abdullah?'

Abdullah's face in the rearview didn't change. 'The emir is a man of great appetite,' he said.

Mason snorted quietly. When I moved my hand into his, he glanced at me, took in my hair, my newly pierced ears, then turned his eyes back to the desert. 'I'm headed back out in the morning,' he said, his voice low.

'I wish you could stay,' I said.

He looked at me. 'Do you?'

Ruthie leaned around me, her breath sweet with mint and pineapple. 'Of course she does. We were just being silly.'

Mason looked from her to me, and I smiled, squeezed his hand, but he seemed almost bewildered, as though he wasn't quite sure who or what to believe.

A mile outside the compound, a white tent as big as a house rose from the desert. In a roped area behind, I could see the milling of horses, hear their nickering calls. Abdullah led us from the Land Cruiser, greeting the other Arabs with elaborate kisses, holding their hands as they talked. I had never seen men kiss one another, never known them to show such easy affection to anyone, wife or child—and I realized that I was listing, my drunken buzz turning to a dull-eyed stare.

'Got some racers back there,' Lucky said. 'I've got my money on that pretty gray mare. Fast-fast.' He repeated the words as though once were not enough to convey the extent of his meaning. 'Bet you a sawbuck.'

Ruthie punched him in the arm. 'You'd better not let anyone hear you say that. You'll get us all caned for gambling.'

'Hell, these boys don't know what real gambling is.' He chuckled and pointed his chin. 'I'm going to check out my meal ticket. Watch your slips, ladies,' he said, and walked from the shadow of the tent.

Mason tilted his head to where a group of American men, bolstered by pillows atop a low platform, sat drinking coffee.

'I'd better get in on that powwow,' he said.

'Remember to stay with the wives.'

I shuffled closer to Ruthie. 'He's mad at me,' I whispered.

'That's just business,' Ruthie said. 'You'll learn to tell the difference.' She stood on her tiptoes, looked to where Lucky and a corpulent Arab man in richly colored robes stood, watching the horses. I saw them bend their heads in discussion, Lucky gesticulating to the gray mare, whose coat shifted from dark to light, like hammered silver in the sun. 'That's Alireza, one of the bigwig Saudi merchants,' Ruthie said in a hush. 'I hope if he's betting, Lucky wins.'

'I thought gambling was against the law,' I said.

'Arabia is like anywhere else,' she said. 'If you have enough money, there's nothing that's not legal.'

I tried to redirect my attention to where the Aramco children knelt in rows, their mothers hovering close, scolding misbehavior, the emir laughing from his elevated chair. Near the front, Candy Fullerton stood over Ross Junior, scowling and pinching his shoulder. Pillbox hat, box jacket, A-line skirt—prim and proper as a Sunday-school teacher. She glanced at me and Ruthie in our formal gowns, and her eyes widened in disbelief.

'Wear it like you mean it,' Ruthie said, and adjusted her bra strap.

I straightened my shoulders, smoothed my taffeta pleats as the emir rose and began making his way down the row of women and children, greeting each one with genuine kindness. He was a big man and seemed little in need of the even larger bodyguards who flanked him, their glowering made more ominous by the bandoliers, rifles, and swords that hung from their shoulders and hips. 'Slaves from Africa,' Ruthie whispered. 'They're free but loyal.' I swallowed my gum, watched as Ruthie gave a slight curtsy and the emir wished good health on her father and her sons, his voice deep and clear.

'Thank you,' Ruthie said. *'Ashkurak.'* The emir smiled broadly and had just turned to me when one of his advisers whispered in his ear and directed him toward the viewing platform.

'I need to find Lucky,' Ruthie said. She spied him near the end of the course, where a loud group of drillers hunched and swaggered, shielding their bids.

'You go ahead,' I said. 'I'm fine.'

She hesitated for a moment. 'Just stay close,' she said, 'or Mason will have your hide and mine too.'

I worked my way through the crowd of men—workers still in their khakis, administrators in dress shirts and black ties, important-looking Arabs in white *thobes*—their words and laughter melding into a single language. It reminded me of a revival, the believers pouring in from neighboring congregations, an enormous white tent blooming amid the stubble of an empty field, the noisy chaos of cars and kids and dogs and, as the evening steamed toward night, the holler and stomp of praise. The spirit descended like a heavenly dove but took up residence with a fierceness that belied its promise of peace: men launched from their seats, trembling and shouting at the top of their lungs; women high-stepped to the altar, heads thrown back, dancing until they fell and lay convulsing with the gift of laughter. Holy Rollers, they called us, but only once did I see anyone roll, and that was Brother Fogarty, who not only rolled

110

but did handsprings up and down the aisle, the tail of his shirt flapping until he flipped to a stop, straightened, pulled out a comb, and smoothed his hair, speaking in tongues all the while. At the end of one long night's service, he was nowhere to be found, but because I was small, I had squatted down and discovered him snoring beneath a pew. Sister Fogarty had given me a stick of Black Jack gum for my troubles, but the taste of anise had made my throat burn, and I had added the wad to the bottom of the children's bench, only to be discovered in the act by my grandfather, who took me back to the church the next afternoon, handed me a knife, tipped the bench, and sat me on the floor, where I pried at the archipelago of petrified gum for hours, wishing that I had left Brother Fogarty where he lay.

A pair of blond saluki hounds barked at the edge of the racetrack as I edged closer. Alireza, the merchant Ruthie had pointed out, blocked my view, and I stood on my tiptoes, squinting through the choking dust that hung in the air mixing with the tarry smell of manure. The horses bunched and spun, their necks arched and tails flashing. Bays and blacks, grays and chestnuts, and a single silver mare, the one Lucky had his eye on, high white hocks and speckled belly setting her apart from the other horses. The Bedouin jockeys in their short robes were lining up their mounts, readying for a bareback run down the slapdash track cordoned off with rope and flags. I felt someone behind me, heard Abdullah at my elbow.

'You didn't get your chance to meet the emir,' he said. He looked from beneath his eyebrows at the men who turned to stare, including Alireza, and I realized how far I was from the other wives.

'Please,' Abdullah said, and directed me away, separating the onlookers like he was parting the sea. When I saw Mason watching us approach, I steadied my step, suddenly more sober as Abdullah worked us forward until we were front and center before the emir. Abdullah offered a few lively words of introduction, and the emir rose to his full height and peered down at me.

'How do you do, Mrs. McPhee?' he asked, and shook my hand.

'How do you do, Mr. Emir?' I responded. I didn't know how to curtsy, but I caught up my gown and gave a slight bow.

'Are you enjoying the festivities?' He rested his fingers together.

'Yes, thank you,' I said, then raised my eyes in earnest. 'I love horses,' I said.

He smiled and dipped his head. 'Please, won't you join us?'

Mason peered at me, on his face a mix of concern and consternation. I was glad when the shot of a pistol turned our attention to the track, and everyone stood to see. The horses swung and lunged forward, riders close against their necks. A roar went up from the racetrack, and Abdullah clapped loudly, shouted a few words of Arabic, then bent close to my ear.

'The emir's horse will win the day,' he said. 'Fortune for us all.' I heard the distinct voice of Lucky let out a whoop, saw the gray mare crossing the finish line a length ahead of the field.

'What are you doing?' Mason stood at my elbow, his voice low. 'You're supposed to stay with the women.'

For a moment, I met his gaze, but when I saw Abdullah look away as though embarrassed, I dropped my eyes. 'I just wanted to watch the races,' I said.

Mason let out a hard breath, nodded to Abdullah. 'You go ahead and take her on home. I've still got some business.'

'But I don't want to go home,' I said.

Ruthie came up beside me, crooked her arm. 'Come on,' she said. 'I'm ready for a drink.' I hesitated, but Mason was already talking with some of the other men. As Abdullah led me and Ruthie to the Land Cruiser, she leaned in close, whispered, 'I wonder what he wears underneath that robe,' but I wasn't in any mood for more jokes. I sat in the back, crossed my arms, and stared straight ahead, a sharp resentment rising along with the crankiness that came with a hangover. 'I wish we could have stayed longer,' I said, louder than was necessary, my eyes on Abdullah's face in the rearview, but he didn't look up.

'You're just a kid,' Ruthie said. 'Forget the drink. I'm ready for a nap.' She rested back her head, looked at me, her eyes half-lidded. 'Listen,' she said quietly. 'It's the transitions that are hardest. When Lucky comes in off tour, we always have to fight at first, but then we get to make up.' She reached for my hand, gave it a squeeze. 'You'll get used to it.'

Abdullah let Ruthie off at her house, and I kept silent as we rounded the corner and idled to a stop in front of my door. Even with the heat, I didn't want to go back into the too-close rooms. I shifted in my seat, looked to where the sun edged the horizon. 'Do you have a horse?' I asked.

He sat stiff, his eyes forward, and now I

113

wondered whether he was mad at me too. He cleared his throat, and I realized he wasn't angry but nervous. 'My family once had a fine mare,' he said carefully. 'Her name was Badra. She was born beneath a full moon.'

'Did you break her?' I asked.

His face came fully into the rearview—the face of the confident man who had first picked us up at the airport. 'Our horses are never broken,' he said. 'They are raised alongside us like siblings.' His dark eyebrows relaxed. 'My father would say, "Children of mine may hunger and thirst, but never my mare."'

I rested my head against the glass. 'I wish I had a horse,' I said.

'But you have a stable of horses.'

'The Hobby Farm?' I said. 'Those funny pants?' I looked out my window to where the fence broke the plain. 'I want to ride out in the desert,' I said, 'like you do.'

He held back a smile, pressed his thumbs against the steering wheel. 'Perhaps Badra.'

'I thought she was gone,' I said, but what interested me more was how different he had become with Mason not around—more vulnerable, somehow, almost timid.

'The emir admired her, and so I gave her to him as a gift.' His face filled with pride. 'She won today's race.'

I leaned forward in my seat, taken with possibility. 'There's no law against a woman riding a horse outside the gates, is there?'

'It depends upon who is with her.'

'You?' I asked.

'Not alone,' he said.

114

I sat quiet, considering my options. 'What about Ruthie? I bet I could talk her into going with us.'

His eyebrows furrowed. 'If not your husband, then your father or uncle or brother or son.'

'I don't have a father or uncle or brother or son,' I said.

'I am sorry,' he said, and I saw his shoulders lift and fall, 'but you are *ghayr mahram,* forbidden to me. And even if I did have your husband's permission to take you into the desert . . .'

'What?' I asked.

He dropped his eyes from the rearview. 'My mother would never allow it.'

I groaned and fell back, sat silent for a long minute before looking out over the compound, its lines fusing in the slackening light. I took a deep breath and rested my head against the side window. 'When will it rain again?'

'As Allah wills.' In the sharp silence, he seemed to be deciding something before softening his voice. 'A cloud gathers, the rain falls, men live. The cloud disperses without rain, and men and animals die.' His face lifted in the apricot dusk, his eyes taking in the neat homes and manicured lawns, the avenues paved with asphalt. He straightened himself, peered straight ahead. 'I should return for your husband.'

I reached for the door handle and stepped too quickly to the asphalt, nearly pitching into the bougainvillea. When Abdullah got out to help me, I held up my hand.

'I'm fine,' I said. I crossed my arms as though the hot wind were a chilling breeze. 'What you said about the rain, was it poetry?'

'The words of Sir Wilfred Thesiger,' he said, 'a British explorer and friend to the Bedu.' He tilted

115

his face away and gathered his robes.

'Abdullah?' I said, and he turned back to me. 'Are you sure we can't go riding?'

He hesitated before returning my smile. 'We shall see,' he said. 'Peace be upon you.'

'And upon you peace,' I said. I waited until the Land Cruiser disappeared before turning for the porch. I started when Faris appeared like a ghost only a few feet away. In the fading light, I hadn't seen him bent near the house's foundation, where he had been deadheading the roses, his red-and-white *ghutra* mixing with the blooms.

'Faris, you scared me,' I said, wondering whether he had been watching me and Abdullah.

He looked at me seriously, then showed me the shears, a fistful of withered petals.

'Yes, I see.' I felt my headache coming back, my earlobes beginning to ache, an irritation at the back of my neck where the sand had sifted into my collar. I surveyed the newer buds, tight and edged brown, the leaves curled. 'They look thirsty.' I knelt and burrowed my finger in the soil, held it up. 'They need more water,' I said, and then louder, as though he might be deaf, 'more water.'

I straightened and entered the house, saw that Yash had cleared the dirty glasses, emptied the ashtrays, and cut a spray of jasmine to sweeten the room before leaving for the day. I showered and lay on the bed, waiting for Mason to come home, halfway wishing he wouldn't. I didn't like the way he was bossing me around, treating me like a child, but what could I do without embarrassing us both? 'It is better to dwell in the wilderness, than with a contentious and an angry woman,' King Solomon had said. Even outside of the church, the few wives

116

I knew who went against their husbands' wishes and brawled with them in public were looked upon with disgust and the husbands with pity. Maybe it was true that the best negotiations were made in bed, but I hated the manipulative nature of pleasing Mason in order to win some favor. It felt like cheating. I could guess Ruthie's response—*Get over it, kid.*

It was past dark when I heard the familiar sound of a basketball hitting the pavement, bouncing, hitting again. I rose, walked to the living room, and cracked the blinds. Mason and Abdullah circled in the vaporous haze of a street lamp, Mason's sleeves rolled, Abdullah's *thobe* lifted and tucked, revealing loose cotton drawers that reached to his ankles. They dodged and dribbled, faked, jumped up and away from each other's raised arms. There was something thrilling about watching without their knowing I was there, as though I were seeing something forbidden through a peephole, their grunts of pleasure and exertion. When they slowed and bent to catch their breath, I returned to bed, still awake when Mason came naked from the shower. I molded myself to his side, touched the softness between his ribs.

'I saw you and Abdullah playing basketball,' I said.

He rested his hands on his chest. 'No competition,' he said, his words clipped.

'Are you upset with me?'

He lay quiet for a moment, as though he weren't sure. 'Just surprised, that's all.'

'It was only Ruthie,' I said, and touched the bowl of his hip. 'She knows everything there is to do around here.'

He exhaled through his nose. 'Seems like you're doing it all at once.'

I rose up on my elbow. 'Guess what I bought,' I said.

'I'm too tired to guess,' Mason said. 'Just tell me.'

'A bikini,' I said, as though the word itself were enough to shock the breath right out of him. 'Do you want to see it?' I asked brightly, then turned on the lamp, went quickly into the bathroom, and pulled on my suit, lifting my breasts to gain cleavage. I opened the door and posed like a pinup, elbows akimbo, then stretched out on my side next to Mason and closed my eyes as he ran his hand down the wale of my waist. When he rolled me to my back and touched his fingers to my nipples and then the thin strip of fabric between my legs, I sucked a quick breath, my hips bucking up. I pushed against him, felt his hand go still. When I opened my eyes, I saw him looking down at me like he had never seen me before.

'Come on,' I whispered. I searched between us, felt the softness there. Mason fell to his back, rested his arm over his eyes.

'I told you,' he said, 'I'm tired.' He reached for the lamp, switched it off.

I stared into the dark, the pleasure draining from me like dirty water. When I touched his shoulder, he flinched.

'Just let me go to sleep,' he said. 'Abdullah's going to be here early.'

I drew my hand away, tucked it between my knees, wondering what I had done wrong. I told myself to leave him alone, that it would be better in the morning, but I could feel him beside me, taut as

118

a wire. I took a deep breath, tried again.

'Tell me,' I said, 'what it's like.'

He didn't say anything at first, and then his words came slow and muted. 'I'm ramrodding a crew of Bedouins who have never worked nine to five in their lives,' he said. 'Every few hours, they've got to stop and pray. Only a few of them speak any English at all.' I saw the silhouette of his arm, his hand running through his hair. 'It's not like any job I've ever had before. I don't know what the hell I'm doing.'

'It's all new,' I said. 'You'll learn.'

'It's not just that it's new,' he said.

I hesitated before touching his face, then kissed the scar at the corner of his mouth. I moved my lips down his throat to his chest, taking my time, until I reached the tight muscles of his stomach, the delicate skin. When he caught his breath, I slid lower, and he jerked like an electrical shock had charged through his bones.

'Jesus, Gin,' he said, and arched toward me. It was nothing like that bottle, nothing at all, and when he was finished, he held me against him so tightly I couldn't breathe. 'Who are you?' he whispered at my ear.

'Just me,' I said. 'Virginia Mae McPhee.' But I wasn't so sure anymore.

CHAPTER SIX

When Yash arrived the next morning, I was already up and in the kitchen, furiously frying the bacon I'd gotten at the pork store. An hour before, I had stepped out with Mason to kiss him good-bye and found all the roses pulled out by the roots, in their place a fresh planting of night-blooming jasmine. 'Faris did it,' I had said to Mason, who had lifted his hands, unmoved. 'He's an old man, set in his ways,' Mason had answered. 'Best to leave it alone.'

I glared at Yash as though he might be in on it too. 'Next thing I know,' I said, 'Faris will be taking over the garden.'

Yash hesitated before pulling up the bar stool. 'It is a piss patch,' he said, 'if you will excuse me.'

'Yes,' I said, 'but it's *my* piss patch.' I dished up our eggs, took a deep breath. 'What do you think I should do?'

Yash poured our cups full of coffee. 'I think that you should let the gardener garden,' he said.

I looked at him for a moment, then dropped my shoulders and pulled up a stool. We ate in silence, sopping the yolk with our toast, until Yash rose to refill our cups. 'It has been a long time since I have had a woman cook for me,' he said.

'What about your wife?' I asked.

He lowered his eyes, pressed the napkin to his mouth. 'That has been many years ago.' I wanted to ask him more, but he gathered my plate, took it to the sink, and ran hot water.

'I've got to write about the Beachcomber's Ball,' I said, and rested my chin on my hands. 'I've been to polka jamborees, but never to a ball.'

'What is a polka jamboree?' he asked.

'You know, polka,' I said. 'It's a dance.'

He looked at me, pleasantly curious but with no recognition.

'Accordion.' I bellowed my arms in and out.

'Concertina,' he said.

120

'And sometimes a tuba.' I blew out my cheeks. 'That's the polka,' I said. 'See?' I stood, took a few short-stepping hops around the kitchen.

Yash regarded me with stern amusement. 'I beg that you do not do that at the ball.'

I stopped, dropped my hands. 'It's the only dance I know.'

He turned back to his chore. 'Perhaps you will have pleasant conversation.'

'Do you know how to waltz?' I asked.

'I was forced to learn while attending school,' he said. 'The British are exceedingly cruel that way.'

'Will you teach me?'

'Mrs. Ruthie will teach you,' he said. 'I'm sure that her experience far exceeds my own.'

'But I don't have time,' I said. 'The ball is tonight.'

Yash raised his eyes. 'And with whom will you be dancing?'

I lifted my chin. 'Whoever asks me.'

'Then he will teach you.' Yash smiled evenly before returning to his cleaning, but now all I could hear in my head was the jumping beat of polka.

'Let me show you.' I removed the sponge from his hand. 'Hold out your arms.'

He glanced at the blinded windows, sighed, then faced me as though presenting himself to a firing squad. I rested one hand on his arm and lifted the other. He brought his palm to meet mine, a good foot of space between us. I began singing nonsense words to the tune of a polka, pushing and pulling him into a two-four shuffle as we hopped out of the kitchen and through the dining room. He never looked down but stared straight over my head. By the time we had swung into the living room, he had

121

taken the lead. We made another turn, knocked the tapestry from the wall, bounced the lamp shade cockeyed, circled the table, and came to a stop.

'See?' I said. 'It's fun.'

Yash rested his hands on his hips, trying to catch his breath. 'It would not be mistaken for a waltz.' He smiled gamely and smoothed his hair. 'Excuse me while I attend to the damage.'

That evening, I took out Ruthie's emerald gown, dabbed each of my ears with alcohol, then swept my hair into a twist, added lipstick and rouge. All I needed was Ruthie's help deciding on shoes. When I heard Yash answer the doorbell, I padded barefoot to meet her. Instead of the lovely yellow sheath, Ruthie wore a straw hat, a sleeveless flowered top tied at her rib cage, and ragged capris. She took one look at me and burst out laughing.

'It's a theme party,' she said, 'a Hawaiian beach bash. Don't you read your own paper?'

I looked at Yash, who looked at me and shrugged.

'We don't have much time,' she said. 'Let's see what we can come up with.'

I followed her into my bedroom, where she shuffled through my closet. 'Nothing,' she said. She considered me where I stood helpless and starting to sweat. 'Yash,' she called loudly, 'bring the scissors!'

I watched as she went at the dress, trimming away the right sleeve altogether and slicing a diagonal line to the left. She cut the sleeve from that shoulder as well, leaving a thin strap, then went at the hem, angling it in a zigzag at midthigh. She held it against me. 'The slip has to go. The bra too.' When I'd gotten them undone, she spun me

122

around and dropped the dress over my head. The crisp material felt rough and alarming against my nipples.

'Ruthie,' I said, 'I can't wear this. If I sit down, it will hike clear up to my Christmas.'

'Your what?'

I pointed down there. 'That's what my grandmother called it.'

'I just cut a five-hundred-dollar dress into rags,' Ruthie said. 'Don't tell me you can't wear it.' She pulled the pins from my hair, fluffed it free of its twist.

'What about shoes?' I asked.

'You're shipwrecked. You don't need shoes.' She pulled me down the hallway, where Yash stood too stunned to speak. Ruthie passed him the scissors. 'Get us a flower, chop-chop.'

Yash came back in with a fragrant white blossom that Ruthie tucked behind my ear. 'Let's go. Linda will have all the men.'

I stuffed my notepad into my purse, then minced across the grass to her Volkswagen, the air cool against my bare legs as we drove through the dark to the recreation center.

'I feel funny doing this without Mason,' I said.

Ruthie huffed. 'The husbands are always off somewhere,' she said. 'In this place, you take what you can get when you can get it.' She parked and checked her makeup in the rearview. 'You've got to love ambient lighting,' she said. 'It covers up any number of flaws.'

'I'm still embarrassed.' I got out and stood at the curb, the warm asphalt sticky beneath my feet.

'Fine,' Ruthie said. 'The keys are in the car if you want to go home.'

The blare of a band echoed across the patio lit with tiki torches and paper lanterns. I hesitated near a hedge of frangipani before following Ruthie across the tough grass and through the entrance to the courtyard, where a group of Filipinos knocked out a brassy rendition of 'Pearly Shells.' Couples looped their way around the marble patio, the men in bright shirts, the women in sarongs and hula skirts, leis stringing their necks.

'See?' Ruthie said. 'You don't look any sillier than anyone else does.' She led me to a table near the bandstand, where Linda sat in a strapless floral dress, talking to a young man in his twenties with rust red hair, his skin a few shades lighter, as though he'd been caught in a rainstorm that bled the color down. He was dressed like a sailor, his white cap set at a rakish angle. He stood to greet us as we approached, but Ruthie stepped right past him and took his chair. 'Thanks, Pat,' she said. 'This is Gin.'

He pulled out the remaining chair for me, and I smelled Old Spice.

'Thank you,' I said, and tucked what I could of my insufficient skirt around my legs.

'Grab us a drink, will you?' Linda pointed Pat toward the refreshment stand, where a young Arab man ladled the punch. She leaned in. 'Reminds me of a nasty dog sniffing around,' she said. 'Just ignore him. He'll go away.'

Ruthie looked over the dancers. 'Get a load of that outfit Candy is wearing.'

I turned carefully so as not to expose more skin than was already showing, saw Candy doing the twist in a coconut-shell bra and a short skirt made of palm fronds that lifted to reveal a pair of scarlet panties. Burt Cane was doing his best to match her moves, the look on his face more pain than pleasure.

'Burt must have left Maddy at home,' Linda said. 'Can't say that I blame him.'

I thought about pulling out my notepad, but I couldn't imagine what I might describe that would make it past the censors. Pat returned and set our drinks on the table.

'How about that dance, Gin?'

'Oh, no,' I said, 'I don't really dance.'

'Of course you do.' Ruthie waved to the bandstand. 'Get out there and hula.'

The musician on the ukulele had picked up the pace and swung into 'Surfin' USA.' Pat held out his hand, and I let him lead me to the dance floor, where we joined the crowd doing the watusi, the monkey, the mash. Pat started jumping from one toe to the other like he was riding a stick pony, and I shuffled my bare feet across the cool marble, arms pinned to my sides. When the song slowed and shifted into 'My Girl' by the Temptations, I made a quick turn for the table, but Pat caught my hand, wrapped one arm around my waist, pulled me against him, and began swaying in a slow circle. I felt my breasts flatten against his chest, his fingers working the curve of my spine.

'Nice dress,' he said. His breath smelled like overripe cherries.

I took the opportunity to step back, put some air between us. 'Your costume is good too,' I said.

'This is my uniform,' he said. 'Just ended my tour and re-upped. Thirty-day vacation, courtesy of Uncle Sam. Visiting family for a few days, then it's back to the Mekong Delta.' He tucked his chin near

125

my ear. 'You sure do smell good.'

I pushed away. 'Listen,' I said. 'I'm just here to take notes.'

Pat ran his gaze from my ankles to my eyes. 'You can take all the notes you want.'

I turned quickly, bumping past several couples as I maneuvered back to our table. When I saw that Pat was following me, I kept going until I'd reached the women's room. I stood in front of the mirror, unable to recognize myself, my hair in waves, the flower at my ear, my shoulders bare. When the door clacked open, I turned on the water, levered some soap, saw Candy Fullerton come in behind me.

'Well, Virginia McPhee.' She sidled up to the mirror, ran a finger beneath each eye.

'Hi, Candy.' I dried my hands and tried not to look at the swell of her breasts pinched beneath the hard husks of coconut.

She moved into the stall, and I heard the dry rustle of her skirt. 'That sailor you were dancing with sure is cute.'

'Pat,' I said. 'He's here on leave.'

The toilet flushed, and Candy reappeared, still pulling up her red panties. 'He's my baby brother.' She leaned into the mirror, ran a tube of red lipstick around her mouth. 'Remember, he's keeping us safe from the Communists. Be nice to him.' She smacked, thrust the tube into the waist of her panties, and looked me up and down. 'Looks like you could use a new dress.'

I gave a little laugh, not sure how funny she meant it to be. She crossed her arms, leaned a hip against the sink. 'Where is that good-looking husband of yours?' she asked.

126

'He's on tour,' I said. 'I'm just here to cover the party for *Sun and Flare*.'

'Sure, hon.' Candy's drawl dipped and slurred. 'We all do what we can for the company.' She cocked her chin. 'Mason is a real keeper, isn't he? So smart and handsome. How do you hold on to a man like that?'

I opened my mouth but couldn't find the words to answer. She smiled, but her eyes stayed flat. 'He knows what he wants. I admire that in a man. That's why I married Ross. He's going to take us all the way to the top.' She checked the mirror one last time. 'I'll call you,' she said. 'We can talk more over coffee.' She clipped out the door, and I counted to one hundred before following, relieved to see Linda and Ruthie at our table.

'I didn't know Pat was Candy's brother,' I whispered. I glanced around to see where he was lurking.

'She's got a whole tribe of brothers. Catholics. They never know when to quit.' Ruthie stubbed her cigarette in the ashtray and cut her eyes to where Candy was already bopping across the dance floor, jerking her arms to the beat. 'She thinks she's a coquette but she's nothing but a tramp.'

I felt a light brush against my shoulder and looked up to see Burt Cane, his brightly flowered shirt ringed with perspiration. 'Ladies,' he said, and focused on Ruthie. 'May I have this dance?'

Ruthie pointed her cigarette at me. 'Ask Gin. She's fresh.'

'How about it, young lady? Care to show an old man some new steps?' He lifted the tips of my fingers and guided me to the floor, where we stood facing each other. When he started wringing his

127

hips back and forth, moving his head in quick jerks, I touched his arm.

'Can you polka?' I asked loudly.

His face lit up. 'I haven't danced a polka since leaving Wisconsin in 'forty-nine.' He took my hand in his, cupped my waist. 'But I bet I remember how.' We waited for the downbeat and dipped into the circle of dancers, weaving our way around and between, taking long strides and kicking behind, twirling until I grew joyfully dizzy and damp with sweat. People stopped to watch, clapping their hands as the band picked up the beat, and I heard myself laughing aloud, like a child spun giddily in her father's arms.

When the song ended, Burt offered a little bow, then escorted me off the floor. 'That was the most fun I've had in a long time,' he said. 'Thank you.' He gave my hand a gentle squeeze and moved back to his table, greeting others as he went.

'You've got to wonder how a nice guy like that ends up with an old bat like Maddy,' Linda said. She pulled at the top of her dress, which settled lower each time she danced.

'She might have been a different woman twenty years ago,' Ruthie said. 'Bottom line is that Burt is a saint. Loyal to a T. He brings out the best in everybody.'

'Hard to believe that about Maddy.' Linda cast her gaze around the room. 'There's no one here worth tempting,' she said. 'What fun is that?'

'Lance Powers just came in.' Ruthie nodded to where two men, one with long sideburns and a full crest of black hair, the other fair and sunburned, hunched over their drinks, deep in conversation.

Linda stood. 'Let's see if I can get his attention.'

Ruthie and I watched her sidle between the chairs, chat a moment at their table before motioning us over.

'What is she doing?' I asked.

'Whatever she has to,' Ruthie said, and rose with her drink. 'Come on.'

The men jumped up to grab extra chairs, held them for us as we sat, and I wished for a wrap, something to cover my arms and legs.

'Gin, meet Lance and Wendell,' Linda said. 'They've got something they'd like to share.'

Lance's dark hair glistened with Brylcreem as he glanced around before lifting a flask and tipping it into our juice. His handsome cheekbones made me think he might be part Comanche or maybe Kiowa. He canted his shoulders Linda's way. 'So, you're a Singles girl.'

'Don't call her a girl,' Ruthie said. 'She's almost thirty years old.'

'Thanks, Ruthie.' Linda's spark of anger made Ruthie laugh.

'So what? We're experienced, that's all.'

Wendell turned his attention on me, and I saw that his nose was blistered raw.

'You're not thirty,' he said.

'She's a baby,' Ruthie said before I could answer.

Wendell lifted his drink, touched it to mine. 'Here's to growing up.'

The second I raised the punch to my mouth and smelled the alcohol, I shivered and lowered it again. Wendell's eyes settled on my breasts, then moved to my left hand. 'Married,' he said.

'To Mason McPhee,' Ruthie said.

'Is that right?' Lance rolled an ice cube around in his mouth, lifted his head to Wendell. 'He's the newbie who got in between Swede and that driller yesterday.'

'Swede has always had a hair trigger,' Wendell said. 'Bedouins just aren't used to being yelled at.'

'Went further than that,' Lance said. 'Knocked the raghead on his ass. Swede will get sent out, sure as hell, but that's better than what he might have gotten.'

'Yeah,' Wendell said, 'like a shiv in the ribs.'

I felt the hair at the back of my neck prickle. 'What about Mason?' I insisted. 'Is he okay?'

'He's more than okay,' Lance said. 'He took the Arab's side, got himself a whole tribe of new friends.'

Wendell smirked my way. 'Next thing you know, he'll be bringing home a second wife.' Everyone laughed as though it were the funniest thing in the world.

Ruthie gave Lance a hard punch in the arm. 'Give her a break, okay? She's just getting used to the place.'

Lance worked his teeth around a toothpick as he considered me, the flaps of his nostrils flaring. 'You might tell your husband that this ain't the game he's used to playing. Rules are different here.'

'Everything is different here,' Wendell said, 'but in the same old way.' He lifted one side of his mouth. 'We're making it up as we go along, carving out our own little kingdom.'

'Kind of like royalty,' Linda said dryly.

'Yeah,' Ruthie said, 'kings and queens of nothing.'

When I felt Wendell's leg bump mine, I drew back, cast a hopeful glance at Ruthie. 'I think I'm ready to go home,' I said.

'It's not even nine o'clock.' She downed another swallow, tapped out a smoke. 'Take the car. Linda is staying over. We'll catch a ride.'

Linda had kicked off her shoes and had her feet in Lance's lap. All around me, people were laughing, having fun. I hated how much I felt like Maddy Cane.

'I guess I'll see you later, then,' I said. I stood, hesitated before turning, wishing that Ruthie and Linda and I had stayed at our own table. I didn't see Pat until I was almost to the exit.

'Where you going, pretty lady?' His cap had fallen to the back of his head, the freckles of his face inflamed, flushed with booze.

I looked back to the table, but Lance and Wendell had ferried Ruthie and Linda to the dance floor. I scrunched my shoulders, suddenly cold.

'I just need to go home,' I said. 'I have that article to write.'

'Oh, yeah,' Pat drawled. 'You're the writer.' He sidled a little closer, ran his fingers down my arm. 'My sister says you're a real smart girl.'

I flinched away and started to step around him, but he moved with me and braced one hand against the wall beside my head. 'How about a nightcap for a soldier in uniform?' He pressed in, his hot breath brushing my neck.

'Excuse me.' The voice that came from behind him was deep and commanding. Pat jerked around, and I saw Burt Cane standing with the stiff posture of a London bobby. 'I believe that the lady is ready to call it an evening.'

The cajoling grin fell from Pat's face. He looked around like he was gauging his chances before snorting and stepping away.

131

'Go ahead, Gramps,' he said. 'She's all yours. About as warm as a block of ice.'

Burt waited for him to pass, then crooked his elbow my way. 'May I?' he asked.

I took his arm, let him lead me. 'It's the Volkswagen,' I said.

'Oh, I know Ruthie's car,' Burt said. 'Come on. I'll be your chauffeur.' He opened my door, took the wheel, knew just where I lived. 'Maddy and I spent a lot of good hours with Buck and Betsy. But that's been some time ago.' He grew quiet, his voice trailing away. When we pulled to the curb, I saw the porch light on, the living room lit from within.

'I think my houseboy is waiting for me,' I said.

'Yash Sharma,' he said. 'He's one of the good ones.'

'Mason says the same about you,' I said.

Burt looked down, then peered to where the glow illuminated the jasmine, opening its fragrant scent to the air, the line of tidy homes, the stars beyond. 'When I first came to Arabia, we lived in tents right alongside the Bedouins. Nothing to do in the desert at night but sit around the campfire, sing songs, and tell stories.' He hummed a single note as though remembering the tune. 'There was this young Bedouin man. He couldn't read, but he could recite *The Odyssey* for hours. I'll never forget that.' He looked to where the flares stoked the coal black sky, and I saw his face lift and fall in the shadows. 'We all believed in what we were doing back then. I'm not so sure anymore.' We sat in silence until he brought his kind eyes to mine. 'Your husband, he did the right thing with Swede.'

'Mason always does the right thing,' I said.

Burt brought up the corners of his mouth. 'I'll

132

make sure your friends get home okay,' he said, and got out to open my door. I swiveled and stood, felt the sharp grass beneath my feet. When I held out my hand, he cupped it in both of his.

'I hope this place is good to you,' he said, then waited until I reached the porch before starting the engine and motoring away.

Inside, I found Yash sitting at the dining table, drinking tea and listening to the BBC.

'You are home early,' he said, pleased.

'I danced the polka,' I said.

Yash gathered his cup and saucer. 'I never doubted that you would.' He stood and dusted his place at the table with his napkin. 'I will clear this and be on my way.'

I said good night before moving to the bedroom, where I stripped off my dress and stepped into the shower, lathering the smoke from my hair, scrubbing my face clean, but I couldn't get rid of the damp feel of Pat's breath at my neck, the voice in my head telling me that I had no business going out without my husband, smoking and drinking and dressed like a tramp. What did I expect would happen? 'The kind of bait you throw out,' my grandfather had warned me, 'is the kind of fish you're going to catch.'

No more, I promised myself, not without Mason, and curled around the kernel of conviction as though I might seed it in myself, force it to grow.

*   *   *

What I attempted over the remaining days of Mason's tour was chaste occupation: I arranged my typewriter at the end of the dining table, knocked

133

out notes on canasta teams and bowling scores. I agreed to join Ruthie for a game of bridge at the home of Lillian Duff, a buxom grandmother with silver hair and a thick strand of pearls at her neck. When we arrived and Lillian asked whether I preferred white or brown, I thought she meant bread. 'She means *sadiqi*,' Ruthie translated, and the other wives laughed. I sat at Ruthie's elbow, uncomprehending as the cards were dealt, trumps, tricks, and strains declared. I ate the few nuts from the miniature paper cup and then the key lime pie cut into slivers. By the time I got home, I was starving, grateful for the hearty beef stew that Yash had waiting.

'Do you know how to play rummy?' I asked him one morning, the only card game I had learned from Mason.

Yash straightened, cocked his chin. 'You will never defeat me,' he said. I had come to understand that his arch demeanor was a kind of teasing, and it delighted me. I found a worn deck of cards inside the cabinet of the hi-fi, pushed aside my typewriter, and dealt us each a hand. We played for an hour, laying down runs and books of aces until Yash held up his palms in surrender. 'I have met my match,' he said. He rapped the cards even, slid them into their box. 'I read your article in *Sun and Flare* about the ball.'

'What do you think?' I asked.

'I think you have a gift for spinning straw into gold.' He rose to gather our dishes, *tsk*ing. 'The day is wasting away. I sit here playing games when I should be at market, finding a fresh chicken for our dinner.'

'I'll ride the bus with you as far as Dhahran,' I

134

said. 'I've got another article to drop off.' I rolled 'Fun Fabrics for Fiestas!' from the typewriter and folded it into an envelope. Yash stood as though perplexed.

'What?' I asked.

'I cannot ride your bus,' he said. 'Only you are allowed.'

'Women?' I asked.

'White women,' he said, 'and their children, of course.'

I stared at him. 'But that's segregation,' I said, remembering Rosa Parks and the Freedom Riders. 'It's illegal.'

'Perhaps in America,' he said, 'but not here.'

I pointed to the ground. 'But this *is* America,' I said.

Yash lifted his shoulders. 'I would have to have *sahib*'s express instruction. You would have to be'—his eyes darted around the room as though searching for an answer—'you would have to be ill.'

'Come on,' I said. 'I'm feeling kind of sick.'

'But, Mrs. Gin . . .'

'I don't care,' I said. 'I'm tired of all these ridiculous rules.'

I waited at the door until he took a hesitant step forward and followed me to the sidewalk. No matter how much I slowed, he remained three paces behind. I stopped, which brought him to a sudden halt.

'I'm not walking in front of you,' I said. 'We can stand here in this heat, or we can get on the bus.'

He took a deep breath, brought himself abreast, and marched with his eyes straight ahead. We turned the corner, and I saw several women already waiting, including Maddy Cane, her hair secured

135

by a scarf knotted tight beneath her chin, fanning herself with a copy of *Sun and Flare*.

'Hi, Maddy,' I said.

She dropped her arm and looked at Yash and then at me. 'What is he doing here?' she asked.

'I've been having dizzy spells,' I said. 'Too much sun, I guess. Mason asked him to ride with me.'

She acknowledged the bow of Yash's head with a slight nod of her own, then turned back to me.

'The Beachcomber's Ball sounds like it was quite the party.' She dabbed her throat with an embroidered handkerchief. 'Burt told me that you two danced the polka.'

'Burt is very kind,' I said. 'I'm a terrible dancer.'

'That's not what I heard.' Maddy flapped her paper. 'He's got a bad heart, you know.'

'I didn't know,' I said. 'I'm sorry.' But I was remembering Burt's jumping rhythm, his enthusiastic sweep around the dance floor, how he seemed less winded than I did.

Maddy looked sideways at Yash, who turned his attention to a nearby shrub. She craned her neck a little closer. 'Your friend Ruthie seems to have enjoyed herself. Doesn't she know how people are talking about her?'

I gave Maddy a weak smile, which seemed only to encourage her.

'She's a married woman, and everyone knows that Linda Dalton consorts with colored boys. That Lance Powers.' Maddy fanned faster. 'If Ruthie Doucet doesn't care about her reputation any more than that, well.' She sniffed and drew her lips into a pucker. 'You seem like a nice Christian girl. I'm surprised that you keep such company. Water finds its own level, you know.'

I felt my face tighten, the last ounce of goodwill leave my heart, my mouth open before I could stop it. 'I'd rather be friends with Ruthie and Linda than some bitter old woman like you.'

Maddy drew back as though I had slapped her. I felt bad but not bad enough to apologize. I heard the chug of the bus and turned quickly, leaving Maddy where she stood. I stepped aboard and found a row with two empty seats, but Yash passed on by, headed for the back. I looked up to see Maddy zeroed in on me.

'Yash!' I snapped. He turned, startled, and I pointed to the seat beside me. He sat down, eyes averted, as though he might be called to task. I sighed with relief when Maddy reluctantly took a seat near the front next to a young mother with two energetic toddlers in tow.

'Thank you,' I said. 'You saved me.'

He peered from beneath his brows to where Maddy sat and whispered, 'From the very bowels of hell.'

I looked at him, surprised, and then felt it coming just as I had in church, a hand-covered giggle that expanded and grew into a hysterical cackle. Yash lowered his head and twisted his mouth to keep the air from escaping his lungs, but his merriment fed mine and soon we were in tears, weak with laughter, even the bus driver smiling into the rearview. Maddy glared straight ahead, and the other wives watched us from the corners of their eyes, except for the two toddlers who jumped up and down with glee even when their mother shushed them.

By the time we stopped in Dhahran, other than a few tittering aftershocks, Yash and I had regained

137

our composure. I walked past Maddy without a glance and stepped off, left Yash to bear the remaining miles to al-Khobar alone.

I visored my eyes with the envelope, took in the hills, the flash of white houses, nicer than any in Abqaiq. Maybe we'll live here someday, I thought to myself, and let the possibility find its gravity. Was that what I wanted? A house on the hill? I looked to the flat desert beyond, the unbroken sky, the shadow of the sea, and felt an undeniable yearning to be out in that open space.

A note on Nestor's door read, 'Back in five,' so I waited, studying the photographs framed on his walls—a caravan of camels shadowed by cirrus clouds that unfolded like wings, the refinery at Ras Tanura, its black cylindrical stacks and squat steel tanks wreathed in vaporous light, the desert transformed into an ethereal kingdom. Prints of high-masted sailing ships along the coast, a stern-faced emir looking out from his palace in Hofuf, boyish princes already weighted with the trappings of wealth, their bare feet buried in sand— even in black-and-white, there was a softness to the scenes, a connection I could almost feel, as though the camera itself were possessed of emotion.

What was it about those images that opened my eyes, made me see in a way I had never seen before? I can look back now and know it was at that moment when I felt something settle, the possibility of who I might yet be fall into place. I wanted to know how it happened, how you could take a hulking storage tank and turn it into a thing of beauty. I tilted my head, made out the photographer's scrawl—Carlo Leoni—and felt something I hadn't expected: envy. I wanted to know what he knew, how to do what he did.

When Nestor returned with a steaming cup of coffee and a sandwich, the stink of egg salad fouling the air, I slid the envelope in front of him.

'It's about fun with fabrics,' I said.

He eked out a smile. 'I'll take a look this afternoon,' he said, pushing a pencil across the lines of a legal pad.

I nodded to the photos on the walls. 'They're beautiful,' I said.

Nestor raised his eyes, settled back in his chair. 'Leoni is one of the best. He loves whatever he sees, and whatever he sees loves him.'

'Maybe I could take some pictures,' I said.

He tapped the pencil against his lips, shrugged, opened a drawer, and pulled out a brand-new Nikon. 'It's yours,' he said. I tucked the camera close. I wasn't about to tell him that I had no idea how to work it, but maybe he could have guessed. 'Do you know how to run a darkroom?' he asked.

'I can learn,' I said.

'Just drop your film. We'll get to it,' he said, and went back to his notes.

I caught the return bus to Abqaiq, took in the shaded faces of the wives, the muted stream of traffic blurring by, focused, then lowered the lens, dissatisfied. What Carlo Leoni had that I didn't was out *there,* where I couldn't go—the open desert, that endless sea. How could I even begin to capture the people and landscape when I was closed up in a house inside a closed compound inside a society and a country that were closed to me in so many ways because I was a woman?

I thought about Carlo's photos, how it was that he could take in so much and all at once, as though his appetite were enormous, his eyes bigger than his head. I put the camera in my purse, looked out the sand-scoured window, and wondered what it would feel like to walk through the world with such ease and affection, if I must first be a man to know.

*　　　*　　　*

The next evening, Mason due home from his tour, I remembered what Ruthie had said: food, sex, and sleep. I let Yash go early, put on a shorter skirt, styled my hair, dabbed a little lipstick, and cued up Ed Ames on the hi-fi. When the Land Cruiser pulled up out front, I met Mason at the door with the martini I had left to chill in the freezer. He took it with a smile, tipped a long swallow, and I tucked my face into his neck. He smelled like something I could almost taste—wet salt, a bitter green, like wind off the sea. When I looked over his shoulder, I saw Abdullah watching us. He met my eyes for a moment before letting out the clutch and driving away.

Mason handed me his glass. 'Why don't you get me a refill while I take a shower,' he said.

I came back with more booze and waited in the doorway of the bathroom until he turned off the water and stepped out, rubbing his head with a towel. He'd never been shy about his body, but it still seemed new to me. I sometimes studied him when he was sleeping: the notch of bone at this throat, the rise of each rib, the strange dark nipples, the swirl of hair like an arrow, the tender muscle that nested in the vee of his legs. He wrapped the towel at his waist, moved to the mirror, and raked a comb through his hair.

140

'Gray,' he said, plucking at his temple. 'I'm getting old.' He rested his hands on the vanity. 'You know what I miss? Playing basketball, I mean really burning up the court.'

I tucked my arms. 'It's my fault,' I said.

'No,' he said, and peered at me in the mirror. 'I knew what I was doing, and I've never been sorry.'

I scrunched my shoulders, made self-conscious by his gaze. 'What happened with Swede?' I asked.

He hesitated. 'How do you know about that?'

'Ruthie told me,' I lied. 'She hears everything.'

Mason grunted, picked up the shaving cream. 'Swede took a dislike to me from the get-go. Thinks the Arabs are good for one thing and one thing only, and that's getting the oil out of the ground.' He lathered his face, wiped one finger across his lips. 'They're doing all the work, making ten cents an hour to my dollar, have no sense how much that oil is bringing in.' He stretched his neck, ran the razor along his jaw. 'When Ross Fullerton called to get my side of the story, he told me that the day a man takes the helm is the day he no longer knows what's going on with his own crew. He said that's why he needs men like me.'

'I saw Burt Cane,' I said, and leaned into his back, circled my arms at his waist. 'He said to tell you that you did the right thing.'

Mason patted his face with a towel, rinsed the sink, and turned to me. 'Lucky wants to take us boating tomorrow. You can wear that new swimsuit. Sexy as hell.' He pulled me close, and I pointed my elbow at the bidet.

'Do you know what that is for?'

He laughed through his nose. 'Yeah,' he said, 'I do.' He ran his lips across my shoulder, then turned

141

me to face the mirror, moved behind me.

'Watch,' he said. I pressed back against him and lifted my gaze as he murmured his pleasure into my ear, but I couldn't keep my eyes from that woman whose hair fringed her shoulders, her lips stained with color, and the man behind her, his head thrown back, his neck exposed, his body arching upward as though he were the one being taken.

CHAPTER SEVEN

The sun was beating down like a pile driver by the time we made Half Moon Bay the next morning. The Bayliner, a Confederate flag pegged to its bow, shouldered in against the wind slap, its outboard churning due east. It was the same red speedboat I had seen in the photo of the Bodeens—the *Arabesque*—maybe inherited, like Ruthie said, one more thing left behind. 'Twin Mercs,' Lucky had boasted as we loaded in. 'Fastest boat on the bay. One of these weekends, we'll take her across the gulf to Bahrain, get the Brits to sell us some rum.'

The wind's direction shifted, the depleting gales blowing off the cool water toward land.

'Executive weather,' Lucky hollered, meaning the kind you wanted when the company hotshots from California decided to pay their visits, but it made for rough seas. He stood bare-chested at the helm with the open stance of a linebacker, hair bristling from his scalp. I clutched my scarf and raised my face to the cottoned sky, the air like a poultice.

'Right about here,' Lucky said, and brought the

boat to anchor. 'Break out the Kool-Aid, girls.'

Ruthie poured the liquor while I unwrapped the picnic Yash had made for us: chapati, rice, cold chicken, chutney. When Ruthie stretched and stepped out of her capris, exposing her racy black bikini, brass rings at her hips and between her breasts, I saw Lucky watching her like she was the sweetest thing he had ever seen. He caught my eye, winked, and I blushed, too shy to strip down in front of him.

Mason helped rig the lines, and I watched the happiness with which he worked, his shirt undone, a red kerchief tied at his neck, the lean muscles of his legs bracing against the cast. Ever since we had launched the boat, he had been questioning Lucky about company politics, who answered to whom.

'You got this triangle,' Lucky said, and touched his thumbs and two fingers together. 'The House of Saud is up here at the top. Smart as hell and mean as sin. When old Ibn Saud decided he was going to rule the peninsula, first thing he did was get the *Ikhwan* fundamentalists on board, then sent them out to slaughter enough Bedu that the sheikhs finally surrendered.' He wrinkled his upper lip, and his voice dipped. 'Then the *Ikhwan* decide the king's being too soft, start making a fuss, so he has to turn around and beat the snot out of them too. Names them his very own militia to keep the peace, gives the real crazies of the group special duties, and that's the *mutaween.*'

'The Virtue Police,' I said, and looked at Ruthie, who held a finger to her lips and shook her head, but I had no intention of saying a word about our adventure in al-Khobar.

'Now Ibn Saud's got the desert Bedouins and

the town Arabs and the religious nuts all where he wants them, and that's the second point of the triangle. Only problem is, he's got no way to develop his new kingdom. Million square miles of worthless real estate but no money in the coffers. He had nothing,' Lucky said, 'until we came along.'

Mason settled back with his drink. 'Why us?' he asked. 'We weren't the only ones wanting in.'

Lucky smugged his mouth. 'A limey or two tried to stake some claim, but they kept to their cabanas, ate their biscuits and drank their tea, wouldn't even take off their piss helmets. What Ibn Saud liked about us Americans is the way we went right to work, eating, drinking, wearing the *ghutra* just like the Bedu. Sun burned us the same color so that pretty soon, you couldn't tell a white man from a darkie.' He leaned in, squinted at Mason. 'The king had requirements that we had to agree to, expectations. He wanted nothing but business, no politics, and we said okay. We beat out the limeys and frogs and wops, just like we always do, and now Aramco is the third point of the triangle. Perfect balance of power, like a pyramid, see?' Lucky clicked his tongue. 'Few years back, old Saud swung a sweet deal, gets fifty percent of all our profit, but the IRS gives Aramco an equal tax break, so it's jake. Keeps the Saudis from nationalizing, which is good for the company'—he winked—'but what it means to you and me, well, that's different.' He tapped out a cigarette. 'Your drill hits petrol, you just might want to say you've found an underground spring, something we don't have to pay for. Know what I mean?' He lowered his face to Mason's lighter, looked up, gave a lopsided grin. 'Oil into water. It's a goddamn miracle is what it is.' He stabbed his hook into a minnow, threw a long cast, settled his cap lower on his forehead. 'Heard you and Swede had a little go-'round.'

Mason flipped his cigarette to the water, ticked one shoulder.

Lucky thumbed his nostril. 'You don't waste much time, do you?'

'Swede was the one wasting time.' Mason leaned back against the gunwale, crossed his arms. 'No reason to treat a man that way because of his color.'

Lucky sucked out an ice cube, let it slip back into the liquor, gave Mason a half smirk. 'Bet you're a college boy, ain't you?' When Mason didn't answer, Lucky chortled and shook his head. 'Swede don't care about color. It's human beings he can't stand. Bossed me just the same when I came up under him, hollering and knocking me around.'

'Saleh Misar stands five-foot-nothing, weighs about the same as one of your legs,' Mason said.

'I hear what you're saying.' Lucky ran a finger across his teeth. 'Thing is,' he said, 'now we got no drilling superintendent, and that's going to pinch everyone right down the line, including me and little Mr. Misar.' He squinted at Mason. 'Swede's been here since before the war, made his friends and made his enemies, but he knew where to slap the grease. That kind of education don't come from no classroom.' He spat on his line. 'Hell, we're feeding the drillers red meat every day. You can stand back and watch them grow. Arabs never had it so good.'

Mason turned his head to the side. 'Not even close to how good we got it.'

Lucky rolled his shoulders, leaned in. 'That pretty little house of yours? Give it to a Bedouin,

145

and he'll trot in his goats, slaughter a few, roast them right there on that nice marble floor.' He settled back on his elbow. 'When I first got here, you couldn't get a full day's labor out of the natives. Doc said they didn't have an ounce of nutrition in them, shouldn't even be alive. We came in, wiped out malaria, developed a vaccine that keeps them from going blind. Put them to work making real wages, showed them how to grow corn and raise chickens, built schools and taught them the alphabet. Turned the Saudi merchants into businessmen, and now we're subsidizing their inventories, buy only from them. We've got houses the Saudi workers can buy on the payment plan. Sounds like a pretty good deal to me.'

Mason lifted the rod tip and settled it again.

'Listen,' Lucky said, and hitched his leg. 'I was born to the canals of the Barataria swamp. One-room shack on stilts, kept the turtles off our toes. Daddy was Acadian stock, right out of Nova Scotia, Mama a mean old German gal.' He circled his drink to take in the bay. 'Kind of like here, people coming in from all over, doing what they was good at. Creoles grew sugarcane, Filipinos netted shrimp, Sicilians harvested oysters, Croats fished for anything they could catch. Irish, Africans, Yugos, Chinese, all mixed up together.' Lucky paused as though to remember. 'Ten years old, got my first job skinning gators for a bohunk named Pohanko. You ever smell gator guts?' Mason shrugged. 'Smells like pig shit, and I did too. That's what my mama said.'

Ruthie looked at me and raised her fist, mouthed the word *pow*.

'Eleven of us kids.' Lucky continued. 'Started

146

getting a little crowded. Took off when I was fourteen. Doubt anyone ever missed me. Went right to the oil patch. They paid me ten cents an hour because that's what they thought I was worth, and they was right. I worked my way up. No one ever handed me a goddamn thing.' He winced with quick pain, straightened his leg. 'Just that fast'—Lucky snapped his fingers—'Saudis got it made.' He pinched one eye closed, gave a single nod. 'I'll tell you this. If they don't like it, they can get on their camels and ride right back into that desert. All the prayers in the world won't get that oil out of the ground.' He squinted a smile, jabbed his thumb down. 'This here is *our* Mecca.'

'Somebody needs a drink.' Ruthie moved across the deck like a figure skater, smooth and precise, and filled Lucky's cup, her shoulders glistening with suntan oil. Lucky lifted his face, looked past her, and his eyes grew big. He reared back, bellowed, 'There!' and I saw Mason's rod bend nearly double. Mason grabbed the butt, arched against the weighted line, reeled in, arched again.

'Bet you got a jack,' Lucky said. 'Take her in a little. Keep the tip up.'

Ruthie clapped her hands. 'He's hooked a good one,' she said, and poured a little more liquor. We cheered Mason on until he had the fish close enough to net, but what came up wasn't a jack or a bonito but a three-foot shark, the cone of its nose edging over the gunwale, its teeth gnashing the line.

'God damn!' Lucky grabbed the gaff, buried it deep in the shark's gills, and hefted it over the rail. Ruthie pulled her feet beneath her and screamed, and I jumped to the stern, forgetting to take pictures as the shark thrashed and twisted.

147

Lucky raised the gaff, brought it down again and again, the blood spraying from the hook in viscous arcs until the shark lay quivering only inches from Mason's toes. I held out my spattered arms and legs, looked up at Ruthie, who let out a whoop and lowered her feet.

Mason wiped his face with his kerchief, flushed with excitement, his eyes as wide as a child's. 'Can you eat it?' he asked.

'Can, maybe. Won't, for sure.' Lucky dragged the shark to the fish cooler, leaving an oily red slick. 'Might be able to trade it once we get back to the bay.' He leaned over the edge and rinsed his hands. 'Some of them Bedouins will eat about anything.'

Ruthie dipped her towel in the water, and I did the same, dabbing at the blood. She lifted her head, pointed east. 'What's that?' she asked.

We all turned to see a column of smoke laddering the sky. Lucky rummaged in the cabin for binoculars.

'Blowout?' Mason asked. Only weeks before we arrived, an offshore explosion had killed three Saudi drillers. The divers who searched had come up shaking their heads. A few days later, the bodies floated in on the landward current, charred skin brined white.

'Think it's just a waterspout, moving away.' Lucky glassed the horizon. 'Got some dhows close by. Pearl divers.'

Ruthie turned to me. 'How about a pearl, Gin? You could make a nice necklace.'

I looked to Mason, who looked at Lucky. 'Can you buy them right off the boat?' Mason asked.

'Nothing you can't buy off the pearlers. They're at the bottom of the barrel.' Lucky lowered the

148

binoculars. 'Might even trade for a shark.'

I held tight to Mason as the Bayliner chopped across the waves to where the dhows, their sails roped tight, studded the water.

'What about us?' I asked. Ruthie had wrapped herself in a beach towel, but her shoulders remained bare.

'We're on Aramco's ticket,' Lucky said. 'Rules are ours.' He reached for the gaff, jellied with blood. 'We'll keep this close, just in case someone says otherwise.'

The anchored vessel we approached was bigger than the others and sat high in the water, its elegant stern and low bow rising to a jutting prow. Ropes, baskets, casks, mended sails, clothes left to dry in the sun—the boat was piled high with everything the crew needed to work, sleep, and eat for weeks at a time. Two dozen men and stick-thin boys in loincloths lined the starboard and port, diving in shifts from each side.

'Hello, the boat!' Lucky hollered. *'Marhaba!'*

The dhow's aging captain, his garments salt-bleached, moved between his divers, aided by a sturdy burled staff. His skin was cured to leather, wrinkled and pinched. When he motioned us forward, Lucky motored in close enough for Mason to throw the ropes, and I was glad for the breeze that carried away some part of the stench of rotting oysters. The men and boys stared at us, their faces slack with amazement.

'He'll offer us food,' Lucky mumbled. 'Take something or you'll hurt the old fella's feelings. Hospitality means more to a Bedouin than to Jesus Christ hisself.'

We picked our way through the clutter and sat

on the rough boards that crossed the boat, where the shy boys brought us mangoes, pieces of fish, and cups of tea. When some of them slid down and disappeared into the water, I held my breath, let it out. It seemed too long before their baskets were hauled up and they followed, gasping, pulling themselves aboard, weary beyond their years.

The captain, whose long name Lucky shortened to Fahad as he translated, had once dreamed of being a boatbuilder, he said, but his clan was not of such rank within his tribe. He gestured at the boys, said he himself had begun to dive at age seven. He told us that forty, sometimes fifty times a day they would be weighted by the ankles and dropped to the bottom, then slip the nooses so that the stones could be hauled up and readied for the next dive. Just as Fahad was indebted to the ship's owner, the boys were indebted to Fahad for food and the unpaid obligations of their fathers and brothers before them. Few had any hope of freeing themselves.

One of the youngest boys, thick hair curling at his brow, arms scaled with parasites, settled himself to sort the oysters, his fingers sheathed in leather, protection against the shells' razored edges. He ducked his head when he saw me watching him. He worked his knife around a mango and offered me a slice.

'Thank you,' I said.

'Thank you,' he said, mimicking my words.

'You are welcome,' I said.

'You are welcome.' He squatted, his knees scraped raw, his feet barnacled with calluses. His dark eyes seemed to fill his small head. He looked behind him to see whether he was being watched.

150

'America, America,' he said.

I couldn't help but smile. 'America, America,' I echoed, and felt my heart shot through with longing. I imagined what my son might have looked like at his age and felt the pining desire to take the boy home, doctor his wounds, feed him hot soup, save him from his lot in life.

He pointed to the bright square of cloth at Mason's neck. '*Ahmar?*' he asked.

'Red,' Mason said, and held the handkerchief out as a gift. The boy hesitated before tying it over his face, then drew his oyster knife and pointed it like a pistol, whispered, '*Cinema?*'

Mason ran his thumb over his mouth to keep from smiling. 'Sure,' he said. 'The movies.' We watched the boy return to his place at starboard, noose the roped stone to his ankle, give us a quick wave, then nod to the older man beside him, who dropped the rock over the side, the boy vanishing with it, the bandanna a brilliant splash.

Lucky smirked at Mason. 'You're a real do-gooder, ain't you?'

'I'm just a soft touch, that's all.' Mason stood, pulled out his cigarettes, shook one loose for Lucky, who eased into a smile, let the smoke laze from his mouth.

'You just keep it up,' Lucky said. 'We'll see where it gets you.'

I moved to join Ruthie, who was looking over the basket Fahad proffered. He held fast against Lucky's rough bartering of the shark: he was Muslim and would not eat fish without scales. He gestured to the binoculars that hung from Lucky's neck.

'What the hell,' Lucky said. 'There's more where

these came from.' He handed over the binoculars, which were passed from one diver to the next, each snatching a second's peek at the magnified world. Even the boy, who had popped back up like a cork, got his turn.

'How about this one, Gin?' Ruthie held a creamy bead between her fingers.

'Perfetto.' The voice came from the bow of the boat, where I saw Carlo Leoni in his scarf and high boots rise like an imp from a sacking of sailcloth. He positioned a Brownie camera at his breastbone, looked down, clicked the shutter, then lit a cigarette in one fluid motion.

'Carlo. Never a surprise.' Lucky introduced us, his voice tight. I watched as Carlo kissed Ruthie's hand, then moved to press his cool lips against my wrist.

'Bella,' he said. *'Sei molto bella.'* He took in my camera, his dark eyes half-lidded. 'We share the same soul, I see.'

'I love your photographs,' I said in a rush. When Ruthie looked at me, one eyebrow lifted, I felt my face turn red.

'And I your beauty, *bella,*' he said. 'Perhaps we can work together someday.'

Lucky growled as though clearing his throat, and Carlo straightened to peer at him, then swung himself up onto a crate coiled with rope so that he stood a head taller. He turned to look at me and Ruthie, raised his chin and then his camera. Ruthie leaned into me as Carlo directed us to move first this way, then that, ordering the boy, still wearing his bandanna, to stand between us. Fahad frowned as he wrapped my pearl in a swatch of leather. When Lucky bent and began unknotting

152

the bow, Ruthie and I stepped back on board while Mason gripped the stern. Carlo helped me, his fingers wrapped around mine, and passed me on to Mason, who steadied me against the roll of water. As we motored off, Carlo stood with his legs spread wide like a swarthy Peter Pan, the tail of his scarf flapping in the wind, then raised his hand and barked a challenge before heeling off his boots, stripping down to his underwear, and diving over the heads of the boys who hung from the dhow's ropes. When he surfaced, he was only yards from our helm. He began a strong, steady stroke alongside the boat, keeping time, until Lucky goosed the throttle and we shot forward, leaving Carlo in our wake. I looked back to see him riding the swell, his mouth open in a full laugh, cheering us on.

'What's his story?' Mason asked.

Lucky cupped a cigarette against the crosswind, pointed it west toward Africa. 'Came over with the Italians from Eritrea. When Mussolini went down, Brits made the colony an internment camp until the war was over.'

'Fascists?' Mason asked.

Lucky nodded. 'Skilled labor. We shipped them in, thousand or so. Wasn't nothing they couldn't make. Something broke, they fixed it. Only problem was they didn't like the Saudis and the Saudis didn't like them. Didn't fit into the Aramco family plan.' Lucky checked his direction, touched the wheel. 'Once we got the Arabs trained, we sent the wops back out, but Carlo, he wanted to stay, had a camera and a way of getting to people. Nailed up a shack on the beach north of Ras Tanura and called it his studio, got in good with the sheikhs by taking their portraits, and the princes took a shine to him. Now he has the run of the kingdom. Hops trains, tankers, camels, boats. There's no one he can't get next to.' Lucky spat tobacco from his tongue. 'Little bastard knows it too. Got to watch him around the women.'

Ruthie and I sat with our backs to the cabin, listening and sipping the last of our drinks. I looked to where Mason stood, more serious now, thinking too much, my grandfather would say.

'I worry about him,' I said. 'It seems so dangerous out here.'

'It doesn't do any good to worry,' Ruthie said. 'When Lucky was in the war, an officer knocked on my door one day, told me that Lucky's plane had gone down.' She shook her head, remembering. 'I fainted, thinking he was dead. Turns out it was only a broken leg.' She huffed a light laugh. 'Lucky is lucky, and Mason is a golden boy. Nothing is going to happen to them.'

I looked out over the water. In twilight, the sky and the sea were the same, no longer blue but striations of purple and pink shot through with blue-white like the inside of an oyster. When the mouth of the bay came into view, Ruthie banged on the cabin to get Lucky's attention and cut a hand across her throat. The boat throttled to a stop, and Mason helped her overboard, feeding the tow rope and skis. We motored slowly until the line straightened and she gave the thumbs-up. The boat churned forward, pulling Ruthie to a stand. Another thumbs-up, Mason passing the signal to Lucky, and we were speeding across the bay.

Dhows dotted the shallows, and I wondered whether the pearlers were watching us, whether

154

what they saw was a woman tethered or simply flying, skin burnished by sun, hair a dark banner against the last fold of light.

CHAPTER EIGHT

This was Ruthie's talent: to take any dog-day afternoon and turn it into something special.

Over the next several weeks, when Mason was on the platform, I spent hours with Ruthie at the pool and hours more with her in my kitchen, eating the meals that Yash prepared for us, drawing him into our conversation. Ruthie's houseboy never returned after finding his bride, and the recent immigrant she hired, a shy young man from Sudan, kept to the farthest corners of the house when we were around, as though he feared contamination. The few times we sat at her Formica dinette to smoke and drink cocktails, flanked by the curio cabinet filled with porcelain bells from various nations on one side, the clock in the shape of a peacock on the other, we both knew something was missing, and we knew that something was Yash.

Mornings, I began to lie in bed and listen for the rattle of his bicycle timed to the muezzin's first call, to regret when the evening song sent him home again. I sometimes felt like a child in his care, and at other times I felt strangely wedded to him, as though I were the husband going off to earn the wages and Yash the keeper of the hearth. When I grimaced at the bitter martini he made me one day when I returned home from the newspaper, he met me at the door each afternoon thereafter with an iced glass of sweet tea and encouraged me to relax, put up my feet while he brought me the mail and finished preparing my meal.

The first time I asked him to sit down to dinner with me, he demurred.

'Why not?' I asked.

'It is not appropriate,' he said.

'You don't believe that any more than I do,' I said, and pointed to the blinded windows. 'Besides, who will know?' I asked.

'Only those we tell,' he said.

'I won't if you won't,' I said.

He considered, his face grave, before reluctantly acquiescing. He sat stiffly in his chair, responding to my attempts at conversation with small tidbits of his life before arriving in Arabia but never anything that I really wanted to hear—nothing more about his wife, about why he had left her behind. As our meals together became more habitual and familiar, we sometimes didn't talk at all but listened to the BBC until he rose to gather our dishes and clean the kitchen before pedaling his bicycle home. When I showed him the pearl I had gotten on the dhow and wondered what to do with it, he took it as one of his errands to have a jeweler in al-Khobar fashion the pearl into a pendant. I hadn't expected him to be so pleased by my delight or so embarrassed when I turned my back to him, bent my head forward, pulled up my hair, and asked him to clasp the thin gold chain. I felt the brush of his fingers, heard his murmured apologies for his fumbling. When I turned to face him, the color of his cheeks had deepened to umber, and he quickly excused himself to the kitchen.

By late spring, the flowers that had erupted from

156

the desert floor were nothing but memory, the purples and pinks and cornflower blues devoured by the camels and goats before they could be burned to cinders by the harsh summer sun. As the heat hit triple digits and Mason's schedule ground into routine, my days became defined by meals, afternoons writing articles for the newspaper, drinks with Ruthie, late nights of reading, sometimes until dawn. After his long absence, Mason's sudden presence felt like an intrusion, a rupture in the space I had made for myself, and I began to understand why Ruthie and Lucky had to fight. Instead of welcoming Mason with open arms, I sometimes resisted his affection, our first round of intimacy a push-me, pull-you bout. When he left again, it felt like I was being torn open, and I would cry myself to sleep, rise the next day back into my other life, begin once again to mend myself against the pain of his absence.

I gave up learning the difference between tricks and trumps, neglected to call Candy about golf, and concentrated instead on my photographs and articles, covering social events, gathering meeting dates, and posting club minutes. I discovered that although the company's children might live in the barren desert, there was nothing that they were denied. They were instructed in marksmanship, archery, and field hockey. They were flown to Lebanon to ski the unlikely snow, sail the Mediterranean, spelunk the Jeita cave. The Hobby Farm stabled the finest Arabian ponies; the Little League teams sported customized uniforms. I interviewed the members of the Dive Club, who had just returned from the Farasan Archipelago, where they searched for silky sharks. I reported the names of Boy Scouts receiving their merit badges and youth delegates selected to attend the national convention in Portland, Oregon, for Teens Aid the Retarded. When the children graduated eighth grade, they left the compound to study abroad at the finest boarding schools and universities in the world, tuition subsidized by the company. 'Little princes and princesses,' Ruthie said. 'They wouldn't know real life if it bit them in the ass.' But when I interviewed a handsome young American man who was visiting after his graduation from St. Stanislaus in Bathurst, Australia—a place he had chosen because of its excellent surf—he seemed less like a scion than a homesick child. 'I didn't want to leave,' he told me, 'but they shipped me out anyway, just like they ship us all out.' He chewed at the rawness of his thumb, where a pinhead of blood welled. 'No one gets it, man. You grow up in the desert, nothing else is real.' I listened, took notes, but I knew it wasn't anything that my readers would want to hear.

When Nestor put me to work drawing the crossword puzzles, I holed up in Mason's study, scouring old editions of *Aramco World,* expurgated dictionaries, and censored encyclopedias. I loved the ephemeral feel of immersing myself in strange knowledge, my awareness of the world enlarging with each down and across, but when I quizzed Yash with my clues, he already knew the answers. 'What do you think I do with my evenings?' he asked. 'I could fill them out in my dreams.'

I carried my camera everywhere, found that things looked different through the lens, and began to understand how Carlo Leoni might come to fancy himself invisible, move more easily through this world. I rode the bus for no other reason than to capture what images I could through the windows: a silver Cadillac sleek as a shark, beside it a donkey carrying three young boys bundled between rickets of wood, their mouths caked with dust; our Muslim driver bowing in prayer alongside the road, each window behind him framing the face of an Aramco wife. I had watched him, remembering my grandfather on his knees beside his bed, in the door of the kitchen, in the field in the middle of pitching hay—wherever the spirit moved him, that was where he fell—and stepped out quietly to take the picture, the women inside scowling their disapproval. I dropped my film off at the newspaper office, waited impatiently for the days it took to be developed, eagerly sorted through the prints. Framed, contained, the desert became more knowable, its variegations and movement captured in split-second shots that I studied like the pages of a primer.

I stopped by the newspaper office one day and found Nestor at his desk, my photographs spread out before him. I was pleased, expecting praise, but he pushed them aside and rested his weary eyes on me.

'Maybe you don't know any better than this,' he said. 'You can't just take photos of whoever or whatever you want unless what you want is to be deported.' He shuffled the pile into an envelope, thumbed down the clasp, and handed it to me. 'I don't want to see these kinds of prints anywhere near here,' Nestor said. 'Do you understand?'

'Yes.' I tucked the envelope against my chest, wishing I had my own darkroom, a private place to do my work without anyone looking over my shoulder.

He took a deep breath, tapped his pencil. 'Maybe it's better if you stay with "Memory Lane."'

'But I want to write about what's happening right now,' I said. 'Something that matters.'

Nestor settled back. 'Just where do you think you are, Mrs. McPhee?' He took off his glasses, rubbed the sore spots on either side of his nose, then pushed forward a photo of a royal-looking Arab man, maybe a sheikh, his son sitting at his knee. 'See anything wrong with it?'

I studied the portrait. 'It looks fine,' I said.

'Except for one very important detail the photographer overlooked.' He pointed to the man's bare feet. 'We can't use it because the censors say it's degrading. What are we supposed to do, buy him a pair of wing tips?'

I stood there, stubborn, my packet of photos clutched tight.

'Listen,' he said, 'I'm not saying you don't have an eye for this. I'm just saying you've got to tighten your blinders. Hunt down Carlo Leoni. See if he can teach you a thing or two.'

I left in tears, not just because I was angry but because I knew that I didn't have any way to hunt down anybody, and especially not a pirate who had the run of the country. I rode the bus back to Abqaiq, found Yash in the kitchen, and sat glum while he made me dinner. He seemed quieter than he had only hours before, and I wondered whether it was because Mason was due home that night, if, like me, he found the transitions the hardest.

'I need an adventure.' I sighed.

'Mrs. Gin,' Yash said, 'you are in Arabia. Do not wish for adventure.'

160

'At least you can drive out of here,' I said.

'I cannot drive,' he said. 'I have never learned.'

'I could teach you,' I said. 'Ruthie would let us use her car. Just around the compound.'

He pinched a smile. 'Let us not forget our experience with the polka.'

I rested my arms on the counter. 'I wish I could explore the desert like Lawrence of Arabia.'

'Ah, you want to go native,' Yash said, taking care as he salted a pot of water. 'It's like an illness among white men of some privilege. T. E. Lawrence, Sir Wilfred Thesiger. They see themselves as golden-haired gods, I suppose.'

'Thesiger? The explorer?' I asked, remembering the rain. 'Abdullah told me about him.'

Yash lifted his eyes, blinked slowly. 'An interesting conversation for you to have with the Bedouin,' he said. He took out a knife, began slicing a carrot. 'Did he tell you about the women who have mapped this land?'

'What women?' I asked.

'Gertrude Bell was one of the greatest Arabist explorers of all time and single-handedly drew the boundaries of Iraq.' He raised his knife like a pointer. 'Did he tell you that Dame Freya Stark trekked the terra incognita of Iran and was the first to locate the fabled Valley of the Assassins?' He flicked the knife. 'Of course not. Women have no place in his history.'

'It hardly matters,' I said, 'if I can't even leave the compound.' I snorted and dropped my chin. 'I just love learning new things,' I said, then tipped my head. 'Tell me about India. All I really know is that is where Gandhi is from.'

'That may be all that you need to know,' Yash

161

said, then lifted his head and scowled at the sound of someone at the door—maybe the shrimp peddler again, thinking me a soft touch. I hopped up to answer it, found Faris clutching a sheaf of dry weeds that he held between us and rattled meaningfully, his wizened face half-hidden in the folds of his *ghutra*. Yash listened and translated as best he could.

'He has dreamed that a swarm of locusts will come from the west and descend this evening.' Faris swept his hand across the yard, uttered a few hoarse words, and Yash nodded. 'He says they will take everything.'

Seeming satisfied, Faris returned to his weeding. I hesitated a moment, then followed Yash out to the back patio, where he had taken the chicken he had gotten at market. I saw that Faris had covered the vegetables with buckets and boxes—anything that he could find.

'You really think the locusts will come?' I asked, wondering whether Faris was only trying to scare me off my garden.

'They always come. If not today, then tomorrow.' Yash motioned at the chicken. 'You can help me. It will occupy your time.'

I sat down and began plucking. 'My grandfather said the locusts in Oklahoma ate the feathers right off the chickens.'

Yash smiled, making quick pinches with his thumb and finger. 'My father said the same of Punjab.'

When the feathers stuck and matted, I wiped my hands on my pants, but Yash remained pristine, his white shirt crisp and unblemished. I thought of my mother sitting on the porch, doing just this thing,

162

how it was in the concentration of chores that she told the stories I remembered.

'What about your wife?' I asked. 'What happened after the fountain?'

'I asked that I might marry her.' He dipped his fingers into the bowl of warm water at our feet and went at the pinfeathers. 'We lived with my family in a top-floor room. My mother would stand on her bed to slap the ceiling with her slipper. 'Enough!' she'd cry. "Enough!"' Yash's face broke into a grin with the memory. 'We found an apartment, very small, but one window looked out over the gardens of an old woman from Goa. She gave us guavas from her trees and bottles of fenny made from the cashew apples she distilled on the slope of the courtyard. We would wake in the morning and know she was brewing by the sweet juice smell. It made us happy and want to make love.'

I blushed in spite of myself, but Yash kept plucking. 'I was not a temperate man,' he said.

'You were young,' I said, 'in love.'

'Young, yes, and in love.' He rinsed his hands, dabbed them against the towel on his knee.

'And then what?' I asked.

Yash looked up, his eyes dark, then stood, taking the chicken with him. 'I will start the stewing.'

I followed him into the kitchen, trailing downy tufts that floated aloft in the slightest movement of air. I stood for a moment, hoping for more talk, but Yash busied himself with sharpening the knife to a fine edge. I sighed, then moved into the living room that felt like a cavern, dark and cool. The house that had once seemed enormous to me now felt small, each room too familiar. I lay on the couch with my book, trying to forget that it was my second

163

time through, that I already knew what came next, and felt the drowsiness of an empty afternoon coming on.

If I dreamed, I don't remember, except when I woke from my nap, it was to what I thought was the static of the television or maybe the radio. I lifted my head and realized it was the sound of the wind rising, sand pelting the house. I moved into the living room and pulled the blinds. The sky was a blur, the light filtered to gray. And then I understood what I was seeing: not the common swirl of dust but the bodies of insects, thousands and thousands of them, a storm of locusts brewing the air.

I knelt on the couch, fascinated. I'd seen the hordes of grasshoppers descend on our neighbor's corn and mow it clean, had swept them into piles on the porch, but I had never seen anything like this. The lawns, the sidewalk, the asphalt—all boiling like lava pouring down the streets. No sun, the streetlights muted, not even the houses next door were visible. The locusts popped against the windows, held for a moment, then fell away to be replaced by a dozen more, their sound a frenzied murmur, like the june bugs I used to catch, tie to a string, and let fly around me, their wings beating up, dipping, beating up, a rhythmic rise and fall, an openmouthed zip of sound. But it was larger than that, a noise that swelled to fill the sky, more like the tornado that had touched down outside Shawnee, when my grandfather had taken me to the dank root cellar. Where the corona of the candle's flame fell away, I could see things moving, spiders, scorpions, snakes. 'Just sit still,' he had said, 'and let me listen.' He was waiting for that sudden quiet that was the heart of the tempest, the train leaving its tracks. I fell asleep against his shoulder and woke up in my bed, the morning sky clear as rainwater.

I slid to sit on the sofa, wondering whether Mason would make it home. I went to the telephone to dial Ruthie, but the lines were already eaten through, and I began to feel a creeping terror, as though the locusts might gnaw their way right through the walls.

'What are we going to do?' I asked Yash. He was tearing up over the onions, wiping his eyes with a sleeve.

'I will bring your tea,' he said.

I hesitated before moving back into the living room, working hard to stifle the sense I had of the air closing in. When a pair of headlights broke the false dusk, I stood at the door, afraid to open it too soon, afraid to wait a second longer. Mason hit the porch at a dead run, Abdullah close behind. We laughed together as they pinched the insects from their clothes.

'It's like a plague,' I said, 'a biblical curse.'

'Locusts are common enough,' Abdullah said. 'If Allah were truly angry, there would be no mistaking it. *As-sahara,*' he said, plucking a locust from his neck. 'That is the desert.' He seemed happy, more like I'd first seen him, as though the hardship of the locusts whetted his good humor.

I gathered the bugs in a paper bag, where they rattled like a sack of snakes, and pitched it out the back door. Yash brought coffee while I stood awkwardly until Mason indicated that I should join him on the couch. Whatever had been their business before they came home,

165

Mason and Abdullah's conversation now moved from the locusts to the prospect of the Dhahran Little League team going to the World Series in Pennsylvania. There was something about keeping quiet, feeling invisible, that caused me to think I might really be, and I half listened, less interested in the details of the discussion than Abdullah's gestures, the way his long fingers articulated the air. Ever since our talk after the emir's banquet, he had seemed different to me, someone I might like to know.

I kept my eyes low, examining his leather sandals, the strong tendons of his feet, then raised my gaze to his shoulders, the place where his collarbone ridged the yoke of his *thobe,* where his *ghutra* hid his plaited hair. I'd seen enough Arabs to know that the drillers' locks were shorn so as not to become tangled in the machinery, but still they wore their *ghutras* tucked or kept their heads modestly capped. Abdullah's long hair set him apart, as though he weren't quite willing to give up that Bedouin part of himself.

I raised my eyes to see Mason watching me, heard my grandfather's voice: *It's not what you're looking at but what you are wanting to see.* I straightened, brought my eyes to Abdullah's face. 'When will it stop?' I asked.

'As Allah wills,' he said, and canted his head to acknowledge my distress. 'It is said that when men were given the gift of song, they forgot to eat and drink and sang themselves to death, so were changed into locusts so that they might sing from birth to the grave.'

'That's cheery,' Mason said.

'Maybe we should all tell stories,' I said, 'like in

166

The Decameron.'

Mason kicked back and crossed his fingers at his chest. 'You two go ahead.' He yawned and closed his eyes. 'I'll just listen.'

Abdullah's face opened with pleasure. 'Who will go first?'

'I will,' I said.

'Will this be a story of love or morality?' he asked.

I thought for a moment. 'Love.'

'A cautionary tale or an adventure story?'

'A cautionary tale,' I said, then changed my mind. 'No, an adventure story.'

Abdullah nodded and sat back with his coffee.

'I once had a horse,' I began. Abdullah looked up, surprised.

'You?' he asked.

'Yes,' I said. 'Where I'm from, women ride horses like men.'

Mason opened one eye. 'Ride them right into the ground.'

I shot him a warning look. 'I mean we sit them like men sit their horses.'

Abdullah furrowed his brow. 'But you said "I." Is this a true story?'

I considered for a moment. 'It's a tale,' I said. 'It's not me but a girl.' Abdullah seemed satisfied, so I went on. 'There once was a girl whose mother had died and who lived alone with her father. They were very poor.' I glanced at Mason, but his eyelids didn't flutter. 'Every night before she fell asleep, she would ask God for one thing.'

'She wants a friend,' Abdullah said, 'because she is lonely.'

'Yes,' I said, 'she wanted a friend, but not like

167

the girls she met at school, who teased her about her tattered clothes and laughed when she cried. She wanted a special friend, the kind who would love her no matter how different she was. So she asked God for a horse. She would sleep in the hay at his feet, and he would watch over her and keep her safe.'

'What about her father?' Abdullah asked.

'Her father . . . her father was very sad. He didn't know how to raise a daughter and wouldn't let her go into town where the other girls were. And so she prayed for a horse. Every night she would pray, and every morning she would wake up and look out the window. She believed that if she prayed hard enough and had enough faith, the horse would appear in the old pasture where her father's mule grazed. But when spring came and the horse had not appeared, she began to believe that God needed a better pasture to put the horse in, and so, as soon as she had finished her other chores, she would go to work mending the fence as best she could with pieces of old wire and rocks around the rotted posts. She pulled the pokeweed and nettles that the mule had left uneaten. She worked each afternoon until her father called her to prepare his supper, and as the days got longer, she went back out after washing the dishes to work until dark. Her fingers were festered with thistles, but still she worked.'

'She will conjure the horse of her very will,' Abdullah said, admiration in his voice.

'She worked and she prayed and she tried to be as good as she could so that God would answer her prayers. She cross-fenced the pasture to keep out the mule, brought water, and sowed the soil with the ryegrass seeds she had stripped from the stalks of nearby fields. Soon, the dirt sprouted green, and she was happy. She sat in her half of the pasture and read her books and dreamed of the horse she would have.'

Abdullah lifted his fingers. 'Has this girl had her first blood?'

I hesitated a moment, unsure of what he meant.

'Yes,' Mason said, never opening his eyes.

'Then it is a husband that she truly wants,' Abdullah said, and winked. 'She only imagines him as a horse.'

Mason's mouth twitched at the corners.

'One morning,' I pushed on, 'she woke as she always did and looked out her window. She blinked because she couldn't believe her eyes. The mule was gone from the pasture, but there was the horse she had prayed for.'

Abdullah sat forward, intent. 'It may be a djinn,' he said. 'She must be wary.'

'It was a horse,' I said, unsure as to whether Abdullah's concern was genuine or if he was teasing me, 'a tobiano paint with a black mane and tail.'

'A stallion?' he asked.

'A gelding,' I said.

Abdullah sat back, smug. 'Then it cannot be her husband,' he said, and I heard Mason snort. I looked from him to Abdullah, feeling as though I were on the outside of some kind of joke.

'He was an old horse,' I went on, 'she could see that right away, and a bit bandy-legged, but when she ran to the pasture, he came to her and laid his head on her shoulder, and she knew right then that God made this horse just for her. His mouth was broken, and his hooves were split, and she worried

169

he'd been hurt, but she washed him and brushed him and told him his name was Sonny and then she fed him the rind of a watermelon.'

'And now he loves her,' Abdullah said, real kindness in his voice, and I smiled.

'Yes,' I said. 'She had forgotten to pray for a bridle and reins and a saddle, but she found an old rope that he didn't mind, and when she jumped one leg over and hitched upright, he held like he'd been a good horse all his life.'

'This is why he was chosen,' Abdullah said. 'Allah is merciful.'

'And so the girl and her horse rode the small pasture, and when she asked her father whether she could ride to school, he said yes, but no farther. She picketed the horse at the edge of the playing field, and he was happy to eat the grass and doze in the sun. The girl knew that she, too, should be happy, but the road to and from school was never long enough, and even with the horse, she was still lonely.'

'She desires a husband,' Abdullah said, and I was sure, now, that he was feigning earnestness. 'Her aunties must find her one.'

'She wants an adventure,' I insisted. 'At first, it was enough for her to explore the nearby fields and farm roads, but in the opposite direction lay the town, where she knew the girls and boys were gathering to drink sodas and listen to music. One afternoon, because the air was warm and all the birds were singing, she let her horse continue past the crossroad. She thought she could deceive her father and tell him she'd stopped to help a neighbor pick plums. She even knew the tree, where she would be high enough on her horse's back to reach

170

the highest limbs, and she would stain her fingers and her mouth with the fruit to convince her father of her lie.'

Abdullah's face took on a truly troubled cast. 'The daughter who disobeys her father in this way, she will be in trouble.'

'This is in America,' I said, even as I realized that what he said was true.

Mason sang under his breath, ' "How ya gonna keep 'em down on the farm after they've seen Paree?" '

'Listen,' I said. 'It's just a story, and I can make it whatever I want. Forget that she's a girl. I'll make her a boy. So now the boy has a horse, and he is the one wanting adventure, and so he goes to town.'

Abdullah relaxed back and nodded at Mason, one corner of his mouth lifting. 'It is better that she is a boy.'

'Fine,' I said. 'It's a boy. So the boy disobeyed his father, rode the horse into town, and went to the soda fountain, where the other teenagers were. He had a Coke and listened to the music on the jukebox and didn't talk much, but at least he wasn't alone. When it started to get dark, he realized how late it was, and he rode the horse to the plum tree and rubbed his mouth and fingers with juice and dropped a few in his pockets. He put the horse away and did his chores before making pancakes for dinner and doing his homework and going to bed early so his father wouldn't ask any questions.' I spoke quickly, the impending lament I had felt when first telling the story turned to frustration. 'When the boy woke the next morning and looked out his window, the horse was gone.' I heard the blood rushing in my ears and remembered it was the locusts' endless chirping. 'And that's the end,' I said.

'But it is not the end,' Abdullah said, and cast a conspiratorial glance at Mason. 'Along with adventure, you promised a love story.'

'He loved the horse,' I said.

Abdullah slanted his mouth. 'A man might write a poem of praise for his horse, but he would not write a poem of love.'

'Finish the story, Gin,' Mason said. 'I bet the boy meets a girl.'

'Why don't you finish it?' I said, sharper than I meant to.

'Please,' Abdullah said. 'I want to hear what happens to this boy.'

I set my jaw. 'Even though he was punished, the loss of the horse only made the boy braver. He began to wait for his father to fall asleep before slipping out and sneaking into town, where he met a girl and fell in love and lived happily ever after. How's that?'

Before they could answer, Yash appeared in the doorway as though he knew I needed intervention. He bowed slightly.

'Your dinner is ready, *sahib*.'

'Abdullah will be joining us,' Mason said.

'You are very kind,' Abdullah said, 'but I do not wish to impose.'

'No imposition at all,' Mason said, and led us to the table before Abdullah could protest further. 'Hey, Yash, check the weather outside. See what's happening.'

Yash seemed relieved to exit the room. He came back to report that the locusts were lessening and that the pin boys from the bowling alley were

172

sweeping them into garbage cans.

'A feast for the Bedu,' Abdullah said. He waited until Mason and I had begun eating before forking a bite of rice.

'Let me guess,' Mason said. 'They taste like chicken.'

Abdullah cocked his head. 'Why would they taste like chicken?'

Mason looked at me and grinned. 'What do they taste like, then?'

'Besides tasting like locusts, you mean.' Abdullah considered a long moment. 'I would say they taste like still-green grain.'

Mason broke into a smile. 'I know exactly what that tastes like,' he said. 'I used to chew the heads to test the fields for harvest.'

'But bugs,' I protested.

'If you remove the legs and wings,' Abdullah said, 'you have a small shrimp.'

I looked quickly at Yash, who raised one eyebrow and turned for the kitchen.

Abdullah rested his wrists against the table's edge. 'To the Bedu, a locust swarm is nothing less than manna from heaven. We eat what we can, then dry and grind them to powder for when food is scarce.'

'You make the most of what you've got,' Mason said. 'We butchered our hogs right down to the bone. Cracklins, chitlins, trotters, jowls. You name it, we ate it.'

'You must come to the tent,' Abdullah said, 'and my mother will fry for you the female locusts full of eggs. They are by far the best.'

'When?' I asked.

Mason cleared his throat. 'I think it's Abdullah's

173

turn to tell a story.'

Abdullah took up his coffee. 'Locust swarms in the desert are too numerous to count, but I remember one especially.' He paused to listen to the rippling drone as though it might call back his memory. 'When spring rains came to Wadi Ab, the caravans stayed for days. The merchants wished to buy our textiles and fine camels and consider our women, but more than that, they wanted to feast their eyes on the beauty of the oasis. I would lie beneath the stars and listen to the men recite poems and tell of their journeys. I planned to join a caravan, travel to distant places, perhaps even Egypt.' He dipped his head. 'I had not yet heard of America.' His voice had taken on the tone of a storyteller, soft and rhythmic. 'I remember that during this season, the emir's representative had visited our settlement, bringing with him promises of gold without measure. Behind them came a group of white men, who camped nearby.' He nodded as Yash poured more coffee. 'Some of our elders believed the Americans had come by the grace of Allah to bring us a life of good fortune, while others believed they were demons. We were amazed by the loudness of their voices and the pinkness of their skin. We knew nothing of their instruments and were filled with curiosity.' He smiled to himself as though amused, then lifted his face and grew more solemn. 'In the days before the locusts, an angry heat had descended, as though the sun meant to burn us to ash. Birds fell like cinders from the sky. There were other omens. The mother of Hammad al-Salib had fallen into the fire, and the skin of her arms fell off like sleeves shorn from a dress. Abu Kareem dreamed that his eldest

174

son, who had gone to work for the Americans, had drowned in the sea and that his body was being beaten against the rocks. The old man had left that morning for Jubail against all persuasion.'

I looked up to see Yash standing in the shadows of the hallway, the coffeepot still in his hands. I caught his eye, glanced at the empty chair, but he shook his head and put a finger to his lips as Abdullah continued.

'That evening, the locusts came with the wind like smoke from Allah's fire. My young sister, tending sheep, spied the black cloud massing on the horizon and came running to tell our father, who ordered us to rope the mare. We gathered in the tent and draped the doorways. We knew the locusts would strip the date palms and grasses, as they always do, but rather than mourning what was lost, my family chose to spend the time just as we have here, drinking coffee and sharing stories.' Abdullah raised his cup to the blinded windows. 'After a time, we opened the tent to find that the locusts had gone except for those that we gathered and roasted over the fire. I led out my mare and fed her a few from my hand.'

'Badra,' I said, and Abdullah nodded. Mason lifted his chin and looked at me. I had forgotten that he didn't know about my conversation with Abdullah in the Land Cruiser.

'I remember that the evening sky had cleared to nothing but stars,' Abdullah went on, 'and the moon rose fat and sated. We slept well that night, as though a purging had taken place, knowing that the locusts come and go like the rains.' He lowered his eyes, touched the rim of his cup. 'Nothing could prepare us for what would be visited upon the wadi

175

the next morning.'

Mason raised his eyes, leaned forward with new interest.

Abdullah took a deep breath, let it out slowly. 'At dawn, we awakened to a noise we had never heard before, louder than the locusts, louder even than the fiercest *shamal*. The children held their ears, and the women wept in fear. It drowned out the cries of our infants. I went with my father to where the men gathered, each shouting louder than the other. It was Hammad who came running from the far end of the wadi, and we feared that his mother had died of her wounds, but when he told us that monsters were tearing the earth, we feared he had lost his mind. We took up our weapons and followed him, but all we could do was watch as the giant machines devoured what remained of the date palms and tamarisks, along with the shade that travelers had sought for thousands of years.' Abdullah half lidded his eyes. 'By the time the sun had set that day, our home as we knew it was gone, and with it the heart of Wadi Ab.'

We sat in silence, Sinatra's voice filling the room. Mason looked down at his hands. 'That shouldn't have happened,' he said. 'I guess this oil company is like any other. Takes what it wants, leaves the people behind.'

'*Inshallah*,' Abdullah said quietly. 'As God wills.' When Yash stepped in with more coffee, Abdullah shook his cup. 'You've been very kind,' he said, and stood to go. 'I hope I may someday return the favor and welcome you to my tent.'

'I would love that,' I said.

'Yeah,' Mason said. 'We'll stop by next time we're on our way to Cincinnati.' He laughed at

176

the look of confusion on Abdullah's face, clapped his shoulder, and walked with him out to the Land Cruiser.

I went to the kitchen to find Yash up to his elbows in soapy water. I picked up the dish towel and began drying. 'Dinner was delicious,' I said.

He considered for a moment, then spoke quietly. 'It is the first time I have served an Arab,' he said. 'They look upon me with disdain.' He wrung a cloth and began to wipe the counter. 'The Saudis do not wish us here except to do the work they see as beneath them.'

'But Abdullah, he's different, isn't he?'

Yash stopped his cleaning to look at me. 'Do you think that an educated Bedouin is any less a Bedouin?' He began scrubbing the counter in earnest. 'I heard what he was saying. He is a noble savage schooled by enlightened beings who misses the Eden he has lost. How very unique.' He glanced up, saw the look on my face, dropped his shoulders. 'Forgive me,' he said. 'I speak out of turn, and he is your friend.'

'No more than you are,' I said, and caught the hint of a smile before he turned away.

CHAPTER NINE

In the desert, this is what I learned: the wind never stops, blowing in hot from the north, a fine talc sifting in from Damascus, Baghdad, Kuwait. It stirs the hems of robes, whips the flags ragged. The Bedu line their eyes with kohl, protection against sun and sand, and still their children walk blinking

177

and blinded, their ankles dangled with red garnets, triangular bits of turquoise, lapis lazuli to ward off evil. The boys' ears studded with stones. The young girls still showing their faces.

As the furnace of late spring forged toward summer, the wind sapped the moisture from my mouth, and the heat that had seemed intolerable became impossible—it staggered you in your tracks, filled you with such dread and discomfort that you doubted your ability to survive. Yash biked in each morning, his crisp shirt clinging to his back. 'It's quite all right,' he said when I worried. 'The faster I pedal, the cooler the breeze.' When he told me that the houseboys, bunked four to a room, had no air-conditioning, I bought him an electric fan at the *suq*, watched him balance it atop his handlebars and weave his way out of the gate, whistling all the while.

Late one night in May, Mason came home wound tight as a top, taking his drink in quick swallows. I sent Yash home and finished cooking our dinner while Mason showered, felt myself caught in the limbo of that transition Ruthie had talked about. He came out rubbing his head with a towel, the dark line of hair down his stomach still damp, and just like that, I was torn between resistance and desire.

I turned to the stove, took the lid off the casserole Yash had made. 'Are you hungry?' I asked.

'Will be.' Mason fingered a cigarette from his pocket. 'Let's go out back, why don't we? There's got to be some stars.'

I replaced the lid, hearing something different in his tone. I followed him out into the yard, where we stood together in the grass, the air like bathwater, the blue-aster sky hewing to black, pinpricked with light.

Mason lifted his head and pointed. 'Tell me the name of that constellation.'

I followed his direction. 'Virgo,' I said. 'The brightest star is Spica.'

He wrapped one arm around my shoulder, pulled me to him. 'How did you get so smart?' He kissed me, kept me close. 'You doing okay?' he asked.

I shrugged. 'Sure,' I said.

'Garden looks swell,' he said.

'Mostly sand,' I said, 'but the spuds love it.' I didn't tell him that I had given up tending the skeletal plants only to wake one morning to find the plot neatly weeded and trenched, a wheelbarrow load of rich compost mulched in, the vegetables already greening under Faris's care.

'Think you can stick it out for a while?' he asked.

I looked at him, sensing some undercurrent of meaning. 'Why?' I asked.

He took another drink. 'Abdullah and I were talking on the way home. He told me that some years back, the Arabs tried to organize, not just the Saudis but the Syrians, Lebanese, the whole lot of them. Fifteen thousand men walked off the job, struck the company to a standstill. Militia shot a few on the spot, arrested the leaders, sent them into exile, and the king outlawed labor unions.' He looked at me. 'You know what they were asking for? They wanted to ride to work instead of having to walk, maybe get a cost-of-living raise every now and then. Wanted washing machines and radios and cars.' He grew quiet. 'They wanted to be like us, imitation Americans. That's the guts of it.'

179

I crossed my arms. 'It's not like Texas,' I said.

'Or it is,' he said. 'MLK had it right. Labor-busting is about keeping the working poor in their place.' He tapped out another cigarette. 'You remember Tiny Doty, the guy who took over for Swede as drilling superintendent?' He tipped back his head, exhaled. 'They've made his position permanent, and Ross says he's considering me to take Doty's place as assistant.' His voice was clear, lighter than it had been for some time. 'What do you think of that?'

'It's great,' I said, but I had no idea what such a promotion might mean. The amount of Mason's salary remained a mystery to me, and what expenses we had were billed through the company. What was more of more?

'Wouldn't have a set schedule like I do now,' he said, 'but at least I'd be home more often.'

I raised my eyes, dropped them quickly, confused by what I was feeling. It was the hours he spent away that allowed me to do what I wanted as long as I was waiting when he returned. 'How long would we have to stay?' I asked.

Mason let out a slow breath. 'If I start working my way up the ladder, we could stay as long as we want to.' He squinted my way. 'The thing is,' he said, 'I'm beginning to see how things work in this place. I'm never going to make a difference sitting on the sidelines. I've got to be in the game.' He rocked me against him. 'Listen, I invited the Fullertons over for dinner tomorrow night. Yash can do the work. All you have to do is look pretty.'

'Ruthie and Lucky?' I asked.

Mason sucked through his teeth. 'Might as well. One way or the other, Lucky isn't going to be happy

180

that they've moved me to the head of the line.'

It hadn't dawned on me to think about it that way—the senior foreman getting passed over for an upstart twenty years his junior.

Mason dropped his cigarette, heeled it out. 'Think I'm ready to call it a day.'

'I'll be right in,' I said, and stayed long enough to find the constellation I had named and name it again, orienting myself, before moving toward the glow of the kitchen, where Mason stood at the window, peering out into the night. I raised my hand, but he turned away as though he hadn't seen me, as though I weren't there at all. I resisted the urge to wave my arms, call out, 'Here I am!' Silly, I thought, and measured my steps to the patio like a lost child, feeling my way through the dark.

*　　　*　　　*

The next afternoon, Mason at a meeting, I tried to help Yash prepare the dinner but succeeded only in getting in his way.

'I can't stand just sitting around and watching someone else work,' I protested.

'You are not required to watch,' he said.

I pulled up a stool. 'I'm not sure I like having servants,' I said. 'It makes me feel funny.'

He raised his eyes. 'Mrs. Gin,' he said, 'my family had three servants, and each servant had a servant of his own. In your next life, who knows? You may go to bed a master and wake up a slave.' He cored a mango and cubed it neatly. 'I would offer to draw your bath,' he suggested, 'but *memsahib* would probably rather do it herself.'

I gave up and trudged to the shower. I took my

time with the razor, running it under each arm and over my legs, a chore I despised, but I wasn't going to take the chance that Candy Fullerton might be smoother than I was. By the time Mason came home, I had pulled myself together: sleeveless silk dress the color of champagne that Ruthie had picked out for me in al-Khobar, high-heeled pumps, the single pearl at my neck, and new matching earrings from the *suq*.

Ruthie and Lucky arrived first, and I was bringing them a dish of almonds when I heard the doorbell ring. Ross Fullerton boiled in like his tail was on fire, blew past Yash, and drafted up to me.

'The little lady!' He lifted his cowboy hat, balding pate shiny with sweat, and kissed my hand. I resisted, pulling away from the wet mash of his lips. I looked over his head, but Candy was nowhere in sight. Yash had bottled a third run of liquor—as smooth as we could get it—and Ross watched with avid attention as Mason poured.

'To the denizens of this charming abode!' Ross knocked back the shot and held out his glass for another. Ruthie drifted to the couch and lifted two fingers. 'Double for me. Easy on the ice.'

Ross dumped down into the easy chair and fixed his eyes to the tapestry. 'Kept Betsy's needlework, I see.'

Mason took the other chair. 'It's a reproduction, one of seven panels in *The Hunt of the Unicorn*,' Mason said. 'This one is called *The Unicorn Is in Captivity and No Longer Dead*. They think the unicorn represents Christ.'

I don't know why I was surprised—Mason had been to college, after all—but I felt the same spark of attraction that I had the first night we talked, as

182

though if I listened long enough, he would fill me up with all that he knew.

Lucky grunted, tucked himself in on the couch beside Ruthie. 'How about you, Ross? Seen any unicorns lately?' he asked, easy, familiar, like he was talking to an old chum.

'Hell, I've seen about everything.' Ross settled deeper, his neck sinking into his shoulders. 'Seen a two-headed calf once, down in Gainesville.'

'Seen a two-headed rattlesnake,' Lucky said, and squinted at Mason. 'Wouldn't you hate to get bit by that sucker?'

Yash bent carefully between us and positioned a tray of salted bread, eggplant raita, and roasted chickpeas. 'The Two-headed Boy of Bengal,' he said.

Ross seemed to notice Yash for the first time. 'How's that?'

'Two heads, connected crown to crown.' Yash straightened but kept his eyes down. 'One head had its entire body. The other ended at the neck, but it could yawn and suckle,' Yash said. 'He was bitten by a cobra and died at age four.'

'Goddamn.' Lucky slapped both knees. 'Now that's a good story.'

Ross settled back into his chair and lifted his glass. 'How about some more of that hooch, boy?'

Yash drew himself upright. 'Of course, *sahib*.' I watched him go into the kitchen, then looked at Ross.

'Yash knows a lot of interesting things,' I said.

Ross hitched the crotch of his pants. 'Not as much as he thinks he does.'

'So, Ross'—Ruthie cut her eyes at me, then canted his way—'is Candy traveling?'

183

'She's got problems with her Pekingese.' He rolled his lips around an almond. 'Told her the desert's no place for a lapdog. Pebbles must have tangled with a wildcat because he came in the house last night, eyeball hung clean out of his head. Slathered it with shortening and popped it back in, but he don't look so good today. Kept Candy up all night with his squalling.' He cleared his throat. 'That damn pirate is coming over tomorrow to take her portrait, and she thinks she needs her beauty sleep.'

Ruthie twitched her eyebrows, and I hid my grin, glad when Yash informed us that dinner was served. We took our places at the table, Ross at the head. It was all I could do to keep my seat and not rise to help with the tureen of curry, the side dishes of yogurt and fruit. Lucky piled his plate with rice and chicken, emptying the small bowls of raisins, sliced bananas, coconut, and chutney, which Yash refilled with growing exasperation. Ross picked over the curry but shoveled in the yams Yash had gleaned from the garden.

'Ross Junior is sure growing,' Ruthie said. 'He'll be headed to boarding school soon.'

'Says he won't go.' Ross ran his napkin down his mouth. 'He's a brat like all the other brats around here. Wants to live on the beach and be a bum. Might should let him go run with the nomads for a while, see how that suits him.'

'I hear you,' Lucky said, and wagged his head. 'These young people coming up today don't know the meaning of paying their dues. We got Joey in the military academy. They'll shape him right.'

Ross sniffed his agreement, wiped his knuckles across his mouth, then cocked an eyebrow at

184

Mason. 'Seven thousand feet in three days.' He let the words weight the air. 'You sure know how to drop a drill, McPhee.'

Lucky slowed his chewing, looked from Ross to Mason.

'It's a solid crew I got,' Mason said. 'Couldn't ask for a better gang pusher than Khalifa Salim, and Saleh Misar might just be the smartest motorman I've ever seen. They're the ones doing all the work.'

'That's right,' Ross said, and leaned back. 'You got to work them as a team.' He flipped open his gold Zippo, snapped it shut, and considered Mason through a waft of smoke. 'You're a tall drink of water. Bet you played ball.'

'Yes, sir.' Mason brought himself to attention.

'Position?'

'Point guard.'

'He was the leading scorer at Shawnee,' I added. 'Full-ride scholarship to Oklahoma State.' I realized too late where the comment would lead and felt myself shrinking back, wishing that I had kept my mouth shut.

Ross lifted his chin. 'Degree?'

Mason didn't flinch. 'I had a wife to support and a job too good to pass up.'

Ross winked my way. 'Looks like you made the right decision on both counts.'

'Anyone been following the Cardinals?' Lucky edged in. 'Bet you wages Bob Gibson is headed for the Hall of Fame.' He leveled his thumb. 'Now, there's a guy your son could learn from. Grew up poor as sin. Rickets, asthma, bad heart—you name it, he had it. Started out with the Globetrotters, but he wasn't like them other colored boys—couldn't stand the clowning. He was serious mean. Bean his

185

own grandmother, then meet her at first base to see if she wanted to make something of it.' Lucky rocked back. 'No, sir. No one messes with old Hoot Gibson.'

'I'm an American League man myself.' Ross snagged an ashtray and puffed his cigar back to life. Yash frowned through the sour smoke as he gathered our dishes. 'Truth is I'd take boxing over baseball any day. Never saw a finer athlete than the Brown Bomber. Nazi bastards went right after him, and now the Communists got our best.' Ross frowned, rolled a speck of tobacco off his tongue. 'Cassius Clay, Muhammad Ali, don't matter what you call him or what color he is, he's still yeller.'

Lucky leaned in, dropped his voice into a lower register. 'You want to explain to me how a man who fights like that can turn tail and run?'

Mason cleared his throat and pushed back his coffee. 'Ross, if you've got some time this week, I'd like to run a few ideas by you.'

'Ideas about what?' Ross asked.

'Working and living conditions mostly,' Mason said.

Ross ran his eyes around the room. 'I'd say conditions are looking pretty fair.'

'I mean for my drillers.'

Ross slid a toothpick between his teeth. 'Did you swap over to Personnel while I wasn't looking? I thought your business was getting that oil out of the ground.'

'That's just what I've been telling him,' Lucky said, eager to agree. 'The Arabs never had it so good.'

Ross didn't take his eyes off Mason. 'Is that what you're thinking, or are you thinking something

186

different?'

Mason opened his palms. 'It's like they say, the biggest problems in the world could have been solved when they were small. If we treat our men right, give them more reason to give us their best, we stabilize the workforce, up production, and everyone wins.' He gave a one-sided smile, dropped his shoulders. 'Hell, I'm just a roughneck. Making the machine work is what I do.'

Ross sniffed, rubbed a smudge from his lighter. 'You're a man of high ideas, McPhee, and high ideas are what made this company. Burt Cane seems to think you're something special. Even put in a good word for you with the board.' When Lucky's head came up, Ross tipped his cigar. 'You'd best let Doucet here teach you a thing or two before you start fixing what ain't broke.'

'Want to hear how your Arab friends fix things?' Lucky pointed his chin at Mason. 'Few months back, couple of tribes started shooting it out right at the base of my rig. Me and the boys holed up and waited until they got their fixing done. Next morning, dump truck pulls up, they throw the bodies in and drive off.' He sat back, looked at Ross, then at Mason. 'It's mighty white of you to offer, McPhee, but them Arabs don't need your help.' He pointed his cigarette. 'And I'll tell you this. Get crosswise with one, and he'll kill you twice for the fun of it.'

Ross raised his upper lip in the semblance of a smile before stubbing his cigar. 'I need to get on home, see how that damn dog is faring.' He lumbered to a stand before I could offer more coffee. 'Mighty grateful, Ginny Mae,' he said, and tipped his hat at Ruthie. Mason saw him to the door, came back, and dropped down next to me on the couch.

'Hey, Yash,' he said. 'Play us some tunes, why don't you?'

Eddy Arnold's voice calmed the room. Lucky settled in the chair Ross had vacated, lit a cigarette, and fixed Mason with a one-eyed squint.

'That's a bigger dog,' he said. 'You'd better watch your ass.'

'If this workforce ever decides to rise up again,' Mason said, 'it's the company that'd better watch its ass.'

Lucky settled his chin on his chest. 'You're acting like you done forgot what side of that triangle you're on.'

'That's just my point,' Mason said. 'The whole triangle is wrong. It sets the workingman against the company and against the king, and there isn't anything balanced about it. If you can't see that, I don't know what else to tell you.'

Lucky ran his tongue behind his teeth, lowered his voice. 'You can tell me why it's you Ross is petting.' There was a moment's silence, as though the sound had been sucked from the room. Mason dropped his gaze to his drink, but Lucky's face didn't change. 'I've been in this place longer than you've been pissing standing up,' he said, 'wrangled more out of those Arabs in a day than most supervisors can in a week. Why you?'

'You're senior foreman,' Mason said. 'Why don't you tell me?'

I looked at Ruthie, who dipped her head but stayed quiet.

Lucky pointed his thumb. 'Here's what I'll tell you,' he said. 'No matter what the Arab workers

188

want, the company makes all its decisions in consultation with the king. If he says jump, we ask how high. It's him the workers got to convince.'

'What's the difference?' Mason asked. 'We've got a king who thinks like an oil company and an oil company that thinks like a king.' He blew out a hard breath. 'The last thing the company wants is nationalization, but if we don't get these workers parity, we're going to have big trouble on our hands.'

Ruthie straightened her back. 'Too much shop talk,' she said. 'Let's have another drink.'

Mason glanced at me, then gave a one-sided grin. 'Hell, Lucky, I'm green as owl shit,' he said. 'Ross is right. I got a lot to learn, and I know I can learn it from you.'

When Ruthie leaned into Lucky's shoulder, he snorted, eased the glass from her hand, drank it empty, and pulled a cigarette from his pocket.

'Listen,' he said. 'I was fourteen, fifteen years old, running a perforating gun outside Thibodaux. I was watching this old farmer breaking his field, been at it all day, gang plow behind a seven-horse team, shires hitched three and four, pulling for all they was worth. Hard as I was working, I believe that gent was working harder. Ate my lunch and kept him timed, an acre an hour, no fooling.' Lucky's speech had melded into a kind of tune whose words I could barely understand. 'Spring, he's wanting to lay a new crop. Must have seen that weather coming, same as I did, because he's hieing that team up one last row. Thunder rolling in from the south, and I'm loading the gun, getting a little jumpy. I got primary explosives, twenty-four shots going in that hole. Don't take much—you're

189

reloading, rig man hits the juice a little too soon, scuffs up some static, and you're a dead monkey.' Lucky pulled on his cigarette, and his voice dropped a notch. 'Hot-hot. Air so wet you could drink it. Start feeling the hair prickling up, but I'm thinking this one last charge, and I'm done for the day, go home and down a cold Dixie.' Ruthie coughed, and he patted her head. *'Sha, sha, sommeil,'* he said, and then went on. 'Wasn't raining, not yet, and I thought that meant something. You know better, same as I do. When the lightning hit, thought I was killed.'

Ruthie rolled her head. 'Not my Lucky.'

'Knocked me on my ass. When I opened my eyes, I seen that old farmer rise up and take off at a dead run, smoking like the devil out of hell, blood pouring from his ears.' Lucky hunched his shoulders, leveled one hand, quieted to a near whisper. 'But them horses, they don't get up. Lightning hit one, tapped right through. All seven went down still tied in their traces, stacked up like cordwood. Even from where I was, I could smell the stink.' He sat for a brief moment, remembering, then pinched out his cigarette. 'I need to get this little girl home,' he said, and helped Ruthie to her feet.

Mason watched him carefully, then stood to hold the door. 'It may be that you and I don't think the same, Lucky, but we're plowing the same field.'

Lucky gave a short grunt. 'You plow your side, brother, and I'll plow mine.' He maneuvered Ruthie down the steps, tucked her into the car, then straightened. 'You're just a pup,' he said, 'but I like your spunk. You tag along with old Lucky, and you'll learn some things. Maybe not what you expect, but you'll learn.'

We watched them drive away, and Mason rolled his shoulders as though shrugging off some ache.

'Are you sore?' I asked, and rubbed his back.

'Not so sore I can't beat you at a game of Horse.'

I raced him to the ball, made my first shot from the left-hand corner just as Yash stepped out onto the porch, headed for home.

'Come on, Yash,' Mason called, and matched my shot, the ball never touching the rim.

Yash's grin broke white beneath the street lamp. He walked slowly to the mark, shot without dribbling, and missed the hoop by a mile, the ball sailing into the dark of the empty lot. Mason whooped and ran after it, but Yash was already waving him off.

'I'm a chess man myself,' he called back. We watched him pedal down the street on his bike, his oiled hair disappearing before the white of his shirt. Mason paused to hear the reverberating chant of the last call to prayer before bouncing the ball my way. I made a jump shot from center, and when he missed his match, I howled, 'H on you!' Lamps in the nearby houses flicked on, then off, but I didn't care. I felt happy, as though the weight of the evening had lifted, as though nothing could touch us there in our small circle of light where the date moths cast their shadows like miniature clouds.

CHAPTER TEN

The sound of the doorbell jolted me awake. Mason groaned, shoveled the covers over his head. I lay

191

still for a moment, waiting for Yash's voice before remembering he had the day off.

I pulled on my robe and stumbled down the hall. When I cracked open the door, wary of who I might find, I saw Lucky, shiny and chipper as though he hadn't just left our table hours before. Behind him, Ruthie waved from the backseat of the Volkswagen.

'Hot as a popcorn fart,' Lucky said. He snapped his lighter, sucked a cigarette to life. 'Good day as any for a picnic.'

Mason came in, still buttoning his shirt. 'Mornings sure come early around here,' he said.

'Waking up is what lets you know you're still alive,' Lucky said. 'Thought we could do some exploring, maybe visit spike camp, show you a thing or two. We got the *sadiqi* juice, but the girls might want something to cut it.'

I looked at Mason, who ran his fingers through his hair. 'Guess we got to do something,' he said.

I ran to change my clothes, then poured a canteeen of water and a jar of the fresh lemonade Yash had left in the Frigidaire, slammed a few cheese sandwiches together, and grabbed a jar of pickles. I followed the men to the little car, a goatskin bag of emergency water hanging from the passenger door, dropped my purse and camera behind the rear seat, and squeezed in next to Ruthie. Mason positioned our lunch in the forward trunk, then squinted into the sharp glare of the sun.

'We're going to swap some sweat today,' Lucky said. When we reached the gate, he saluted Habib without stopping.

'Better tell him where we're going,' Mason said.

'Where we going?' Lucky lipped his cigarette.

'We're wildcatters, ain't we? Bird-doggin'. Just following our nose.'

The stinging wind that whipped through the windows was no relief from the heat. I had gathered my hair beneath one of Mason's cotton handkerchiefs, and still the strands pulled free. We followed the asphalt a few miles northeast toward Dhahran before forking left onto a packed sand road. Within minutes, the Volkswagen was the sole object in sight. Only flares broke the horizon, and soon they, too, were gone. A few outcroppings of dark rock, clumps of camel brush, long stretches of cracked sand flats flanked by hilly *jabals*. When the road gave way to meandering drifts that snaked away in front of us, Lucky got out and scouted a thin line of oil.

'Tanker leaks the valve just a smidge, leaves a nice little trail for us to follow,' he said, and unscrewed a flask, took a long swallow and then another. I saw the way Mason watched him, the wary cast of his eyes.

The deeper we got into the desert, the deeper the sand. Even with the big tires, we bogged. Every mile or so, the men piled out and pushed while Ruthie steered us clear. The oil marker disappeared, then appeared again as the sand whisked one direction and then the other. My mouth filled with grit, and I licked my lips. When Mason handed me the canteen of water, I drank until he tipped it down. 'Better save some,' he said. 'We're a long way out.'

Lucky grunted and pointed to a tall tamarisk. 'How's that look for a picnic, girls?' He pulled the emergency brake. 'Biggest goddamn parking lot in the world.'

I couldn't wait to escape the sweltering car.

193

Ruthie jumped out and ran ahead of me, kicked off her shoes, rolled her pants, and scrambled to the top of the nearest dune. I focused my camera, caught her laughing and leaping down the sand face in leggy strides. The shelter wasn't much—more filter than shade—but we spread two blankets and arranged the food while Lucky poured the drinks. Without Yash's attention, our lunch seemed scant: a dented can of peaches that Ruthie had brought, a few dry sandwiches, the pickles that puckered my mouth.

'Wish I had a river to jump into,' Mason said.

Lucky rested on his elbow. 'Arabia used to be covered with streams. One of the biggest ran right through here. Wadi Sahaba.' He plucked up a small rock worn smooth as glass, worried it against his thumb. 'Sand is like water. Wears down everything,' he said, and pitched the stone away.

Even in the heat, it felt good to lie next to Mason, drowsy in the open air. When Ruthie and Lucky began kissing, I snugged my head into the crook of Mason's shoulder, embarrassed and a little excited by their shushed giggles and moans. I realized what I wasn't hearing—the songlike call to prayer that marked the day's progression. When a bustard broke from behind a dune, wings set, its call a harsh bark of alarm, Lucky sat up to study the direction of its flight.

'Wonder what's eating that guy.' He peered to where the bird had risen, then motioned to Mason. 'Let's go see what we got.'

Ruthie moved to my blanket, and we watched the men disappear around a hillock of sand. We shared a cigarette and sipped at the spiked lemonade. The tart drink made my mouth drier than it already was, and I chased it with water as hot as the air. I kept my eyes on the place where I'd last seen Mason.

'Should we be worried?' I asked.

Ruthie followed my gaze. 'Only if we hear someone scream.'

'I don't think Mason or Lucky would ever scream,' I said.

'I wasn't talking about them.' Ruthie lay back, her dark glasses reflecting twin pinpoints of sun. I wanted to shrug off my worry as easily as she did, but I felt exposed without Mason, overwhelmed by the sense that Ruthie and I were marooned, vulnerable and alone.

'What would you really do if something ever happened to Lucky?' I asked.

'I would have Joey to go back to,' she said, then grew quiet, and I knew she was thinking of me.

'If something happened to Mason, I think I would stay,' I said. 'Maybe get a job and live in Singles like Linda.'

Ruthie smirked. 'You wouldn't be single for long,' she said, 'not in this crocodile pit.' She brought the cigarette to her lips. 'How's the love life these days?'

'Good,' I said, 'unless Mason is too tired or in his study.'

She opened her eyes, looked at me. 'What does he do in there, anyway?'

'Paperwork, I guess.'

'Drillers don't have paperwork,' she said. 'They're roughnecks, not engineers.' She exhaled, lowered her voice. 'I probably shouldn't tell you this, but Lucky can't read. He bluffed his way into the service. I tried to teach him, but it just made him mad.' She lifted her shoulders. 'He might act

195

like he doesn't understand, but he knows why he'll never get promoted.' She flipped her cigarette to the sand. 'Don't say anything to Mason, okay? It's hard enough for Lucky as it is.' When I nodded, she pulled up her blouse, exposing a lacy brassiere, rolled to her stomach so that the sun hit her back, and rested her head on her arms. 'I'm kind of glad he's not ambitious like Mason, you know? We have more than we need already.'

'I don't think it's about more with Mason,' I said. 'At least not more money or things. He just wants to make a difference.'

Ruthie drew up one side of her face. 'An idealist,' she said. 'Gee, we haven't had idealism around here since 1952. Really, it's kind of sweet.'

I raised my head to the sound of voices, saw Mason and Lucky reappear, followed by a man riding a large white donkey. Ruthie sat up quickly and pulled down her blouse. The Bedouin waited until Mason encouraged him forward before dismounting and greeting us.

'This here is Sahid,' Mason said. 'Says he's traveling alone, hoping to find work at Ras Tanura. He's got a hell of a long way to go.'

When Mason passed Sahid the canteen, he swallowed and grimaced and swallowed again, then gratefully accepted the cigarette that Lucky offered.

I showed Sahid my camera. 'Okay?' I asked. He smiled as I focused, his teeth stained with coffee, his nose a broken line. How old was he? I wondered. Forty? Sixty? When he looked at Ruthie, she pulled the blanket's corner to cover her bare legs. He gestured, said something that made Lucky burst out laughing.

'Hey, babe!' Lucky said. 'He wants to know if he

196

can marry you. He's willing to barter the donkey.'

'You're the ass.' Ruthie rolled the blanket to her waist, grabbed the can of peaches, and pitched it at Lucky. He used his pocketknife to jack open the tin and spear the peaches one by one. Sahid took each slice in his fingers, paying no mind to the flies that hovered at his mouth. The men conversed for a minute longer, Sahid's face growing more serious as he swept one hand along the horizon before saying his good-byes and leading his donkey north, stopping once to bend and tunnel his finger in the sand, revealing a sprout of green grass, which the animal cropped in one bite. Sahid looked back at us, seemed to consider, then bore west as though he were suddenly sure of his direction.

'We'd best head back,' Mason said, moving to help gather what food remained.

'So says Sahid.' Lucky visored his eyes against the sun cutting the *jabals*. 'Thinks there's djinn in this place.'

Mason weighed the water bag in his hand, then scouted the dunes, and I saw the dark edge of worry crease his brow. Lucky slapped the dust from his pants.

'Okay, gals,' he said. 'All aboard.'

If the heat had seemed stifling before, it now seemed unbearable. Sweat chafing beneath my arms, the taste of cheese and hot lemonade souring in my throat, I closed my eyes, breathed the hot wind as Lucky geared us between the towering mounds of sand.

Mason pointed across the dashboard. 'That way,' he said.

'Better get your bearings, son,' Lucky said. 'We're headed right.'

'We don't want it to get dark on us,' Mason said.

Lucky flicked his cigarette out the window, growled a laugh. 'You worry like an old lady,' he said. He skirted a garden of black rock, took a pull off his flask.

'Let the girls have some,' Ruthie said. She reached forward, then passed the flask to me, but I shook my head.

'What about water?' I asked.

'We got plenty,' Lucky said.

'We got what's left in the bag,' Mason said. Lucky looked at him and then away.

We topped a razor-backed dune, a pennant of sand blowing from its peak, and rode the slip face like a wave, only to stall again. Each time the car sank to its hubs, we got out to dig and push until we were grimed and exhausted. Ruthie dropped her face into her hands.

'Let us rest for a while, will you?'

Lucky clicked off the ignition, and the sounds of the desert settled around us. The call of strange birds was followed by a high catlike keening, and I remembered the story Mason had told me of a Bedouin at the gate, begging for help because some wild animal had dragged his child from their tent. By the time the trackers found what remained of the boy, they had only a leg bone to bury.

'Still got a few good hours of daylight,' Lucky said. 'Worse that can happen is we sleep right here. I got to piss.' He opened his door and moved behind the car, toeing the depth of the sand into which we'd settled, then stuck his head back in the window. 'Come on, McPhee. Let's crawl up and get sighted,' he said. 'Pistol is beneath the seat, ladies. Just make sure you're not pointing it at a white man.' We watched them scamper up the slope, then stand straight against the deepening sky.

Ruthie leaned against my shoulder. 'I just want to go home.'

'Maybe they'll send someone to find us,' I said, then remembered we hadn't told Habib where we were going.

A shout came down from the dune, and I peered into the distance until I made out the form of a camel, a man looming high on its back, rifle slung across his shoulder, dagger tucked at his waist. The camel knelt at the Arab's command. I thought at first it was Sahid, but I could tell by his upright carriage that this man was younger. He offered Mason and Lucky his own goatskin bag before gesturing toward the Volkswagen, and I heard their voices rising in laughter.

Ruthie ducked to see out my window. 'What's he saying?'

'I don't know, but it seems okay.'

The men trekked back to the car, Mason in the lead. He pulled open my door. 'Sahid sent help,' he said, and pointed to the camel. 'You two ride. We'll walk.'

I grabbed my purse, hung the camera around my neck. 'Where are we going?' I asked.

Mason lifted his eyebrows. 'Guess we're going to meet Abdullah's family.'

The man pulled back his *ghutra,* and I felt my heart jump with recognition.

'So you have come for my mother's fried locust,' Abdullah said. When I saw the flash of his wide smile, I laughed aloud, resisting the impulse to hug him like a long-lost friend.

While Ruthie gathered her shoes, Abdullah led

me to where the she-camel rested, placidly chewing her cud. She gazed at us from beneath her long lashes, then turned away, indifferent.

'It is not like a horse,' Abdullah said, 'that a boy might ride without reins.'

'I can do it,' I said, and clambered on.

Abdullah looped the rope in his hand, stepped close. 'I am truly sorry,' he said quietly. 'It is a weak father who uses a horse to punish his child.'

I straightened myself atop the camel, embarrassed that I had been found out. 'It wasn't my father,' I said. 'It was my grandfather.'

'Allah is merciful,' he said. 'There will be another horse for you.'

Ruthie approached and climbed on. 'I hate these things,' she said, and the camel laid back its head as though on cue and gave a long, excruciating bellow. With Abdullah's command, it began to rock forward, then back, bellyaching all the while. Ruthie clutched at my waist and squealed, Abdullah encouraging her to hold on, and we began the slow, jarring plod through the dunes, Mason and Lucky following in our tracks, sand filling their worthless shoes. I focused on the rope leading to Abdullah's hand, felt as though I were being towed like a skiff across the water.

Ruthie brought her chin to my shoulder. 'I think Abdullah's got a crush on you,' she said.

'Don't say that,' I shushed. 'He's just a friend.'

Ruthie snorted. 'Remember what Marilyn Monroe said? "If you can make a girl laugh, you can make her do anything."'

I turned as far as I could to glare at her, but she had fixed her eyes on that place where the dunes vectored. I followed her gaze, saw a large

200

rectangular tent appear, pegged out across a salty flat, black except for a single runner of white that wrapped it like a ribbon. Low and narrow, open along the front, it leaned into its poles with sturdy resolve against the prevailing wind. Long-eared goats grouped and broke before us as the camel groaned to her knees, mewling for her calf.

Two women emerged, covered head to wrist in black scarves, a striking contrast to the colorful patterns of their ankle-length dresses. Soft black masks with square holes framed their eyes like miniature windows. One hung back, cradling a young toddler wearing nothing but bits of strung stone, and I wondered whether Abdullah had lied to me about a wife. At his instruction, she handed the child to the older woman and set to work at the camel's flank, filling an enameled bowl with milk. I hesitated but drank when she held it out, licking the froth from my lips, as rich and salty as smoked cheese.

'This is my mother, Fatima,' Abdullah said, 'and my sister, Nadia.' The relief I felt surprised me— not his wife after all. He rested his hand on the baby's head. 'My niece,' he said, his voice resonant with affection, and she grinned up at him, paddling her feet with delight. I wondered where the father was, how many family members shared the small tent, how many mouths Abdullah had to feed.

Fatima directed us to the door, where Ruthie and I left our shoes and entered the area divided into sections by striped draperies: women, children, and the kitchen on the left, men and guests on the right, an open gathering place in the middle lined with goat-hair rugs and pillows. Abdullah hung his long sword and rifle on the center pole before arranging the coffee urn and building a small fire to roast the beans, and I remembered what Yash had told me: the highest compliment you could pay a Bedouin was that he made coffee from morning till night.

Inside the room kept private by a flapped blanket, the air smelled of wet wool, dung smoke, and the particular musk of women. Fatima urged us to sit and checked that we were hidden from the men before she and Nadia shed their veils. Nadia was younger than I'd expected, only a girl, her hair and eyebrows jet-black. She smiled, revealing a flash of white teeth, and I grinned back, noting with pleasure her resemblance to Abdullah.

Fatima, possessed of a stately authority, sat ramrod straight. Black hair reddened with henna that rouged her temples, kohl-lined eyes, a faded blue script of tattoos along her forehead and chin, fingernails stained with dye—she looked both elegant and sinister as she watched us arrange ourselves among the cushions, assessing our every move as though she were calculating our worth.

Ruthie bumped my shoulder. 'Remember to tuck your legs so that the soles of your feet don't offend them. Arabs are touchy that way.' I folded my knees modestly under Fatima's appraising gaze as Nadia offered us a bowl of sticky dates, which we ate like candy, licking our fingers. When Ruthie opened her purse, Nadia leaned forward, curious. What was a purse, and what did it carry? Ruthie pulled out a pack of cigarettes, passed them around, then popped open her Zippo, eliciting a whoop of delight from Nadia. When we had smoked them down to the filters, Fatima and Nadia began to talk among themselves, pointing to our blouses and

202

slacks, sometimes moving close to rub the cloth between their fingers. Nadia rose with the sleeping child in her arms and knelt at my side. Could she touch my hair? I pulled off my kerchief and tried to finger out the tangles, but she stopped me, laid the little girl in my lap, and reached for a wooden comb. Gently, never a snag or a pull, she worked the strands from top to bottom, her rhythmic concentration like a lullaby, thin bangles of gold tinkling at her wrists, a small circle of ink like a single black coin tattooed into her palm. I cradled the soft blanket, studied the baby's round face, ears pierced with lapis, dark lashes and rosebud lips. When she woke, her eyes—brown irises set in deep blue coronas—studied me with such intensity that I shivered and handed her back to Nadia, my chest aching.

When the dates came around again, I shook my head, and the women looked disappointed. 'Good, good,' I said, and rubbed my stomach. The sand beneath me had molded to my body, and I settled myself a little deeper into its hold. A pleasant silence filled the room as Fatima began working the loom, her wooden shuttle polished by decades of spinning and weaving, and I felt myself drift, lulled by the low voices, the shush of thread against thread, the long-ago memory of rainy afternoons, my grandmother cutting old clothes into squares, pinning, and stitching remnants of shirts and flour sacks into Flying Geese; my outgrown nightgowns and the least faded swatches of my calico dress snipped and puzzled into Nine Patch and Snowball. I'd fall into my nap and wake to find a limp stack of scraps blocked and basted. By first frost, I'd have a new quilt at my chin, soft and familiar.

I raised my eyes when I heard Nadia speaking directly to Fatima, who shook her head decisively. Nadia patted her mother's arm, imploring until Fatima sighed, dropped her weaving to her lap, and took the baby. Nadia rose and pulled on her head scarf, then made motions like she was swimming and reached for my hand. I looked at Ruthie, who shrugged.

'We must be near the shore north of Ras Tanura,' she said. 'We're lucky we didn't end up in Kuwait.' She lay back and closed her eyes. 'You kids go ahead. Us old ladies will take a nap.'

I thought I should ask Mason, or at least tell him, but I let Nadia lead me to a gap in the tent's back wall, and then we were moving out of the shadows, the sun a waning glow, the sand warming my feet. Nadia's fingers seemed small in mine, but her strength kept me upright as we both staggered, laughing and breathless. When we topped over the dune, I stopped. It was as though the world had fallen away, the sand flowing into the sea.

Nadia tugged at my hand before letting go and running toward the water. A few yards from the shallow lap of waves, she took off her scarf and pulled her hair free of its braids. She touched one finger to her lips—this would be our secret—then dropped her dress and folded it neatly at her feet, giggling and motioning for me to do the same.

How could my modesty be greater than hers, this girl who walked through her life cloaked and veiled? I fumbled at the buttons of my blouse, embarrassed. Since my mother's death, no one but Mason had seen me naked, not even when my son was born and the doctor had groped beneath my hospital gown without once looking at my face as

204

though he, too, were ashamed.

Nadia soothed my distress with girlish laughter, lifting the camera from my neck, helping me to bundle my clothes, averting her eyes to allow me what privacy she could. This time, when she took my hand and began pulling me forward, I hesitated. 'I'm afraid,' I said. 'I don't know how.'

She encouraged me, holding my arm, reassuring. I could hardly feel the warm water at my ankles. When we were in to our knees, Nadia stopped to cup handfuls and pour them over my shoulders. I trailed her until we were up to our waists. When the water rocked me off my heels, she leaned into the sea, let her feet kick up. *'Ta'alay ma'ee!'* she said, and I knew she meant that I should follow her.

I bent my knees, submerged to my neck, and made a few bobs to test the buoyancy of my body, felt Nadia take my hands and lead me deeper until I could no longer touch bottom. When I panicked, she calmed me and ferried me after her as she floated on her back, legs fluttering. I lifted my chin and sputtered, resisting the urge to jerk free, thrash my way back to shore. The moment I quit fighting, I felt my body rise, as though my resistance had some weight of its own. Like my own skin, that water, and after a time I couldn't tell where it ended and I began. Only Nadia's hands kept me tethered, or I might have floated away. When I felt her body shift, I closed my eyes and let myself go, surprised to feel the loose bed come up beneath my feet. The sea was at our chins, our hair spreading out around us like the fine roots of mangrove. She was happy, I could tell, so happy to be teaching me to do this impossible thing.

'Ashkurik,' I said. 'Thank you.'

She smiled, held my eyes for a moment before pushing away. This time, she swam in earnest, long strokes that took her out to open sea. I wanted to call her back, tell her she was going too far, but what did I know of her world?

I waded to land, wrung my hair before pulling on my clothes, then sat in the sand and watched for any sign of her, sure that a rising swell was the round of her shoulder, a ripple the dark fan of her hair. In the fading light, the phosphorescent glow of brine shrimp played across the waves like sheet lightning, and I let out a breath when Nadia finally emerged, her breasts round with milk. She dressed and motioned me to follow, and it was then that I lifted my camera to capture her moving ahead of me, cresting the dune, her black silhouette against the sky, her unveiled face turned toward me like an orphan moon.

When we reentered the tent, we found Ruthie and Fatima in careful silence. Nadia took the child, who gripped her mother's hair as Nadia pressed her close. She laid her hand on my arm.

'Sadiqati,' she said.

'My friend,' I said, and a smile broke across Nadia's face. When I unclasped the small pearl from my neck and held it out to her, she looked from me to Fatima, and they exchanged anxious whispers.

'Now you've done it.' Ruthie yawned as she gathered her purse and scarf. 'If they can't give an equal gift in return, it will be a dishonor.'

I stumbled over my words, trying to make them understand. 'Please,' I said, 'for the baby.'

When Fatima finally voiced her approval, I gently laid the gold chain around the child's neck, then gripped Nadia's hand. I gathered my camera and followed Ruthie outside, where the men waited. I looked at Abdullah and smiled my happiness, and he smiled back before bringing the camel around.

Ruthie and I remounted, the camel's buck and heave more familiar now, like the persnickety habits of a mule. Abdullah handed me a stick and showed me how to tap its neck to guide it in lieu of reins. When his fingers grazed mine, he looked away quickly and busied himself with the rope. Ruthie pinched my waist. 'Told you,' she muttered.

By the time we reached the Volkswagen, the rising wind had blown troughs around the tires, and it tipped precariously. With the help of ropes and the camel, Abdullah and Mason broke the axles free, and Lucky steered the little car to a cracked salt flat.

'*Allah kareem,*' Abdullah said. 'God is kind.' He kissed Mason's cheeks, held his shoulders in an affectionate embrace until Lucky honked the horn, and we piled in. This time, I welcomed the snug closeness of bodies, warmth against the desert's descending chill. The discomforts of the day were nothing compared to the delight I had felt in Nadia's company, an accidental adventure that, more than anything, I wanted to make happen again.

Lucky waited until we lost sight of Abdullah before reaching beneath his shirt and sliding the pistol onto the dash.

'Took it along just in case,' he said. 'Never know who you're going to run into out here.'

Mason looked at him like he had lost his mind. 'And who did we run into?'

'Abdullah.' Lucky nodded. 'He's all right, but you never know. Some of them's good and some of them's bad, just like all people is. One lays a finger on my wife, I'll shoot him standing up. And that includes Abdullah.' He pinched shut one eye. 'Don't tell me you wouldn't do the same.'

Mason glanced at me. 'Guess it's not something I plan to see happen.'

'You're in Arabia, partner,' Lucky said. 'You'd better be armed and ready when that plan of yours breaks down.' He flicked his cigarette out the window. 'You think you've got the world by the tail, but you're forgetting one thing. This ain't your world.' He let the words settle before snorting. 'Listen,' he said. 'If there's one thing I'm aiming to teach you, it's how to stop being so damn serious.' He pointed past the stand of acacia lit by our headlights. 'If we can believe your buddy Abdullah, we got a straight shot right out of here.' He thumped the stick into low, loosened his shoulders, and crinkled his eyes. 'Old Sahid, he saved our bacon, didn't he? Him and his sorry-assed donkey.'

When that rolling Cajun laugh came up from Lucky's belly, Mason smiled in spite of himself, and I felt my own spirits lighten. Lucky broke into a chorus of 'Camptown Races' and steered us toward the flattening horizon as we all joined in, following the road headed south, guided by the flares marking home.

*   *   *

I was at the table the next day, dressed in a cool cotton housedress, my feet bare, typing an article on the Garden Club's annual bulb sale, when Mason

208

bent over my shoulder. 'How about we catch a movie before I head back out?' He leaned in closer, put his mouth to my ear like he was whispering a secret. '*Irma la Douce* is playing. Adults only.'

I shrugged him away. 'I'm almost finished.'

Mason touched the pile of photos I had spread out next to me, picked up a few of the clandestine shots I had taken from the bus. 'These are really something,' he said.

I ducked my head, pleased by his praise. 'If Nestor won't run them, it doesn't matter.'

'Maybe some other magazine,' Mason said. 'Maybe *National Geographic*.'

'Really?'

'No reason not to try.' Mason gazed at the photographs a moment longer before moving his focus to the one I had taken of the hands hung from the post. He squinted and cocked his head just as I had: a skeletal tree at first, a few blackened leaves.

'That's outside the police station,' I said. 'Ruthie told me it's how they punish thieves.'

'I've seen it.' Mason settled into his chair, fingered a cigarette from his pocket. 'In Arabia, it's all Old Testament, an eye for an eye. You kill someone, by accident or intent, they've got to even the score. What they have here that we don't is plain old mercy. The person who is wronged can forgive, and everything is settled. Family, friends, even a stranger can pay blood money to spare a thief, which means it's the poorest who bear the brunt of it. Kind of like everywhere else.' He tapped the photo. 'My guess is those fingers belonged to someone who was hanging on by the skin of his teeth.'

209

I thought of Baby Buckle, then looked at the article I had written—bulbs, for heaven's sake. I sighed.

'I tell you what,' Mason said. 'I'll set up a file drawer for you in the study. A career girl needs her own space.' He leaned back, crossed his fingers behind his head. 'We should plan that road trip before it gets any hotter.'

'Maybe Ruthie and Lucky can come with us,' I said.

Mason thought for a moment. 'I don't expect Lucky to be happy about my being up for promotion,' he said, 'but it seems like he's got some other burr under his saddle. Can't sit still during meetings, up and down, smoking like a chimney. Won't even look at the reports, just pushes them on by.'

'Ruthie told me,' I said, 'he can't read. She says that's why he'll never get promoted. He doesn't want you to know.'

'Huh,' Mason said. 'Well, I'll be damned.' I could see him thinking about it for a long second before he stretched, yawned expansively. 'Guess I'll kick back for a while,' he said.

I found him a few minutes later, barefoot and shirtless, already napping on the couch, one of those people who can fall asleep anywhere, and I remembered Brother Fogarty, snoring beneath the pew. I studied Mason for a moment, one arm tucked behind his head, the other resting on his chest, all the care gone from his face, the scar at the corner of his mouth that never tanned. If not for the possibility of Yash walking in, I might have stretched out beside him like those first nights of our marriage spent on the single bed, just to feel that closeness.

Instead, I changed into my work clothes and headed for the garden. I was on all fours, breaking over the onion greens to keep them round and sweet, when I heard someone behind me. I thought it might be Faris, come to shoo me away, but I looked to see Mason stretching, scratching his bare belly.

'That's a sight I like waking up to,' he said. 'Don't stop on account of me. I'll just sit back and enjoy the view.'

But now I was self-conscious about showing him my backside, even if some part of me liked having him watch. 'Maybe I'll dig some spuds,' I said. I rose and found the spade leaned against the wall where Faris had left it and cut it in behind one mound. When I levered the handle, half a peck of potatoes erupted, perfectly whole and unblemished. I knelt and dropped them into a basket. Mason lowered himself to the ground beside me, and I leaned into the light musk of his body, familiar and distracting. I loved to mouth the cap of each shoulder when he stood naked before me, test my teeth against the tensile strength of his skin, and I wanted to do that now, nip him a little too hard.

'We've got enough spuds to feed Coxey's Army,' he said.

I rubbed the waxy jackets, remembering the caked red clay that clung to the tubers back home. 'They come up so clean,' I said.

He took out his pocketknife, pared me a crisp slice. 'Just a little appetizer,' he whispered against my throat. He moved his mouth over mine, and I felt his hand work beneath my blouse and under my bra.

211

'We'd better . . .' I tried, sure that Faris was watching.

'Yeah'—Mason grinned—'we'd better.' He gathered the basket against his side and stood, pulled me up with him. 'Do you remember that tune by Little Jimmy Dickens?' He broke into a chorus of 'Take an Old Cold Tater and Wait,' and I laughed, remembering how it felt to live the truth of the song, communal Sunday dinners and not enough chicken to go around, being shuffled outside with the other children to wait for whatever remained, sometimes nothing more than the last hard scrapings of gravy, the neck and often the feet, fried crisp enough to gnaw on.

'Do you think we're done being hungry?' I quieted my voice. 'I mean really hungry?'

He touched the corner of my mouth and smiled. 'Yeah,' he said, 'I think we're done.'

We were turning for the house when a terrific explosion rocked the air, nearly knocking us to the ground. I gripped Mason's arm and looked up to see the birds lift from the trees. At the south fence, where the flares flamed red, a cloud of black smoke boiled up, and then we heard the shrill alarm of the disaster whistle cut through the haze.

'It's the stabilization plant,' Mason said. He pulled me into the kitchen, where Yash stood wide-eyed and motionless over a pot of steaming rice. Mason yanked on a shirt. 'You two stay here.'

He was out the door and running for the gate, me right behind him, when another blast dropped me to my knees. A brilliant ball of fire rose into the sky, casting light and shadow across the faces of the people spilling from their houses to watch.

'Mrs. Gin.' Yash was helping me to my feet,

212

urging me back to the house. 'It is best if you stay inside,' he said. 'There may be an evacuation.'

I stood, saw the other men racing to the plant. A smaller explosion, and then another, the oily smoke spreading across the compound as the siren blared and the Volkswagen came ripping down the street. Lucky stopped just long enough to drop Ruthie before taking off again. She grabbed my hand, and we huddled together on the porch.

'I should get my camera,' I said, but she shook her head.

'Security would confiscate it,' she said. 'This is nothing that anyone wants to see.'

Yash urged us inside, but we stayed where we were for another hour, then two, keeping watch like sailors' wives. We drank the sweet tea he brought us and smoked until the only light in the sky was the belt of flame that surged and retreated, bright as a prairie fire. Even after the call went out that the blaze was under control, the eruptions continued, each brewing another belch of oily smut that rode the searing breeze, greasing our skin.

'There they are,' Ruthie said, and I saw the Volkswagen rounding the block. Mason got out, covered with soot, and groaned when I tucked in against his chest. Lucky held Ruthie in his arms, nodded at Mason.

'That boy there,' he said, 'he's got some *cojones*.' He grinned, his teeth white against the smudge of his skin. 'Wasn't no one else willing to run in on that fire and cut that valve. If it wasn't for him, this whole place might have gone up in smoke.'

I looked up at Mason, but he shook his head. 'Couldn't have done it without your help.'

'Hell,' Lucky crowed. 'We was like Pancho and

213

the Cisco Kid.'

Mason ran his hand through his hair. 'Think I'm ready for a shower,' he said.

'Get yourself some rest, pard,' Lucky said. 'The next round is on me.'

'We'll talk more tomorrow,' Ruthie said, and gave me a quick hug.

Yash waited at the door with a highball, which Mason drank in one long draft.

'Go on home, Yash,' Mason said, and handed him the empty glass. 'It's been a long day. We can take it from here.'

I believed I wouldn't be able to stand it until Mason told me, until I knew some part of what he knew, but I was learning the ways of men, their silence and refusal to speak of important things, things they believe too complicated for their women to hear. I waited, giving the liquor time to do its work. When he slumped to the sofa, laid back his head, I eased down beside him.

'The pipe ruptured,' he said. 'That first explosion trapped five Arabs.' His breath smelled smoky, like he had inhaled the gas flare's fumes. 'Burt Cane ran in first, tried to shut off the valve.' He blinked slowly. 'They're every one of them dead.'

I remembered the joyous polka around the patio with Burt, the words he had offered me—*I hope this place is good to you.* They sounded wistful now, as though he already knew, as though he had been saying good-bye. I leaned into Mason, caught a whiff of burned hair—his eyebrows, his arm hairs singed to ash. He felt too hot to touch, as though the least scuff of friction might set him aflame.

'But you did it,' I said quietly. 'You shut it down. Cisco and Pancho, like Lucky said.'

214

Mason held up one blistered hand. 'More like Quixote and Sancho,' he said, 'tilting at windmills.' He brought the cigarette to his mouth, held the smoke so long that I felt the ache in my own chest. He exhaled all at once, leaned forward, covered his face. 'Goddamn it,' he said, then pushed himself up with such force that it rattled the ice in our glasses. I watched him disappear down the hallway, heard the door of his study bang shut.

I sat for a moment, then went to the door, knocked lightly. 'Mason?'

'I'm okay,' he said, his voice muffled. 'Why don't you get the bed warmed up for me,' he said. 'I won't be long.'

I wanted to find some way to comfort him, but I did what I was told and went to our bed, warming it against the chill of the air-conditioned room. The world felt emptier, my place in it less sure, as though gravity were letting loose its hold, and I held to Mason's pillow as though it were my anchoring weight, breathed in, fighting against the grief I felt for Burt, the fear when I imagined Mason forcing his way through the flames. Maybe it was better not to know, I told myself, to go through my days like the other wives seemed able to do, calmly ignoring how dangerous the men's work was—a miracle that they came home at all.

*   *   *

They held Burt's memorial in the Oil Exhibit building, standing room only, the remains of his body ready to be flown out even as the Arab dead were buried by their families in graves made of sand. As I sat between Mason and Ruthie and listened to

215

one man after another offer his memories and his praise, I kept my eyes on Maddy, slumped in her folding chair.

'They've got her drugged,' Ruthie whispered. 'She's not even blinking.'

After the service, Mason stepped aside to speak quietly with Tiny Doty, whose eyes were rheumy with exhaustion, and I followed Ruthie to where Maddy was receiving the sympathies of a long line of women. We shuffled forward a step at a time until I stood before her. She looked up through her bifocals fogged with tears.

'I'm so sorry,' I whispered, then moved a few feet away to wait for Ruthie, who gathered Maddy's hands, covered them with her own, and leaned her mouth to the older woman's ear. They stayed that way for a long time, Ruthie bent and whispering, Maddy crying and clinging to Ruthie as though she might go down if she didn't have someone to hold on to.

Mason and Lucky waited for us, leaned against the back wall and smoking.

'How about that drink I owe you?' Lucky asked Mason.

'Maybe tomorrow,' Mason said.

Lucky tipped back his head. 'You sick?'

'Come on, Lucky.' Ruthie tugged at his arm. 'We all need a break.'

Even though it was still early, once we were home, there seemed nothing to do but go to bed. Mason stretched out beside me and rested his arm across his eyes.

'Those pipes rotted through,' he said. 'Tiny Doty told me. How could the company let that happen?'

'The sand,' I said, 'or maybe the rain.'

216

He shook his head. 'There's no excuse,' he said. 'None.'

I felt every muscle in his body tense. I rose to my elbow, whispered, 'Roll over,' and settled astride the small of his back, began working my thumbs at the base of his skull, beneath his shoulder blades, pushing into the springy softness between each rib, laddering my way down his spine. I hesitated when I felt him flinch, thinking I had hurt him, and rested my cheek in the nook of his neck, heard the hitch in his breath as though he might be crying. Even after I knew he was asleep, I lay there, inhaling the milky scent at the nape of his neck. When, finally, I slid to the side and tucked in against him, he moaned in his dream and rolled away, and I felt the air cool between us, heard the sharp ticking of the clock.

A crystal ball, a shew stone, and I might have lingered next to him a little while longer, but I took up my book, the pages ahead like a promise that all could be made right again, and I wonder now— was it youth that allowed me to believe that my hours were lined out before me like coins I might pluck up and carry in my pocket to spend? There was always the morning after night, the lunch after breakfast, the muezzin's call endlessly spilling out over the compound.

Burt Cane's death was a sadness, but he was an old man, wasn't he? And Maddy Cane was nothing like me.

217

CHAPTER ELEVEN

Was it the next morning, or the next (so many of them the same—the room sulfured with light, the birdsong, the muezzin's first call to prayer, Yash tinkering in the kitchen) that I woke to the sound of something strange yet familiar? I opened my eyes, saw Mason's side of the bed empty, and tried to remember what day it was, whether he was on the platform or in the shower. Time is like this in the desert, the hours slow and weighted as though the sun passing over were a brilliant boulder lumbering across the sky. Mason's absence had become more familiar to me than his presence, and I was sometimes startled to find him there beside me and would lie very still, examining his face as though to memorize his features, as though there might come a time when I would no longer be able to recognize who he was.

I rolled to my back and listened, trying to make out what I was hearing. When the door to the bedroom swung open, I jerked up the covers, thinking for a ridiculous moment that it was Yash, but then I saw Mason. Instead of the company-regulation khaki pants and button-down, he wore jeans and a white T-shirt, cigarettes rolled in the sleeve, like he was that farm boy again.

He flicked his lighter, sly-eyed me through the smoke of his cigarette. 'We seem to have us a regular rodeo outside,' he said. 'Abdullah says someone put in a request for a ride.' And then I recognized the nickering and chuffing of horses.

I didn't even bother to shower, just rifled the

drawers, pulled on a pair of Mason's jeans and then my mother's boots, arching my toes against their familiar crease and bend. I tied my hair in a blue scarf that I thought might match the sky, added film to my camera, and stepped out into the heat. Abdullah, dressed in the belted robe of a Bedouin, stood at the head of three glistening horses, their long tails swishing, Faris hovering close by, ready with a shovel to move their manure to the garden. Abdullah loosened the lead of the gray mare, brought her to me.

'Badra,' he said quietly, his voice tender. 'She will carry you well.'

I held out my palm, let her snuffle and lick, then touched the silver velvet of her muzzle. When Abdullah nodded, I grabbed a hank of mane and swung myself up onto the thin cushion of leather that served as a saddle and adjusted my sitting bones to fit her back, which was narrower than Sonny's had been, just right. Instead of reins, Abdullah handed me a single rope connected to the left of the bangled headstall so that the horse gave to that side like a goat kid trained to a post. A young black mare whose hide rippled in the heat stomped and settled as Mason pulled himself up. I saw Abdullah watching the mare's ears flick back and knew he was judging her mood just as she was judging Mason's.

Abdullah took the basket lunch Yash proffered, set it on the grass, and pulled it apart. When he held up a checked tablecloth and cast it aside, Yash crossed his arms.

'You will have sand in every bite,' he pronounced. Abdullah paid him no mind but stored our lunch in a rough satchel that he slipped over his

219

head and shoulder, adding only a single canteen.

'We'll need more water than.that,' Mason said.

'We will find water.' Abdullah mounted his own muscular bay and moved her forward, Badra following, Mason bringing up the rear. We clipped down the asphalt, children coming from their yards to watch, cars pulling to the side, until we reached the gate, where Habib exchanged a few jolly words with Abdullah, reached up to shake each of our hands, and waved us through.

I rode easy on the gray, rocking my hips to her smooth gait, the twist of tension at the base of my spine unwinding. When Abdullah led us off the road and pointed us south, into the heart of the desert, Mason, too, seemed to relax and began humming 'Home on the Range' as the mares found their footing, their shoes solid-plated for protection against the rubbled rock. The heat that in a car felt like an affliction came tempered by a constant breeze. I lifted my camera and saw what Carlo must, the boundaries of the world falling away. A small jerboa hopped in front of us, and I caught it in midleap, a mouse except for the cartoonishly long ears, legs, and tail. Each time I shuttered, Badra's ears clicked back then forward, but she never hesitated, steady in her march.

We rode until the sun scorched our shoulders. By the time Abdullah directed us to a narrow island of tamarisk, my rump was aching. We wove our way through the trees on a barren path that led to an open flat mounded like the mouth of a volcano—an ancient well ringed by centuries of stone and camel dung.

'Sure this well is yours?' Mason asked. 'I don't want anyone taking shots at us.'

Abdullah responded to Mason's ribbing with a sideways grin. 'It has belonged to my tribe for as long as man has thirsted.'

'Adam's ale,' Mason said. 'I could use some of that.'

Abdullah dismounted, and I looked around for a place to tie Badra.

'Bring her here,' Abdullah said. 'We will have our water.' He uncovered a large skin bucket and rope, looped the end around Badra's neck, and dropped it down the black shaft. He urged the horse forward until the bucket reappeared, then motioned us to drink.

Mason spat and wiped his mouth. 'Too briny for me,' he said, then moved away. I could tell by his bowlegged stance that he was galled and would be raw by the time we got home.

I cupped my hands, dipped them into the water. 'It tastes like the sea,' I said, and Abdullah smiled his approval.

I stowed my camera and laid out our lunch while the men reclined in the thin shade, the ground-tied horses dozing close by. I tore the chapati and offered the dal, which Abdullah accepted graciously. I finished a sweet slice of melon, wiped my hands down my jeans, and surveyed the hazy horizon. 'I could live like this,' I said.

'Bet you'd miss running water,' Mason said, 'miss our nice soft bed.'

Abdullah looked up quickly, as though the mention of the bed were a naughty detail.

'I survived without them before,' I said.

Mason stripped a straw of dry grass and worried it through his teeth, raised an eyebrow Abdullah's way. 'Women never appreciate what you do for them.'

'That's not what I mean,' I said, then caught myself. I didn't want to have some silly spat in front of Abdullah, who had taken the makings for coffee from his pouch, gathered brush and dung, and fanned a fire to life. When I raised my camera and asked permission, he lifted his face, and I took a few photos, then simply studied him through the lens because I could, as though I weren't really looking even as he gazed back at me, his eyes unwavering, and I felt my heart pick up speed. When Mason cleared his throat, I didn't look around but stowed the camera, then moved to kneel beside Abdullah.

'Teach me how to do that, will you?' I asked.

I stayed close as he showed me how to roast and grind the fistful of beans, their fragrance like the taste of green cherries, then filled a small brass urn with water and set the coffee to boil, pinched a bit of cardamom. His bag was like a magician's hat, from which he pulled three cups.

'It is tradition,' he said, 'for the host to take the first swallow so that the guest'—he nodded at Mason—'won't fear poison.' He sipped, waited a moment, then rolled his eyes and keeled over sideways.

I rocked back on my heels and laughed, then looked to Mason, who was watching us, his mouth a thin line.

Abdullah recovered and filled the other two cups. I sipped at mine, swabbing the bitter taste away with a bite of chapati. Mason knocked his back like it was a shot of whiskey, then rose. 'Gotta see a man about a horse,' he said. Abdullah peered at him quizzically until Mason stepped behind a clump of bushes.

'How is your mother?' Now that Mason wasn't there, I could ask. 'Nadia and your niece?'

Abdullah moved his eyes to the coffee, poured us each another cup. 'It is difficult to speak of our troubles,' he said.

I canted my head. 'I've had some of my own.'

He nodded, grew pensive. 'My sister is the youngest of four wives,' he said. 'Her husband is a member of the Alireza family.'

'The merchant,' I said.

Abdullah worked his jaw, studied his cup. 'He is my mother's uncle's cousin. Had my father known that such bitter fruit could grow from the same tree that had sweetened my mother, he would never have allowed the marriage. My sister has divorced him, but he refuses and is demanding her return. She won't go.'

'She shouldn't have to if he is mean to her,' I said, remembering the story of my grandmother, her sock of pennies.

'If she does not return,' Abdullah said, 'Alireza will come for the child.'

My heart hit the cage of my chest, just the way it had when my grandfather had first come for me.

'He can't do that,' I said.

Abdullah looked at me. 'According to our law and custom, the child belongs to the father.'

I heard Mason come up behind us, saw Abdullah draw back and grow silent. I leaned in. 'Bring Nadia and the baby to the compound,' I whispered. 'They can stay with us.' I wanted to say more, but I stood, dusted my hands, and looked beyond the trees. 'Is it okay if I ride Badra?' I asked. 'Just around the edge?'

Abdullah glanced at Mason before nodding his head. 'Be watchful of snakes,' he cautioned.

I raised my shoulders. 'Can't be any worse than copperheads,' I said.

'Just stay close,' Mason said, his voice low, 'real close.'

I clucked as I approached Badra and held out the melon rind. She moved fluid as mercury, lipping the fruit from my fingers, the other mares gathering close, snuffling. When I swung up and onto her withers and directed her out of the trees, she pranced and shimmied, kicking up sand.

'I know, girl,' I said. I held her to a walk, thinking about Nadia. I had no idea what Arab law had to say about women divorcing their husbands, what rights Nadia might have, if any. I wanted to believe that Abdullah would take care of his sister, and I imagined him on his horse, sword drawn, ready to defend Nadia against the awful Alireza.

Badra threw her head, and I patted her shoulder to calm her, then checked to see that we were out of sight before gathering two handfuls of her mane. I lay low on her neck like I had seen the jockeys do and squeezed my knees tight around her barrel, felt the engine of her haunches bunch and release, the first rough leap forward, and then her body planing out like we were skimming the sea.

I squinted against the onrush of air, the wind pulling loose my scarf before I could catch it. Badra lengthened her stride as I whooped my joy into her ear. I'd set my sights on a distant acacia, alone in its stand against the sky—just far enough, the men would never know—but we reached the tree faster than I could have imagined. I sat back, tucked my bottom, gave the rope a gentle pull. 'Whoa,' I said, then again, 'Badra, whoa!'

But Badra didn't whoa. We ramped right past the acacia, and now I was tugging hard. No real saddle, no bit to clamp down, and as I hauled back on the rope, I felt my balance tip, my center give way, and I rolled off in a backward somersault. I landed on my back, knocked the wind right out of myself, and sprawled flat. I lay still, sucking air, inventorying injury, then pushed myself to a sit and watched Badra disappear behind a low dune.

I brought up my knees, rested my elbows, dropped my head. It had been years since I'd been thrown from a horse, and that had been Sonny, who once startled sideways as I walked him up the county road, then broke into a bucking run that left me hanging by one boot until my foot pulled free. I'd hit hard, but I was just a girl, and I jumped up before I knew I might be hurt. It took me a minute to discover what had spooked Sonny: in the barrow pit, a broken-backed mutt, spun aside by a passing car, lay panting, its teeth drawn back in a rictus grin. I had caught Sonny and gone for my grandfather, thinking he might save the dog. *A mercy,* he had said as he raised the shovel. It was the sound of the bit through bone that never left me.

I emptied the sand from my boots, then rocked back, peered skyward, took a deep breath. I stood with a groan, began slogging back to where a pale twist of smoke wreathed the treetops. Some part of me wanted to follow Badra, take my chances in the Empty Quarter with the hyenas and snakes rather than face Mason's anger, present Abdullah with the news that I had lost his beloved mare. By the time I reached the well, my neck and chest were damp with sweat, my shirt wicking my skin. Whatever

225

wind had caught my scarf had carried it far away, and my hair had whipped and knotted. The two remaining horses whinnied at my scent, and the men looked up from their coffee. Mason stood, his eyes wide, and took me by the elbows.

'Are you okay?' he asked.

'I'm fine,' I said. 'Just bruised, is all.' I turned to Abdullah. 'She bolted,' I said.

The concern on Abdullah's face eased into amusement. 'Badra does not bolt,' he said, and leaned back on one elbow, 'but you owe me no apology. It is the emir's prize mare you have lost.'

Mason let out a hard breath. 'Great, Gin. That's just great.'

'I'll take one of the other horses,' I said, 'go look for her.'

'The hell you will.' Mason planted his hands on his hips and looked at Abdullah. 'What should we do?'

Abdullah lifted his cup. 'We should drink our coffee,' he said. 'Badra will come back to water. It is only a matter of time.' He nodded in the direction from which we had come. 'I will lead you to Abqaiq and return for her. It is nothing.'

Mason sniffed and spat. 'We'd better get going then.'

'Haste comes from the devil,' Abdullah said. 'We will finish our coffee.' He shifted his gaze away from Mason's quick look and began to chat pleasantly, naming the various landforms, telling us which tribe lived where, the invisible routes his people had traveled for centuries. I sat down a ways from Mason and watched Abdullah trace the flight of a kestrel with his hand, the small raptor flushing a tight flock of turtledoves that spilled away from

226

us, wings clapping. He recalled for us the names of famous falcons he had witnessed at the hunt, how the sheikhs who owned them prized the birds above all else. I wanted to raise my camera, capture him resting so easy, his fingers inscribing the air, but I didn't dare, not because of him but because of Mason, who sat with his back stiff, dark-browed and sullen.

'It's so beautiful,' I said. 'You must love it here.'

Abdullah offered a patient smile. 'No Arab loves the desert,' he said. 'We love water and green trees. There is nothing in the desert, and what man needs nothing?' He looked at Mason, then focused on the dying fire. 'Now we see how wrong we were.'

'No wrong that can't be made right,' Mason said. He straightened, and I sensed some shift, his face animate again. 'You know as well as I do that the company has you over a barrel, and they'll keep you there until you stand up, say you won't take it anymore.' He took up a stick, poked at the embers. 'You're the owners of this plantation. One of these days, you're going to wake up and realize that.'

Abdullah's gaze sharpened at the tone in Mason's voice. 'We are not sleeping,' he said, then glanced my way before dipping his head, measuring his words. 'When I returned to Arabia with my education,' he said, 'I went into the field and offered my opinions. Mr. Fullerton acted as though what I said mattered, and he took note, but when I began to ask questions about certain operational inconsistencies and reporting, he refused to answer. Within a week, I was no longer an engineer but a driver for the Americans. He claimed that my translation skills were too valuable to waste.' He picked up a small rock, weighed its heft. 'Whether

227

they are Saudi or American doesn't matter. The princes fatten at the banquet while we beg scraps at their feet.'

'Amen,' Mason said. He flipped his cigarette to the fire and peered at Abdullah. 'The way I see it, nationalization is the only way you're ever going to get a fair shake. Once you get your own people trained and educated, Americans will be as useless as the Italians, expedient labor you can ship back out.' He squinted one eye. 'Just don't say you heard it from me.' When Abdullah didn't respond, Mason sat back. 'You're right,' he said. 'We can talk more about this later. We just need to enjoy our coffee.' He held out his cup. 'You know why Arabian horses hold their tails up so high?' When Abdullah hesitated, Mason quirked his mouth. 'So the wind can blow in their ears and out their asses.'

Abdullah stared at him for a moment, then broke into an appreciative laugh. I felt the mood lift and was grateful, but then Abdullah shifted and looked at Mason, new seriousness in his eyes.

'The explosion at the stabilization plant,' he said. 'Two of the men who died were my cousins.'

Mason rested his arms on his knees and nodded. 'I'm sorry,' he said.

Abdullah glanced at me as though he wasn't sure he should continue in my presence. When I dropped my gaze, straightened the hem of my shirt, he continued. 'The pipes ruptured because they were not sound,' he said.

Mason nodded. 'The company should never have allowed that to happen.'

'Why,' Abdullah asked, 'was it allowed to happen?'

'The pipes, you mean.' Mason pushed out a

228

breath through his nose, raised one shoulder. 'Laziness, procrastination. Failure to oversee operations.'

Abdullah studied him for a long moment, and I could see that he was gauging Mason's sincerity. 'No man can serve two masters,' he said, and Mason brought up his eyes.

'Who do you mean?' he asked.

'You are senior staff,' Abdullah said, 'a company man, yet you claim allegiance to the Arab workers' cause.'

Mason flipped his cigarette to the fire. 'We both know that if you shut down the pipes, you shut down the money. I'm not saying it's an excuse.'

'No,' Abdullah said, 'there is no excuse for causing an innocent man's death.'

Mason looked up, squinting against the light. 'Causing?'

'What do you call it when repairs are ordered and paid for but never made?' Abdullah asked. 'What do you call it when deception puts money in the pockets of the rich and results in the death of the poor?'

Mason held his gaze. 'I call it business as usual,' he said.

'Not here,' Abdullah said. 'Not until the oil came.' He looked away, then back at Mason. 'My cousins died because of greed. I want to know whose purse their blood has filled.'

'You think someone was skimming?' Mason asked.

'I don't think,' Abdullah said. 'I know. It is why I am a driver instead of an engineer.'

Mason hesitated, then lit another cigarette, let out a slow breath. 'It would have to be someone in

Maintenance,' he said. 'Supply.'

'Buck Bodeen,' I said, and both men looked at me as though they had forgotten I was there. 'He was the department head in Abqaiq. Maybe he got caught,' I said. 'Maybe that's why he and Betsy had to leave.'

Mason stared at me for a moment, then gave a slow nod and dropped his eyes to the fire. 'Just not soon enough,' he said. He turned to Abdullah. 'Who would have taken those orders?'

Abdullah looked at me, his face drawn. 'My cousin and brother by marriage,' he said.

Mason tipped his cup. 'Alireza,' he said, and Abdullah nodded.

'He is a dangerous and brutal man,' Abdullah said. 'He is no favorite of the emir.'

We all sat in silence a long moment. When both men again turned their eyes my way, I knew what they were thinking—that they had made a mistake by speaking of such things in front of a woman.

'I won't tell,' I said, 'not even Ruthie,' but my grudge against Alireza was growing by the minute.

Abdullah dipped his head once, then moved to snuff the fire and scour the cups with sand before packing them carefully with the last of the food. Mason climbed on the little black mare, grimacing as he settled his sore seat, then reached down and pulled me up behind him. When Abdullah mounted the bay and led us out of the trees, I took a final look back, hoping I might catch some glimpse of Badra hightailing it toward us, unwilling to be left behind, but all I saw was the tamarisk stand and the acacia tree that had been my goal. By the time we filed back into Abqaiq, the sun had drifted toward the horizon, and I knew that Yash was already gone

230

and that Abdullah would be searching for Badra by moonlight.

I peered up at the sky, knew just where the guiding stars would be. *I could go with you,* I wanted to say. *I could help you find her,* but I knew I would never be allowed. Mason's mood had grown more sullen, and I knew he was angry—at Buck Bodeen and Alireza, at the company, at me.

I was showered and in bed when he came from his study, still carrying the drink he had been refilling since we arrived home. He stood in the doorway, considering me from a distance, his face half in the shadows.

'You let her run, didn't you?' he asked, his voice flat.

'I'll be more careful next time,' I said. 'I promise.'

'There's not going to be a next time,' he said. 'You want to ride, you go to the Hobby Farm like the other wives.' He turned and disappeared down the hallway.

'Never let the sun go down on your wrath,' his mother once told me, her single piece of advice before we left Shawnee, but I didn't care. The days that I had imagined with Mason as a comfort now seemed more like a trial. *I wish he'd just leave,* I said to myself, and the thought startled me. When had I begun to wish him away?

I didn't realize I had been asleep when I woke later that night, still alone in the bed. At first, I thought that it was the sound of the horses that I heard, but then I made out the low murmur of men's voices. I pulled on my robe, walked down the hallway, and peered around the corner. Abdullah had returned and sat with Mason at the dining table, his *ghutra* folded away from his face.

231

I saw how his glistening black hair fell against his shoulders, beautiful, but not like a girl's—like an animal's, I thought, or maybe a kind of man I had never seen before—and I remembered the story of Samson and Delilah. What would it feel like to hold that hair in my hands?

'Mason?' At the sound of my voice, their heads jerked up, and Abdullah's face opened with surprise.

Mason leaned back, let out a heavy sigh. 'Gin, for God's sake, will you just go back to bed?'

Abdullah looked quickly at Mason, a flash of disapproval crossing his face before he pulled his *ghutra* close. 'Badra is safely home,' he said. 'I wanted to return this.' He pulled my blue scarf from inside the fold of his *thobe* and laid it on the table.

'Thank you,' I said, and drew my robe a little closer. 'Are you talking about the explosion?' I asked.

Mason lifted one hand, let it drop. 'Bodeen is gone,' he said. 'Alireza is untouchable. Like fingering ghosts.'

I folded my arms. 'Do you want coffee?' I asked.

'Coffee would be good,' Mason said without looking, and I knew that he was still angry with me.

Abdullah lowered his gaze as I walked past him and into the kitchen. I pulled out one of Betsy's tea towels—this one Friday—and considered its stitch as I waited for the pot to perk, wondering again what had happened to Sunday, whether Betsy had known or even suspected what her husband was up to all those hours he spent in his study, building his ship in a bottle—and that is when I remembered the red leather book.

232

I found the volume in its place, the ledger sheets still pasted in back. I held it for a moment, hopeful that my hunch was right, not only because I wanted to help Mason and Abdullah, but because we now had this enemy in common: because of Alireza, Nadia was in danger, and Burt was dead. I arranged a neat tray with three cups and saucers, sugar and cream, added a plate of Yash's macaroons, and tucked the book beneath my arm.

'*Ashkurik,*' Abdullah said as I placed his coffee in front of him.

'You're welcome,' I said, acting as collected as I could in my bathrobe. I held out the book to Mason. 'Take a look at this,' I said. 'The last few pages.'

He peered at me for a moment, then took the volume, rested it on the table, and flipped to the end. I took my chair and watched him read down one page, and then the next. 'This is it,' he said. 'Bodeen kept a record.' He looked at Abdullah with something like amazement. 'It's been right here in my own house the whole time.'

I wanted to say that it wasn't his house, not even Bodeen's, that it all belonged to the company, but the look on Abdullah's face as Mason moved the volume in front of him kept me quiet. He wasn't eager or satisfied but grim as he took the book, and I realized that what he was seeing wasn't numbers but the lives of his people reduced to scribbles on a page.

'Bodeen put in a requisition for supplies,' Mason said, dragging his finger down the column, wrinkling his forehead, 'but it looks like he pocketed half the money, gave the other half to Alireza.' He pushed back, and the skin around

233

his mouth tightened. 'It's not just about graft. It's about what's wrong with this company,' he said. 'It's all tied together. Put the least skilled, lowest-paid workers on the front line. Something like this happens, there's always more where they came from, right? Pay a little blood money and walk away.' He tapped the ledger, raised his eyes to Abdullah's. 'I'm not done with this,' he said. 'Not by a long shot.'

Abdullah held his gaze a moment, gauging Mason's conviction, but Mason didn't have to convince me of anything. He would never walk away from a wrong that needed to be made right. Not Mason McPhee.

'What about Lucky?' I asked. 'Maybe he can help.'

Mason slid his eyes away. 'It's hard to say where Lucky is in all this,' he said. 'Right now, it's just between the three of us.' He closed the book, handed it to me. 'Put this back where you found it,' he said. 'It's been there for this long. It will keep a while longer.' He stubbed his cigarette. 'Abdullah and I still have some business to take care of,' he said, and I realized I was being dismissed.

I never liked being bossed, but there I stood in my nightclothes. I took the book to the study, slid it into place. Instead of going back to bed, I turned off the light and sat in Mason's chair, listening to the muted voices of the men. No matter how pretty I was, no matter how smart and brave, it would never be enough to earn me a place at that table.

What if this were my study? I wondered. My job, my salary, my house? Because Ruthie was wrong— we weren't earning more money than we knew what to do with. Mason was. I thought of my photos in

234

the file drawer and felt just like that: as though a little bit of room had been made for me, a slip of space that I should feel grateful for.

CHAPTER TWELVE

Mason woke me the next morning by standing at the foot of the bed and rocking the mattress with his knee. When I opened my eyes, I saw him in his boxers, buttoning his khaki work shirt from bottom to top. 'I want you to stay inside the compound until I get off this tour,' he said, twisting his cuffs.

I sat up and tried to focus. I thought it was because I had let Badra run, or maybe it had something to do with Alireza and Bodeen, but Mason shook his head. 'We got bigger concerns. Word just came down that something is heating up between Egypt and Israel. Probably only a bunch of saber rattling, but it could turn serious.' He flapped his pants from their fold. 'Some of the men are already flying their families out to Rome. If you can't promise me you'll stay in this compound and mean it, I'm going to send you out right now.' He strapped on his belt, picked up his duffel, and slapped on his cap before stepping close, lifting my chin. 'And not a word about Bodeen and the ledger, okay?' When I gave a confused nod, he peered at me for a moment, then kissed my forehead and walked out of the room. When I heard the Land Cruiser grind into gear, I pulled on my robe and moved my pout to the kitchen, where Yash kneaded bread.

'I don't even know what this thing with Egypt

235

and Israel is all about,' I said.

'It is about territory,' he said, and gave me a ball of dough to round and flatten. 'The gentiles will not allow the Israelis to have more, and the Israelis will take no less.'

It dawned on me that I was living in the Promised Land. 'The Valley of Abraham,' I said.

Yash nodded. 'Christians, Jews, Muslims, all claim Abraham as their father, and see what a happy family it has made.' He tightened his lips. 'Since the creation of Israel, there has been conflict at the borders, but Egypt is amassing troops, and Israel will not be intimidated. The Arabs who have spent centuries attempting to destroy one another will gladly join together against the Israeli colonizers.' Yash grew pensive. 'Years ago, the British, in their ineffable fashion, promised Faisal a united Arab nation, then pieced out Israel and Palestine behind his back. He doesn't show himself to be a vengeful man, but one wonders about the fury of his dreams.'

I remembered my grandfather's fiery sermons from the book of Revelation. 'The Bible says that the Antichrist will bring all the gentiles together,' I said, 'and then comes the Tribulation.'

'If memory serves me,' Yash said, 'it entails a great deal of pain and suffering.'

'The Seven Seals and the Four Horsemen of the Apocalypse,' I said, 'and pestilence.'

The doorbell rang, and Yash looked up at the clock's early hour. 'Ah, yes,' he sighed.

Lucky busted in before either of us could reach the hallway, brandishing a bottle, Ruthie nudging in against him, looking like she hadn't slept a wink.

'Genuine Cuban rum is what we got here,' he

236

announced, 'straight from Bahrain.' He knocked back a swallow and hissed through his teeth. 'Damn, that's fine.' He handed me the bottle and looked around. 'Where's that husband of yours?'

'He had an early meeting,' I said. I took a drink of the rum, found it surprisingly sweet.

Lucky's smile tightened. 'What meeting?'

I lifted one shoulder. 'Maybe it's about Israel and Egypt,' I said.

'Hell,' Lucky said, dropping back and cutting his eyes at Ruthie. 'I talked to the fellas at the airbase, and they say it's a big fuss over nothing. The militia has it under control.'

'That's a bunch of bullshit, and you know it,' Ruthie said, and took the bottle. 'When have these people ever been under control?'

'Listen,' Lucky said, 'I've got my sidearm loaded and my machete nice and sharp. Arabs want to come over that fence, I say let them come.'

She rolled her eyes toward me, her skin pale in the harsh light of the kitchen. 'I'm headed to the airport, Gin. They're flying me out.' She lowered her face, her voice distant and strained. 'They're always shipping us out somewhere.' She handed me the bottle, lit a cigarette, and I saw that her hand was shaking as she rubbed her temple with one thumb. 'I have such a headache,' she said. 'It must be the rum.' She let out a breath. 'I've got to use the bathroom before we go.'

Lucky waited until she was out of earshot before looking at me from beneath his brow. 'She needs to get on out of here for a while,' he said. 'I don't want no one giving her a hard time.' I took another drink, then passed the bottle to him, looked down, and wiped my cheeks. He rested his hand on my shoulder, gave it a gentle squeeze. 'That's the girl,' he said, then straightened and looked at me with new seriousness. 'Listen, sis, there wasn't no meeting this morning.' I brought up my eyes, and his face took on a pained expression. 'That boy of yours is on some kind of crusade, and I'm worried he don't know what he's getting into. I told him he'd better leave it alone, but he won't listen.'

'He won't listen to anybody,' I said.

'Stubborn as a mule,' Lucky agreed. 'Ruthie don't like how tight a rein he keeps on you.' He took another drink of rum and passed the bottle to me, like we were toasting good times. 'What's he up to, anyway? I mean besides all this rabble-rousing about labor. He's got some big bone he's chewing on.'

I had forgotten how smooth real liquor could be, how it could wash down any misgivings I might have about breaking another of my promises to Mason. I took a big swallow, passed the bottle back, and lowered my voice so that Yash couldn't hear.

'Mason thinks that Buck Bodeen was cooking the books, skimming money from Materials Supply,' I said. 'That's what caused the explosion at the plant.'

Lucky peered at me for a moment and then grimaced and wagged his head. 'Bodeen,' he said. 'Always trying to run the numbers.' He nodded once. 'You tell Mason I'm behind him on this all the way. Anything I can do, he just says the word.' He straightened when we heard Ruthie come out of the bathroom. He considered the bottle, took a last drink, then handed it back to me. 'Keep what's left for when this mess is over,' he said. 'We'll have us a fine celebration.'

'We're leaving the Volkswagen,' Ruthie said.

'Lucky has his pickup, and there's no reason you shouldn't use the car while I'm gone.' She tugged at Lucky's hand, and I moved with them to the door, where Ruthie hugged me hard. 'If things get too bad,' she said, 'you can always come to Rome. I'll take you shopping. Via Condotti is the best.' She lifted her shoulders. 'I just hope they'll let me back in.' She looked out over the compound. 'I don't know what it is about this place,' she said. 'At first you don't want to come here, and then you never want to leave.'

Lucky pulled her close, and she leaned her head into his chest, wiped her eyes. 'Let's get this over with,' she said, and I watched them get in the pickup and drive off down the road, then took one last drink from the bottle before taking it to the kitchen. When Yash came in, he found me at the counter, eating almonds and staring drunkenly at the blinded window, wondering what it would be like to be with Ruthie in Rome.

'Ruthie is leaving,' I said as though to myself. 'Flying to Rome until this is over.'

Yash considered my words, then tied on his apron. 'It is a good day for *saag* and roti,' he said.

I sat at the counter, glum and silent, and watched him mix spinach with onion, garlic, ginger, and chickpeas. He fried several rounds of bread dough before moving them beneath the broiler to puff, then pulled them out with his tongs, spread one with ghee, and handed it to me.

'It is good to have comfort,' he said, 'in times of tribulation.'

I breathed in the turmeric and coriander, then lifted the napkin to my face, but too late—Yash had already seen that I was crying.

239

He stood awkward in his apron, then squared his shoulders like a soldier bringing himself into formation. 'Perhaps some more rum,' he said, 'in your tea.'

I shook my head, blew my nose into the napkin, which brought up Yash's eyebrows. 'I'm sorry,' I said. 'It's just that everything feels so wrong.'

'Remember where we are,' Yash said.

'This isn't funny,' I said.

He eased out a breath. 'No,' he said, 'it is not.' He tilted his head. 'If not rum, perhaps rummy?'

I smiled a little and stood to get the deck of cards, but Yash held out his hand.

'First,' he said, 'you will finish your lunch.'

'Who are you?' I asked. 'My mother?' He didn't answer but simply went on about his chores, and I finished my lunch and felt better.

*   *   *

Except for Ruthie's absence and my detention, that day and the next passed like so many others: I read, worked on crosswords for the paper, puttered in the garden, watched TV with my feet up while Yash vacuumed the carpets, and played more games of rummy than I had in the totality of my life. Not a single mention of Israel appeared in the *Sun and Flare* or any other paper we could read, but we listened to what news came over the radio, caught bits of President Nasser's inflamed speeches accusing Israel of hostilities and then Moshe Dayan's equally adamant rebuttals.

'Who is telling the truth?' I asked Yash one day over lunch, but he shrugged.

'The victor will write the history,' he said, rising

240

to resume his dusting, 'but the truth we may never know.'

'Maybe I'll go for a swim,' I said. I had been watching the children at their lessons, and, when they were done, sliding into the shallow end to mimic their movements.

Yash nodded his approval. 'An excellent decision,' he said. 'The moist air is good for your lungs.'

'Do you know how?' I asked.

'Of course,' he said. 'It was a part of my education. I excelled at water polo.' And then, as if reading my mind: 'It is a game for boys, so it will do no good to ask me to teach you.'

'Abdullah's sister is teaching me,' I said. 'To swim, anyway. I met her when Lucky got us lost in the desert. We might still be there if Abdullah hadn't found us.'

Yash straightened and looked at me. 'Did his mother feed you her famous locusts?' he asked.

'Just dates,' I said, 'and lots of tea. But I loved it, Yash. It felt so good to be out *there* instead of stuck in this house all day.'

'I'm sure that I wouldn't know,' he said.

'But even if you can't drive, you're a man. You can go wherever you want,' I said. 'And I bet you've ridden a horse before.'

'It will come as a shock,' he said, 'but the Arabs did not bring forth the horse from their own spit and a handful of sand.' He rested his elbow at his waist. 'I would wager that the Manipuri horses of India have carried soldiers into more wars and raced to more victories than any breed in history, including your Bedouin's precious Arabian ponies.'

'He's not my Bedouin,' I said, but I secretly liked

the sound of it.

Yash sniffed and went on. 'The Manipuri came with the Tartar invasion, as did the game of ground polo.' He looked at me. 'Surely,' he said.

'I know,' I said. 'I've seen it on TV. But I bet women can't play that either.'

'Not so,' he said. 'As far back as the fifth century, in Persia, in China, women and their horses have competed on the polo field.'

'Then I want to learn,' I said, and glanced at him before lifting my cup. 'Maybe Abdullah will teach me.'

He saw that I was teasing him and tucked his mouth to the side before growing more pensive.

'In the military, I rode a fine horse.' He nodded, remembering. 'But it is different here for me than it is for you. You think of me as a free man, but even if I had the means to buy or borrow a horse, I am not at liberty to come and go as I please.'

'You make it sound like you're a slave or something,' I said.

Yash looked at me with a kind of fondness, as though he found my ignorance endearing. 'Slavery was abolished in this country five years ago,' he said. 'We are now called houseboys and maids.' I watched him push through the swinging doors into the kitchen, then turned back to my lunch.

'Yash?' I called.

He cracked one door. 'More coffee?' he asked.

'I just wanted to say thanks,' I said. 'Sometimes I forget.'

'*A votre service*,' he said. He lifted his nose. 'French, I can teach you.' And he let the door pip shut.

242

*   *   *

Instead of walking to the recreation center that afternoon, I drove the Volkswagen as though a few blocks might gain me some distance. Without Ruthie, the camp felt even smaller, as though it were closing in around me. The pool was empty, the Arab workers standing about with little to do but watch. Whenever my eyes met theirs, they looked away, and I felt an unease settle into the pit of my stomach. The Bedouin boys at the snack bar, the old Arab we called Tommy who ran the movie projector, Faris in my garden, Habib at the gate— they were part of my every minute, made my life in that place possible. I remembered Abdullah's words: *We are everywhere, part of everything, beginning to end.*

I practiced swimming underwater, came up for a breath, and saw Candy Fullerton mincing toward me in a lemon-drop bandeau and matching mules, her blond hair pushed back by a polka-dot band. I groaned when she waved brightly and settled her beach bag on the lounger next to mine. I climbed the short ladder and wrapped the towel at my waist, wanting more than anything to make a quick exit, but I took a deep breath and settled in beside her, thinking that she, if anyone, would know what was happening outside the gates.

'What's going on out there, anyway?' I asked.

She stopped applying Coppertone long enough to look at me blankly.

'Israel and Egypt?' I said.

'Oh, that.' She flapped her hand, then dug through her bag for her compact. 'You live here long enough, you don't pay attention to that stuff

243

anymore. If it gets too bad, they'll evacuate.'

'Ruthie already flew out,' I said.

'It's just as well. She doesn't really belong here, anyway.' When I stiffened, she brought up her mirror, applied a thick layer of white cream to her nose. 'Don't get huffy. I'm just saying she doesn't fit in, that's all.' She rolled out her lipstick, bowed her mouth, and made three perfect swipes of pearly pink. 'Maybe now you'll have time for that golf lesson,' she said, and smoothed the pouch of her stomach. 'I haven't had a putting partner since Betsy flew the coop.'

I waited for a moment, thinking that I could ask her about Buck Bodeen, remembered what Mason had said about keeping quiet. I rolled my towel and pulled on my dress. 'I really need to get home,' I said.

'Too bad,' she said. 'Your tan is fading out.' She pushed up her breasts and dipped a finger into her cleavage as though she were checking its depth. 'Carlo Leoni is retaking my portrait this afternoon. The first time, the light was all wrong.' She hardened her mouth. 'Maddy told me you brought your houseboy on the bus.'

'I was sick,' I said.

'Next time, just stay home.' She pushed on her dark glasses, then lifted her chin. 'Not that you care,' she said, 'but I got a telegram from my mother. Pat's boat got hit. They flew him out to Japan.' She jerked her head. 'It wouldn't have killed you to be nice, you know.'

'I'm sorry,' I said, but she acted like she didn't hear. I stood for a long moment before turning for the exit. As bad as I felt about Pat, I was glad to be back in the Volkswagen, glad to be leaving Candy

244

behind. Back home, I found Yash in the kitchen, frowning down at a large manila envelope.

'What is it?' I asked.

He handed it to me. 'I am not in the habit of opening your personal correspondence,' he said, his voice notched with irritation.

I tore the flap, pulled out the photo that Carlo Leoni had taken of me and Ruthie on the dhow, the Arab boy tucked at our knees, all of us smiling, close to laughter, and in the corner in flowing cursive: *Amo le mie due belle ragazze! Carlo.*

'Who delivered this?' I asked.

'The pirate,' Yash said.

'You know him?' I asked.

'I know of him.' He bent to check the drip of the still, adjusted the coil.

'He's not a pirate,' I said, 'not really.'

'If he is not a pirate'—Yash straightened and looked at me—'then what is he?'

'A great photographer.' I held out the print. 'See?' But he waved it away.

'Virtue is in the subject, not in the man who captures it.' He pulled out a can opener and punctured a tin of tomatoes.

'Did he say where he was going?' I asked.

'Sometimes it is better not to know,' Yash said, then reluctantly cast his eyes to the back porch. 'He has asked for coffee.'

I hesitated a moment before rising. When I swung open the door, I jumped back like I had stepped on a snake. Carlo sat on the step, placidly smoking. He flipped his cigarette to the grass and stood to face me, the brow of his green scarf stained with sweat, his shirt unbuttoned down his chest, his camera hanging heavy and loose.

245

'*Bella,*' he said, 'I knew you would come.'

I pressed my hand to my chest, tried to quiet the hammering. 'I wanted to say thank-you for bringing the photo,' I said.

He reached for my fingers, held them at his lips, peered up at me. 'You are like a madonna, you see. It is in the young boy's eyes. I want it to be cherished.'

I felt a giggle coming on, heard Yash make a coughing noise behind me, and eased back my hand.

'I have an appointment,' Carlo said, looking around as though the yard stretched for miles. 'I wonder if you might help me find my way.'

I remembered Candy and her portrait and then thought of the Volkswagen parked at the curb, the rare chance to talk with Carlo about his photographs. I wouldn't be going far, I told myself, only inside the compound.

'I'll be right back,' I said, and went in and grabbed my camera, ignoring the look of disapproval on Yash's face. Carlo followed me to the car and opened my door, watched me slide in before walking slowly around, a diminutive swagger, and settling into the passenger seat. When I glanced at the dagger that rode his hip, his eyebrows leaped and settled. 'An unarmed man is like a castrated bull, good only for slaughter,' he said, then laughed when I popped the clutch, killed the engine, and started it again. 'Ah,' he said. 'You drive like an American.'

I smoothed out in second gear and kept our speed at a steady ten miles per hour. 'What's going on out there?' I asked. 'Anything new?'

Carlo struck a match. 'There is nothing new. It is

246

a story as old as the sands.' He waved the match in an extravagant gesture of extinguishment, inhaled deeply. 'Israel has attacked Egypt and destroyed its air force. The Bedouin Militia has been called in to protect Aramco's compounds from Arab *malcontenti,* but it will be over soon enough.' He considered me from the corner of his eye. 'You Americans worry that in the face of your Zionist sympathies, the Saudis will banish you from the country.'

'I'm not worried,' I said. I hit third gear, took a left without slowing, fearing I would never get us started again if I stalled. Carlo let out a low laugh and pointed toward the rec center.

'We should stop for a swim,' he said casually, 'to relax.'

'I don't think you're allowed in,' I said.

'Nonsense,' he said. 'Who can refuse me?' He eyed my bare arms. 'I can tell by the strength of your shoulders that you are a strong swimmer.'

'I'm learning,' I said. I drove even more slowly as we approached the center, pulling to the curb behind a pickup in hopes we wouldn't be noticed. I couldn't imagine what rumors Candy would spread if she spied me in Carlo's company.

Carlo cocked his head and gazed at me, a cigarette between his teeth. 'I have seen your photographs,' he said. 'There is a spirit in them, a spark of genius.'

I felt my cheeks pink, the smile break out across my face before I could stop it. 'I've still got a lot to learn,' I said.

He ran his tongue over his molars, flared his nostrils. 'Let Carlo teach you.'

I stared straight ahead, gripping the steering

wheel as though I might be torn away. 'When?' I asked.

He measured the horizon. 'The sun is right,' he said, 'and now is always the right time.'

'What about your appointment?' I asked.

'It will wait,' he said. He gazed at me, his eyes half-lidded. 'I could take you to my studio, show you how to use my darkroom. *Mia casa è tua casa, sì?* It is business between professionals.'

I held my breath, my head swirling with possibility and a chance to get back at Candy. I considered Carlo's face, open now, as though he were allowing me to see all that I wanted—the noble breadth of his forehead, the chasteness of his intent, the way his eyes lifted when he smiled.

'You'll have to drive,' I said. I swung open my door and went around to the passenger side, but Carlo remained in his seat. He pinched his cigarette, let out a slow curl of smoke, and squinted up at me.

'Tell me, *bella*,' he said. 'Where is your husband? You know I would need his permission.'

I felt myself flush as though I were the one who had been caught in flagrant seduction. I held his gaze for a moment, then rummaged my purse for a scrap of paper, wrote a few sentences, and signed Mason's name. 'There,' I said.

Carlo considered the note. 'You are crazy,' he said. 'Sorrow for me, I value this in a woman.' He slid out, eyeing me as he passed, eased into the driver's side, and tapped the car into gear. When we reached the gate, he stopped and presented the paper to Habib as though he himself were convinced of its authenticity. They exchanged a few sentences of Arabic, Carlo's voice loud with good nature as he gestured my way and then at the note, until Habib stepped back and watched us pass. I craned around to see him peering after us as though he wasn't quite sure what had happened.

We broke out onto the road in first, the transmission screaming, until Carlo bucked us into second, then third and fourth, the Volkswagen rattling with speed. He never slowed as we headed up the highway that would lead us north but dodged and darted, hunched and gesticulating. *'Stupido! Idiota! Imbecille!'* I turned my attention to the landscape flying by: low-lying hills, piles of stone, animals grazing on scrub—I might have believed myself back in Shawnee. I looked at Carlo, leaned over the wheel like Odysseus guiding his ship through the straits, wind furling his scarf, and felt my own hair tugging free. I held to the window frame, but he swayed with the car, loose and easy.

'I didn't bring any water,' I said.

'Did you bring your camera?'

'It's in back,' I said.

'Then we will survive.'

I looked toward the horizon, took a deep breath to settle my nerves. What am I doing? I thought. If the company caught me, I'd be on the next plane out, and Mason could lose everything he had worked for. But the farther we traveled from Abqaiq, the less worried I was, as though the desert itself might protect me, take me in. When low black shadows broke the sandy swales like a fleet of black ships, I pointed, and Carlo nodded.

'Bedu,' he said.

'Have you ever visited them?' I asked, searching for the tent with the single white stripe.

'Many times,' he said. 'They are like family to

249

me. In the beginning, we Italians lived here like *Roma*, like Gypsies, *sì*?' He gestured to the air. 'We were divided into camps by race and nationality.'

'Segregated,' I said, and he nodded.

'Saudi Camp, Indian Camp, Italian Camp, all of us clustered around American Camp like beggar dogs.' His face took on real seriousness. 'The king allowed the import of Italians on one condition: that our food and housing remain poorer than that of the Saudi laborers.'

'Not an easy trick,' I said.

He lifted his shoulders. 'To the Americans, we were all of us coolies,' he said, and the corners of his eyes creased. 'Yet they came to the Italian camp for our spaghetti and our wine. We had once fought as enemies, but now we celebrated each night as though we had ended another war, dancing until dawn.' He chuckled. 'The single girls, how they swooned for me!'

I tried to imagine a younger Carlo. 'Were you a pirate then?' I asked.

He clucked his tongue. 'I was born a pirate,' he said.

I laughed, sucked my lips, tasted salt, told myself not to think about water. I reached for my camera, placed the lens at the edge of the open window, and adjusted the shutter. An acacia, a jut of rock, the common sky—nothing I could frame until a gazelle broke the plane, zigzagging before us like a rocket on springs. Three camels appeared in the distance and watched our approach with lazy curiosity. I snapped a shot as we tracked by.

'What do you see in the camels?' Carlo asked.

'I don't know. Just that they are there, I guess.'

'That is no reason to waste film,' he said.

'Their shape,' I said, 'their color.' I considered for a moment. 'The way they stand like a three-dimensional triangle. A pyramid. They aren't casting shadows, just the dark patches beneath their bellies, like little pools of oil.'

'*Buono.* I like how you learn,' he said, and I felt a spark of pleasure.

'Ruins?' I asked. 'Is that what we're looking for?'

He held out his hand. 'It is all ruin,' he said, then motioned that I should pay attention. A series of wavelike dunes captured the light in an apricot pool. Each second, the division of sky, sun, and sand shifted, demanded that I adjust, open, allow a shadow, make it disappear. When I turned in my seat and focused on Carlo, he drew himself upright.

'I am *piccolino,*' he said, 'a small man. It is up to you to capture my *grandezza.*' He gave me his profile, peering into the distance, then slowly turned his eyes on me, and I felt a jolt of expectation, as though something were about to be revealed.

'Am I a robber?' he asked roughly, and lifted his chin. 'Perhaps.' He pinched his eyebrows, darkened his gaze. 'A beggar? Never.' He creased his broad forehead. 'Always remember that seeing is not knowing. You are *piccola,* but I will teach you to be big.' He relaxed, lit a cigarette. 'There is a diver,' he said, 'who works on the drilling platform to secure the pipes underwater, a fellow Italian from the coast of Amalfi. A big man with fists like *this,*' he said, and placed his own fists together. 'As a boy, he worked with his kinsmen to haul the big boats to harbor with the strength of his bare hands.' Carlo paused, caught in a moment of wonder. 'What a thing it must have been to pull a ship from the sea!'

'Like landing a leviathan,' I said, remembering Jonah's whale.

'Yet he is afraid,' Carlo said with some pity, 'of the smallest spider and must be rescued and calmed like *una bambina*.'

I looked out across the desert, empty as any ocean. 'It's strange,' I said. 'I feel safer out here than I do inside the compound.'

'That is because you think you have somewhere to run,' he said, and winked. 'Like Carlo, you are a rascal and live by your wits.'

I rolled my eyes, but the truth was that I liked being compared to Carlo, his sense of invention and adventure. I porpoised my hand through the current of air, thought about what I knew of Carlo's life.

'Is it true,' I asked, 'what they say about you?'

'That I'm a great photographer?' he asked, but I saw the amusement in his face. He tilted back his head, gave me a rapscallion smile. 'I have captured the affection of an American beauty who is foolish enough to love me and keeps me clothed. I have my studio, my camera, my dagger. It is enough.'

'Do you ever get lonely living on the beach by yourself?'

'Who among us lives without loneliness?' he asked.

I thought of my nights without Mason, then opened my purse and took out the cigarettes, handed one to Carlo. 'Do you know Abdullah al-Jahni?' I asked.

'I have known him since he was a boy,' Carlo said. 'He used to come to my studio, curious and unafraid. We pretended great battles with our weapons.'

252

'I like him,' I said, 'and his sister, Nadia.'

'Ah, I remember her.' Carlo smiled with the memory. 'She took the veil so young. Maybe because of her father's death, maybe because her face captured the hearts of too many men.' He grew more serious. 'They never should have married her to that ruffian Alireza.'

'He's rotten to the core,' I said.

'Alireza is a dangerous man,' Carlo agreed. 'It is better that Nadia has returned to her family. She is safer there.'

'She wants a divorce,' I said. 'Can you do that in Arabia?'

'Easier than in Italy,' he said. 'We must plead our case to the pope himself, but here it takes little more than the speaking of the words 'I divorce you' three times. Still,' Carlo said, 'a man of Alireza's reputation would find it a great insult.'

'Abdullah told me that Alireza is going to take away her baby,' I said. 'I don't care what the law says. It's not right.' I was surprised by the sharpness of my voice, the orphan's grief flooding back. I thought for a moment that I should tell Carlo about the scam, that maybe he would help, but I turned my eyes back to the desert, held my tongue. 'Nadia is teaching me to swim,' I said more quietly.

'*Splendido,*' Carlo said, his humor restored. 'You and I, we will swim together.' He began singing what I thought must be some kind of opera, his voice rising and falling with the wind, and I felt the sadness blow away, laughing aloud with Carlo when his voice broke at the highest note. 'An aria,' he said. 'I am no Caruso, but I have the passion.' He looked at me. 'Photography is like poetry, but poets we must also be.'

253

I smiled, laid back my head, closed my eyes, and let the wind cool me. I didn't realize we were nearing Dhahran until Carlo began to gear down. I looked to where he pointed and saw a queue of official vehicles parked along the sandy shoulder of the road that led to the main gate.

'Hide the cameras,' he commanded. In the distance, I could see flames leaping, and then I heard the shrill call of the disaster whistle.

'Another explosion,' I said, but Carlo shook his head.

'No. It is something else.' We slowed as a Bedouin militiaman, bandoliers strapping his chest, separated himself from the cluster and waved us down. Carlo narrowed his eyes, took out the note I had written, and drew out his dagger, laid it alongside his leg, said, 'Don't speak a word, *bella.*' I gathered my scarf over my hair, pulled it across my face, tucked it at my throat as the man approached.

Carlo handed him the paper and gestured to the road, joking and offering cigarettes, but the man remained unsmiling as he bent to peer in at me, then walked back to confer with his fellows. Carlo's voice grew more serious.

'Listen to me,' he said. 'These are not local men. I have no sway with them. If they threaten to arrest us, you must act furious. Say that I am your driver, that your husband is an important Aramco executive, that he will be angry when he finds out your virtue has been questioned. It won't matter that he can't understand you.'

'I'm not afraid,' I said.

Carlo nodded to where the guards conferred. 'If you don't fear for yourself, then fear for me.'

We watched as the guard walked back to the car.

254

I pressed my shoulders straight, readying myself to act their superior, someone who might make them pay. The man leaned into Carlo's window, and I could smell his sour breath as he barked a few words. He glared at me, then dropped the paper into Carlo's lap and stepped away. We crept forward until we had cleared the queue, and I heard Carlo let out a sharp sigh.

'Mio Madre,' he said. 'You have taken years from my life, and the day is not yet over.'

'But it worked,' I said. 'We fooled them.'

He looked at me sideways and allowed a grin. 'If you are a good clown, they accept you as a clown.'

'What did he say is happening?' I leaned out my window and peered across the sand to the compound's boundaries, struck again by how much like an island it was, a fenced oasis moated by sand.

'The protests have spread to Dhahran,' Carlo said, peering through the windshield. 'These are university students. You have educated them well.'

'But why the compound?' I asked.

'Because of Aramco's ties to Israel,' he said. 'They want King Faisal to stand with his Arab kin and join the oil embargo.'

As we approached the turnoff leading to the main gate and guardhouse, I pulled out my camera. 'Drive closer,' I said.

'Pazza,' he said. 'I knew that you were a crazy woman.' He checked his rearview before steering us off the road and parking in the shaded lee of an ancient tamarisk. Above the wail of the siren, I could hear the pop and sizzle of small explosions. Maybe it was the adrenaline that allowed me not to think of the risks I was taking, or maybe it was Carlo's earlier praise that made me bold, or maybe

it was nothing more or less than my being that stubborn girl I had always been, acting first, willing to suffer the consequences later, but more than anything, what I wanted was to be where whatever was happening was happening.

I opened my door, whispered, 'Come on.'

'Where?' Carlo asked.

'I don't know,' I said. 'Just follow me.'

'I am a pirate,' he hissed. 'I have no need for a navigator.' But he trailed me anyway. We looked around before striking out across the sand, then hunkered our way along the fence that enclosed the compound, scrabbling forward against the pitch of rock and sand, the vacant desert on our left, on our right the bunkerlike buildings, the shouts of men, the slap of someone running down the street. Smoke twisted above us, settled like garland in the limbs of acacia. A hundred yards north of the administration building, the Dhahran hospital crowded the fence, three stories of shaded windows reflecting back the sun.

'There is nothing here,' Carlo whispered. 'We should return before we are discovered.' I ignored him and pushed against the wire, hoping for give. How many fences had I climbed over, scooted beneath, wiggled through? But this one was different, several feet higher than my head, barbed at the top, chain link dense enough to keep out the jackals and svelte foxes.

'Wait,' Carlo said, and pulled me back. I peered ahead, saw a flurry of movement dusting the sand.

'It's an animal,' I said.

'Yes,' Carlo said, 'but what kind?' We bunched close, creeping forward until we could see where the fence had been cut and broken through. In the

256

mesh of wire, a large red dog struggled, caught by a slender hind leg—someone's Irish setter, bolting from the noise. She lifted her head, feathered tail wagging, and gave one light bark as we approached.

Carlo examined the breach in the fence, but I was focused on the dog, her long muzzle, deep chest, narrow hips, the blood that matted her haunch. When I knelt beside her, she licked my cheek and whined. The sharp wire had hooked her through the hock. I held her leg, feeling for a way to work the wire loose, but the pain made her jerk from my hands, whimper, and snap.

'Help me,' I said to Carlo. 'It's going to take us both.'

He shook his head. 'Leave her,' he said. 'To them, dogs are unclean. We are already risking too much.'

An explosive concussion split the air, and Carlo ducked as though the hospital might come crashing down on our heads. I thought about Linda, wondered if she had fled the compound, saw Carlo peer up, searching the windows as though he shared my thoughts. He drew his dagger, motioned to the cringing dog. 'Kneel on her neck,' he said.

'Don't kill her,' I said. I was remembering the dog in the ditch, my grandfather's shovel, the *chunk* of metal against bone.

'Do as I say,' Carlo insisted, 'before we lose more time.'

I stroked the dog's sleek head and rested my knee against her neck. A strangled scream of terror broke from her throat as Carlo gripped her leg, made two shallow cuts, and pulled the wire free. When I sat back, she jumped up as though sprung from a box and bolted in a single leap, disappearing into the desert like a coppery wraith.

Carlo wiped his knife. 'Now she will be eaten by hyenas,' he said.

'Better than dying here.' I stood, rested my hand against the mangled fence, looked back at Carlo. 'Mason is going to kill me if he finds out about this,' I said.

'I believe he will have a fight on his hands,' Carlo said. He pulled back the wire, giving me clearer passage, then followed me through the gap.

We pressed ourselves against the hospital's walls, freezing whenever we heard a voice, until we came into the clear near a corner of the administration building, its windows busted. In the parking lot, three fire-blasted sedans lay overturned and smoldering, releasing a tarry smoke. When I lifted my camera, Carlo touched my shoulder and pointed down the street toward the louder shouts and rumblings, the chaos of concentrated commotion. I moved in front of him, but he caught my arm. 'Let me go first,' he said, and crept forward until we could see a handful of Arab youths pitching rocks and bottles, chanting their slogans. A clutch of Bedouin militiamen watched from a distance, their faces rouged by the glow of a storage shed that had been set aflame.

'Why aren't the guards stopping them?' I whispered.

'Why would they?' Carlo said. 'They are all Arabs and will not turn on each other if they have an enemy in common.' He knelt on one knee and focused on the rioters.

'But we're not the enemy,' I said, 'and they're destroying the compound.'

'It is not their compound,' he said, 'and you are

258

their enemy's friend.'

I peered past him to the shadowy faces of the militiamen, who stood at ease. The chief lit a cigarette, threw his match to the gutter, and rested against the hood of his Jeep. I edged ahead of Carlo, crouched behind a hedge of frangipani, its fulsome sweetness perfuming the air, and crept forward until I was within fifty feet of the guardsmen, ignoring Carlo behind me, his voice low and insistent, calling me back.

I rose against the trunk of a date palm, my camera at the ready. As intent as they were on the violence, I reasoned, they wouldn't notice me. I adjusted my lens to take in the rioters, one with his arm cocked, ready to pitch a large rock, even as the leader of the militia calmly watched, on his face a look of pedestrian curiosity. I followed the arc of the stone, saw it hit a window of the Oil Exhibit building, the glass explode into a shower of fragmented light. I held my ground, capturing the smile that broke across the chief's face as the shards spangled the street. The protestors turned, raised their arms in triumph, and I zoomed in on their faces, masked in the folds of their *ghutras,* took several quick shots. In that second, Carlo was at my elbow, and I saw the chief peering my way.

'Run, *bella.*' Carlo pushed me so hard that I stumbled forward before regaining my balance. I thought I could hear his feet hitting the ground behind me, or maybe it was the camera banging against my chest or my heart pounding in my ears, because when I looked back, I saw him still there, squared off with the militiamen, gesticulating wildly. His voice carried on the air, a hectoring mix of English, Arabic, and Italian even as the

259

chief approached, his weapon at the ready. I cut through a lawn, dodged around parked cars, didn't stop until I reached the hospital, where I flattened myself against a wall shadowed by palms.

How can I explain the strangeness of being caught in that limbo between the silent desert and the riotous calamity filling the streets? I hesitated another moment, but what could I do? I didn't think that the rioters or militiamen would hurt me, but I knew that if caught with my camera, I would be turned over to the company, who would send me out and maybe Mason too. I told myself that Carlo could clown his way out of anything because I couldn't bear to contemplate the other possibilities: that he could be beaten, jailed, shipped back to Eritrea because of me.

I stepped through the fence and followed its boundary to where Carlo had parked the Volkswagen in the shade of the tree. The car creaked when I opened the passenger door and slid in as though it, too, were protesting my presence. I peered toward the breach in the fence until I saw a shadow separate, break free. Carlo ran to the car, motioned me into the backseat, and took the wheel. 'Stay down,' he commanded, and gunned us onto the road.

I crouched on the floorboard, my knees crammed to my chest. 'Where are we going?' I asked.

'My studio,' he said.

I braced myself against the seat, felt the air cool my back, damp with sweat. I lifted my face so that he could hear me. 'I'm glad you're okay,' I said.

'They try to scare me, but they forget how big I am.' He growled a laugh. 'They know that I have

260

the protection of the emir.' He lit a cigarette, and I saw his eyes in the rearview lift. 'We have lived to see another day, *bella*,' he said, 'and now we have our story to tell.' He inhaled deeply and took up the aria where he had left off, filling the small car with his boisterous vibrato. Half an hour later, he slowed and turned right, and we bounced across the bermed road and railed a long path through the sand before pulling to a stop. I peered out from between the seats, saw a small building on the beach, and then Yousef's taxi.

Carlo squinted, geared down. 'Someone welcomes us home,' he said. He got out, and I heard him speaking in Arabic, Yousef answering, and then the passenger door swung open, and Carlo levered the seat. I clambered out, saw Yousef leaned against his Chevy, the brim of his hat shading his face.

'Howdy,' he said.

'Howdy,' I replied. I couldn't imagine what he must have thought of me as I followed Carlo toward what looked like a hobo shack, the skull-and-crossbones flying above. The studio was more solid than I had expected, built of large automobile packing crates nailed tight against the winds that stung my ankles. I wasn't sure who might be inside, but when Carlo swung open the planked door, I saw Linda Dalton in her nurse's uniform, sitting on a narrow cot. Before I could begin to wonder what she was doing in Carlo's studio, she arched her eyebrows.

'So,' she said, 'imagine my surprise.'

I heard the hint of jealousy in her voice, looked from her to Carlo and back. 'We were just taking pictures,' I said.

261

Linda's mouth hitched. 'I bet you were.'

'Really,' I said, and felt my face redden. 'Nothing'—I grimaced—'nothing like *that* happened.'

Linda crossed her legs, tilted her head my way, ignoring Carlo. 'I wouldn't tell anyone,' she said. 'You'll ruin his reputation.'

Carlo cupped her face in his hands and kissed each of her cheeks. 'You are safe,' he said, 'and now I am happy.'

'I was just leaving to deliver X-rays to Abqaiq when the riot broke out.' Her eyes softened, and she looked up at Carlo. 'It won't kill anyone if they're a little late.'

Carlo winked my way, then motioned me to the cot beside Linda, brought us each a warm Pepsi. The hut was surprisingly cool, filtered light coming in through two saw-cut windows bedizened with translucent shells, illuminating the prints tacked to the whitewashed walls.

'What a lucky man I am,' Carlo said, lifting his bottle, 'to be in the company of such beautiful women.'

Linda offered me a cigarette. 'Maybe it's a good thing that Ruthie flew to Rome,' she said. 'My neighbors marked their house that they were Muslim and ran off.'

I lowered my voice. 'We sneaked in through the fence,' I said, 'and took pictures.'

Linda's eyes snapped once. 'Are you crazy?' She turned to Carlo. 'I thought you of all people would know better.'

Carlo stroked the point of his beard that lifted and settled like the back of a cat, and his tone grew more serious. 'They took my camera.' He turned up his palms as though showing us how empty they were. 'I will enter a plea with the emir, but I fear it is hopeless.'

I considered only a moment before pulling out my Nikon, still holding the film of the riot. 'Until you get yours back,' I said.

He hesitated before shaking his head. 'I cannot,' he said. 'It is the extension of your very soul.'

'Oh, cut the crap, Carlo,' Linda said. 'Just take the damn camera. Gin can buy another one in Khobar. You're the one who doesn't have the money.'

Carlo pouted at Linda, his eyes half-lidded. 'You are beautiful, *amore mio*. How I adore you. You make me forget my pain.' He puffed his chest, held out his hand. 'If not for you, I would be nothing but a poor pirate.'

Linda stood, slapped the wrinkles from her uniform, and jerked her chin toward the door. 'Come on, Gin. I've got work to do.'

'Wait.' Carlo grasped her arm, turned her toward him. His gaze had sharpened. 'Stay with Carlo awhile longer. I will show you my photographs.'

'Jesus, Carlo.' Linda snatched her arm away. 'I'm not one of your little girlfriends.' She settled her shoulder, looked at him from the corner of her eyes. 'You're pathetic, I swear.'

'I am,' Carlo said, his eyes gone soft. '*Tu sei la mia stella polare.* I am always lost without you.'

I felt something give in Linda and knew just what it was. 'I'll meet you outside,' I said, and pulled the door closed behind me. I looked to the taxi, where Yousef thumbed back his hat. He met my eyes before shaking his head and sliding back into his nap.

I sat in the sand, rested back on my elbows, and watched the water, the thin lines of dhows graphing the horizon, heard the distant sounds of traffic along the highway. A jet, its contrail feathering across the blue dome of sky, reflected a spark of sun. I breathed in the air, tart as a penny, and it came to me that what I was feeling was a kind of solitary pleasure I hadn't known since I was a girl. In that moment, I allowed myself to imagine that I could be like Carlo, bluff my way through the world, make myself into a pirate who could come and go freely, revel in the unfettered air. I was almost sorry when Linda appeared, carrying her sturdy nurse's shoes and shushing through the hot sand in her white nylons, regal as a clipper ship. I rose reluctantly and followed her to the taxi. Yousef, roused from his stupor, waited for us to brush off our feet before closing our doors. He had deflated the oversize tires to give us more traction, but still we skittered and slewed.

'What about the Volkswagen?' I asked.

'Carlo will drive it back.' Linda bobby-pinned her white cap, furiously tucking the loose strands of hair, then shoved on her sunglasses. She smelled sweet and warm, like summer molasses. 'I can't believe you gave him your camera,' she said.

When I started to remind her that she was the one who had convinced him to take it, she waved her hand.

'I know, I know. He always does that to me.' She sucked on her cigarette. 'For God's sake, don't tell Ruthie. She'll never let me live it down.' She picked up the envelope of X-rays and groaned. 'That's just swell,' she said. 'They're melted.'

The road was less crowded than usual, Yousef

264

able to stay in a straight line for miles at a time. Linda looked out her window. 'I don't think the rioters want to hurt anybody. They kept apologizing for the inconvenience. Really, they're not very good at it.' She gave a quiet laugh. 'My houseboy told them to leave me alone and lied that I had children inside. Guess I'll have to keep him after all.' She laid back her head, let the smoke rise from her mouth. 'I don't know what it is about Carlo. Gets me every time.'

'It must not be money,' I said, 'like the Moroccan.'

'The Moroccan was DOA,' she said. 'Money doesn't put the moxie in the man.' She turned her face to me. 'But Carlo, he has moxie in spades, doesn't he?'

'Yes,' I said, 'and he's funny and brave and romantic and kind.'

Linda took off her dark glasses, her eyes wistful. 'You don't think I'm foolish for dating a pirate?'

'No,' I said. 'Besides, he's not a pirate. Not really.'

'Sometimes, I like to pretend that he is,' she said, then shook her head. 'He flirts with all the women, makes everyone think he's some kind of Casanova.' She lifted her shoulders. 'But he's just a force of nature.'

'It's like his photography,' I said. 'He loves whatever he sees, and whatever he sees loves him.'

'Yeah,' she said, and turned her eyes back to the road, the sharpness of her features easing, 'that's it exactly.'

It was nearing dusk by the time we reached Abqaiq. Yousef drove me all the way to my door before dropping Linda at the clinic. I stepped in and knew by the savory smells that Yash was making dinner. He hurried to usher me inside, his face pinched with worry, and I heard the local radio announcer's excited Arabic.

'If you had told me what time you would return,' he said loudly, 'I would have had your meal ready.'

'I don't need a lecture, Yash.' I pulled off my shoes, not caring how much sand I dumped. 'I get enough of those when Mason is home.'

He straightened, cut his eyes to the living room, and I saw Mason enter from the hallway, his hair still wet from the shower. He didn't even acknowledge I was there, just sat down on the couch, lit a cigarette, and lifted his chin to Yash.

'What's the latest?' he asked.

Yash snapped to attention. '*Sahib*, King Faisal has agreed to join the embargo. Aramco is forbidden to ship oil to the United States or Britain. All incoming flights are being diverted to Rome.' He moved with my shoes to the door, turned them upside down, shook them vigorously, and continued his report. 'The Saudis are threatening to nationalize if the U.S. continues its support of Israel. The king assures Americans protection'—he kept his gaze on his task—'as long as they remain inside the compounds.'

Mason glared at me. 'I need a drink,' he said, and disappeared into the kitchen. When I heard ice dropping into a glass, I turned to Yash.

'What is he doing home?' I hissed.

'Mrs. Gin,' Yash said, and lifted his hands, 'there is a war.'

I set my mouth. 'You're eating with us,' I said. 'Don't even bother to argue.'

I sat and waited with my hands in my lap until

Mason came to the table. He hesitated when he saw the three place settings, then took his chair at the head. 'Are we expecting company?'

'Just Yash,' I said, and arranged my napkin. 'I don't think it's safe out there for him.'

Mason looked toward the closed doors of the kitchen, then back at me. 'Where in the hell have you been all day?'

I slathered two rounds of *dosa* with ghee, laid one on his plate. 'I was at the club,' I said, my heart racing, 'playing cards with Candy.'

He settled his eyes on me. 'You've never been any good at lying, Ginny Mae,' he said. 'What I'm beginning to wonder is just how much you're lying about.'

I opened my mouth, shut it again, afraid that I would dig myself deeper. Mason picked up his bread, set it down.

'Do you think I'm the one who makes up the rules around here? You can be mad at me all you want, but it doesn't change a damn thing.' He leaned in. 'You're going to get yourself in trouble and pull me right in with you, and then where will we be? Back in that Oklahoma oil patch, that's where.' He lowered his voice. 'I don't need you drawing attention right now. I've got an inside lead on the deal with Bodeen and Alireza, someone I think might listen to what I've got to say, and I don't want you messing it up.'

I sat very still, like I had as a child when I believed I might make myself invisible, grateful when the kitchen doors swung open and Yash appeared, bearing a deep dish of steaming butter chicken. He hesitated for a moment until Mason motioned him forward. Yash never met our eyes as he took his place at the table, his carriage polite enough to demand that we be civil. We ate in silence for a few minutes until the sound of my own chewing was about to drive me mad.

'Yash,' I said, and he looked up, a little alarmed. I gave him an encouraging smile. 'Why don't you tell us more about India.'

He pressed his napkin to his mouth and cleared his throat. 'I must say that this current situation has reminded me a bit of my own country's history.'

I let the tension ease from my shoulders. Such an introduction could only mean a long oratory. I glanced at Mason, whose eyes were fixed on his food as though he couldn't stand the sight of either one of us.

'The 1947 British partition of India,' Yash continued, 'produced one of the largest human migrations ever recorded. A multitude of Muslims journeyed north to their new home of Pakistan, the Hindus and Sikhs south to their new India, and as they passed, they slew one another by the thousands.'

Mason's eyes flicked up for a moment.

'My family had a private car and was in no danger, but I vividly remember the refugee trains. It was bedlam, the people tearing at one another to climb on board.' Yash paused, seemed to go more deeply into himself, his voice a little quieter. 'Along the route of migration, a family of Muslims that had fallen behind the caravans huddled and wept. We slowed to allow a few goats to be herded from the road, and I peered into the faces of the dying old man and his wife, propped among their few belongings. He was nothing but bones, his only covering a scrap of dirty linen at his loins. His eyes, rolled to the heavens, terrified me, but when I pointed him out to my father, he said it would be better that they all died that way.' He lowered his eyes. 'I suppose that like most people, he viewed those he had set himself against as animals. It is the only way we can justify our survival over their destruction.'

'Is that what Gandhi said?' I asked, but Yash shook his head.

'It is what experience teaches,' he said. 'What Gandhi said was that the idea that the world's religions must be separated was for him a denial of God.'

Mason considered Yash as though he were seeing him for the first time, then pushed back his plate. 'What is your take on the riots?' he asked.

'A minor form of revolt.' Yash graciously took the cigarette Mason offered.

'You know what Martin Luther King said, don't you?' Mason popped his lighter. ' "A riot is the language of the unheard." '

Yash drew in a breath. 'Truly, in the long history of occupation,' he said, 'the Arab-American experience is extraordinary. No war has been waged, no genocide enacted, no peoples enslaved. The land has remained in the hands of the kingdom, as has the government and its affairs,' he said, 'yet it remains a form of colonization.'

Mason nodded. 'Corporate colonization.'

'And with colonization comes resistance,' Yash said. 'One wonders if the Americans won't regret their temperate regard for this country's sovereignty. It is a point of great hubris, believing that you can control what you first do not conquer.'

'Nationalization would allow the Saudis to take

269

control of the company.' Mason squinted at Yash. 'Isn't that what these riots are really about? The Arabs want us out, want to claim what's theirs.'

'It is about all of it,' Yash said. 'What matters in this case is that both the United States and Israel believe that they are exceptional, that they are God's chosen people. In this way, they have yoked their destinies. Whoever rises up against one must rise up against the other, and that is the Saudi dilemma.'

'You don't think we can bridge that divide?' Mason asked.

Yash tensed his lips. 'The Bedu have a saying. "I against my brothers, I and my brothers against my cousins, I and my brothers and my cousins against the world."' He stubbed his cigarette, glanced at his watch. 'It is late,' he said, and rose with his cup. 'I will finish my cleaning and be on my way.'

'Let me help.' I stood quickly and gathered our plates, refusing to look at Mason. I wasn't sure what he would say to me once we were alone, but I knew I didn't want to hear it. I followed Yash into the kitchen, helped him wash, dry, and put away the dishes, and for once, he didn't protest. He stowed his apron, and I saw him to the door.

'Be careful,' I said.

'*Shubh ratri,*' he said quietly. 'Sleep well, Mrs. Gin.' He balanced his bike. 'I will wait to hear the lock.'

I closed the door and released the bolt, listened to the creak of his bicycle become more distant. I went back to the table, but Mason kept his eyes on his whiskey.

'I'm just going to bed,' I said. When he didn't respond, I turned down the hallway, showered, and lay between the sheets, guilty and confused. The war seemed distant and impossible, secondary to my own little world of turmoil. Mason was always showing up when I least expected him, and it dawned on me that I could never really know where he was, what he was doing, when he might catch me by surprise.

I flipped my pillow, pressed my cheek to the cool side. I had never considered my marriage to Mason a mistake, but I was beginning to wonder—who might I have been if, instead of getting into Mason's car that night, I had finished school, somehow gone to college, gotten a real job? Someone like Linda, single and free to make love to a pirate if I wanted.

I rolled to my side, twisted the sheet beneath my chin. 'I could have been a stewardess for Pan Am,' I said aloud. I didn't care whether Mason heard me, didn't care whether he came to bed or not, I told myself. I didn't care whether he ever came to bed again.

CHAPTER THIRTEEN

On the ninth of June, less than a week after the war had begun, it was over. I sat in the welcome cool and listened with Yash and Mason to the broadcast of President Nasser's speech, blaming the Americans for Egypt's loss to Israel, but whatever trouble still brewed outside the compound never made it past the Abqaiq gate. Within a matter of hours, it seemed, the avenues were again filled with delivery vans and company cars, the swimming pool bustling with mothers and toddlers back from their

271

forced vacations. Ruthie, her voice full of the old bravado, called to say that, like many of the wives who had evacuated, she was taking an extra week or two to do a little shopping, Israel's victory over Egypt a welcome excuse for a holiday.

Since the start of the war, Mason's time at home had been taken up with endless production meetings that lasted well into the evening, the company in the throes of new imperatives, as though pumping more barrels into the rift left by the war might seal King Faisal's allegiance.

'What about Alireza?' I asked Mason one morning.

'It's not like I can just show up at headquarters and file a complaint,' he answered. 'I've got to be careful. Put this in front of the wrong people, and I might as well burn that ledger and hop the next plane out of here.'

I looked down, worried my ring finger. 'I hope they put him in jail,' I said.

Mason shook out a cigarette. 'I'm guessing they won't do a damn thing to Alireza,' he said. 'He's too big, too powerful. My interest is in setting things right, making the company stand up and take responsibility. This is just the kind of thing that will put more pressure on Aramco to make concessions, bring more attention to the workers' cause.'

'If Alireza got in trouble,' I said, 'maybe Abdullah's sister could get her divorce and keep her baby.'

'The rules are different here,' he said. 'There's nothing I can do about that.'

'Then who is going to help her?' I asked. 'She's just a girl.'

'She's also a Bedouin,' he said, and ran a knuckle

272

over his lips. 'Best that you leave all that go, Gin, and take care of your other business.'

But what other business did I have? No assignments from Nestor, no camera, no Ruthie. I spent the remaining days until Mason left for the launch chafing at the emptiness of time marked by meals, the muezzin's call, the company's noon whistle that broke the day in two. I hounded Yash in the kitchen, considered the still's steady percolation. Was it any surprise that so many Aramco wives slept the mornings away, claiming headaches brought on by the heat?

'I'm bored out of my mind, Yash, I swear,' I said.

He ran a rag around the rim of a water glass. 'You can take your photographs.'

'I can't,' I confessed. 'I gave my camera to Carlo.' When Yash raised his eyes, I shrugged one shoulder. 'What's for dinner?' I asked. 'Mason won't be home until late. Looks like it's just the two of us.'

I helped him set the table, chatting about my plans for next year's garden until he became more relaxed, and we ate in easy conversation, Yash swirling his after-dinner coffee as though it were wine, sharing humorous stories rife with the gossip of houseboys: Swede's wife, her arms and legs like brittle sticks, had stashed bars of Ex-Lax in her freezer and taken enemas twice a day, while chunky Edna Doty, twice the width of Tiny, had a drawer full of bright red garter belts and wide-paddled brushes that never touched a hair on her head. Whatever secrets the wives hoped to shelter, the houseboys discovered, each servant's discretion tempered by his treatment at the hands of his mistress, and I wondered what Yash had told them about me.

'Which reminds me,' Yash said, 'Mrs. Fullerton called. It seems she scheduled you a golf lesson yesterday afternoon, but you failed to appear.'

'Candy Fullerton,' I said, 'is not a nice person.' I gave him a sideways look. 'What do you know about her and Carlo?'

'Nothing that is not true.' Yash ticked an eyebrow. 'She may have fallen under the rake's spell, although it's most likely that she tripped him first.'

'She's the manager's wife,' I said, wondering whether Linda knew. 'I can't believe she would do that.'

'It is convenient to believe that we are above all vices but our own.' He listed his head to the side. 'Do you know,' he asked, 'that to test his vow of celibacy, Gandhi brought his virgin grandniece to his bed, had her remove all her clothing, and lay with her through the night? His followers were shocked.'

'I wonder what the grandniece thought,' I said.

Yash smiled. 'He was an old man by then. Perhaps she teased him cruelly.' He took a drink of his coffee, drew back into himself. 'But I'm sure that this is not the kind of story you wish to hear.' He rolled his mouth. 'It is difficult to compete with your friend the Bedouin.'

'Oh, I don't know,' I said. I pinched a piece of chapati. 'What else you got?'

'Perhaps adventure.' Yash looked into his coffee. 'Or maybe a love story.' He ran his fingers along the tablecloth like he was reading Braille. 'You have asked me about my wife.'

'You must miss her,' I said.

'I do.' He furrowed his brow. 'She died giving birth to our son.'

'Oh, Yash,' I said, 'I'm sorry.' I waited a heartbeat, the bread going dry in my mouth. 'But your son, he lived?'

'Yes, he lived.' Yash's shoulders bunched, released. 'But I couldn't bear to see her face in his and drank to blind myself. I lost my commission in the army, our home, and when they took my son from me, I lost everything.' He inhaled through his nose, let it out slowly, as though trying to regain his control. 'When I read of the call for servants in Arabia, it seemed a way to escape my sorrow, which is how I have come to be here, a sober man but no more happy.' He paused for a moment, then rose to gather our dishes. '*Sahib* will be home soon.'

I didn't say what I was thinking, which was that it hardly mattered. Mason and I had spent the days since the war in mutual disregard, as though we were the ones in détente. Each morning, I waited until he left before rising, kept my nose in a book if he showed for lunch, went to bed early when he arrived back home. He seemed happy enough to ignore my sulk, and I was counting the hours until he would leave again. The truce between us might have held if not for Candy Fullerton.

*   *   *

I came home from my swim at the pool that Saturday to find Mason in the bathroom, freshly shaved and showered. I watched him part his hair, combing the wave from front to back.

'Another meeting?' I asked, but he shook his head.

'We're going to the Fullertons' for dinner,' he said.

'But it's your last night home,' I said. 'We could go see a movie.'

'A movie isn't going to tell me what I need to know.' He pulled on his shirt and buttoned the cuffs. 'Better get ready,' he said.

Just do this, I told myself. Tomorrow, he'll be gone.

I showered, put on makeup and fixed my hair, then pulled on the little black dress that I had bought at Fawzi Jishi's when Ruthie had insisted that every girl should have one. I stopped in the living room long enough to pick up the photo taken that day we had boarded the pearling dhow. Despite his disparaging comments about Carlo's talents, Yash had mounted the photograph in a lovely bamboo frame. It made me happy to see Ruthie beside me there, both of us laughing into the sun.

I rode in silence as Mason drove the Volkswagen to the Fullertons', the engine chattering to a stop in front of their flat-roofed bungalow lush with flowering shrubs, its veranda spiked with tiki torches. He pulled the emergency brake, turned his face without looking.

'Let's not rock the boat,' he said. 'This is important to me.'

I sat with my hands in my lap. 'I know,' I said.

He took a deep breath and stepped out to open my door. When his fingers brushed my elbow, I felt a little shock—the first touch we'd had in a week. Before we could make the porch, I heard a dog yapping, and Ross came booming out.

'Sit, sit,' he commanded, and directed us to a

276

circle of wicker chairs arranged around a low table, then motioned to the Syrian houseboy. 'Bring it on, Henri.' Henri came with mint juleps, a bowl of nuts, and a layered tray of tiny cucumber sandwiches alternating with red radishes pared into petals and filled with dollops of dilled mayonnaise, bacon, and olives. 'Candy's putting on her war paint,' Ross said. He adjusted his crotch and crossed his legs. 'You're looking mighty nice tonight, Ginny Mae.' Mason glanced at me, as though he had forgotten to notice.

'Thank you,' I said, and pulled my wrap over my bare arms, relieved when the conversation turned to baseball. I surveyed the porch, remembering the summer nights when my grandfather had moved our chairs outside to take relief from the heat. The cooling air, the coming darkness, all gave comfort to the concerns of the day, and he would take up his fiddle, pull the bow, tune his voice to the note, begin slow and easy. He sang out into the open of the cotton fields, sang with the cicadas' chorus, and I would watch the lightning bugs star the sky, the happiest I ever was in his company.

'Ever been to the Derby?' Ross didn't wait for our answers but doubled his chin, took a sip of his julep. 'Fastest two minutes in sports. Proud Clarion came out of nowhere to take it this year, thirty-to-one odds. Made somebody happy, but not me.' He held a lighter to Mason's cigarette. 'Bet you're not a gambling man, are you?'

'No, sir,' Mason said, 'can't say as I am.'

'Just as well.' Ross bit the end off a big cigar and squinted up at Mason from the folds of his cheeks. 'Guess Doucet's the one's got that vice.'

Mason looked down, rubbed a thumb against his

277

glass. 'Guess we all have to have one,' he said.

'Wife like yours, I might not need any other.' Ross kinked his lip my way, then reared back when he heard Candy come out the door. 'Here's the girl. I was beginning to worry. Your drink was losing its ice.'

'I had to put Pebbles and Ross Junior to bed.' Candy flounced down in a drift of White Shoulders. 'We're going to dine al fresco,' she cooed at Mason. 'Won't that be romantic?' She turned to scowl at Ross. 'Are you going to smoke that before supper?'

'And after,' he said, bellowing his cheeks.

'It stinks.' Candy pursed her mouth at the lip of her julep, sipped, and frowned. 'How's yours, Gin? I can have Henri make you a new one.'

'It's fine.' I took a quick swallow, tried not to wince at the bite of raw alcohol.

She lit her cigarette, blew a stream of smoke. 'Is Ruthie still in Rome?'

'Another week or so,' I said.

'She'll have all new clothes.' Candy cut her eyes at Ross, pulled a pout. 'I wish someone would take me to Rome.'

'You got more clothes than you know how to wear.' Ross motioned to the low table. 'Have some nigger toes.'

'Brazil nuts,' Mason said, but kept his voice light. I obediently took a handful and busied myself cracking their thick shells, grateful for the distraction, until Henri stepped over to tell us that the first course was about to be served. We moved to the table covered with Irish linen and set with Nippon china straight from Japan, more crystal and silverware than I'd seen in one place. While Henri filled each of our bowls with a ladle

278

of mushroom soup seasoned with sage that smelled like the rain-swept desert, I kept Candy at the corner of my vision, following her lead: this spoon, that fork. I bladed a pat of butter and moved it to my smallest plate before cutting it to spread on my roll. When she lifted her spoon, dipped it into the soup and away, brought it to her mouth in a precise trajectory, I did the same, resisting the urge to slurp, take in a savory mouthful. She tapped the corners of her mouth with her napkin.

'I recognize that dress,' she said, and waved her spoon. 'I had my eye on it, but Fawzi wouldn't barter.'

'I got a good deal,' I said. 'He threw in a slip.'

'You must have had Ruthie with you,' she said. 'She knows how to Jew them down.' She squinted a smile as Henri positioned our salads and then an elongated silver platter holding an entire fish garnished with lemons and surrounded by onions and small red potatoes, a currant where its eye once had been. 'It's only hamour,' Candy said, 'but it was all that was fresh.'

We watched as Henri skinned and filleted the fish with the skill of a surgeon. I looked at Mason, who was sopping his soup bowl with bread, intent on his conversation with Ross about a new spike camp that had been pitched deep in the Empty Quarter. I touched his leg, but he ignored me.

'Men,' Candy said sotto voce. 'They're animals, I swear.' She sat back as Henri filled our plates. The fish course was followed by miniature cups of lime sorbet, and I was relieved that the meal was coming to an end, until Candy eyed the way I ate the icy scoop in two bites. 'Better slow down,' she said smugly. 'We're only halfway through.'

279

Henri made room for the standing rib roast, a steaming boat of au jus, creamed horseradish, potatoes au gratin, new peas and pearl onions floating in cream.

'Pile it on there, Henri,' Mason said, smacking his lips in an exaggerated fashion.

'You're liking that, aren't you, Mr. McPhee?' Candy said.

Mason swallowed a mouthful of potatoes. 'Best meal I've had since leaving Texas.'

'You're just saying that.' Candy leaned toward him and offered her cleavage. 'I'm sure that Gin is the best cook in the world.'

'Gin's got other things going on,' Mason said. 'Yash is the one who takes care of the kitchen.'

Candy fluttered her hand. 'Houseboys just get in the way of good home cooking.'

'I like Yash's cooking,' I said. Something about the way they were talking made me feel like I wasn't even there.

'I'm a meat-and-potatoes man myself.' Ross leveraged his belly, patted it fondly.

'We've still got dessert,' Candy said. 'Cream puffs and fresh berries.'

Henri dutifully appeared with the pastries, each powdered and wearing a little skirt. I worried mine around its lacy plate, sure I couldn't eat another bite, but Mason licked at his so lewdly that I blushed. He washed it down with black coffee and took the cigar Ross offered, biting off the end and spitting it away as though it were an everyday thing.

'Bring us some more of that hooch, boy,' Ross said to Henri. 'Don't bother with the fancy stuff.' He leaned in. 'I've got a joke for you. So this Texan walks into a bar . . .'

280

'Oh, God,' Candy groaned, 'not this one again.' She held her hand to the side of her mouth. 'Don't listen, Gin. It's nasty.'

Ross squared himself up. 'Texan goes into a bar and hollers, "Drinks all around! My wife just gave birth to a twenty-pound baby boy!"'

Candy rolled her eyes and looked away.

'Now,' Ross said, 'everybody in the bar is happy as hell, congratulating ol' Tex, marveling at the size of that baby, saying, "We sure do grow 'em big in Texas!" which is true.' Ross chomped down on an ice cube. 'Week later, here comes Tex back for a beer. Bartender says, "Tell me, Tex, how much does that boy of yours weigh now? Must be big as a bull." Tex shakes his head, all sad-like. "Down to twelve pounds," he says. Well, now the bartender is worried. "Is he sick?" he asks. "Has he had the diarrhea?" Ol' Tex takes a big swig of beer, wipes his mouth, and smiles a proud-daddy smile. "Nope," he says, "just had him circumcised."'

Ross rocked back, laughing so hard he choked, but Candy repositioned herself, cocked her shoulders. 'I thought we were going to be civil tonight,' she said, and tipped her chin toward Mason. 'Ross has big news, you know.'

Ross's guffaws lapsed into a winded *whoosh*. He reached into his back pocket, pulled out a handkerchief, and wiped his eyes. 'That's right,' he said, and blew his nose. 'Thought we might talk about what comes next for you and your little gal here.'

Candy looked at Mason, the shadows of her face flickering into a flirty smile. She drained the last of her julep and motioned to Henri for a refill.

'Now'—Ross buckled his brow, grew more

281

serious—'some might say you don't have the experience. Some might even say you should have been the one sent out instead of Swede Olson.' He grunted as though pained. 'Burt Cane, he thought you were something special, and that's worth a lot in my book.'

Mason took the drink that Henri offered, set it down.

'I know you've got your sympathies,' Ross said. 'You've told me your concerns, but you know as well as I do that productivity is our top objective.' He worried a molar with his toothpick, sucked it clean. 'We're training the Saudi boys, getting them educated, easing them in. Bring them along too fast, they'll founder like a horse on spring grass.'

Mason worked his jaw, looked at me, then back at Ross.

'Well,' Candy said, 'are you going to tell him or not?'

Ross pulled a big puff from his cigar. 'McPhee, I've made my decision. I'm putting you up for promotion to assistant drilling superintendent.' He reached out, slapped Mason's shoulder. 'Play your cards right, son, and you're on your way to the big house.'

Candy bounced and clapped. I attempted a smile, but all eyes were on Mason, who broke into a wide grin and raised his glass before taking a long pull on his cigar. In that moment, he wasn't the man I had married but somebody else—a man on his way somewhere I wasn't sure I wanted to go, someone I wasn't sure I could trust anymore. I sat forward in my chair.

'Maybe we should take some time to talk about this,' I said.

Mason's grin faltered, but Ross crooked his cigar. 'That's right,' he said. 'I want you all or nothing, McPhee.' He cocked his mouth. 'And you don't want to be letting this little girl get too far away from you. Young bucks will be on her before you can say scat.'

Candy stared at Ross like he had dropped in from outer space, then broke into movement all at once, pushing back her plate, tipping her glass until the ice hit her teeth, lighting a cigarette, and waving it at me.

'I can't believe,' she said, 'I can't believe you have to think about it.'

'Now, sugar.' Ross gave a sideways smile. 'I'm sure they'll make the right decision.'

Candy pinched her lips around her cigarette, the tick of her shoe coming faster. 'Maybe it's Gin who thinks she can do better.'

I opened my mouth to answer, but Mason cut me off. 'If I commit to this job, I commit all the way. A lot of good men have given the best years of their lives to making this place work, and if I say yes, I mean to be one of them.'

'That's the spirit,' Ross said.

Mason relaxed back, fingering his cigar, but I set down my drink. I couldn't stand another minute of Ross, of Candy, not even of Mason. 'We really need to go,' I said.

Candy's eyes flashed in the torchlight. 'I've seen your pictures in the newspaper, Gin. They're very nice. You should have brought your camera.'

Mason glanced at me, murmured his agreement, relieved to move the conversation along. 'I told her she should send some to *National Geographic*.'

'Ask her where her camera is,' Candy said.

283

Ross beetled his brow. 'Here, now. Let's have some more *sadiqi* juice.'

'Ask her,' Candy said.

Mason peered at Candy for a moment, then slowly moved his eyes to mine. 'Where's your camera?' he asked.

I held Candy's gaze. For a heartbeat, I thought I might lie, but it was her smirk that made me more angry than afraid. 'I gave it to Carlo Leoni,' I said. 'Security confiscated his.'

Candy slanted her mouth. 'Ross told me that you were right in there with the action, Gin, just you and Carlo, running around the desert in Ruthie's Volkswagen. Must have been *loads* of fun.'

I looked at Ross, who screwed up his face like an apology and scratched a thumbnail across his forehead.

Mason sat still for a moment, then carefully stubbed his cigar. 'We're keeping you folks up awful late.' He stood with Ross and shook his hand. 'If you're offering me the promotion, I'm saying yes right now.' He turned to Candy, pressed her fingers between his. 'That was a blue-ribbon dinner, ma'am. Mighty fine.'

Candy cocked her hip, said, 'Any ol' time, Mr. McPhee,' then cut her eyes at me. 'You haven't even asked how Pat is doing. I know he's dying to hear from you after all the fun you two had at the ball.'

Before I could answer, Mason gave a final nod good-bye, gripped my elbow like a rudder, and piloted me to the car. We sat in silence as he throttled us home, working the stick shift like he was levering iron. When I started to speak, he held up his hand.

'Don't,' he said.

'If you'll just listen to me, I'll tell you the truth.'

'What the hell makes you think I want to hear it?' He punched the Volkswagen around a corner and hit the curb in front of our house. 'You're going to bollix this up for everybody.'

He slammed his door, ignored mine, and I followed him across the grass, dragging my wrap through the dew. 'Maybe you would rather have Candy for a wife,' I said loudly. 'I saw the way you looked at her. She's nothing but a tramp.'

He turned, his face flushed. 'You're acting like you don't have a lick of sense in your head,' he said. 'You're starting to make me crazy.'

'Crazy?' I said. 'You think I'm making you crazy?' I slapped my chest. 'What about me, Mason? You don't know what it's like, being stuck in this place day after day.'

'From what I'm hearing, you don't either.' He banged open the door, and I trailed him through the living room and into the bathroom, where he pulled off his shirt, stripped his belt, then cranked the shower. 'You've got this big house, nice furniture, Yash waiting on you hand and foot. What more do you want?'

I peered at him, let my hands drop. 'You've changed, Mason,' I said. 'I don't even know you anymore.'

His mouth hardened, and he took a step toward me. 'I'm still the same guy I was the day we got hitched,' he said. 'I'm the guy who is working his ass off so that you can get your hair done and buy your jewelry and wear your pretty clothes. I'm the one who is paying for this roof over your head.' He pointed his finger. 'You'd better look in that mirror if you think that I'm the one who's changed.' He glared at me for a moment before turning to the shower.

I stood, staring at the curtain he pulled between us, and felt my anger turn to a paralyzing helplessness. I looked at myself in the mirror—my mouth drawn down, my shoulders slumped. The marble floors, the double closet with its cache of new outfits, the enviable bidet—I hated it all. I willed myself to move into the bedroom, to go through the motions of readying for bed, to take off my clothes, pull open the dresser drawer, and take out a fresh nightgown.

What was it about seeing my unmentionables there, so neatly folded and carefully arranged, that broke the spell? The cold despair that had numbed me gave way to a rage that seized me like a fit. I jerked the drawer from its slides, turned it upside down, and dumped it on the floor. I kicked my underthings into a maelstrom of nylon and satin, straps akimbo, leg holes gaping, my slips lacing the lamp shades, my stockings flagging the curtains. I moved to Mason's underwear drawer and scattered his boxers and T-shirts and socks across the room. I heard the shower turn off, Mason step out. He came up behind me, pulling on his pants.

'What are you doing?' he asked, his voice rising into a higher key. 'Stop.'

But I couldn't stop. The dresser emptied, I moved to the closet, ripped shirts and skirts from their hangers, winged our shoes against the walls, then turned my attention to the bed. I snatched the sheets from their moorings and dragged the blanket down the hallway like the skin of an animal, Mason following a few steps behind, hollering for me to stop, *just stop*. I paused at Betsy Bodeen's tapestry, the unicorn in its pen, and jerked it to the floor, scuffing it beneath my bare feet until the threads frayed. The record albums were next—Buddy Holly, Petula Clark, The Supremes sailing obliquely against the blinds. The couch pillows whumped to the floor, cushioning the crystal ashtray but not the ginger-jar lamp, which shattered into a dozen scarlet pieces. Had the shades been open, the neighbors might have seen me in my all-in-all, raging from room to room like the madwoman I had become. I didn't pause to think of Yash, all his hard work come undone.

'You're acting like a spoiled brat,' Mason said. He made a grab for my arm, his grip tight enough to hurt. 'When are you going to grow up?'

I turned on him. 'Do you want me to grow up? Is that what you want me to do?' I jerked my arm away. 'What if I told you that I made love to Abdullah?' I said. 'How would that be? Maybe I'm not your little girl anymore.'

It wasn't the anger in Mason's face that made me wish I had held my tongue but the shock of pain that took its place, as though I had slid a knife between his ribs—his mouth an open wound.

'You're crazy,' he said, as though he was truly confounded. 'You're plumb crazy.'

His confusion fed mine, and I hit him in the chest with my fists, not like the girls in the movies, but as hard as I could, like I was driving nails, and it knocked the breath right out of him. He stood stunned for a moment, then grabbed my shoulders and shook me like a rattle. I pushed away, stumbled to the floor, and Mason straddled me, pinning my arms.

287

'Get off,' I demanded. I wanted to spit, to bite him so hard that he bled.

'Tell me it's not true,' he demanded. When I wouldn't answer, he leaned down, his hot breath in my face. 'Tell me.' I growled into his mouth, bucked my hips and twisted my legs, but I couldn't budge him and felt the shame and frustration stinging my eyes.

'I hate you,' I said. I gritted my teeth, bit the words into pieces. 'I hate you.'

He went still, and his grip on my wrists loosened. He straightened slowly, moved his weight to his knees, then stood. I looked up to see him peering down at me, his eyes dark with hurt.

I pushed myself up and ran to our bedroom, slammed the door, and curled on the bare bed, feeling like I might shatter into a thousand pieces. I was sure that I heard the front door open and close, Mason leaving the house, going somewhere I couldn't follow. Maybe he would go to Ross, I thought, tell him to ship me out, that I was no use to anyone anymore. I heard the seconds of the clock louder than the thrum of desert crickets huddled against the still-warm foundation and then the steps in and out of the kitchen, the hi-fi click on, Sinatra start in low.

Twenty minutes, maybe thirty, I lay listening, hoping for the sound of Mason coming down the hallway to say how wrong he was. I imagined what I would say: *Don't touch me, go drink your whiskey, just leave me alone.* And then, as the air in the room cooled, I thought I might allow him to lie down with me, warm me against the chill. Finally, miserable and shivering, I pulled on my robe, felt my way through the dark, and found him sitting

288

bare-chested on the couch, the liquor bottle close at his side, the ember of his cigarette growing bright, then fading again. There was something about seeing him that way that made me feel sick inside. He was a man that any woman would want, wasn't he? Working so hard to do what was right. 'A real keeper,' Candy had called him. Why was I always getting in his way?

I sat down beside him, pulled his fingers into mine. 'I'm sorry,' I said, wondering whether he was too drunk to hear. 'You know I didn't mean it.'

He didn't look at me but took a slow drag off his cigarette. 'I'm never going to be enough for you, am I? Don't matter how hard I try, never enough.' He let out a breath, smoke rising like vapor. 'I was your one-way ticket out of that Oklahoma hellhole. Don't you think I know that?' He lifted the bottle, wiped his mouth. 'Maybe this is where you want to get off.'

I sat very still, remembering how I had wished him away. The thought of being left alone, or of being shipped back home to live on my own, suddenly terrified me.

'That's not true,' I said. 'I need you, Mason.'

'You don't need me,' he said. 'You've never needed me.' He fixed his eyes on the dusky wall. 'Do you remember when I brought you home from the hospital? You wouldn't let me near you, wouldn't even let me sleep in the same bed. I spent all those hours on the couch, listening to you cry.' He brought his eyes to meet mine, the lines of his face etched with shadow. 'He was my son too, Ginny Mae. He was my son too.'

The light in the room shifted—a car or maybe dawn coming on—and I felt as though I was at the

289

edge of something awful. How could I undo what I had done?

I moved from the couch to the blanket I had dragged from the bedroom. 'Here,' I said, and patted the floor.

He slid to his knees beside me, his hands hanging limp, as though he didn't have the strength to lift them.

'Help me,' I whispered, and reached for his belt, but he stopped me.

'You've got to tell me,' he said, 'about Abdullah.'

'Please.' I hushed and kissed him, felt his lips soften. I wanted to appease him but still keep him guessing, keep whatever power this was I had over him. I opened my robe, pressed my breasts against his bare chest, and lay back, pulling him with me. He rested his weight on his elbows, hovering over me.

'Tell me the truth,' he said, his eyes holding mine. All my resistance had turned to desire, but still I refused, pressing my shoulders to the floor, arching up to meet him. When he entered me, he did it slowly, holding himself back, and I clenched my teeth as he rocked into me, moving me with him. 'Tell me now,' he whispered at my mouth, 'and I'll believe you.' When I wouldn't answer, he pushed deeper, and then I couldn't stay quiet anymore.

'No,' I said, 'I didn't.'

'Promise me that I'm the only one,' he said, 'no one before, no one after.'

'I promise,' I said. 'Only you. Ever.'

I felt the muscles in his back tense, his breath catch and hold. I wanted to pull him in, push him away, call out and cuss him, but all I could do was come with him, and then what power did I have? I opened my eyes to the dark ceiling, remembering that first time in Mason's car, how the frost had starred the windows and our breath fogged around us, how I always gave in too soon, and if that wasn't need, what was?

It was hard to let go, to separate ourselves. Mason reached for his cigarettes. He seemed himself again, as though our lovemaking had set things right in his head. He drew me to him, and I tucked in, rested my ear against his chest, heard the steady march of his heart.

'I needed that,' he said, and held his cigarette to my lips. I inhaled, let out my breath.

'You know that I'm never going to be Candy Fullerton,' I said.

'And I'm never going to be Ross.' He gathered my hand in his. 'Listen,' he said, 'I'm going to quit telling you what you can and cannot do. Doesn't do me any good anyway.'

'I want to explore,' I said, 'take pictures like Carlo Leoni.'

'I hear the road to Riyadh is a real adventure,' Mason said. 'When I get back in camp, we'll load up some food and water and plan an expedition, maybe take a tent, do a little camping, eat by candlelight. How does that sound?'

'Like a start,' I said.

He ran his thumb over my knuckles. 'I've been thinking,' he said. 'Someone knew what Bodeen was doing but covered it up, and I'm betting a hundred to one that it was Ross Fullerton. He may even have ramrodded the deal with Alireza.' He lay quiet for a moment, then lifted his cigarette, let out a slow breath. 'Lucky's right about one thing,'

291

he said. 'These are bigger dogs.' He rolled his face to mine. 'Not a word to anybody about any of this, okay? Wrong person gets wind, we could all be in big trouble, and we have no idea who that wrong person might be.'

I should have told him right then that I had spilled the beans to Lucky about Alireza and Buck Bodeen, but I didn't want to make him angry again, to lose what ground I had gained.

'Promise me you'll be careful,' I said.

He lifted my hand, kissed it, then rocked himself up, pulled me to a stand, and gathered the blanket from the floor before leading me to the bedroom. We made a nest on the mattress and spooned together, slept that night tucked so tightly that I thought I couldn't breathe.

'No,' Mason would whisper whenever I squirmed for a little more room, until I quit resisting, let my body meld to his.

'Freedom is one of imagination's most precious possessions,' Yash once said to me, and still, I did not listen.

CHAPTER FOURTEEN

Mason left for the launch early the next morning, kissing me so long at the door that I heard Yash clear his throat in the kitchen. 'See you in two weeks,' Mason said, pinching my bottom. I batted him away, both of us giggling and smooching the air.

Even before Mason and I had risen from our haphazard bed, Yash had the living room tidied,

292

the lamp replaced with one from the spare room, our breakfast on the table. I ate with my eyes down, embarrassed to hear him snapping fresh sheets. When I went back to the bedroom, I found the drawers reorganized, every dress and shirt rehung as though the night before had never happened. The one small thing out of place was a ribboned package on my pillow. I opened the velvet box, lifted the diamond ring, and slid it on next to my wedding band. I lifted my hand like I had seen other girls do, flashing it in the light, but all I felt was a kind of numb appreciation, like I had earned the gift through some marginal favor.

I remember how those next two weeks were hot beyond words, steaming the breath from my lungs. I sat stagnant in the living room, watching TV, reading, unable to bear the torture of stepping outside. I was glad when Linda Dalton stopped by, dressed in her nurse's uniform and carrying my camera.

'I bought Carlo a new one,' she said, 'extra lenses and everything.' She held out a packet—the photographs I had taken that day in the desert. 'Carlo says you should hide them,' she said. 'We don't want you getting deported.' She shook her head when I asked her to stay for lunch. 'X-rays to deliver,' she said. 'They'll melt in the heat.'

I saw her to the door, then sat at the table and opened the packet. The apricot desert, the three camels arranged like a pyramid, Carlo's brooding profile, and then the shots of the riot, the cars overturned, the shattered windows. I remembered the charge of adrenaline, the background of smoke and glittering glass, the chief leaned lazily against the hood of his Jeep, the protestors with their fists

293

full of rocks—for that moment, at least, I had been on the other side of something more than a simple fence, had crossed the divide into another kind of life.

I spent an hour in Mason's study, poring over the framed map, tracing the few roads, measuring the two hundred miles of desert road from Abqaiq to Riyadh, imagining the photographs I would take whether Nestor wanted me to or not.

When Ruthie called from Rome that evening to say that she was catching the next available flight back home, I told her about the diamond ring, how strange it made me feel, and she laughed. 'You've got it good,' she said. 'Now all you have to do is learn to enjoy it.' And I realized that she was right. What did I want that I couldn't have? It was beginning to dawn on me that if I played my cards right, Mason could be my advocate, my traveling companion, the one who could open the doors instead of closing them. All I had to do was learn the rules of the game.

*   *   *

The day before Mason was due back in camp, I drove the Volkswagen to the pool, enjoying one last turn behind the wheel before Ruthie returned home. Once in the water, I concentrated on letting go of the panic that filled my chest whenever my feet couldn't find bottom. I paddled my way from one side of the shallow end to the other, avoiding the small talk of the young women who chatted over the heads of their children, wondering if I should feel glad that I had so little to anchor me. When the wind picked up, the mothers gathered their towels and herded their broods out of the water, and I welcomed the chance to have the pool to myself, ducking under, holding my breath to escape the stinging sand. The Arab boy who manned the snack bar looked at me with sympathy when I gave up and made my way to the exit.

'*Shamal,*' he said, and pointed to the sandstorm darkening the horizon.

I followed his direction, saw what could have been a tsunami of muddy water, or the choking smoke from a wildfire, a cyclone of sand boiling toward us. By the time I arrived back home, my eyes were burning, and I squinted through the grainy light, saw the Land Cruiser parked in front of the house, Abdullah at the wheel. I hesitated at the curb, wondering whether the storm had forced Mason home a day early, whether I should stop and say something to Abdullah, but the biting sand drove me inside. Yash met me at the door, ready with his broom.

'Where is Mason?' I asked, shaking the sand from my hair.

'Mr. Mason is on the platform,' Yash said. 'He returns tomorrow.' I knew by the way he refused to meet my eyes that he was hiding something.

'Then why is Abdullah here?'

He sighed in resignation. 'It would seem that you are being watched.'

I trailed him into the kitchen, rich with the steam of the stock he was reducing, my tea already steeping. 'What do you mean, watched?'

'I didn't want to say,' Yash said, 'but I have seen the Bedouin most every day since Mr. Mason left, driving by, sometimes parking at the end of the block. I can only assume that *sahib* has pressed the

295

Bedouin into duty as'—he widened his eyes and lifted his shoulders—'a tracker, I suppose. I hear it is what they are good at.' He pinched a bit of salt.

I stared at him for a moment, then slid to the stool. I couldn't believe that Mason had tricked me so easily. I looked down at the ring, folded my hands away.

'This is ridiculous,' I said.

Yash hummed and nodded, then stirred the pot and sniffed. 'You see how we have this in common.'

'What?' I asked.

'You and I, Mrs. Gin, share a history of oppression, I at the hands of the British, and you at the hands of men.'

'I'm not oppressed,' I said.

Yash regarded me. 'You cannot leave this compound or this country without the permission of your husband. You cannot drive yourself to the market or enjoy a cup of coffee at the public café. You are liberated then.' He snapped his fingers. 'Very well.' He looked at me with an air of exasperation. 'Don't you see that we men are all the same? We wish to spread our seed on fertile soil, keep our plots free of weeds and our harvests pure, bring forth white man from white man, Sunni from Sunni, Brahmin from Brahmin. We protect you from the advances of other men, not in your interest but our own. We will readily kill you before we share you. It is the story of all mankind.'

'What?' I asked, and wrinkled my nose. 'Why are you saying all this?'

Yash paused, let the sharpness of his shoulders ease. 'You are right. It is not appropriate,' he said, and sank his hands into the dishwater. 'What occurs between husband and wife is no one's business but

296

their own.'

And then I remembered the dresser drawers upended, the shattered lamp. I dropped my face into my hands and groaned.

'He can't just sit out there all day,' I said. 'He'll roast.'

'He is a Bedouin,' Yash said. 'They come fully cooked.'

'But I don't want him watching my every move,' I said, my frustration turning to anger. I thought for a moment, then rose and pulled a Thermos from the cupboard, filled it with hot tea from the pot, and added sugar.

'Now where?' Yash asked.

'Not far.' I moved to the entryway and stepped out into the *shamal,* cracking my eyelids just enough to see my way to the Land Cruiser. The storm might have been a blizzard, the pelting sand stinging my face like ice, but I was determined to confront Abdullah, to let him know I knew what he and Mason were up to, that I didn't like it one bit. I didn't even think about taking my usual place in back, just rapped my knuckles on the passenger window and opened the door, which swung out hard, clipping my wrist. I pulled my way into the seat and used both hands and all my strength to wrestle the door closed. I wiped my face, tears streaming, and looked up to see Abdullah staring at me, eyes wide.

'It's okay,' I said, 'just sand.' I held out the Thermos. 'I thought you might like some tea.'

He hesitated before taking it. 'Thank you,' he said quietly. He pushed back the folds of his *ghutra,* and I saw that his hair had been cut to the collar. I felt a wash of anger and regret, as though

297

something had been taken away from me. When he saw me looking, his eyelids fluttered as though he were ashamed.

'Why did you cut your hair?' I asked.

'Mr. Fullerton,' he said quietly.

'Do you always do what he tells you?'

Abdullah didn't answer but poured a little tea into the top of the Thermos. In place of a *thobe,* he wore the khaki work pants and shirt prescribed by the company, and the outline of his body seemed different, thinner than I had expected.

'So is this what you're going to do whenever Mason is gone?' I asked. 'Sit here and watch my door all day?'

His eyes clicked up, then down. He licked his lips and blew across the cup's edge but didn't answer. The air inside the Land Cruiser was close with the smells of diesel rags, the work sweat of men, and the woody scent of Abdullah's cologne, or maybe it was only his skin. He seemed more shy than he had before, hesitant to look at me, and I wondered what Mason had told him. The thought that they had plotted this out, that Mason's conciliatory words were a lie all along, made me sweaty with resentment. I looked out the window, the street and houses hidden by the brown skein of sand.

'I hate that fence,' I said, and pushed back against the seat, crossed my arms. 'It's supposed to keep us safe, isn't it?'

'From what?' Abdullah asked.

'Hyenas,' I said, then turned to face him, 'and Arabs throwing rocks.'

I could tell by the quick flick of his eyes that I had startled him. It dawned on me that he might have been part of the riot, his *ghutra* wrapping

298

his face like the mask of an outlaw, and the idea pleased me, a secret we might share.

'In Texas, they probably thought you were an Indian or something,' I said. 'You know, like an Apache.'

He rested his cup on the dashboard, where it fogged the windshield. 'They thought I was a Mexican,' he said, 'and treated me with contempt.'

'At least you got an education,' I said. 'That's more than I have.'

He looked at me fully for the first time. 'And where has it gotten me?'

I pulled in my chin, cast my eyes around the cab, and lifted one hand. 'Here,' I said.

He snorted, then drew back, as though he had shown some part of himself he hadn't meant to reveal.

'What?' I lifted my hair, felt the moisture at the back of my neck. 'Do you think that you're the only one who has ever felt put upon? I bet you've never been switched for cutting the sleeves from your dress.'

Abdullah's eyes took on new focus. 'Have you been denied sweet water?'

I met his gaze. 'Have you been told that you can't leave the camp because you're a woman?'

'I can't live inside camp because I'm an Arab,' he said.

'I can't drive to your tent because I'm a girl,' I said, 'and you men won't allow it.' I bunched my fists into my armpits. 'I hate that word, *allow.*'

'I hate that they call me a coolie when they think I can't hear.'

'You're not a coolie,' I said. 'You're a petroleum engineer.'

299

'I was,' he said.

I pressed back against the seat. 'We're both just a couple of hicks from the sticks,' I said. 'We should be grateful for what we've got.'

'Being a driver for the Americans isn't the contribution I had expected to make,' he said.

I ticked my shoulder, drew my mouth to the side. 'And neither is this,' I said, 'is it?'

He looked at me quickly, something in his face I couldn't quite read. We both fell silent, listening to the *shamal* keen around us, scouring the metal. The Land Cruiser bucked and shuddered, and I was glad for its anchoring weight, but Abdullah tightened his grip on the steering wheel like he was fighting to keep us on course.

'Alireza came to the tent,' he said, and the creases around his eyes deepened. 'He has taken the child.'

I sat up and glared at Abdullah as though the fault were his. 'Why would you even let Alireza near your tent?' I asked. 'Why didn't you take that rifle of yours and head him off at the pass?'

The line of Abdullah's mouth flattened, and he spoke with such calm that it made me want to scream. 'Above all else, Bedu value bravery, democracy, and hospitality. Anyone who approaches a Bedu tent requesting shelter is welcomed and given three days and three nights of food and drink before being asked the reason for his visit.'

'That's great,' I said. 'You open your door and invite the robber in.'

A look of pained confusion came into Abdullah's eyes. 'We abide by the code of *dakheel*,' he said. 'The harmony of the tent cannot be violated. If

300

someone, friend, stranger, or even my worst enemy, comes to my door, I am honor-bound to take him in and defend him with my life for those three days, even above the lives of my own family.'

'So you would protect Alireza,' I said, 'but let your mother and your sister die.'

'Or my son,' he said simply. 'It is against our teachings that Alireza would take his daughter from the milk of her mother's breast, but he is not an honorable man.'

'And what about you?' I asked. 'What kind of man would let Alireza do such a thing?'

Abdullah looked up in a flash of anger. 'What do you think would happen if I had denied Alireza his child? Do you think I would be seen as some kind of hero?' The muscles of his face tightened against the anger he didn't want to show. 'Alireza is a powerful man. If I tried to fight him, I would bring punishment down upon my head and upon the heads of my mother and sister.'

I leaned in as close as I dared. 'Alireza would have had to shoot me dead before I'd have let him take that baby away.'

'And then you would be dead,' he said, 'and he would still take the child. You could be proud of that.' He pulled back into himself. 'Your husband is right when he says that we must resist revenge, aggression, and retaliation.'

'He's always saying stuff like that,' I snorted.

'Martin Luther King said it first,' he said.

'You and Mason and your Martin Luther King,' I said. 'Why don't you tell me what the reverend has to say about the rights of women?' I asked. When he didn't answer, I snorted and pushed back against the seat, crossed my arms, and propped my knees

301

against the dash as though I meant to stay awhile. I saw his eyes settle on my legs for a moment before cutting away, and felt a twinge of satisfaction until he reached for his tea, drank it in one swallow.

'Thank you,' he said, and handed the empty cup to me.

I hesitated before screwing down the lid, dropping my shoulders. 'I just can't stand it,' I said, my words nearly lost to the sound of the storm, 'feeling so helpless. I don't want to think of myself that way.' I looked at him. 'And I don't want to think of you that way either.'

'To be humble is not to be helpless,' Abdullah said, 'but to submit to the will of Allah.'

'I don't need another sermon on humility,' I said.

'It is life that will teach you what you least want to know,' he said.

'And what if I want to know it all?' I asked.

'Then your life will be long,' he said.

I looked out my window, saw a weak flicker through the sand, the porch light flashing on and off.

'I've got to go,' I said.

'Wait,' he said, and reached into his shirt pocket, brought out a small braid of horsehair. 'I made this for you.'

I took the fob, running my fingers over the silken strands of Badra's mane. 'It's beautiful,' I said. 'Thank you.'

He flushed, pleased and embarrassed, and I wondered for the first time whether Yash had been wrong, whether Abdullah had come to my door of his own accord. The possibility buzzed in my chest, filled me with a furtive anticipation.

'Do you like chili?' I asked. 'I mean Texas chili,

302

no beans, so hot it will burn the hair right off your chest.'

Abdullah stifled a smile. 'Yes,' he said, 'I like chili.'

'I'll bring you some,' I said. 'Tomorrow for lunch?'

The corners of his mouth lifted. 'I will be here.' He started to say something more, then tightened his lips.

'What?' I asked.

He took hold of the steering wheel, lowered his voice. 'I am glad for your company,' he said.

I smiled, slipped the fob into my pocket, then dropped my shoulder and opened the door. A choking gust blew up around me, and I leaned into the wind. Yash met me in the entryway, but I ignored his scowl. He was right: the last thing I needed was another man telling me what I could and could not do.

I flopped down on the couch and turned on the television, trying not to think about Abdullah and Nadia and her baby, unable to think about anything else. When Yash came in with his feather duster and began another round of attack against the sand that had become his life's battle, I looked up.

'You didn't have to flash the porch light,' I said.

He lifted the crystal ashtray, kept his eyes on his work. 'You did not have to take my tea to the Bedouin.'

'He was thirsty,' I said.

'Bosh.' He repositioned the lamp, straightened its shade. 'In your perception of him, he can suck honey from the rock, I'm sure.'

I noted the sharp movement of his elbows, the blade of his back turned to me. 'You're mad at me,'

303

I said.

Yash's movements slowed for a moment and then became more purposeful, the feather duster whipping up a current of air that fluttered the curtains.

'It is inappropriate,' he said, his voice tense.

'That you're mad?' I said.

When he turned, I saw his mouth drawn down. 'Do you think that this is a game, Mrs. Gin? A story from one of your romances?'

The sharpness of his tone sat me up straight. The hurt hit me first and then the anger. Who did he think he was?

'I don't think you should be talking to me that way,' I said.

Wind rattled the door, pelted the windowpane with sand. He held my eyes for a moment, then dropped his gaze to the floor. 'Dinner at six, *memsahib*,' he said quietly, and turned for the kitchen.

I sat for a long moment, listening to the familiar sounds of his work, smelled the first warm waft of garlic and bay leaf, but I refused to feel bad about any of it. I rose, turned off the television, then stood in the silence of the living room, thinking of Mason somewhere in the middle of the sea, and felt a sharp resentment that he had left me here alone, a houseboy and a Bedouin for company.

I moved to the dining room and waited for Yash to serve me, which he did without comment. I didn't ask for my water to be refilled but simply expected it, and it was. My dinner plate disappeared, replaced by a caramel custard that I ate with a dainty spoon. As I drank my cup of coffee, I looked toward the swinging doors that separated me from the vibrant utility of the kitchen, then down at the diamond ring. Maybe I'm being cruel, I thought, a coward, or maybe this is just the way it's supposed to be.

I left the dishes to Yash, sat on the couch with the novel he had found for me at market. He moved quietly into the entry, rested his hand on the doorknob. 'Good night, *memsahib.*'

I lifted my head to the racket of the *shamal.* 'You're riding your bike?'

'Not riding,' he said. 'Pushing.'

I lowered my eyes. 'Be careful, then,' I said.

When the door clapped shut against a gust, I shivered in the room's sudden chill, rose, and turned down the AC. I thought about Nadia, the wind wailing through the seams of the tent, her arms empty.

If I could drive beyond the gates, I thought, or if I had a horse, I would find some way to rescue the baby from Alireza. I considered Carlo, but even if he agreed to drive me out into the desert, what did I expect him to do? Draw his dagger, be the pirate he only pretended to be, some swashbuckling hero from one of the novels I read? Maybe Abdullah was right—maybe it was more about pride than it was about honor, but where did one end and the other begin? No matter how much MLK and Mason and Abdullah and Yash complained about their various inequities, none would ever know what it was like to be a mother whose child had been stolen away.

I worried myself into a headache, finally took a shower, put on my nightgown, went to bed, and waited for the hours to pass. I wasn't sure what I would say to Mason, but knowing that Ruthie would be home soon brought some comfort. I

305

wondered what she would think about Abdullah waiting outside my door—if, like Yash, she would believe that Mason had stationed him there, or if she would think he was flirting with me. One way or the other, she would tell me to keep Mason guessing. Because I was learning, wasn't I? How to hide my hand. How to keep myself from folding too soon.

*   *   *

It wasn't the wind that woke me the next morning but Yash rattling down the hallway. I looked to the window, saw the light still muted, the air thick with dust, the gale just beginning to wane.

When I heard Yash's knock, I pulled myself up in bed. I didn't look up as he positioned the breakfast tray across my lap but kept myself formal and composed like I thought Scarlett O'Hara might, the mistress of the manor. I flapped open my napkin. 'Has Ruthie called yet?' I asked.

'The lines are down because of the storm,' Yash said. 'There is no reception of any kind.'

I shrugged my shoulders. 'I'm going to make chili for lunch,' I said.

He didn't respond but poured the fragrant tea, then straightened, his face perfectly blank. 'When you are ready to receive her, Mrs. Fullerton is waiting.'

'Oh, no,' I groaned. 'She's here now?'

'She will wait.'

I sighed, pushed the tray aside. Yash looked away as I pulled on my robe. 'She probably wants me to join some club,' I said.

Candy sat prim in her Sunday best, knees

306

together, teacup balanced. She scooted forward when she saw me.

'Oh, Gin, it's awful,' she said, her eyes brimming. 'I'm so sorry.'

I stopped, my knees gone soft in their sockets. 'What?' I asked. 'What has happened?'

Candy looked from me to Yash. 'Doesn't she know?' When Yash lowered his eyes, she slid back to the sofa, turned her gaze on me. 'The plane went down last night in the storm. They found it this morning in the bay.' She folded her fingers as though in prayer. 'Forty-two dead, all from Dhahran and Ras Tanura, excepting Ruthie Doucet. They say she got the last open seat out of Rome.' She looked at me and blinked against her tears. 'God was calling her home.'

The muscles of my cheeks bunched, but the cry didn't come, just a hoarse expulsion of air.

'You poor thing.' Candy rose, steered me to the chair, and took the tray of tea from Yash. I numbly accepted the cup she offered, let her tuck the napkin beneath my chin. 'As soon as the wind dies down, they'll bring in the Dive Club. At least they'll find her,' she said, and pleated her lips. 'I passed Lucky on the street, drunk as a skunk. Someone should call security.' She pulled a scarf from her purse and floated it over her hair. 'I brought my Irish casserole. Tell Yash it's already seasoned.'

Yash waited until she was out the door before coming to stand beside me, his voice low and earnest. 'I'm so very sorry, *memsahib*.'

I stared at the window, felt as though my language had left me. 'I hate her,' I said, and began to cry. I thought of the people going about their familiar routines, survivors smug in their good

307

fortune—not them this time, but someone else. I knew that if I had gone to Rome with Ruthie, I might have been on that airplane too, but the idea that I had escaped some awful fate brought no comfort. I looked at the photo that Carlo had taken of me and Ruthie and the boy, all of us smiling so openly into the lens, and remembered Ruthie telling me about Lucky's plane going down, how nothing would ever happen to him. Instead, it had happened to her.

My head felt too heavy for my neck, and I rested it back against the chair, closed my eyes. 'I need to find Lucky,' I said as though to myself, 'before Candy calls the guards.'

'It may be better for you to rest,' Yash said gently. 'Take some tea.'

I rocked my head. 'I don't want to just sit here and cry,' I said. I looked up to see the helplessness on Yash's face. 'I'm okay,' I said, but it was a lie that neither of us believed.

I stood and made my way down the hall to the bathroom, where I washed my face in cold water and changed into my clothes. Yash held his silence as I stepped out the door into the still-gritty air, startling a hedgehog from my path. The compound seemed muted, the only sound the faint bark of a dog let out to howl into the dregs of the storm, the Arab workers sweeping the sidewalks clean. As I walked the few blocks to the recreation center, I checked the vacant side streets and yards for any sign of Lucky, then stopped at the empty pool laced with sand, where a Bedouin boy ran his long-handled sieve through the water, undaunted by the endlessness of his task. It was too early, but I pointed to the theater and asked anyway. 'Cinema?'

When he nodded and pointed, said, *'Yum Yum Tree,'* I stepped to the lobby, cracked the swinging doors, and peered in, the bright screen illuminating the emptiness. As my eyes adjusted, I saw Lucky's silhouette, dead center, as though he had ciphered his way through the rows. I felt my way through the dark aisle and folded down the seat beside him, but he didn't look at me, his face flat as putty in the reflected light.

'This is the scene where he goes after the little blonde,' he said, his words thick and cadenced. I smelled his breath ripe with moonshine, saw the pistol rested on his thigh. He tipped his head. 'Tommy, back there on the projector, second time he's played this through. He'll do that for his old buddy and a riyal.'

'Lucky,' I said.

'Shhhh,' he said, the darkness of his eyes lost in the hollows of his face. We sat in silence for a long moment, listening to the heightened voices, the rollicking music, until he pulled a flask from his pocket and lifted it to the screen. *'Sadiqi,* my friend.' He took a swallow, clucked his tongue. 'When I first came to Arabia, you could buy real Kentucky bourbon right off the street,' he said. 'There's never enough anymore.' He coughed, a quick spasm, lowered his chin to his chest. *'J'ai gros coeur.* I feel like crying, you know?'

He sat very still, then tilted forward, hunkering in on himself. When I touched his back, he winced as though his skin were bruised. He took a deep breath, lifted his face to the screen, transfixed by the catapulting color, Jack Lemmon's scarlet smoking jacket, the turquoise sheaths and golden chiffons of the girls.

'Wasn't but fifteen the first time I pitched off a rig,' he said. 'You get used to it. Sand don't hit no different than dirt.' He rolled his shoulders, leaned back, and closed his eyes as though he had fallen into prayer. 'Just a few more years, I'd have had enough money to buy my way right out of this desert, take my Ruthie down to Florida, buy us a place in Sun City.'

I looked at my lap, laced my fingers together, and had a sudden memory of my mother teaching me to make the church and the steeple, all the people folded inside. Lucky opened his eyes, stared blankly at the screen.

'When Brother Bodeen went down,' he said, 'I thought I was okay. Figured I'd just lay low for a while, you know? Let things smooth over.' He nodded once. 'Only thing I didn't plan on was Mason McPhee.'

I looked at him through the smoke that rose into the projector's beam, remembering the bottle passing between us, how I had told him the details of Mason's crusade, never considering that Lucky might be the wrong person, and felt my stomach knot.

'I told him, "McPhee, you'd better leave it alone," but that boy never listen, never know when to leave good enough alone.' He grew still, his voice almost wistful. 'Then they come, they say, Doucet, this your doing, they say, you got to fix this. They think I'm the one who busted the game.' His breathing became faint, a raspy exhalation. 'Then no one would listen to Lucky no more.' He moved his hand over the pistol, and I saw his fingers tighten. He pointed it at the screen, breathed out a little puff of smoke. 'Pow,' he said softly. 'Pow,

pow.' He sat still for a moment, then tucked the gun at his waist, lifted his chin, called out, 'Shut her down, Tommy.' When the screen went dark, he pulled himself to a stand.

'Wait,' I said. 'Where are you going?'

'Back to the swamp,' he said. 'This desert's got all it's going to get out of Lucky Doucet. I ain't got no more to give.' He looked down at me, and rested his hand on my head like a blessing. I felt the rough calluses, the broken knots of his knuckles as he stroked my hair.

Petite soeur,' he said, his words so quiet I could barely hear them. 'Little sister, that's what she called you.'

'Please, Lucky,' I said. 'Tell me what is happening.'

He held my eyes for a moment, then focused on the wall behind me, nothing there but the faint red glow of the exit sign. 'Always doing the right thing,' he said, almost in a whisper. 'Never once saw him turn tail and run, not even when them pipes exploded, blew them Arabs sky high.' He moved his head back and forth as though in wonder. 'I'm saying, We got to get out of here, but he marches right in, dragging that piece of scrap metal like God's holy shield, telling me to stay back, stay back.' He paused as though in wonder. 'Did he tell you how hot it was?' he asked. 'Did he tell you how that fire sucked the air right out of our lungs?'

'No,' I said. 'He never told me.'

'I thought we was going to die, sure as hell,' Lucky said, 'but he just hunches down, goes right at it, like he's got some devil to kill. What choice I got but to tuck in there with him, piss running down my leg?' He snorted, then nodded in grave assessment.

311

'He's a bigger man than I'll ever be,' he said, and I saw his shoulders rise and fall, the hinges of his jaw loosen as though he were fighting to set loose the words. 'Maybe,' he said, and let out a long breath. 'Maybe me and the *Arabesque* got one last race to run.' He let his hand drift from my head, then started up the aisle. I heard the door open, turned to see him looking back at me, but I didn't have time to ask him anything more before he let the door clap shut. The air conditioner kicked on, and I sat alone in the humming quiet of the theater for a long time, then rose from my seat and walked out into a morning shocked by sun into stillness, the light burning white enough to blind me.

CHAPTER FIFTEEN

What can I say that I knew for sure as I walked those few blocks home? Only that Ruthie was dead and that Lucky's words had filled me with a dark foreboding that I had no way to make sense of, while all around me Abqaiq went on about its daily business. The school bell rang, calling the children to their desks. Soon the noon whistle would blow, the muezzin's song would fill the air, and we would eat our lunch and take our coffee and imagine our evening meals.

I turned the last corner, saw the Land Cruiser just pulling away, and remembered the chili I had promised Abdullah. I wanted to run after him, call him back, tell him about Ruthie and all that Lucky had told me, but it was too late. I turned to see Yash sitting on our porch, peering south toward the

Empty Quarter.

'*Memsahib,*' he said when he saw me, and stood up quickly to hold the door. I followed him into the kitchen, sat at the counter, and watched him begin to prepare my lunch, balancing a pineapple by its stem, making quick diagonal cuts to remove the eyes, the miniature trenching like a ribbon winding the fruit. His knife was the only sound until I mustered the will to speak.

'Yash?' I asked quietly.

'Yes, *memsahib?*'

'Do you believe in God or Allah or whatever your people call him?'

He hesitated a moment before gentling his gaze as a physician might. 'You miss your friend,' he said.

'It's not just that,' I said, and wiped my cheeks with my knuckles. 'I'm sorry about what I said before.'

'I have been impertinent,' he said. 'It is I who must apologize.'

'Please, will you just call me Gin?' I said, and saw his face soften.

He rested his knife. 'May I move your tea to the dining room?' he asked.

'Our tea,' I said, and he dipped his head once. We went to the table, where he pulled out our chairs and filled our cups. Who else did I have to turn to? Who else could I trust?

I pinched the tablecloth, trying to find a way into my questions. 'I need to be honest with you about something,' I said. 'I hope that you will be honest with me.'

'Of course, Mrs. Gin.'

'Something is happening,' I said. 'I'm afraid that

313

Mason is in trouble.' I looked to see his response, but his face didn't change. 'Tell me what you know about Lucky and Buck Bodeen.'

He cleared his throat. 'Mr. Bodeen and Mr. Doucet drank together. They spoke a certain kind of French they believed I didn't understand.'

'I found Lucky at the theater,' I said. 'He told me that he and Buck Bodeen were cheating the company out of money.'

'Yes,' he said. 'With Alireza.'

I stopped, surprised, but why? All that dusting, tidying, making order, that hearing of everything. I realized that Yash must have known all along.

'What if Mason decided he was going to tell someone?' I asked. 'What if Lucky said he'd better leave it alone, but then Mason didn't?'

Yash's eyes came up, sharp and sudden, a look that cut to the quick of my fear.

'Tell me what you're thinking,' I said.

'I think that you should speak with Mr. Mason and tell him what Mr. Doucet told you.' Yash held my gaze. 'Tell him that the wrong people know that he has made a discovery.'

I looked at the clock. Mason was already on the return launch, unreachable. Hours would have to go by. Yash saw the look on my face.

'Maybe some rum,' he said, but I shook my head. 'Rummy, then,' he said, got out the cards, and poured more tea. The news of Ruthie's death, Lucky's words in the theater—already, it felt like the day had stretched on forever, like we were marooned in some kind of tea party hell.

What else could I do but take up the cards that Yash so carefully dealt? We played one round and then another. I began counting the drips of the still.

314

How many seconds to fill one bottle?

'My mother often said that a patient soul endures what heaven ordains,' Yash said gently.

'I don't believe in heaven,' I said. 'I don't believe in anything anymore.' I dropped my hand. 'I can't stand just sitting here playing cards like nothing is wrong. I've got to talk to Mason.' I covered my eyes, afraid I was going to cry.

Yash sat quiet for a moment, then lay down his cards, stood, and beckoned me to follow him to the hallway, where he opened the doors of the linen closet.

'Let us fold,' he said.

I looked at the towels and sheets. 'But they're perfect,' I said.

He reached in, swept each of the shelves clean, then motioned me to sit before joining me on the floor. I stared at the pile, too much like the chaos I was feeling, then took up one of the towels and doubled it down the way Yash had always done, surprised when he stopped me.

'As you were taught,' he said.

It took me a moment to remember—three down, three across—and Yash followed my lead. The soft cloth in my hands, the repetitive motion that necessitated a simple concentration—I felt my fingers find their rhythm, my shoulders let go their cramp.

'When Mason gets home, I'll tell him what Lucky said.' I nodded to assure myself. 'Mason will know what to do.'

'Of course he will,' Yash said. 'He is an intelligent and reasonable man.'

'And Lucky was so drunk,' I said. 'He wasn't thinking straight because of Ruthie. He probably

315

didn't even know what he was saying.'

'Quite possible,' Yash said.

I tucked my chin to still the tremor of my words. 'I wish I weren't so helpless,' I said.

'The fact is that you are a woman,' Yash said, 'and in possession of great power.'

'What power?' I asked.

'Your desire for knowledge,' Yash said. 'It rattles the gods to their bloody core.'

'It got us cast out of the Garden,' I said miserably, and smoothed an embroidered pillowcase. Yash took up its twin, ironed it against his thigh.

'Do you remember,' he asked, 'that there was another tree in that garden?'

I thought for a moment, trying to recall. 'The Tree of Life,' I said.

'And what would have happened if Eve had eaten of that tree as well?' When I couldn't answer, he bent in as though sharing a secret. 'She would have lived forever.' He straightened, matched the corners of the pillowcase. 'Immortal and wise, your Bible says, 'as one of us.' That is why Eve was banished, you see—not because of her error but because of God's fear. She is your heroine.' Yash lifted his chin. 'Remember that strength does not come from physical capacity but from an indomitable will.'

'I like that,' I said.

'So do I,' Yash said. 'If not for Gandhi, I would have no words at all.' He considered the pile of linens covering his knees. 'I began as a warrior, but see how meek I have become.'

'You've always seemed brave to me,' I said.

He leveled his shoulders. 'Now see how readily I

316

rise to the praise of a woman.'

I laughed a little, grew somber again. I folded the pillowcase over, wondering at all the hours Betsy Bodeen had labored with her needle and thread.

'But women, we're always punished, aren't we?' I asked. 'For wanting to know, I mean.'

Yash matched the selvage of a towel, worked it even, laid it on the top of the pile, and grew quiet. When I looked at him, I saw his eyes fixed on the empty shelves. 'My wife wore a perfume that was undetectable unless I was very close to her,' he said, his voice distant, 'like the first bloom of a shy flower. Not even the desert has taken that memory from me.' His gaze dropped to his hands, and he pressed his palms against his thighs. 'I remember nothing of my mistress.'

I lifted my eyes. I had imagined Yash as an ardent young lover, even his bitter grief the dark matter of romance. I had never considered that he might have been unfaithful to the woman he had wooed and won.

'You've asked me to be honest,' he said. He closed his eyes, and when he opened them again, I saw how deeply he had gone inside himself. 'The truth is that I returned home one evening from a liaison,' he said, 'and my wife suspected my indiscretion. She insisted that I tell her everything, and when I refused, she would not let me into our bed.' He fell silent, his fingers curled against a washcloth. When he began to speak again, his words were hushed, almost a whisper. 'I believed that it was my right as her husband, and I forced myself upon her.' When I lowered my gaze, he nodded gravely. 'Yes,' he said, 'now you see what kind of man I really am.'

317

'We all make mistakes,' I said quietly.

'Please, Mrs. Gin,' he said. 'Do not embarrass us both by excusing my actions.' He dropped his chin, shaped the cloth's corners. 'My son was conceived that night. My wife bore the pregnancy like a burden. When the child was born, it was as though the seed of rage I had planted split her in two. They could not stop the bleeding.' He pressed the square with both palms, raised his eyes. 'You asked if I believe in God. If not, why do I curse him?'

'My grandfather believed that cursing God will buy you eternity in hell,' I said.

'A thousand hells are owed me, then.' Yash drew another washcloth to his knee, but his fingers had lost their purpose. 'Perhaps now you will hate me as I hate myself.'

I looked away. 'I could never hate you,' I said, and gathered myself, my words hesitant. 'I wasn't married when I got pregnant, but I meant for it to happen. Maybe so I could escape, I don't know. When the baby died inside of me, it felt like I was being punished, like it was what I deserved, but I never considered what it might do to Mason. All I could think about was myself.'

We sat in silence, listening to the steady drip of the still, until Yash shoveled a tower of sheets between his hands, stood, and placed them in the closet. When we had restocked all the shelves, he pushed back his shoulders, took a sharp breath through his nose.

'I believe we have confessed enough sins for one day,' he said. He tightened his lips, and I saw his eyes fill with tears. 'Your questions have dislodged the cork from the bottle,' he said softly. 'I cannot stop thinking of her.'

318

'Your son is still there,' I said. 'You could go back and see him.'

He offered a pained smile. 'It is not like in America,' he said, 'where you can be forgiven. Guilt is one thing. There is no redemption in shame.'

I watched him turn and make his way into the kitchen, all the starch gone from his spine. I worked my way through the remaining linens, trying not to think about anything but the task in front of me. At the bottom of the pile, I found the missing Sunday tea towel, still stretched on its small hoop, its appliqué unfinished, the needle and floss pricked through the cotton.

It seemed like years since I had sewn anything, but when I pulled the needle free, its feel was familiar, and the chain stitch, the running stitch, the cross stitch came back to me. I bent over the towel, following the zigzag pattern of the blanket on which the little Indian boy sat cross-legged, smoking a peace pipe on his day of rest. I knotted the thread, bit it close, released the hoop, and felt a small satisfaction, as though I had finished what Betsy Bodeen had begun.

Just be patient, I told myself, and heard my grandfather's words: 'In order to move the world, you must learn to be still.' He had meant the hours I might spend in my prayer closet, but I never knelt long enough to pink my knees. Now I had no choice but to wait for Mason to come home, just as I had been doing since the day we married, only now I had this awful fear to keep me company.

I rose, found my book. Every few minutes, I checked out the window for Abdullah, hoping that he would reappear, park at my step like a guardian at the gate. Our conversation during the *shamal* seemed strange to me now, as though, like Dorothy and her tornado, I had dreamed my way through the storm. The Volkswagen remained outside my door. With Ruthie and Lucky gone, who would come to claim it?

Yash and I worked on the dinner together, which helped to pass the time: chicken and walnuts in creamy gravy, okra with onions and spices, and, always, the rice. Our hesitance in the kitchen had turned to habit, our movements efficiently timed, but as the evening wore on, an uneasy silence fell between us. Yash glanced at the clock, and I knew that, like me, he was expecting the door to swing open at any moment, Mason to haul in.

That hour went by, and then another. The gravy thickened in its pan, the rice clumped, and still neither of us said what we were thinking, not a word about what could be wrong, as though to speak our fears might make them come true.

'Maybe I'll go for a quick swim,' I said.

Yash nodded his agreement and covered the dishes. 'This will keep well enough in the oven.'

I drove the few blocks in the Volkswagen, hoping that, like washing a car to bring on rain, my leaving the house would draw Mason home. The suntan lotion in the jockey box, the residual sweetness of Ruthie's perfume brought her back to me, and I tightened my grip on the wheel. At the pool, I slid into the lukewarm water, miming what I remembered of Nadia's grace as the moon broke free of the flares and plied its light alongside me. If I narrowed my vision, I could almost believe I was outside of the compound, swimming in the sea beneath the desert stars—easier to believe than my memory of the theater, Lucky hovering over me like a barbarous saint. I took a deep breath, ducked under water, and stayed there as long as I could until the only thought in my head was breaking the surface, breathing again.

When I arrived back home, the porch light seemed too bright, and I squinted against its glare. I didn't have to go in to know that Mason wasn't there. I sat for a long time with the windows rolled down, taking in the night air, the crickets, the strange bark of an eagle owl hunting the grass, until I knew that Yash would be worried. He met me in the hallway, his face etched with a kind of intense concern I hadn't seen before. He urged me inside, locked the door, and motioned me into the kitchen as though someone might hear.

'What?' I insisted, my voice sharp with alarm.

'While you were gone,' he said, 'two militiamen came to the door, asking for Mr. Mason.' He turned on the burner, ran water for tea, and I saw the sweat beading his upper lip.

'Did you tell them that he's on his way home?' I asked.

'They say he was not on the launch,' Yash said.

'Then he's still on the platform,' I said, but Yash shook his head.

'Then where is he?' I asked.

Yash set the tea to steep. 'They say he is nowhere.'

'That's ridiculous,' I said. 'Everyone has got to be somewhere.' The simplest of answers to a child's riddle.

'We will take some tea,' Yash said.

'I don't want tea,' I said, and rapped the counter so hard that Yash jumped. 'I want to know where Mason is.'

He took a patient breath. 'I hope that I may teach you two things while living in this place,' he said gently. 'The first will be to maintain your manners even in the face of crisis. The second will be to hold your tea.'

He placed a cup and saucer in front of me, but I sat unmoving, trying to remember everything that Lucky had said. It wasn't just panic or fear that I felt but the sensation of my mind floating away, as though my head had come unhinged, separated itself from my body.

'Something has happened,' I said.

'Perhaps he has only gone to Bahrain,' Yash said, 'taken an impromptu holiday.'

'He wouldn't do that without telling me.' *Not Mason McPhee.*

Yash didn't respond but positioned my plate of food, warm from the oven. I watched him roll up his shirt cuffs, run hot water over the dishes.

'What if he doesn't come home?' I asked.

'If not today, then tomorrow,' Yash said. The thought of his leaving, of facing the coming hours alone, brought with it a wave of panic.

'We have the extra room,' I said. 'Maybe you could just stay.'

Yash hesitated for a long moment, then dipped his head. 'Of course, Mrs. Gin.'

I ate what I could for him, then stood with my plate, and we washed the dishes together before going to our separate rooms, offering our soft good nights, and closing our doors quietly against the other, the air a tender bruise between us.

CHAPTER SIXTEEN

If these were your two choices—to be paralyzed by fear and helplessness or to rise up, lash out—which would you choose? Always I had been willing to take my chances, survive whatever consequence came my way, and this time was no different.

That willful girl I had always been came back into me as I lay through the night, trying to make sense of what was happening. If Mason had been delayed by mechanical breakdown or bad weather, the company would know where he was and wouldn't have sent the militia to our door. No part of me was willing to consider that he had simply taken some kind of joyride to Bahrain. It was Lucky's words that rang like a threat—*that boy never listen.* By the time the sun broke the horizon, I believed I couldn't wait any longer. Someone knew where Mason was, and I was going to find out who.

I rose before Yash, made scrambled eggs and bacon. He came into the kitchen, smoothing his hair, his shirt and trousers rumpled, as though he had slept in his clothes. He sat at the counter, and I took the seat next to him, piled our plates with food. I tore my toast in half, dunked it in my egg.

'You eat like a boy,' Yash said. 'I fear what you are about.'

'I have a plan,' I said.

'A plan? You are acting out of character,' he said, but his droll humor came tinged with regret.

'Mason is out there somewhere,' I said, 'and I'm going to find out where.'

'I fear that I have encouraged you in this,' he

said. 'You should let me glean what I can from the other houseboys.'

'And what are you going to tell them?' I asked. 'That your *sahib* didn't come home? That his wife is worried?' He dropped his gaze, and I saw what he was thinking: I had no idea the trouble I might get into. 'I'm not afraid of Alireza,' I said.

'It is not only Alireza,' Yash said, and I saw his lips tense. 'I'm sure that you are being watched even now.'

'Who is watching me?' I asked. 'Do you mean Abdullah?'

'Perhaps,' Yash said. 'All I know is that if an intelligent and ambitious young man such as your husband were fomenting an agenda of solidarity among the Arab workers, it is difficult to imagine what measures the company might take to stop him. Mr. Mason's efforts to uncover Alireza may provide his enemies the opportunity they need.' He brought his eyes to mine. 'The company knows he is missing. If he has gone into hiding, they may hope that you will lead them to him. Why else hasn't Mr. Fullerton or some chaplain come to your door?'

I sat quiet, trying to comprehend what he was telling me, who I could trust. 'What am I going to do?' I asked.

Yash rotated his coffee cup like he was positioning a dial. 'I can hardly believe I am going to suggest this,' he said, and raised his eyes. 'Petition the pirate.'

'Carlo Leoni?'

'Do you know of another pirate?'

'But I thought you despised him.'

'The fact remains that he has the run of the kingdom.'

324

'I can ask Linda,' I said. 'Maybe she has heard something.'

'There is a sense of desperation in the air,' he said. 'It may be more dangerous than we know.' He held my eyes for a moment, then lowered his gaze. 'Perhaps there is time for one more story.'

I wanted to say no, that I didn't have time, that I had grown impatient with stories except the one that lay in front of me, but Yash's solemn face kept me silent.

'The friend of my own youth was Amar,' he said. 'We drank together, gambled together, visited certain women together.' He blinked, suddenly shy. 'Those were our salad days.' He hesitated. 'Shall we smoke?' He lit our cigarettes, then grew quiet, touched his thumb to the ashtray. 'We were in the army,' he said, 'and were sent to the northern border. There were fifty in our troop, marching toward our ordered position. At forty-nine hundred meters, the Himalayan cold is inescapable. Many of us were suffering altitude sickness.' He inhaled slowly, as though remembering the struggle to breathe, and I saw something shift in him, his shoulders take on weight.

'The Chinese had emplaced one thousand soldiers on the highest ridges.' He looked at me as though to explain, said, 'The elevation favors defense.' I nodded, urging him on. 'When they attacked with mortar fire,' he continued, 'we entrenched, believing we were safe for a time, but when I looked at Amar, I saw him huddled in the mud, blood running from his ears, the result of oxygen deprivation.' Yash paused, remembering. 'The battle was hopeless, and we began to retreat. The Chinese honorably held their fire, but Amar

325

would not rise, sure that they would murder us as we fled. When I tried to pull him up, he pointed his rifle at me.' Yash dropped his eyes. 'I believed he was delirious. I brought my own rifle to bear and ordered him to march, but I was bluffing, of course. I would not kill my dearest friend.' I thought his story had ended, but he gathered his breath, lifted his cigarette. 'When the shot rang out, I thought I had been hit by enemy fire, but it wasn't my blood. Amar had placed the muzzle beneath his chin. His face was gone, but he was still alive.' Yash closed and opened his eyes. 'And then, of course, I had no choice but to kill him.'

I held still for a long moment, wondering why Yash was telling me this, why now. 'There was nothing you could have done,' I said.

'Still.' Yash touched two fingers to the crystal ashtray. 'I wonder whose commander I thought I was.' He brought his eyes to mine. 'Fate and folly sometimes meet. How will you know the difference?'

'Maybe I won't,' I said, and then more quietly, 'Are you afraid that you'll get in trouble for helping me?'

The look on his face eased into an enduring smile. 'They say it is better to die in the company of friends than to live in the company of enemies.' He lifted his cup. 'We are comrades, you and I,' he said. 'Let us be brave. *A la sature!*'

I reached for my own cup and met his toast. '*A la sature!*' I echoed, and drank the last of my coffee, felt the weight of the moment return. 'Yash?' I asked. 'What will all this come to?'

His smile never faltered. 'The education of Mrs. Gin,' he said, and then he grew more solemn.

'Please be careful,' he said, and lowered his eyes. 'If something were to happen to you, I would never forgive myself.' When I stood to go, he rose with me, reached into his pocket, and held out his hand, dropped a fistful of riyals into my palm. 'It is all I have,' he said. 'I wish it were more.'

I closed my fingers around the coins. 'I'll be home before dark,' I promised, then surprised us both by giving him a quick hug. He held to me for a moment, then straightened, cleared his throat. 'Perhaps my mother's masala lamb for dinner,' he said, then sat back down and pretended concentration on stirring his tea.

I gathered my scarf, packed my bag with my camera, a canteen of water, a pack of cigarettes, my notepad, my pen, Yash's riyals—I believed that I was prepared for anything. I stepped out into the heat, battling the impulse to jump in the Volkswagen and gun it right through the gate, like Ruthie had said. I looked back to see Yash standing in the doorway. He raised his hand, and I waved back, but he didn't move, and I could see him there, peering after me, until I turned the corner and was out of sight.

At the bus stop, I ignored the few wives who looked my way, their faces full of pity over the news of Ruthie's death. I had no idea whether they had knowledge of Mason's absence at all. Wasn't every wife's husband gone?

I considered my few options. The bus didn't go to Carlo's shack on the beach, and even if it did, the driver would never drop me there alone. I looked to the taxi stand, where Yousef regarded me from beneath the brim of his hat, and wondered whether he would risk my passage.

327

I stepped over quickly, handed him a cigarette and a few riyals. 'Carlo Leoni,' I said under my voice.

Yousef looked at the cigarette, then tucked it behind his ear. 'Dhahran,' he said loudly, and I looked around, saw the wives openly staring.

'Dhahran,' I said, following his lead, and he opened my door.

The taxi smelled like stale smoke and a perfume I could almost name. Even through my pants, the seat branded my legs, and I hiked up my knees. Yousef steered us toward the gate, where he stopped and exchanged easy words with Habib. I closed my eyes, wrapped my arms around my bag, and drew it close until we were out on the road, then let my shoulders relax and lifted my face to the hot wind. When Yousef peered into the rearview, I pulled out another cigarette for good measure and handed it to him over his shoulder.

'*Ashkurik,*' he said. His gaze came up to meet my eyes, and he grinned. 'No one loves tobacco more than a Bedouin.'

I blinked, trying to hide my surprise. 'You speak English,' I said.

'Little bit,' he said, and snugged the cigarette behind his other ear.

I settled back against the seat and wondered at all that Yousef might have heard as he ferried the men, wives, and single girls back and forth across the desert. I looked out at the cars speeding by, the jalopies, donkeys, and camels crowding the shoulder.

'Do you know where my husband is?' I asked.

'No, ma'am.'

'Abdullah?' I said.

328

'My cousin,' Yousef said.

'Will you take me to him?' I asked.

'I don't know,' he said.

'Do you mean you don't know where he is?'

'I don't know.'

I slumped back, looked out at the road stretching before me. Even if I found Carlo, located Abdullah, where did I think that might lead me? Even al-Khobar seemed impossible, distant as the moon. If Mason was hiding, he could be anywhere, nowhere I could go. I felt the panic edge back in, and what good was that? 'You only think you know what you're doing,' my grandfather often said to me, and maybe he was right. It wasn't that I felt brave or righteous in my quest—it felt like the only choice I could make, the only action I could take. I wasn't afraid for myself, maybe because I believed that the worst that could happen would be that I would be deported, flown out. The one thing I knew for certain was that I would never leave without knowing where Mason was, without at least trying to find him, without discovering the answers to my questions. I remembered Lucky in the theater and wished that I had clung to him until he told me everything that he knew—the not-knowing, for me, was worse than death.

When Yousef reached the familiar turnoff, he stopped, got out, and let air from the tires, then steered us onto the packed sand, and we wove our long way to the shore, stopping just outside Carlo's door.

'Will you wait?' I asked, and when Yousef nodded, I offered him another cigarette, but he held up his hand, pointed to the two behind his ears.

I swung out and crossed the hot sand. From inside the shack, I heard Carlo singing the same aria I'd heard that day in the car. I knocked, called, 'It's me. Gin.'

The voice went silent, and I heard the sound of whispers and shuffling before Carlo came to the door barely buttoned and missing his scarf, his hair loose, the broad dome of his forehead shiny with sweat.

'*Bella!*' he said. 'You are a surprise.' He glanced behind him, then back at me, and I heard a voice from inside.

'Come on in, Gin.' Linda sat on the cot in nothing but one of Carlo's blousy shirts, her beehive undone, platinum hair falling across her shoulders. Her nurse's uniform lay neatly folded across a fruit box, topped with her starched white cap. She crossed her bare legs and lit a cigarette. 'Get her a Pepsi, Carlo. She's thirsty.' She patted the space on the cot next to her and motioned for me to sit. 'How are you, sweetheart?' she asked. 'I've been worried.' She took my hand in hers, and her eyes filled with tears. 'We're going to miss her, aren't we?'

I nodded and took the warm bottle that Carlo offered, tipped a swig, felt it bubble against the back of my tongue, my nose stinging until my eyes watered.

'Thank you,' I said. Carlo focused on me for a moment before looking away, and that was when I understood that he knew.

'What are you doing all the way out here?' Linda asked. '*Sun and Flare?*'

'I'm looking for Mason,' I said.

Linda glanced at Carlo, who busied himself with

330

the buttons of his shirt, and her face grew more serious. 'Why?' she asked.

'He's missing,' I said. It sounded so ridiculous that I almost disbelieved it myself. *What do you mean, missing?* 'He was supposed to be home last night, but Security says he never boarded the launch.' I turned the bottle in my hands and began to tell them everything—about Lucky and Bodeen, Alireza and the ledger, Mason's suspicion of Ross Fullerton and Yash's warning about the company. Linda listened without interrupting, as though absorbing the information required for diagnosis, then moved her sharp gaze to Carlo.

'Did you know about any of this?' she asked.

Carlo fixed his eyes on a small wall mirror, tying his hair. 'It is only as she says. That is all that I know.'

'That is the biggest lie I've ever heard come out of your mouth,' Linda said.

Carlo chuffed a single word I couldn't understand, then began tucking his shirt, flush with exasperation. 'The Arabs, the Americans, they are no different. They skim, they cheat, they give with one hand and take with the other.' He slapped his bare feet against the floor, puffing bigger with each breath. 'The company'—he threw his fingers into the air—'*la famiglia,* is ruled by scoundrels who call themselves heroes and heroes who prove themselves scoundrels. How it is that anyone is ever surprised is beyond me.' He looked at me hard, but when he saw the stricken look on my face, he made himself small again.

'I'm sorry,' he said more quietly, and looked at Linda as though for permission.

'Just tell us,' Linda said, and wrapped one arm

331

around my shoulder as though we were in this together. Carlo paused, judging our fortitude, took a few steps to his right and then his left, trying to find his mark.

'I had been sent to take photographs of the drilling platform's progress.' He lit a cigarette, shook his head. 'The company sees every new piece of machinery, every inch the drill drops, as worthy of record. They mean to write their own history.' He scratched a thumb behind one ear, and I saw something in his manner that I couldn't quite read—a mix of hesitance and agitation.

'The wind had been rising for hours, and I feared it might strand me.' He stopped his pacing and rested his eyes on Linda. 'I was thinking of you,' he said. I saw the way he shifted his gaze to the light of the window, taken by the memory already imbued with the beauty and horror of myth. 'I stood at the railing, and something in the water caught my eye. I looked down, followed the cables' trajectory into the sea. I thought at first that it was a tarp or a dhow's lost jib.' He lifted his cigarette, held it just shy of his mouth, as though he had lapsed into some fugue, forgotten what he was about. 'And then I saw that it was a woman, her face turning to the sun and then back to the sea. What I remember most is the school of little fishes that darted and hid in the lee of her body.' He held his breath for a moment, then lifted his shoulders as though there were no help for it. 'And then she was gone, torn loose by the waves.' He averted his eyes. 'I told no one. What business is it of mine? Trouble would surely follow.' He blinked hard. 'A few days later, a pearling dhow found her washed ashore.' When he stopped in his pacing and rested his eyes on mine, I

332

tightened my grip on Linda's hand. 'Dear *bella*,' he said, 'it was the body of Abdullah's sister.'

More than sadness or grief or even disbelief, it was a choking anger that filled my chest. 'Alireza,' I said.

'But it isn't Alireza the authorities are looking for.' Carlo resumed his pacing shuffle—more a harried clerk than a pirate. 'Four Arabs have come forward to claim that they witnessed her in the company of an American man.'

'That would be suicide,' Linda said, and Carlo grimly nodded. I watched his lips, the rush of blood filling my ears.

'It's Mason,' I said before he could utter the words. 'He's the one they are looking for.'

'That can't be true,' Linda said. 'Who would ever believe such nonsense?'

Carlo dropped his eyes to mine, his face heavy with regret. 'Whether it is true that Alireza murdered his wife out of spite or opportunity,' he said, 'we may never know, but it is no secret that your husband was a threat to him. Doing away with his wife and casting blame on Mason would kill two birds with one stone. The four witnesses?' He shrugged. 'They could be poor men lying to feed their families or simply to save their own skins.'

'Mason must be hiding somewhere,' Linda said, her face hot with insistence. 'He's not in the hospital. I know that.'

When Carlo didn't answer but resumed his erratic pacing, Linda stood, grabbed his arm.

'Look at me,' she said. 'You tell this girl what you know right now, or I'm walking out of here.'

'It does no good to offer false hope,' he said, but when Linda didn't budge, he nodded to me. 'Your

333

husband was on the platform,' he said, 'and then he wasn't. It happened before the girl was found. It made no sense, the sea was too rough, but I saw it myself. A private boat came for him.' He blew a long breath. 'When I saw it was Lucky Doucet at the helm, I had no doubt that trouble would follow.'

I sat for a long minute, saying nothing because Carlo had been right in his trepidation: what I felt was the shock of hope. When I saw the look of pity that passed between Linda and Carlo, I pushed myself up and gathered my bag. Linda took my arm.

'What are you going to do?' she asked.

'I'm going to find Abdullah,' I said. 'We can get that ledger and take it to the emir. He's got to help me find Mason.'

Linda began to gather her uniform. 'I'm going with her,' she said. But Carlo caught her arm.

'No,' he said.

Linda wrested her arm away. 'What is the matter with you?'

'You must listen to me,' he said, an edge of desperation sharpening his words. 'There is too much that you don't understand.'

'Don't lecture me, Carlo.' Linda sat down and tugged on one nylon, clipped it to her garter.

Carlo's shoulders sagged, and he looked at her with resignation. 'Abdullah has already joined the search,' he said, then dropped his eyes away. 'It may very well be that he doesn't mean to save her husband but to kill him.'

'That's not true,' I said, as though his words were a simple lie. 'They're friends.'

'The truth is,' Carlo said gently, 'that Abdullah will have no choice. He will be honor-bound to avenge his sister's loss of virtue or risk alienation at the hands of his tribe, which for a Bedouin means death.'

I stared at him, felt Linda find my hand, hold on.

'Maybe you should just stay here,' Linda said, 'until we can figure this out.'

'No,' I said, and pulled away. 'There's not enough time.'

'Carlo,' she said, 'for God's sake, go with her.'

'She is safer without me,' he said. 'They will be looking for any excuse to detain her.'

'Who?' she asked. 'Do you mean the militia?'

'The company,' he answered. 'Alireza. They all have reason to want her gone.'

Linda slowly moved her eyes from his to mine before wrapping me in her arms. I sagged against her until I felt myself beginning to tremble. Carlo took my hands in his.

'Vai con Dio, bella,' he said. 'Remember that you are young and beautiful. You need never be alone.'

His words hung in the air between us. He meant to comfort me, I think, or maybe it was his way of telling me what he believed: that the end of the story had already been written. I held his eyes for a heartbeat before pulling the door tight behind me. Somehow, I knew it would be the last time I saw him, that the image of Linda languorous in her pirate's shirt would be the final memory I would have of her. But I didn't let myself think of this then. How could I? I could wail my madness to the desert, or I could keep my wits and my will about me. It wasn't stoic resolve that I felt but a numbness that allowed me to think of nothing but what came next: I would get into the taxi, go back to Abqaiq, tell Yash all that I had discovered, find Abdullah,

335

the emir, and then, and then . . .

I looked out across the sea to where the dhows rode the uneasy waves, and I remembered the Arab boy, the mango he had fed me, how he had wanted nothing more than to go to the movies. I touched my throat where the pearl had rested and thought of Nadia moving so easily through the water, her face sheened by moonlight, and then her body pounding against the pilings, her clothes torn away. How easy she was to sacrifice. What, after all, was the worth of one Bedouin girl?

I knew I was going to be sick. I fell to my knees in the sand and retched until my stomach was empty. I was afraid that Carlo and Linda might see me and insist that I come back inside, or that Yousef might decide that I needed to be in someone else's care. The only weapon I had was control, my ability to convince everyone that I was okay, that I could do this, that I knew what it was that I was doing. If I broke down, then that was what I would be— broken, another helpless woman who could be put on a plane and flown far, far away.

I covered the bile with sand, sat back on my heels, then took a tissue from my bag, wiped my mouth. I stood, covered my hair with the scarf, and walked to the car, where Yousef was waiting to open my door. He averted his eyes as I slid into the backseat, and I wondered why I felt I could trust him. He could drop me anywhere, deliver me to anyone's door, and I would be helpless to stop him. I stared at his face in the mirror, the Stetson Ruthie had insisted on.

'Ruthie,' I said. 'I miss her.'

His eyes came up. 'So do I,' he said.

He shifted the car into reverse, hit the gas, and

swung us into a lurching half circle before dropping the car into gear so fast that we skittered forward across the sand and kept a head of steam until we hit the road. I leaned back, closed my eyes. I couldn't believe that what Carlo had told me about Abdullah was true—I wouldn't believe it. I thought back to the movie theater, replayed the scene with Lucky, the way his hand had rested on top of my head, how the shadows had shifted across his face. I imagined him at the helm of the *Arabesque,* the fastest boat on the bay, his stance sure again as he steered into the waves, the hours that it would take him to buck through the storm, the extra fuel he had the foresight to bring, enough water and whiskey to get them through. He was grinning into that wind because he had made the decision to do the right thing, to undo what he had done. Redemption, and wouldn't his Ruthie be proud?

When the hair on the back of my neck prickled, I turned to peer behind us, suddenly sure that we were being followed, and felt Yousef give the car a little more gas. It seemed a lifetime since I had left the compound, yet nothing in the desert had changed. Only as we approached Abqaiq did I see the outlying buildings with new eyes: somewhere among the portables and poor apartments, Yash lived his life separate from me. I tried to imagine him biking out of the gate, going to his thin bed, the fan I had given him oscillating the air, and I remembered nights in Oklahoma too hot to sleep, how my grandfather would wet a sheet and hang it over the open door, how I would lie awake and wait for the smallest breeze. When I thought of the harsh words I had said to Yash, I wanted to cover my face in shame. How could I have forgotten who

337

I was, that place I had come from?

Habib met the taxi at the gate, smiling until he bent down and saw me in back, and then something like sadness came into his face. I listened to the quiet words he exchanged with Yousef, sure that they were talking about me. When Habib stepped back, Yousef motored forward, rounding the corners with great care as though I were made of glass and might shatter. I was glad when he pulled to a stop in front of my house, grateful that Yash would be waiting with his tray of tea.

Yousef got out to open my door, and I saw him focus on something behind me. I whirled around, but it was only Faris, who stood with a trowel in his hand. His eyes were not on me but on Yousef, and I heard him speak a few hoarse words before turning, headed back to the garden.

'Memsahib,' Yousef said as he waited for me to exit the car, and I raised my eyes. He looked away for a moment, then down at his boots. 'You should return,' he said, 'to your real home.'

I peered past him to the blinded windows. 'Inshallah,' I said quietly, handed him the last of the cigarettes, and stepped to the porch.

The entryway gave me my breath back, the cool air chilling my skin. I left my bag on the console, went into the living room, and collapsed on the couch. I already knew what Yash was going to say: that I should rest for a while, eat a little something, that I needed my strength. He would bring us our tea, I would tell him all that Carlo Leoni had told me, and together, we would decide what came next.

I heard ice drop into a glass, heavy steps come from the kitchen, and looked up to see Ross Fullerton, in his hand a deep shot of whiskey.

338

'Virginia,' he said, his voice nearly jolly. 'Virginia Mae McPhee. Mind if I sit?' Before I could answer, he lowered himself into the chair, settled his hat atop his knee. A welter of sweat ringed his forehead.

I sat up straight, working to keep the surprise from my face. 'Where is Yash?' I asked.

Ross pulled out a half-smoked cigar, rubbed it around in the ashtray. 'I sent him on out,' he said. 'Back home.'

'But I haven't had my dinner,' I said, as though that were the thing that mattered.

'I bet you can make yourself a sandwich.' He grimaced a smile. 'Houseboys are a dime a dozen around these parts. One starts riding the ladies' bus, forgetting his place, it's time for him to move on.' Ross's upper lip jumped like it was hooked to a string. 'Candy told me he spent the night here with your husband gone, but sometimes she imagines things.'

I looked to the kitchen. I wanted to leap up right then, shout throughout the house, believe that Yash would appear around the corner at any moment. I wanted to say that it was all my fault, to take the blame, but I knew it wouldn't change a thing. I could feel Ross watching me, gauging my reaction.

'Where is Mason, Ross?' I asked. 'Where is he?'

Ross shoveled deeper into the chair. 'Well, now, I was hoping you might tell me.' He pooched his lips, rubbed his fingers and thumb together. 'It's not uncommon for a man to need some time to think things over.' He lit his cigar, gave it a long pull. 'Only thing is, we made a deal, and now he's left me in a lurch.' He squinted, then heaved a pained sigh. 'Hell, Ginny Mae, he's got us all

339

confounded. Maybe he just took a powder, lit out for the territories. Wouldn't be the first roughneck I've seen do it. Run like the nomads that way.' He moved the cigar from one corner of his mouth to the other. 'All I know is that his passport is sitting in Dhahran.'

I saw the way he flattened the beefy expanse of one hand against his knee, like he was covering a card. I knew better than to trust him. I kept my eyes down, rubbed the knobs of my knuckles—pretending the timid company wife I could never be.

'Are you going to make me leave?' I asked.

'You're part of the family, Ginny Mae. You know that Mother Aramco takes care of her own.' He studied me from the fleshy puddles of his cheeks, then looked around the room. 'Knew Buck Bodeen since the beginning,' he said. 'He was a friend, a good one.' He squinted one eye shut and sighted down the crease of his hat. 'When I found out he was mixed up with Alireza, I knew it was big trouble. I had to get him out of here.' When I looked up, Ross wiped his nose, cleared his throat. 'Thought I had more time to get things back in order, get the plant working the way it needed to be, but I was wrong.' He raised his face, his jowls sacked with regret. 'It's as much my fault as anyone's that Burt Cane and those other men are dead. The best I can do now is try to set things right. I trust you'll help me out, tell me what you know.'

'I know that Lucky was in on the deal,' I said.

Ross blinked once. 'Who told you that?'

I hesitated, not sure how much I should reveal. 'Lucky told me,' I said, 'after Ruthie died.'

340

He rolled his tongue, shook his head. 'Goddamned Cajuns,' he said, almost to himself, 'always running the endgame.' He cast his eyes to the ceiling, ran his hand back and forth over his head like he was buffing a shoe. 'Damn it,' he said. 'Damn it to hell.'

He grew quiet, and in the momentary silence, I heard the rhythmic pull of Faris's rake across the lawn.

'I'm afraid there's been some trouble,' Ross said, and looked at me with his hangdog eyes, let me see just how sorry he was.

'The girl they found dead,' I said.

He tilted his head to see me better. 'What about her?' he asked.

'She was Abdullah's sister,' I said. 'I know they think someone killed her, but Mason didn't do it. He's being set up.'

'Set up.' Ross clicked his jaw to one side and then the other. 'Now, where would you get an idea like that?' I could tell by his tone, the flatness of his gaze that he knew just where I had been, that I had been talking to Carlo. A cold dread prickled up the back of my neck as he pulled a handkerchief from his pocket and blew his nose. 'Here's the thing, Ginny Mae,' he said. 'If that boy of yours thought he could waltz into this mess and play sheriff, well, that would be some special kind of foolishness, and maybe all the reason that Alireza needed to kill that girl.'

I focused on my fingers, twisted the diamond ring, and felt the rasp of sand underneath. The corners of Ross's mouth arched into a cramp, and he poked the handkerchief back in his pocket.

'What I'm saying is that if you got any

341

information that might help me, you'd better give it right now, because I'll tell you this—' He nodded and his voice graveled. '—if we don't find that husband of yours first, we might not find him at all.'

I moved my eyes to the floor, afraid that Ross could somehow see that I was thinking about Lucky and the *Arabesque,* the last hope I had. He studied me for a long moment, fingering his cigar, then took up his hat.

'Heard the gales hit ninety during that last *shamal,*' he said, 'waves running twenty feet. You'd have to be a brass-balled cowboy to wrangle that ride.' He ignored the shock that crossed my face when I realized he must already know about the boat and rocked himself to a stand, wincing with the effort. 'This place saps the vinegar right out of you,' he said. He paused beside me, tapped two heavy fingers against my collarbone. 'Probably best if you stay inside, lock your doors.' He clucked his tongue as though it was a pity. 'Desperate men,' he said. 'I've seen them do some desperate things.'

I heard the door swing open, click shut. A hot breeze shot through, scattering the ash of his cigar. I stared at his empty glass until I could focus again, remember my plan. I would take Bodeen's ledger, find some way to reach the emir, get to Alireza before he or anyone else could get to Mason.

I rose and went to the study, pushed open the door. Why was I surprised at what I saw? The books pulled from their shelves, the drawers dumped out, the files rifled, my photographs tossed aside. The miniature ship lay in the shards of its bottle, the mast snapped in two. The red leather ledger was gone.

How long did I stand there, dazed, unblinking,

before going back to the entryway, already knowing what I would find? My purse, my identification card, my camera and film, the few riyals Yash had given me—Ross had taken them all. I slumped against the wall and remembered my mother in the last throes of her life, taken by morphine, the wildness in her eyes gone dull, like the eyes of the animals my grandfather killed for meat. More than anything, I wanted to escape the pain and confusion, find that smoke-gray place of nothingness.

Please, I thought, and realized that I was praying.

I willed myself upright and moved through the house, past the familiar furniture, the hi-fi, the tapestry on the wall. I opened the blinds on every window and watched the hot light spill in.

Set it all afire, I thought.

Burn it all to ash.

CHAPTER SEVENTEEN

The everyday rites of survival, the actions that become ritual—so often, they are what saves us.

I remember how I took Ross's glass to the kitchen and scoured it with soap until it squeaked and smelled like lemons. I brewed a pot of tea, raised the cup to my face, and breathed in, wishing I had drunk every drop that Yash had offered. In the refrigerator, I found what remained of the curried shrimp he had made for me and savored it like a last meal. I remembered the liquor in the cupboard that Lucky had brought from Bahrain, how he said we would celebrate when all this was over, and poured myself a shot. I raised the glass, whispered, *'A la sature,'* and swallowed it down.

I went to the linen closet, pulled out a folded towel, then stopped to consider the tapestry: a flowering field of French knots and raised roses, tight satin stitches filling the body of the white unicorn. I ran my fingers along the silken thread, thought of all the hours Betsy Bodeen had sat in this house, plying her needle and thread even as her life was unraveling just as mine was now. What had the unicorn meant to her, captured as it was in its small pen? *A representation of Christ,* Mason had said, *alive again.* When had I ever known such faith?

I took a shower so cold that my teeth chattered and my lips turned blue, rubbed myself dry, pulled on Mason's work shirt and jeans, dropped the fob Abdullah had given me in my pocket, and toed into my mother's boots. I combed my wet hair, tied on a scarf. I knew I was going somewhere. I didn't know where that somewhere might be.

The knock at the back door startled me with expectation, and then fear, but it was only Faris, standing there like a delivery boy, holding out a fistful of beets from the garden. I took them, felt their greens nettling my arms.

'Thank you,' I said, and then lowered my face, wondering how it could be this that made me cry. 'Do you want water?' I asked. 'Sweet water?' But he just peered at me, his eyes clouded with cataracts, and ran his tongue over his wrinkled lips before motioning me out the door. I followed him around the house to the front yard, where he stopped and pointed. A quarter mile beyond the fence, a wavering image shifted and disappeared, only to appear again—a black tent pitched like a mirage against the backdrop of sky. The familiar leanings and ropes, the single white stripe—even from a distance, I knew it was Abdullah's.

I wasn't sure what Faris had expected me to do, whether he was surprised when I began walking, then running down the street, the beets falling from my arms. He didn't call after me, didn't do anything but watch me go. The few cars that passed gave me wide berth, the drivers and passengers peering out at me like I was someone's lost dog. Habib must have heard me coming, my mother's boots clopping the asphalt, because he stepped out and sucked in his belly. I didn't have my purse, my identification card, but I knew that, for better or worse, he would recognize me.

'I have to go to the tent,' I said.

Habib peered back at the compound, his gaze more serious. 'Do you think it is all right if you go to the tent?' he asked.

'Fatima is there,' I said. He waited as though he needed something more. 'Yes,' I said, raising my voice, impatient. 'I think it is all right if I go to the tent.'

He considered a long moment, then nodded and stepped back. I looked to the road open before me. The urge to run that I had expected to feel wasn't there, only a pounding awareness of the sun beating down. I struck out across the wind-sculpted desert, my boots slewing sand. The goats set up a ruckus as I approached, the camel and her calf bawling until Fatima appeared. I stopped several yards away, breathless and damp with sweat.

'Peace be upon you,' I called, and Fatima raised her veiled face, her graying eyes holding mine. I

345

thought for a moment that she might deny me, send me back through the gate, but she motioned me forward, and I heeled off my boots before entering. The coffee roaster and urn, the pillows and rugs— all arranged just as they had been before, but no sign of Abdullah, the center pole empty of his rifle and sword.

Fatima took off her scarf, her hennaed braids falling to her waist, and began to make our tea, and I remembered what Abdullah had told me about the code of Bedouin hospitality and *dakheel*, wondered for the first time whether Abdullah might have taken Mason in. I looked into the tent's shadowed corners, saw nothing but the pillows and rugs, Fatima's loom, felt my hope husk away. We sat across from each other, quietly sipping through the ritual three cups, my impatience quelled by the memory of Yash's admonishment that I must learn to hold my tea. When Fatima gestured to the space beside me where Ruthie might have been, I lowered my eyes. I didn't know how to speak of any of it, didn't know whether I should say Nadia's name, what Fatima might tell me if she could. I looked up, saw the grief and confusion on her face mirroring my own, heard her murmur as though she understood.

'Abdullah?' I said, tentative, unsure. 'Do you know where he is?'

She didn't answer, but after a moment, she reached for a small bronze box, opened its lid. She held out her fist to me, and I felt the pearl necklace flow into my palm like sand.

I wanted to tell Fatima that I was sorry, that something had gone terribly wrong, but all I could do was bring the chain to my neck, clasp it behind. In the silence that settled between us, I heard the nicker of a horse, the calming voice of a man. I followed Fatima's gaze and saw Abdullah silhouetted against the sun. He wore the full garb of a Bedouin, his *ghutra* wrapped at his throat, his robe belted, a dagger at his waist. I hadn't thought I would be afraid, but I was.

He lifted his chin and studied me for a moment before stepping away, and I heard the sound of a fire being struck, smelled the smoke that carried with it some hint of incense, and then the coffee being roasted, like the burning of summer's dry stubble. When Fatima mimed as though drinking, pointed me to the open center of the tent, and took up her weaving, I rose slowly as though I were the one stiffened with age.

'*Ashkurik,*' I said, and the corners of her sad eyes lifted.

Abdullah stood at the fire, a brass urn and two cups before him. He gestured to his right, where a rug had been spread and dusted free of sand.

He wouldn't serve me this way, I reasoned, if he meant to hurt Mason. The idea that he might do so seemed suddenly absurd, a drama only a pirate would pretend.

I looked to where Badra grazed a small clutch of brown grass, her back still marked with the dark sweat of her ride. I pressed my fingers against the horsehair fob in my pocket like a charm and took my place, tucked my feet, and waited until Abdullah lowered himself to the sand before looking up. It seemed impossible that we had ever spoken, that there was a language that we shared, that we had told each other stories and teased. I watched as he tended the small fire, each movement precise,

347

efficient, and remembered my grandfather—
each morning, the four sticks of kindling split and
feathered, laid atop a twist of paper, the single
match struck, the wait to add another piece of
wood to the stove, and then another, never rushing
no matter how icy the room. 'Do it right once,' he
would say, 'or do it twice wrong.' It was a lesson I
seemed never to learn.

Abdullah poured our coffee—another three
servings before I shook my cup in the mute gesture
that meant enough. He stirred the fire, then
elbowed back into a bolster and crossed his fingers
at his chest. I saw him glance at me quickly, then
away.

'You never brought our lunch,' he said.

It took me a moment to remember: *Texas chili,
no beans,* Abdullah just pulling away as I came back
from the movie theater. That moment seemed years
ago, and I gave a strange laugh that set my teeth to
chattering.

'I wish I had a cigarette,' I said.

When Abdullah reached inside the placket of
his robe and pulled out a pack, I realized that I had
never seen him smoke before. I steadied my own
shaking hand as he held the lighter to my cigarette,
then his own. He reclined again, let out a slow
breath, the smoke rising to the soft wind that raised
the folds of his scarf, revealing the round of his ear,
the nape of his neck. I watched, oddly mesmerized
by the tensing of his jaw, the configuration of his
hands. His calm was nothing new to me—he was
every man I had ever known, resolute against any
show of emotion. I believed that my only hope was
to match my stoicism to his, to earn my place at the
fire, to not be exiled to the weaker world of women.

'Yash is gone,' I said, 'but you probably already know that.' When he didn't respond I looked down at my hands. 'Ross took the ledger,' I said. 'It's all the proof we had.'

'It doesn't matter,' Abdullah said. 'None of it matters anymore.'

'But it does,' I said. 'Mason is your friend. You know he has always been on your side.' I fought to keep my voice from rising. 'You know what those four men are saying isn't true. Someone paid them to lie.' I let a moment skip by. 'And you know who it was who paid them.'

He blinked his eyes away, then glanced to where Fatima sat in the shadows, weaving with the unhurried efficiency of someone who has learned to bide her time.

'It was during the *shamal*,' he said quietly. 'I had gone into camp, hoping only to see you. When you brought me the tea, I thought it was fate, and I left the compound happy.' He balanced the cup in the center of his hand. 'When I returned to the tent, I found my mother weeping. She told me that Nadia had gone to the shore. I tried to follow, but the storm filled my eyes with sand.' The lines around his mouth tightened. 'There was nothing I could do to save her,' he said. 'It is better that she gave herself to the sea.'

He paused, and in the silence, I heard the sound of Abqaiq's schoolchildren float in on a torpid current of air, mixing with the muezzin's call.

'She drowned herself,' I said—a possibility I hadn't imagined but now seemed so clear. 'Because of Alireza,' I said. 'The baby.'

Abdullah rolled his cigarette against a stone. 'They have found the *Arabesque* run aground,' he

349

said, 'just north of Jubail.'

'Then they made it,' I said. 'They survived the storm.' When he didn't answer, I felt a claw of new fear scrabbling to take hold. 'You would tell me . . .' I trailed off, blinking against the dark edges of my vision. 'Please,' I said, 'just tell me the truth.'

He lifted his face, looked to the east. 'There is something happening here,' he said, as though in a dream. 'It is something that nothing, no one can stop.'

'I don't know what that means,' I said. 'Why won't you just tell me? Why won't you say if he's dead?'

'Because I can't say,' he said.

'Why? Why can't you say?'

'Because I don't know.' He considered his empty cup. 'All around the boat, the wind had swept the sand clean. The trackers had no trail to follow.' He looked toward the compound, the smutty flares warbling the air, then lowered his gaze. 'I have brought you Badra,' he said.

I looked to where the mare had dropped her head and dozed, her ears tenting forward to catch the tenor of our voices, her breath sculpting a small bowl in the sand.

'A horse?' I asked. 'Do you think that a horse is what I want from you?'

'It was your husband who asked to buy her, but the emir is a generous man. Because you admired her, he has sent her as a gift.' His eyes came up to meet mine. 'Mason is gone, Gin. He isn't coming back.'

It wasn't only what he was saying to me that shocked me into stillness but the sound of my name in his mouth.

350

'I don't understand,' I said. 'I don't know what you are telling me.'

He offered his words like a heaping of small stones. 'I am telling you that even if Mason survived the *shamal*, there are men who will not let him live, and there is nothing I can do to stop them.' He lifted one hand tentatively, as though in offering. 'I am telling you that you can stay,' he said, 'here with me.'

Stay here. I met his gaze because I couldn't look away, and I wonder now: What did he see in my face?

I staggered up, trying to stand, but the sand caught my heels, and I fell to the edge of the fire. The stink of burned animals took to the air, the skin of my right arm singed before Abdullah could grab my wrists and snatch me up. I tried to wrench myself free, saw the look in his eyes, a mix of excitement and fear, and I thought he might pull me close, hold me against him, and what then, I ask myself now. What then?

'Abdullah.'

It was Fatima's strong voice that broke the spell. She stood unveiled in the open door of the tent, her chin lifted.

'Abdullah,' she said louder, the word like a command, and I felt him let go. He looked at me, then dared to rest his palm against my cheek before turning to where the mare waited, tied to nothing but sand. He grabbed a hank of her mane, pulled himself up. No word, no kick of his heels or snap of the reins, just his body leaned forward, and they were moving away so fast it did me no good to call, though I did, again and again, for Badra to come back, to wait, to please wait for me.

EPILOGUE

Where does it end, that arc that traces the path of our days, ascends, ascends, then begins its sure decline? A heroine's journey, a cautionary tale— only later can we look back, try to make sense of what story we are living, give it some meaning that might redeem the choices we have made.

I can tell you that Fatima came to where I lay, curled and howling by the fire, that she knelt beside me like a mother might. I looked up, saw her eyes heavy with an acceptance I could not bear.

'Will you tell me?' I whispered. I clung to her hands. 'Won't you please tell me where he is?'

She rose silently, urging me up with her. I wanted her to soothe me, salve my burns, tell me that Abdullah would return, but I pulled away and left her there, left all that was left for me to leave. I stumbled across the sand, down the road, and back through the gate, Habib silently watching.

Just inside the door of my home, a grim American man I had never seen before was waiting. He handed me my passport, along with a one-way ticket, an envelope of strange money, and told me to take what I wanted, that I wouldn't be back. I packed no bags, took nothing but what I wore— Mason's shirt and jeans, my mother's boots, my scarf—and he drove me to the airport without another word, put me on the next plane to Rome.

I remember nothing of that flight except the stewardess touching my shoulder, handing me a sandwich that I held until she came and took it away. A car was waiting for me, another silent man, who took my passport before he dropped me in front of an ancient stone building and handed me the single heavy key. I stood alone, looking up and up, and began to climb the stairs, one floor, and then another, and another, ascending to the rooms that have held the past three years of my life.

I remember how I lay on the thin mattress as the hours turned into days, rising only to fill my mouth with water, use the toilet. I believed that I wanted to die, but it was my hunger that goaded me to take some of the *lira* and go back down to the street, where I found a little market, bought a round of bread and a wedge of hard cheese, then sat on a bench overlooking the Tiber and cried as I ate it all. I began walking the city like I had first learned to drive—around one block, and then another—never caring that I might be lost, until the street opened out into a kind of courtyard, and I stopped, amazed.

Have you seen the Trevi Fountain? The waters spill out, the great marble seahorses riding the foam. At the edge of the pool, a large sculpted vase is said to once have hidden a stubborn barber's lowly sign. They call it the *Asso di Coppe*—the Ace of Cups—and I leaned against its base, numbly counting the coins, all those wishes for return, and wondered, Why here? Soon, I would know: the tall buildings, the labyrinthine avenues—in the Great Fire, there was no escape, and people died by the thousands in these very streets because they had nowhere to run.

Those first weeks in Rome, returning to Arabia was my obsession, as though I might yet find my way through the maze of fear and confusion my life had become, rescue Mason, save myself. I petitioned the embassy for a new passport, told

354

them that my husband was missing, that I needed to find him, but they shook their heads as though deaf until, finally, I stood mute, the other people in line staring at me as though I might be crazy. And wasn't I? Even if I were allowed to return to Arabia or even Shawnee, whom did I think I might find there? Better that I remain where they have sent me, surrounded by a sea of people who have taken me in like the orphan that I am, who urge me to eat, eat, who light their candles and remember me in their passionate prayers.

I believe it would please Carlo to know that, like him, I have learned to make my way through this world by taking the portraits of those who consider themselves important. They seek me out, hang their likenesses on the walls of their villas, but most days, I carry a simple Rolleiflex hung beneath my scarf. I can walk any avenue, see ruins in every direction, the ancient domes and fractured pillars thrusting up from the marble floors and ruptured canals, the ancient cathedrals marshaling the town. I turn a corner and there is another piazza with a bench or two, a belled wall, where I sit with the elders, their ineffable patience stretching through the sultry afternoons. They have nothing but time, it seems, to watch, to listen, to study the sky, to gossip meanly about their neighbors as though I were just the one to hear, and I snap the shutter, catch their faces unguarded as they contemplate the gush of water from the mouths of stone fishes. Young mothers push by with their prams, and I wonder how my life might be different if I could find my way back to that first night with Mason, start over again.

I say this aloud to Apollonia, the old woman who sits on the bench next to me, whom I have come

355

to know like the seasons here—slowly and with anticipation. 'Never regret,' she tells me, 'or your life will end before it's begun.' I don't tell her that there are times when I wish it were so but breathe in the comfort of her smell—hot wool and ripe lemons—as she talks to me of her dead husband, her seven children and nineteen grandchildren. She thinks that I, too, am *vedova de guerra*—a widow of war, and maybe I am. She points out the handsome young men who walk by, wearing their lust like a golden skin, and makes bawdy gestures that only we can see. She loves to hear my Arabian tales. I have imagined for her every possible outcome to this story, and the impossible, too—that my heroine looks up one day and sees her lost love, that faint scar, those blue, blue eyes. He was only wounded, had gone into hiding—'He didn't want to endanger her, so he stayed away as long as he could bear,' I say, and Apollonia nods.

'A good man,' she says, 'who made a bad mistake.'

I want to tell her that maybe I am the one to blame, that if I hadn't told Lucky, he and Mason and Nadia might still be alive, but it is a story that no one would want to believe of me, not Virginia Mae McPhee.

When Apollonia takes my arm and we walk past the young sweethearts strolling the bridges, the businessmen covering their mistresses in the backseats of cars, the old lovers hand in hand, taking their *passéggiata,* I think of Carlo, imagine that he and Linda have married, that they live in a white stucco house just north of al-Khobar, large windows to catch the sweet salt breeze, three dark-eyed daughters who someday will grow taller than their father. Perhaps he has given up his pirate's guise, thrown off his silk and heavy boots, taken on the cotton undershirts and soft shoes of an old man. Maybe one day, I think, he will find me, teach me how to eat tripe, introduce me to his cousin's cousin, show me how to grow big again. But it is Apollonia who presses her warm hand to my heart, tells me that the boat of my soul has known many waters, that I am still worthy and true, and an unexpected hope stabs into me.

Most evenings, in the little *ristorante* near the river, I take my wine in short glasses, take whatever Fausto, the surly owner, brings from his kitchen, and it is always good. I love the forest mushrooms most of all—morels in the springtime, porcini in the fall—and Fausto loves me, although he has his *consorta* upstairs who bangs her heel against the floor when he lingers too long at my table, and I think of Yash and his young wife making love to the brewing juice of cashew fruit, lewd and promising on the morning air. There are times when I wish I could travel to India, find Yash if he is there or find what remains of his family, trace his blood and know it again, but what would I tell his son? *We danced*, I might say. *He taught me so many things.* Orphaned himself, abandoned, set aside, what would he care? Perhaps he would hate me as I sometimes hate myself.

Too often, I forget that Ruthie had a son, that she lived every day with his absence, that wherever he is, he must now live with her death and his father's, too. Because I believe that they are all dead, don't you? *The last open seat, one last tour, one last race to run*—I sometimes feel as though I am the last one left to tell the story, and where is

357

the mercy in that?

You are wondering about Abdullah. I don't know what to say. I could have loved him, I think, or I did. I keep the short braid of Badra's mane in a box made of abalone with other precious things: a fistful of small pebbles the color of cinnamon that I emptied from my mother's boots, the necklace with its single pearl—all that I have to remind me that I once lived there, where the sand meets the sea.

There are times when I wonder whether it is simple solitude that I seek, whether that is what drew me to the desert, the tent, whether what I wanted from Abdullah was anything more than that. Some part of me has always believed that I need only myself to survive—that part that Mason recognized early on—but what woman has ever known such agency and could move through this world without the aid and protection of men? What choice do we have but to try? Every time a woman sins, my grandfather said, she falls again, and I say that in doing so, she claims sovereignty over her actions. See the two sides of me, then: repentant and refusing to repent. Everything in my life is different, yet nothing has changed.

*   *   *

Like Dickens in his London, the night's such dark thoughts keep me awake, I walk. The city never chills like the desert at dusk, but last winter, in the throes of insomnia, I stepped out, looked up, and thought that the stars were falling. The snow hit my face like sparks from a fire.

I had almost forgotten those winter mornings in Shawnee, my bedsheets iced to the wall. How

358

my grandfather would wrap me in a blanket and carry me to the kitchen, where the potbellied stove moaned its misery so that I didn't have to. He would tuck me into my chair, rest his hand on the top of my head. 'You are a fine girl,' he would say, as though the cold had melted his heart. And then he would pray and spoon the porridge, test it against his own lips before moving it to mine. 'Eat, eat,' he would say, and then he would bundle me in wool, sit me on the mule, and lead me to school through the ghostly fields. When the last bell rang, I would find him waiting, ready to tug my hat over my ears, snug on my mittens, and we would follow our own trail home.

Who knows where grace resides? That night in Rome, the miraculous snow coming down, I stopped when the Gypsy fortune-teller called to me. She had no table, only the slick flint road to lay her prophecies upon, and I crouched before her. The card came up, an open palm holding a golden chalice, the *Asso di Coppe*. 'Cups are the suit of the heart,' she crooned, 'of family, of love. Do you have someone to forgive?' she asked me, her eyes clouded with age. 'Do you want to ask forgiveness?' She smelled like the last wilted petals of jasmine, the desert after a rain. She took my fingers, clasped them in hers. 'We are all wanderers on this earth,' she said. 'It is never too late.'

I let her peer into my face, then slowly drew my hands away. I pulled off my diamond ring and dropped it to her blanket like payment for my sins. I was blocks away before the regret turned me around, but what did I expect? She was a nomad, after all. She had taken her cards, taken my ring, rolled up her blanket, and was gone.

How long did I search the *vias* and nearby piazzas for any sign of her before I found myself on an unknown avenue whose walls were bolted with forged iron? In an upstairs window, its arched panels opened to the cold air, a light shone through, and I could hear the voices of the choir, practicing their songs of communion. A slender *osteria* anchored the corner, and I hesitated before giving up and walking in, past the old bachelors taking their late meals, to the handsome young barista who followed me with his smoky eyes. *'Una bottiglia di vino rosso, per favore,'* I said, and maybe it was the bitterness in my voice that caused him to bring me the bottle already uncorked. When he offered two glasses, I shook my head, said, *'Solo una.'* He took in my sadness but would not take my *lira* no matter how much I insisted. I asked whether I was his evening's charity, but he said no, that if I did not accept the wine, he would have to drink it himself, and that might lead him into temptation. He lifted one eyebrow. *'Tu sei la mia salvezza,'* and though I felt like no one's salvation, I raised my chin, said, *'Grazie,'* and turned for the door before he could see my tears.

Outside, the stone street was cobbled white, and I stepped carefully down the narrow walk. I brushed the snow from the curb, across from the church window, sat down, and lit the one cigarette I allow myself each day, already wishing for another. The doors along the avenue were barred, the roadway free of traffic, not even a bicycle winding the icy street. I wrapped my scarf around my ears and tipped the wine that warmed my throat as the voices rose, the beautiful voices, pouring out through the open window with the light, which was

360

golden, so sacred that I believed I had to witness its genesis.

I hadn't set foot in a church since leaving Shawnee, and never a church like this one. I rose and stepped to the entryway, but the door was locked. Late at night, and all of the doors of Rome were locked tight. When I lifted my face, the snow shut my eyes. I opened my mouth, took the flakes on my tongue. I stood with my hand gripping the latch. I couldn't let go. Dear God, I thought, let me in. The snow is falling. The stars are burning.

All I ever wanted was to know.

ACKNOWLEDGMENTS

Before I offer my gratitude to the many people who had a role in this book's creation, I want first to acknowledge that, though this story relies upon and incorporates historical elements, it is very much a work of fiction, its characters and situations conjured from my imagination. The Saudi Arabia of 1967 is gone, a place impossible to go back to, and those readers who are familiar with that land and time may find certain of my details and logistics inconsistent with their memories and experiences. Those readers who know the contemporary Arabian landscape, populated by high-rises and luxury hotels, may find it difficult to imagine that the eastern edge of the peninsula could ever have been so barren. Likewise, the political, cultural, and religious environment of Arabia has changed a great deal since the 1960s. Because of the closed nature of the Saudi society and the doctrine of exceptionalism that directed early Aramco, I often found it difficult to access truly objective accounts of life inside (and outside) the American compounds and oil towns. What I offer you, then, is Gin's story as I have invented it. All my hours of reading and research brought me to a new appreciation of just how complex the relationship between the United States and Saudi Arabia is. If, as Yash says, the events in these pages add up to the 'education of Mrs. Gin,' they also represent the education of this author. Outside of the political gravity of what I discovered, the one impression that remains with me is the spirit of genuine friendship that developed—and continues to develop—between those Arabs and Americans who have worked together over the years.

While researching and writing this story, I have relied upon a blessedly generous circle of family and friends. To Robert Wrigley, the poet who has my heart, shares my tent, and muses with me in our aged hot tub, another glass of champagne to all those nights with our bodies in the water and our eyes on the stars as we trekked through the imaginary desert together, following the windblown trail of this story. To our children, Jace, Jordan, and Philip, and my mother, Claudette Barnes, thank you for your gift of time, support, and inspiration. My aunt and uncle, Coleen and Wayne Cook, and my cousin Terry Cook, whose memories of their years in Abqaiq spurred this story—thank you for the time you gave me, answering my endless and sometimes odd series of questions. William Tracy, former contributing editor of *Aramco World*, offered his expert reader's eye and Arabian memories—thank you, Bill and Marjorie, for your confidence, coffee, and cookies. Lois Wolfrum, who lived and worked as a Singles girl in Arabia, brought to this story her love of the Saudi people and her flag of fierce independence. I relied heavily on an engaging personal online journal written by Aramco expat Colleen Wilson, who, even in the face of personal hardship, took time to offer me details of her experience in the camps. Other Aramcons, including those with whom I connected on Facebook, impressed me with their deeply felt love of Arabia and its people.

Sayantani Dasgupta endured a long series of my embarrassingly uninformed questions about India and responded with endearing patience, as did Bharti Kirchner, whose culinary expertise I relied upon and who generously read and responded to sections of the manuscript. Morning conversations with my sister-friend Claire Davis about writing and every other thing in our world became my daily bread, and her uncanny ability to pull me up, dust me off, and point me in the right direction kept me from losing my way. To my Free Range Writers—Collin Hughes, Buddy Levy, Lisa Norris, and Jane Varley—thank you for twenty years of rare trust, good friendship, and hard reads. To Jeanne Amie Clothiaux and Kelly Madonna Quinnett—may the Three Tall Women forever meet to wonder, imagine, and create.

Grazie mille to the Rockefeller Foundation at Bellagio and the Liguria Study Center at Bogliasco for the glorious gift of time and space, and to my resident mates there, thank you for sharing with me your intelligence, humor, and creative energy. Thanks to my colleagues and my students at the University of Idaho for their faith and support.

To my editor, Jennifer Jackson, and my agent, Sally Wofford-Girand, who have journeyed beside me as I made my way through the desert—a thousand thanks for your steadfast direction and reassurance. Many thanks, too, to family members and friends who offered their memories, knowledge, insights, and encouragement, including Greg and Judy Barnes, Keith Browning, Brittney Carman, Betsy Dickow, Anthony Doerr, Bob Greene, Robert Coker Johnson, Annie Lampman, Brian Leekley, Sam Ligon, Martin Mallinson, Daniel Orozco, Joy Passanante, Brandon Schrand, Mark Spragg, Jess Walter, and Gary Williams.

A very special note of gratitude to the independent booksellers who keep me in their hearts and on their shelves.

Finally, I have researched a small library's worth of material over the years of this book's composition and have been informed and directed by the novels, memoirs, scholarly texts, government reports, articles, journals, letters, diaries, blogs, and oral histories I have read. I want to make special mention of the brilliant Italian photographer Ilo Battigelli, whose artistic (not personal) life inspired the creation of my character Carlo Leoni. You can learn more about Mr. Battigelli's masterful photographs and biography through the searchable archives of Arab News (http://archive.arabnews.com), Aramco Services (http://www.aramcoservices.com/news-publications), and the Center of Research and Archiviation of Photography (http://www.craf-fvg.it/eng/index.asp).

Along with archival issues of Aramco (now Saudi Aramco) publications—*Sun and Flare, Aramco World*, the 1960 edition of *The Aramco Handbook*, and the 1981 edition of *Aramco and Its World*—the following is a list of selected sources that I found particularly poignant and from which I drew details and descriptions of life in the desert: *The Belt*, by Ahmed Abodehman; *In the Land of Invisible Women: A Female Doctor's Journey in the Saudi Kingdom*, by Qanta A. Ahmed, MD; *At the Drop of a Veil: The True Story of an American Woman's Years in a Saudi Arabian Harem*, by Marianne Alireza; *Islam: A Short History*, by Karen Armstrong; *Out in the Blue: Letters from Arabia—1937 to 1940: A Young American Geologist Explores the Deserts of Early Saudi Arabia*, by

Thomas C. Barger, former president and CEO of Aramco; *Brownies and Kalashnikovs: A Saudi Woman's Memoir of American Arabia and Wartime Beirut,* by Fadia Basrawi; *Nine Parts of Desire: The Hidden World of Islamic Women,* by Geraldine Brooks; *Big Oil Man from Arabia: From Camel Back to Cadillac—or the Amazing Adventures of Aramco, the American Overseas Oil Company That Is Transforming Saudi Arabia,* by Michael Sheldon Cheney; *The Wahhabi Mission and Saudi Arabia,* by David Dean Commins; *The Arab of the Desert,* by H. R. P. Dickson; *A Bedouin Boyhood,* by Isaak Diqs; *Guests of the Sheik: An Ethnography of an Iraqi Village,* by Elizabeth Warnock Fernea; *The Qur'an,* translated by M. A. S. Abdel Haleem; *Behind the Veil: An Australian Nurse in Saudi Arabia,* by Lydia Laube; *Seven Pillars of Wisdom,* by T. E. Lawrence; *Lawrence of Arabia,* directed by David Lean (from which comes a slight paraphrasing of 'No Arab loves the desert. We love water and green trees. There is nothing in the desert and no man needs nothing,' spoken in the film by Feisal); *Honey and Onions: A Life in Saudi Arabia,* by Frances Meade; *Home: The Aramco Brats' Story,* a documentary film by Matthew Miller, Todd Nims, and Zachery Nims; *Playing in the Dark: Whiteness and the Literary Imagination,* by Toni Morrison; the *Cities of Salt* trilogy, by Abdelrah-man Munif (which inspired Abdullah's description of the destruction of the wadi and a play on this quote: 'You go to bed a warrior and wake up a slave'); *Black Tents of Arabia,* by Carl R. Raswan; *Sea-son of Migration to the North,* by Tayeb Salih; *Discovery! The Search for Arabian Oil,* by Wallace Stegner, who first described the American explorationists as 'tinkerers and gadgeteers'; *A Vanished World* and *Arabian Sands,* by Wilfred Thesiger ('A cloud gathers, the rain falls, men live. The cloud disperses without rain, and men and animals die'); and *America's Kingdom: Mythmaking on the Saudi Oil Frontier,* by Robert Vitalis (which includes an extensive bibliography and in which I found the quote, '[A] King who thinks like an oil company and an oil company that thinks like a King,' attributed to United States State Department desk officer Richard Sanger). Mason's articulation of what the Arab workers were striking for is a paraphrasing of a quote from a 1955 *Time* article titled, 'Alchemy in the Desert,' reported by Keith Wheeler.

Additional selected and suggested titles include *Crescent, Arabian Jazz,* and *The Language of Baklava,* by Diana Abu-Jaber; the writings of Ayaan Hirst Ali; *The Girls of Riyadh,* by Rajaa Alsanea; *Opening the Gates: A Century of Arab Feminist Writing,* edited by Margot Badran and Miriam Cooke; *Sleeping with the Devil: How Washington Sold Our Soul for Saudi Crude,* by Robert Baer; *Disfigured: A Saudi Woman's Story of Triumph over Violence,* by Rania al-Baz; *Thicker Than Oil: America's Uneasy Partnership with Saudi Arabia,* by Rachel Bronson; *Oil, God, and Gold: The Story of Aramco and the Saudi Kings,* by Anthony Cave Brown; *Struggle and Survival in the Modern Middle East,* edited by Edmund Burke III; *Passionate Nomad: The Life of Freya Stark,* by Jane Fletcher Geniesse; *A Land Transformed: The Arabian Peninsula, Saudi Arabia and Saudi Aramco,* by William Facey, Paul Lunde, Michael McKinnon, and Thomas A. Pledge, and edited by Arthur P. Clark and Muhammad A. Tahlawi; *Daughter of*

Persia: A Woman's Journey from Her Father's Harem Through the Islamic Revolution, by Sattareh Farman Farmaian; *The New Encyclopedia of Islam,* by Cyril Glassé; *The Price of Honour: Muslim Women Lift the Veil of Silence on the Islamic World,* by Jan Goodwin; *The Writing on My Forehead,* by Nafisa Haji; *The Reluctant Fundamentalist,* by Mohsin Hamid; *Mother Without a Mask: A Westerner's Story of Her Arab Family,* by Patricia Holton; *The Jewel of Medina* and *The Sword of Medina,* by Sherry Jones; *Black Light,* by Galway Kinnell; *The Kingdom,* by Robert Lacey; *Some Girls: My Life in a Harem,* by Jillian Lauren; *Veiled Half-Truths: Western Travellers' Perceptions of Middle Eastern Women,* edited by Judy Mabro; *Not Without My Daughter,* by Betty Mahmoody; *Reading Lolita in Tehran: A Memoir in Books,* by Azar Nafisi; *Among the Believers: An Islamic Journey,* by V. S. Naipaul; *The Energy Within: A Photo History of the People of Saudi Aramco,* edited by Kyle L. Pakka; *Persian Girls: A Memoir,* by Nahid Rachlin; *Harem Years: The Memoirs of an Egyptian Feminist (1879–1924),* by Huda Shaarawi; *Sandstorms: Days and Nights in Arabia,* by Peter Theroux; *Arab Women: Old Boundaries, New Frontiers,* edited by Judith E. Tucker; and *The Prize: The Epic Quest for Oil, Money & Power,* by Daniel Yergin.

'Boredom is the desire for desires' is a paraphrase from Leo Tolstoy's *Anna Karenina.*

CHIVERS LARGE PRINT –direct–

If you have enjoyed this Large Print book and would like to build up your own collection of Large Print books, please contact

Chivers Large Print Direct

Chivers Large Print Direct offers you a full service:

• Prompt mail order service

• Easy-to-read type

• The very best authors

• Special low prices

For further details either call
Customer Services on (01225) 336552
or write to us at Chivers Large Print Direct,
FREEPOST, Bath BA1 3ZZ

Telephone Orders:
FREEPHONE 08081 72 74 75